A
LIGHT
IN THE
FOREST

ALSO BY MELISSA PAYNE

The Secrets of Lost Stones

Memories in the Drift

The Night of Many Endings

A LIGHT IN THE FOREST

A NOVEL

MELISSA PAYNE

LAKE UNION PUBLISHING

Text copyright © 2022 by Melissa Payne
All rights reserved.

Published by Lake Union Publishing, Seattle

www.apub.com

Amazon, the Amazon logo, and Lake Union Publishing are trademarks of Amazon.com, Inc., or its affiliates.

ISBN-13: 9781662503689 (paperback)
ISBN-13: 9781662503696 (digital)

Cover design by Adrienne Krogh
Cover image: © Robsonphoto / Shutterstock

Printed in the United States of America

To my father, Charlie:
I wrote this book with you never far from my heart.

CHAPTER ONE

Vega

Colorado
April 2021

Vega stood in the middle of the kitchen with her left arm bound so tightly behind her back the tendons in her shoulder gave way to a sharp pop. She closed her lips to keep a moan inside.

"Don't laugh at me." Her boyfriend, Zach—fingers so tight her hand had gone numb. No hint of lightness in his words. A cruel angle to his jaw. Not the man she'd met a year ago, on a warm day in October when she'd been camped at a state park. He'd just finished a mountain bike ride. She was putting hers away. He was cute, handsome in an unassuming way. Ruggedly sexy. But in this moment—with his hand crushing her wrist, using his strength to intimidate her—he was someone else. A stranger in his skin.

Her head buzzed, her senses assaulted, overwhelmed with the smallest details.

Warm air from the cooling oven.

Sleet in wet taps against the window.

Broken glass at her feet. Orange juice sticky across the counter.

Riley crying from the pack 'n play on the floor behind her.

Her pulse raced, panic twisting knots into her stomach. Her mother's voice in her head. *Run.* Frenetic energy raced down her legs and into her arm that hung free by her side. His other hand rested casually on the counter by his untouched plate of food. Like this was a normal morning. Like his hand squeezing her wrist hadn't just destroyed what she'd hoped would be an idyllic life. He yanked her arm, and electric shocks raced through her shoulder.

She started to buck against his grip, a wild desperation to free herself racing through her body. She knew what men could do to women. Had felt a sickening suspicion about Zach growing. He wasn't special. Or different. He was exactly what her mother had warned her about.

She grabbed the grapefruit spoon and stabbed his hand on the counter. The spoon bounced off the hard bone, hardly breaking the skin, but he grunted, releasing her, and for a second, she felt relief and even a traitorous hope that it would break whatever spell had turned this man into a monster.

He punched her in the stomach.

She couldn't breathe. Pain in her belly. White spots blooming in her vision. Urine wet on her pants. She crumpled to the ground, arms pressed into her gut, and leaned her back against the pack 'n play.

A bloodied napkin landed on the floor by her feet, followed by the flutter of an empty Band-Aid wrapper. The front door slammed shut.

She breathed in, but it came out a sob. Her hair reeked of burned meat. And when she lifted her hand, she noticed a bracelet of reddish-blue fingerprints marring the skin of her wrist. She stared at it.

Vega knew what this was. Had seen the bruises, the fear in the slouched backs of other women. But she'd never felt it herself. Her mother had spent her entire life trying to help women in situations just like this. And Vega had grown up helping her.

She turned her wrist, winced at the pain that shot up her arm. She brought her knees up, arms hugging her shins, and recoiled when she spied the napkin. White linen, ruined by spots of blood so red it looked fake.

She touched her face. Smelled the sweet thickness of maple syrup in the grooves of her fingertips. Her stomach turned, and she covered her mouth with her palm, afraid she'd be sick.

A loud ringing in her ears and her mother's voice in the cotton inside her head, muted but firm.

Run.

But Vega couldn't move, scrambling to find sense in what had happened.

She'd made breakfast for him. Gotten up early to do it, despite the hours she'd been awake with Riley, trying to calm his agonized cries, soothe him back to sleep. She'd kept the door to the baby's room closed; Zach had to be at the store early that morning. He needed his sleep. The more Riley had cried, the more she'd felt the gulf inside her widening. She was a terrible mother. Couldn't help her own baby. Her C-section scar had healed, but it remained a constant reminder of the life she'd brought into the world, and the epic failure she was at caring for that soul.

If only her mother were alive.

Her thoughts walked drunken lines in her head, unorganized, scattered by the shock that turned her skin to ice.

She'd put the bacon in the oven instead of frying it on the stove because she'd had Riley strapped to her chest, calmed at last and asleep, with his body pressed against hers. She didn't want the splatters of hot fat to scald his tender flesh.

She'd made french toast with fresh blueberries, had been heating the syrup and forgotten about the bacon. It was fine—charred a bit. She'd set a place on the island for Zach: cloth napkin, matte-gold fork and knife, a small spoon with the sharp tines on the end for the half grapefruit he liked every morning. Steaming cup of coffee and fresh-squeezed orange juice perched on the edge of the place mat. Newspaper folded open to the business section.

It was how he liked it and how she liked it too. Having lived on the road with her mother for her entire life, it still felt like she was playing house. And a little like she'd betrayed her mother. But it was exactly what she'd wanted: a home, a family, a place to let her roots grow deep.

Zach said that while they both might have come from nothing, they didn't have to live that way. Said it mattered how she kept house—the dishes they ate off, the meals they cooked, the linens they slept on. Their home was modest, tiny but neat, in an old neighborhood at the base of the foothills. The kind with mature trees, not the new developments with cookie-cutter lots and tiny shrubs. Vega loved it.

But Zach wanted more. One day, he dreamed, they'd have a mountain home made with cool metals and warm woods, marble countertops, and a fireplace in the master. A home with gates and a quiet Tesla to drive, one for each of them. *But I don't need all that,* she'd laughed, snuggling into the curve of his arm, legs entwined. *I like my old van.* She hardly drove it anymore. It was the one she'd grown up in with her mother—an old conversion kind made into a camper—and it held all her memories, the good and the ones laced with her discontent. Her desire to stay put that had breached some kind of unspoken agreement between her and her mother. Still, it was the only thing she had left of Renee, and she'd never get rid of it.

Zach had kissed her neck. *That eyesore won't be allowed in our new neighborhood. Too ugly.* He'd tickled her and she'd brushed it aside, thinking he was kidding. Assuming it had been a joke.

Blood on the napkin ignited flashbulbs of memory. His anger over the bacon. She'd laughed because it was a ridiculous thing to be angry about. But something had awakened in his eyes. A slug hiding in the dirt. One she couldn't see until she'd swept away a layer of soil to expose it. Like the time he came home drunk and pinned her up against a wall. She'd pushed him away; he'd stumbled, hit the back of his knee on the coffee table, and fallen to the floor. Shook his head, stared at his hands, and disappeared inside their bedroom. She'd slept on the couch.

Don't laugh at me.

She'd laughed again, not heeding the slug. *It's bacon. Don't be such a snob.* And turned away from him to pick up Riley, who'd started crying again. Before she could, he'd grabbed her hand and yanked her back, twisting her around until she faced him with her arm pinned behind her, his hand squeezing the bones of her wrist, a painful popping in her shoulder. His eyes were hard and serious. She wanted to scream, but she couldn't move. Loathed the thought that she'd ignored the warning signs, had allowed herself to believe that Zach was different.

Don't talk to me like that.

It had shocked her, and she'd almost laughed again. Of all people, Vega should never have found herself in this situation. Not after the life she'd shared with her mother. One spent opening back doors to show women and children and others a way out. The two of them female vigilantes in a world of abusive men. Vega had grown up seeing the truth of what happened behind closed doors. But in her mission to save victims of domestic violence, her mother had insulated Vega from experiencing anything for herself. She'd kept them forever moving, never staying anywhere long enough to make friends.

Vega stared at Riley; her body shook. How had she let herself ignore the doubt that had haunted her quiet moments? The too-tight grip on her arm when she'd giggled at Zach's attempt to button Riley's jammies. The press of his lips when he saw her "like" a photo of his high school friend at a Rockies game on Instagram. Her chest heaved. How had she let herself stay with a man like Zach?

Run.

It's exactly what her mother would tell any woman in this situation.

In the pack 'n play, Riley squirmed, brought his legs in and out, restless, uncomfortable for some reason that Vega didn't understand.

She had no experience with babies, and her mom, who knew everything, was gone. Her face was dry, but her eyes burned.

A wisp of Vega's mother in the space beside her, and her voice slid into Vega's ears.

There are some men you run from.

It ignited something inside her, and Vega pushed to her feet, yelping from the sharp pain that spidered through her shoulder and arm, cradling it to her stomach while she threw clothes into a bag. Her breath came in rapid huffs that made her feel dizzy.

A dog barked from down the street, another from next door. Sentries warning her of something coming. She slung her bag over her injured arm, picked up Riley with the other, and ran to the van. Rain and snow turned her lips cold, her teeth chattering. Her hands fumbled to clip in the car seat. She slid Riley into the seat, kissed the tip of his nose, and stared into his eyes. "I'm sorry." She wiped tears from his face, the same from hers, and slid the van door shut; it was loud in the quiet morning. Warm yellow glows lit the windows of her neighbors' homes. Her heart thumped against her chest. Zach's parents' house was only three doors down. It was still dark.

She scrambled into the driver's seat and turned the key, pressing her foot on the gas. It revved, and she waited for the old engine to warm, whispering, "Come on, come on." Craned her neck to look around, jumped at a figure walking toward her. She gripped the steering wheel, thought of the loaded gun her mother had always kept in the glove compartment but never used. The same one Vega had asked Zach to hide in the attic the moment she'd brought Riley home, having nightmares of her baby finding it. The figure came closer. Her skin prickled. A man in a hooded raincoat, dog on a leash. He gave her van a quick glance before hurrying past.

Vega slumped over the wheel, pressed her forehead into the plastic, and told herself to breathe past the pain in her stomach and the disbelief that tightened her throat.

Zach had been different when they first met. Quick to anger, sure—she'd seen it once when his bike chain popped off during a particularly steep ascent. He'd thrown the bike down the trail. But that had been about a bike, she'd thought. Not a person.

If she was being honest with herself, there'd been a time when she thought the spark between them had waned. She didn't know; she'd never had a boyfriend and was reminded of this inexperience by the self-doubt that pecked at her confidence. But then she'd gotten pregnant, and everything seemed better. Happier. Hopeful. And when something did happen—Zach screaming at her because she'd smiled at the guy delivering pho, pinching the tender flesh of her side because she'd forgotten to use the good silverware when his parents came over for dinner—he was sorry. He was always so sorry.

The windshield wipers swished thick slush off the glass. The sky hung low over everything, matching the heaviness across her shoulders.

A car drove slowly down their street, headlights bright in the dim morning. She squinted, adrenaline racing into her fingertips. She tapped the wheel. Was that Zach's car? From the bench seat, Riley cried.

Again, her mother's voice, insistent, panicked. *Vega, go!*

She released the emergency brake and pressed the gas, the van sliding on the slushy pavement, then catching and fishtailing forward.

CHAPTER TWO

VEGA

She had to stop at a rest area in Kansas. It wasn't far enough for Vega, who felt the prickle of Zach chasing after them between her shoulder blades. But Riley had been crying nonstop since she'd left the foothills, and in her hurry, Vega hadn't properly buckled the carrier into the seat and had noticed it jiggling loose a few miles back.

It was late morning, and the cold spring air raised goose bumps along her arms. Vega carefully slid Riley out of his seat. His body was both soft and rigid, and she nestled him in the crook of her arms. She couldn't stop shaking, and it seemed to upset him more, because the volume of his cries intensified, adding to the prickles of anxiety that wormed through her muscles.

Before having him, she hadn't held many babies—a handful, maybe, but only for a short time while a woman hurried around her home, collecting clothes or packing a bag. Vega's mother had always given her a job to do when they were helping someone leave, and when she was younger, holding a baby seemed like an important one. Her mother had given her a warning too: if something happened, run to the van and hide.

Vega's breathing was too shallow. *Nice and slow.* Her mother would gently pat a woman on the back, rub small circles, her voice soothing. *Pack warm- and cool-weather clothes; don't forget essentials: medicine, Social Security cards, underwear, toothbrushes, contact numbers.* Vega rocked her arms, felt the baby's cries vibrate against her chest. She couldn't remember what she'd packed. She'd thrown some things into a bag, but it hadn't been much. All these years helping others, and when it came down to it, she hadn't learned how to help herself.

From the cup holder in front, her phone buzzed, vibrating against the plastic. It had been buzzing for the last hour, but she didn't have to look at the screen to know who it was. Zach was the only person who ever texted her. She grabbed the phone, glanced at the screen. A mix of Snaps, texts, and voice mails. The most recent text read:

We're both so tired from the new baby. We need to be more patient with each other.

The message was followed by a string of emojis: hearts, a kiss face, a sheepish one, more hearts.

The screen blurred. Her mother's voice. *The classic abuser,* she would have said. *Controlling, manipulative, charming at all the right times.* A sob stuck in her throat. She leaned her head against the side of the van door, staring down at her son, whose pink lips curled around his cries. She kissed his forehead. Why had it taken Zach's fist for her to leave him? What was wrong with her?

She sat on the edge of the van floor—feet on the ground, jiggling Riley up and down—and for the first time, the enormity of what she'd done hit her with such a force she let out a gasp. Where was she going? How would she take care of Riley on her own? What would Zach do when he realized she'd left?

She opened the driver's-side door, slid her fingernails along the carpet under the seat. It lifted away easily. Stuck into a divot in the floorboards was a waterproof plastic bag. Inside the bag were cash—not much, but more than she had on hand—and her Social Security card, along with Riley's birth certificate, which she'd added only a few weeks before. Her mother had always hidden anything important and taught Vega to do the same. It was a hard habit to break and one she'd almost thought silly, given her new life with Zach and the baby. But on the night Zach pinned her against the wall, she'd sneaked out after he'd gone to bed and added Riley's paperwork to her own. That night, she lay beside Zach, her leg muscles tense, lungs tight, and when Riley woke up crying, she spent the rest of the night in his room, rocking him.

She pocketed the money, replaced the bag, and made a bottle. Riley's soft gulps were loud in the van. His eyes searched her face while he ate, still that dark blue from when he was born but starting to get lighter. Maybe he'd have green eyes like her mom. He was peaceful when he ate. The crying happened soon after and never seemed to stop. She'd been a mother for a total of two months, and she knew so little. She swallowed past a lump. Her mother had been alone, too, and she'd figured out how to do it. Vega had no choice but to do the same.

She always missed her mom the most in the quiet moments with Riley. Or when she needed someone to talk to. To ask for advice. Hear her voice. Grief spread thick over everything that had happened since. And when it threatened to suffocate her, she thought of her unusual childhood. One of brightly colored adventures, their lives a blur of truck stops and campsites, learning how to use her hands to build, fix, and make things work. No day exactly the same. Her mother couldn't stay in one place for long, and as soon as a job ended, her desire to put miles on the van returned. This was the crucial difference between them: as Vega grew older, she craved boredom, stability, and a home.

Tears stung her eyes, as they often had since her mom died. Vega's life wasn't the same without her. And to think she'd once thought she could make it on her own. The last thing she'd said to Renee was a ghost that appeared in her dark and loneliest moments: *I think I'd like to stay put for a while.* She hadn't said it in anger, wasn't trying to upset Renee or make a point. Vega had been twenty-three and wanted to try living on her own terms.

They'd just finished a two-week job in Silverthorne and were enjoying the stillness that came from a day off. Vega had joined her mother outside the van where they were camped in the woods. Pine trees rose above their spot; wind sifted through the needles, making a soft whooshing sound. A bird called out. Vega had just handed her mother a cup of strong coffee and sank down in a chair, tipping her head back to stare at the deep-blue Colorado sky. Tapped her feet on the dirt, nervous.

Heard there's a maintenance job open at the high school.

Her mother hadn't responded, and Vega deflated, worried it would end with Renee saying no and Vega giving in. But this time she felt different—a desire to find her own path growing, a quiet anger spreading inside her heart. She breathed in and said what she'd rehearsed. *I love you, Mom, and I'm grateful for all our adventures, but this is important to me.*

Waited for Renee's typical response: *Life is lived in motion.*

Silence.

Vega stared into her mug, gripped the ceramic with her fingernails. *I-I'm going to do it with or without you.*

But Renee didn't respond, and Vega wondered if this time would be different. If her mother would have a change of heart. Or if Vega would actually have the guts to follow through with it on her own. The silence was heavy, and Vega couldn't bring herself to look at Renee.

Her mother's coffee cup had dropped to the ground, pine needles floating in black liquid sludge. Renee looked funny, staring at the coffee on the ground. Something about her face was off. Like melting clay. One eye lower, the edge of her mouth bent into a frown.

Mom?

She never spoke again after that. And a few months later, she was gone, Vega's heart in pieces and her decision to stay in one place made for her. It wasn't much later when she met Zach, and she was so hungry for something to fill the emptiness that maybe she ignored her gut, overlooked the warning signs.

Riley sucked the bottle dry, and Vega hoisted him up to her shoulder, patted his back. She pulled out her phone, fingers hovering over the screen, and something heavy pressed against her chest. She had no one to call.

It rang and Vega jumped, dropping it on the ground. Zach's face appeared on the screen beneath a few specks of dirt. Handsome, that perfect blend of angular jaw with just enough of a five-o'clock shadow to give him a man-of-the-outdoors look without overdoing it. Her stomach curdled at the image; she touched her wrist, felt the pull of her incision scar on her abdomen, tender now from his assault.

The call went to voice mail. She picked up the phone, and a Snap popped up on the screen. She clicked on the icon—it was an image of his face, lips pursed in a kiss. She clicked the button to turn the screen off. The phone had been a gift from Zach when she first moved in with him. She'd never had one so nice before. They'd sat on his front steps, his arm draped around her shoulders. He'd clicked on something called Find My.

This way I'll always know where you are. He'd kissed the spot just under her ear. *You never have to be alone again.*

She'd snuggled against him, hand on her belly. Her baby would have the home she'd always dreamed about. But her smile had wavered. Something about the way Zach had said it, the possessive grip of his arm, gave life to a tiny seed of doubt. She'd brushed it away. Her mother had doubted all men. That didn't have to be Vega's story too.

Riley let out a loud burp. Another ping on her phone. A text this time that unfurled across her screen. **What the fuck are you doing in Kansas? Bring my son home or I'm calling the cops.**

Panic gnawed into her belly.

Ditch the phone. It was one of her mother's cardinal rules. *If they can find you, they will.*

She pictured her Bitmoji on Zach's Snap Map. The chilled air breathed goose bumps across her skin. He could see where she was. She clicked on the app and found something called "Ghost Mode" that hid her location.

The phone rang again with Zach's picture, and her grip weakened as she thought of his words from all those months ago. *I'll always know where you are.* She fumbled with the phone, trying to remember what he'd clicked to get to the Find My app. She'd had a phone before, but it had been cheap and affordable—no bells and whistles like this one. Finally, there it was. Inside an icon that looked like a bike sprocket. She slid the "Share My Location" button to Off, and her lungs finally opened. Another buzz, another threatening text, and Vega powered off her phone and tossed it into the cup holder like it might sting her. Couldn't shake the feeling that he could see her, hear her, find her.

She laid a blanket across the floor and carefully settled Riley on top, quickly unbuttoning his blue jammies to change him. Her stomach in knots, hands shaking. She didn't have the money to replace the phone, not yet. And without an idea of what she was going to do next, she didn't feel like she could ditch it until she could get another one.

From a handmade box on the floor, she pulled a diaper and the wipes. She thought of Zach calling the cops. It was ludicrous. She'd show them her bruises, tell them everything. He was the horrible person, not her.

But her mother never involved the police. She refused, even when Vega questioned her about it. Said that in her experience, it caused more trouble than good. Told her about a woman whose abusive husband got her arrested for defending herself. Twisted her words, intimidated her, charmed the police. The woman ended up in jail, signed a confession just so she could get out instead of facing a long judicial process, had to take anger-management classes in order to be around her children again.

Vega pulled the tabs on Riley's diaper closed, zipped up his pajamas, and held him to her chest, horrified to think of losing him to Zach. She stared out across the rest stop parking lot to the plains that spread flat for miles and miles. Her body hollowed. Where could she go? She thought of the loose coalition of women who had worked with her mother from time to time. One could procure an ID and other paperwork with some advance notice; another secured cash as needed. Renee had been the one who helped women leave. And Gwynne, the only one Vega had ever met—she was the counselor, the one who followed up, made sure the people they helped were doing the best they could. Vega had lost touch with Gwynne after Renee died. Ashamed she hadn't carried on where her mother left off. Confident that she'd never need her help anyway.

She touched her forehead. *Idiot.*

She chewed on her tongue. *Think.* What was her next step? *Find a safe place.* It was a checklist of questions. *Do you have family you could live with? Money stashed away somewhere? A safe place he doesn't know about?* All these years, she'd listened to her mom prepare women for a life on the run. Never thinking it could be her.

Renee had been far from a typical mom. Built her career by hand, literally, as a very skilled handywoman. Her business had been targeted toward female customers, she'd told Vega, because women needed someone they could trust to come into their homes. *How come they trust you?* she'd asked once.

Her mother had nudged her gently with an elbow and smiled. *Because I'm not a man.* It had been a truth that Vega had been raised on. Like *vegetables are good for you, too much sugar is bad,* and *most men are dangerous.* Vega had let it sink in.

Men are dangerous.

They'd lived in Renee's van and traveled wherever there was work. Sometimes staying a few months in one location, other times only a few days. It mattered less about the work and more about her mother's need to move on. Vega always sensed it coming because it typically happened after one of Renee's frequent nightmares.

There was a picture that Vega had framed and hung on the wall of the van, near where she and her mom used to sleep. One that she'd taken of her mother at work—face still with concentration, kneeling, a tool belt cinched around her waist, hair under a bandanna.

Hand me the flat head, would you, peanut?

Sometimes the work was straight up—installing a new faucet, painting the house, landscaping. There wasn't much Renee wouldn't take or couldn't do. She was a hard worker, diligent and fair, and she was always the lowest priced. It was, Vega understood as she got older, one of the many reasons they lived on the road. It was the cheapest option. And the safest, according to Renee.

Hold the paintbrush at an angle, got it, V?

But there was another side to her work, one that Vega didn't see until she was old enough to understand the early-morning calls, the hurried escapes. As a little girl, Vega grew anxious for the women, could feel the fear that swirled around the ones who ran. It made her cling to her mother.

Ring the doorbell and give her the envelope, okay?

Okay. She'd been ten at the time, and they'd been in Montana, working jobs in Billings. Word of mouth spread quickly, and once Renee picked up one job, she'd usually snag a few more. This one had been so easy—unclogging a kitchen drain—that Vega had wondered why Renee had taken it.

If the husband answers—

Tell him I'm selling Girl Scout cookies, I know. Her leg muscles felt twitchy, pierced with a nervous energy.

This wasn't unusual. Sometimes they gave women and their children rides to places or thick envelopes like this one. The women had suitcases stuffed so that the zippers were nearly bursting, or the children clutched trash bags and one stuffed animal. Sometimes all her mother did was sit at the kitchen table after a job and listen while the women cried. Some women had bruises—finger-size, on their forearms or biceps, along their jaws, circling an eye. It's why Renee worked only when the husbands or boyfriends had left for the day or an evening out. It was all carefully planned.

On that day, her mom had sat in the driver's seat, frowning at the house in front of them. An early-morning glow hit the roof, sliding down the eaves as the sun rose. Vega held the big yellow envelope in her hands and played with the silver clasp, opening and closing it.

What's in here, Momma? She'd never asked before. She wasn't sure why, other than it seemed part of the job and it felt silly to question it, like asking why she painted a house or used a hammer to pound in a nail.

Her mother had looked at Vega and smiled, but it didn't reach her eyes. She'd touched Vega's chin and softened, like Vega reminded her of something good.

A way out, she had said.

That day had gone terribly wrong. But it was the first time Vega understood what her mother really did—and when she truly believed what Renee had always told her: men were dangerous and couldn't be trusted.

Riley squirmed against her and she patted his back, inhaled his milky breath. There was a painful pull in her shoulder from where Zach had twisted her arm. Her mother's lifetime of work and Vega's longing for a family had trapped her in a similar life as the women they'd helped.

She placed Riley back into the carrier. His eyes pinned to her face, and Vega felt the weight of his innocence, his implicit trust. "I don't know what I'm doing," she whispered.

A state-trooper car pulled alongside her van, and a female officer with dark hair and easy dimples got out of the passenger side, smiling at Vega and rubbing her hands together. "It's cold today!" she said, and her eyes drifted to Riley in his car seat, who was moving his little fists in the air, warm under a blanket Vega had tucked around his body. Vega fiddled with the blanket, needing something to do to hide a sudden nervousness that fluttered through her hands.

The officer smiled at Riley. "Snug as a bug, aren't you?"

Her gaze slid from the baby to the state of Vega's van, the tools organized in handmade crates that were bolted to the floor, a mattress in the back, plates and silverware in plastic storage tubs. When Renee could afford it, she'd purchased a trailer to store all her tools but had kept the bins inside the van to organize their living space. At Zach's request, Vega had gotten rid of the trailer when she moved in with him. There'd been no room to store it, and he didn't want it permanently parked outside.

Vega felt her pulse beating fast in her neck. She slid the van door closed, gave the trooper a smile that felt stiff and insincere. "Better get back on the road while the little man has a full belly."

The woman blinked and Vega bit the inside of her cheek, her mind turning over Zach's threat. Had he already called the cops?

"Have a safe trip," she said, and moved toward the bathrooms.

Vega breathed out and flung open the driver's door, buckling her seat belt and starting the van all at the same time. She needed to get far away from Zach, somewhere she could breathe without fear knotting her stomach. She couldn't think this close to him.

Her back tires squealed when she accelerated, and Riley started to cry. Where should she go? Her hands gripped the steering wheel, thighs jittery with indecision and panic. When she turned the dial to warm the van, her eyes caught the postcard clipped to an air vent. A picture of a town called Crystal, somewhere in the hills of Ohio. She'd found the postcard when she was little, snooping around the van on a snowy day, bored and curious. It had been stuck inside one of the clothing drawers her mother had built under the bench seats in the van. She'd thought it was the prettiest picture—nothing in the West looked that green—and asked if she could hang it in the van, like people in houses do with pictures. Her mother's jaw had tightened, and Vega bit her nail, worried she'd be in trouble for snooping.

Instead, her mother had touched her face, eyes gentle. *Why would you want to hang a picture of a nothing town full of nobodies and bullies?*

Vega put her hands on her hips. *How come you keep a picture of a nothing town with a bunch of nobodies and bullies?*

Her mother laughed, and it had poured over Vega like the coolest rain on the hottest day. She didn't know then that she was a sassy child. There were no other kids around to compare herself with.

Renee had dipped her chin as though Vega had won. *Fair enough. I keep it to remind me why I left and why I won't ever go back.*

Vega accelerated onto the highway, her shoulders tense but her decision made. A nothing town full of nobodies sounded like the perfect place to hide.

CHAPTER THREE

VEGA

Ohio
April 2021

The town didn't look anything as advertised. Vega tapped the picture in her hand and held it out, away from the baby's head, so she could study it again. It was an old postcard, wrinkled and worn, the kind with a stamp on the lower corner that read HELLO FROM CRYSTAL! It wasn't a real picture, more a drawing made to look like a picture. And it was a total lie.

Riley mewled against her chest, wiggled his skinny arms, and then burrowed his tiny head deeper into the soft carrier Vega wore strapped to her body. She rocked from one foot to the other, patted the baby's tiny back, and locked a yawn inside. Her eyes were gritty and dry from lack of sleep. Every time she'd closed her eyes, the scene from her kitchen stained the darkness.

Now that she had stopped driving, the fear that had trailed her from Colorado caught up, lurking behind her, tracing cold fingers down her back. She looked again at the postcard and shook her head. It showed a beautiful sun-dappled stream lined with trees that were thicker and greener than anything she'd ever seen in the West. Quaint buildings peeked through the leaves, as though a bustling little town lay just out of sight, serenaded night and day by the babbling of the clear, clean water. She used to stare at the picture while her mother put miles between their last job and the next. Imagined herself standing ankle deep in the bubbling water, the leaves filtering the sun and shading everything green.

She lowered the postcard, frowned at the muddy half-paved street and paint-peeled buildings in front of her. A few of them abandoned with shattered windows and splintered siding; the handful of others housing an odd collection of stores: pottery, herbs, recycled—no, what was the term . . . *up*cycled—jewelry, a post office, a restaurant that looked like it was only open for lunch, and a store with a front window full of tiny stuffed animals. Steep hills with trees that hovered over the street blocked out much of the weak midwestern sun, giving the light a bluish hue.

Her mother had hardly ever talked about her life before Vega. But as Vega grew older, she'd pressed her for information. Where was she from? Who were her parents? Her mother never talked about Vega's father. And when Vega did ask, Renee was cryptic. Vega worried the truth was that her mother had run from Vega's father. And she didn't want that to be true. She wanted to believe that she and her mom were different, too strong to be in dangerous relationships.

Vega had loved their life as nomads, but over the years, their transience, their total lack of family outside of the two of them, had made her desperate for something to anchor to, even if it was only in the past. Once, when Vega was eight, she'd woken to the sound of rain pelting their van, wind battering the metal, making it rock and creak like it might fold in half from the onslaught. A strike of lightning illuminated her mother's sleeping face. Thunder followed, so loud she thought her eardrums might burst. *Mommy!* she'd screamed, and in the next flash of lightning, she saw her mother's eyes wide open, and she pulled Vega close, arms strong around her.

Vega had pressed her face against her mother's chest, felt the beating of her heart beneath her cheekbone, couldn't fall asleep while the storm raged and didn't want her mother to either. *Do you have a mom and dad?*

A sigh that pushed against Vega. *Of course I do, silly.*

Do you have a brother or a sister?

She made a sound in her throat, like she might cry. *I had a sister.*

What was she like?

A pause and Vega went rigid, thought her mother would stop talking; then she kissed the top of Vega's head and tightened her arms around her. *She was funny and sweet, just like you.*

Later, when Vega was playing hide-and-go-seek with her stuffed animals and snooping again, she'd found a picture inside her mother's drawer—one of a girl sitting on the steps of a giant yellow school bus surrounded by a forest. The girl slouched against the side of the stairwell, cigarette in one hand and a lazy smile on her lips, her other arm extended, middle finger raised at the camera. Vega had gasped; it was her mother, young and vibrant and giving someone the finger.

Vega had lain on her stomach and stared at the picture. This was a side of her mother she'd never seen. It felt like time traveling, and Vega had wished she knew more about the girl. There was a hardness in her eyes but also something unbound, something free. On the back, handwriting she didn't recognize: *Crystal 1995.* She wanted to bring the picture to her mother, ask her to tell her stories about that girl, but something stopped her, and instead, she'd hidden the picture under the socks in her own drawer.

But now, standing in the real Crystal, she didn't feel a link to her past. Her skin itched from two days on the road and lack of sleep. It had taken much longer than she'd expected to get here. There had been middle-of-the-night stops to find simethicone, diapers, wipes that didn't burn Riley's little bottom, and a pacifier because she'd dropped one in the parking lot of a truck stop and couldn't bear to put it back into his mouth, even after she'd cleaned it off.

She'd tried to drive through the night, but she couldn't keep her eyes open despite Riley's cries and had to stop several times to walk the baby in circles to try and calm him, to get him to nap as soon as he stopped. Gas pains, she finally learned once she'd quickly turned on the phone to google *why does my baby cry so much?*

The door to the herb store opened, and a woman appeared, wearing a loose jean dress with a large American flag embroidered across the chest, gold stars along the hem. She squinted at Vega. "Sounds like your baby has colic."

Vega held Riley close, straightened her shoulders, unsure how to respond. "Is there a motel around here?" She hadn't seen one on the way into town. Her body ached, and the lack of sleep buzzed in her head along with an undercurrent of worry. Her money would run out soon if she didn't find a way to make some. And now that she was here, she was at a sudden loss. What was her plan?

The woman folded her arms. "This isn't the city." She said it like it was something Vega should have already known. "There's no parking on Main Street. It drives customers away."

Clouds collected overhead; a breeze shot down the road, making the sign above her door creak on its hinges.

Vega shifted, patting the baby's back. He stiffened his little arms and legs, cried harder. Tears stung her eyes. She'd driven all this way and now what? She looked at her van. It had been her home for years, but sleeping in it one more night was a giant step backward for her and Riley. She wanted him to know what it felt like to have an actual roof over his head. She bit her lip, felt everything pile on top of her and, for a moment, thought she might collapse from the weight of it all.

Another door opened—this one black lacquered with a polished window—underneath a sign that said EVE's PLACE. A man walked out, smiling at Vega and shaking his head. "I'll be damned."

She stiffened.

"I told her there's no parking on Main Street, Heff," the woman said, still in her doorway.

Heff gave the woman a smile. "We've talked about that, Jane. It's just your preference, which, I regret to inform you, doesn't count as the law." He approached Vega. "Eve said someone was coming today."

Jane gave a loud huff. "You choose to fraternize with sin. Think of your soul, son."

The man was tall, with honey-blond hair and bright-blue eyes. "Thank you for your concern, Jane, but my soul's just fine. It might do you some good to examine your own, though. Pretty sure the Bible mentions something about loving neighbors."

Jane's face hardened, and she disappeared inside her store.

The man turned to Vega. "I'm Heff."

Vega, who had watched the exchange utterly confused, replied automatically. "Vega."

He pointed to the postcard in her hand. "That's a Crystal antique." His voice was low and rumbly, and the baby relaxed against her like the man was telling them a bedtime story. "Carl painted that picture years ago and turned them into postcards and magnets. He wanted Crystal to be the next up-and-coming artist town." Heff laughed like he and Vega were old friends sharing a joke, talking as though it were part of a longer conversation and Carl were another old friend.

She took a step back, immediately suspicious, and slid the postcard into her bag. Her head swam, and she wished she'd stopped in Columbus, where there'd been a zillion motels she could have stayed at. At least given herself some time to regroup. Her single goal had been to get here, and now that she was, she realized she hadn't thought much beyond that.

On the door he'd just walked through, Vega saw a sign stuck to the glass: APARTMENT FOR RENT. Her heart fluttered. Renting was out of the question, but maybe they'd consider a short-term stay, like an Airbnb kind of deal. She pointed at the sign. "You have a place to rent?"

He craned his head to see where she was pointing, then turned back, smiling. "The only one in town. It's not big. Just a one bed, one bath with a small kitchen and a living room–slash–dining room. But it's got a walk-out porch with a view of Main Street that you can't find anywhere else in town. You could put a chair out there for some indoor-slash-outdoor living space." He handed her a business card.

She studied it, the words bleary, her body so tired it had sucked all the moisture from her eyes. It was simple—underneath his name, a string of words that read, Your local real estate agent/deputy/ local artist. "You're really into slashes." The normalcy of the conversation felt at odds with the rising anxiety that tugged at her bowels. Flashes of Zach's face, the feel of his fist in her gut were playing on repeat in her head.

"I suppose I am," he said, and pointed his thumb over his shoulder. "The apartment's above Eve's Place."

Eve's Place was the only building with a fresh coat of paint. Big black lettering outlined in gold arced across the wide storefront window. Inside, the cozy store displayed outdoor gear, taffy, coffee, and small bins of produce. Against one wall was a tiny bar, big enough for four people to sit elbow to elbow, with a shiny espresso machine on the counter and a domed ice-cream cabinet on the floor. "Is it furnished?"

"It sure is. Furniture's seen some days, though. 'Course, so has the apartment. It's in one of the original buildings in Crystal. Probably dates back to the late 1800s."

She tapped Riley on the back, stood straighter. "Would you consider renting it for a night?" With the money in the van, she should have enough for a night, plus some left over. She looked at the dirt from the half-paved street crusting the bottom of her boots; a town like this couldn't be that expensive.

"I'll have to run it by Eve, but I don't see why not. You seem like you could use a break."

Vega jiggled Riley, whose crying had returned. It rattled her eardrums. The man looked at her, head tilted, something like pity in his eyes, and she stiffened, brushed a piece of hair from her forehead. She must be a sight, with her road-wrinkled and stained clothes, screaming infant, and bags under her eyes.

"But I'm pretty sure Eve will have no problem renting for one night. She's new here like you."

Vega raised an eyebrow. "You give a store away to all your newcomers?"

The baby's legs jerked when Heff laughed. Vega started to bounce up and down on her toes, rubbed circles on Riley's back.

"Around here, if you aren't born in Crystal, then you're new until the day you die. I wouldn't say Eve's a newcomer—she moved back here five years ago. She's just a little different than some folks remembered. But that's her story to tell." He smiled fondly. "Makes the best cappuccino this side of the Appalachians, sells local produce, and if she's in the mood, she might even tell you what's in your future." He lifted his eyebrows. "Eve died once. I mean, really died—heart stopped pumping blood, brain waves kaput and everything. But she wasn't all the way dead, see. She'd just gone on to the other side, and when she came back, well . . . she was changed for the better."

Vega patted the baby's back and waited for the man to wrap it up. She wanted to sleep, she wanted peace, she wanted a moment to breathe that wasn't inside her van. But the man seemed to talk in pages, and she wasn't sure if he'd reached the end of page one.

He leaned closer, like he was sharing a secret. "It's taken a few folks around here some time to welcome Eve back."

"Why?"

He pointed at her. "Exactly. And that's the problem with closed-minded folks, isn't it?"

The baby wiggled his little fist, grabbing a piece of her hair. Vega didn't respond, waiting instead for the man to answer his own rhetorical question.

"Because change scares them so dang much, doesn't it?" The man wasn't much older than her, but he spoke with an odd mixture of black-and-white movie star meets millennial. "Anyway," he said, "the house coffee is the best, too, if you're not on a cappuccino budget." He lifted his eyes, indicating the upstairs apartment. "You might want to be careful with the little one up there."

Above the store was a tiny porch, with a railing so low that it might come to her knees and big enough for maybe one chair if it could fit through the slim french door.

"That railing is too low for him. I can ask Eve about a baby lock for the door."

She looked down at Riley's tiny body pressed against her chest—his cheek smushed against her, eyes drooping low—and rubbed her finger along his velvet skin. "The baby can't crawl or open doors yet."

Heff shook his head, like she'd surprised him or something, still smiling as if she were the most interesting person he'd ever met. She took a step back. Her mother had taught her enough to know that men could not be trusted. And Zach had made her question her own judgment.

But the man stepped back, too, and Vega couldn't tell if he did it to give her space or to mock her. "Okay, then," he said. "That's a true statement for sure. Does your baby have a name?"

Vega hesitated, wanting to tell the man to mind his own business. He was probably the type who touched pregnant bellies without asking or pressed a hand along a woman's hip, chummy and assuming. But it was late, the mist was hardening into rain, and Vega needed to rest because she didn't think she could drive another mile without falling asleep and crashing. The idea of a place with a bed where she could lie beside Riley—a solid door with a lock, a bathroom, if only for a night—was all she wanted. She wrapped her arms around the baby and stood a little taller. "Baby," she said.

He dipped his head. "Smart," he said. "Get to know the little guy first, find out who he is before you make assumptions. I like it."

She had no idea how to respond. The man was so comfortable in his own skin that he wore it like a silk robe. Vega had never felt that way. Her skin was her armor, the only way she'd felt protected in a world of dangerous people, where her only family was her mom and the van her only home. That and her spiky blonde hair and black leather jacket and the tattoos that curled up both arms and across her chest, tickling her neck and snaking down her thighs. Zach had been the only person she'd let inside her armor, and that was a mistake she promised herself she'd never make again.

There were soft lines around the man's blue eyes, and he wore a thick blue-and-green-plaid shirt, untucked over his jeans, and muddied work boots. Nothing to indicate he was the police. "Where's your badge?" she said.

He stuck his thumbs into his jeans pockets and laughed. "I'm more of a volunteer. A part-time official. Lots of people have left these parts over the years, so funding for a full-time deputy dried up." He sighed. "We have a fellow who comes through town a couple times a month. I suppose you could say I'm a Band-Aid for the times when he's not here."

She looked around. A single stoplight swung on a heavy black wire. The light changed to red. There was not a car in sight. "For who?"

His laugh was a deep baritone that made the baby wiggle his arms. "Crystal doesn't seem like much, but it's a good town, good people. There's just some who want to keep to themselves, others who want to see it grow, and a few who don't quite agree on a path forward." He gestured at the storefronts. "We're in the middle of an art revival, though. We have at least two artists selling their work at Eve's now. And that doesn't even include me. I tell you what, it's driving tourists to our town. There was a guy in last week who bought one of my bottle-cap openers. And some woman a few months ago who bought one of Carl's paintings. So, pretty successful, I'd say."

Vega didn't know how to respond. She patted the baby's back and struggled for something to say. Nothing came to mind.

Heff waited a second longer than was comfortable so that the silence hung between them, broken only by a handful of raindrops hitting the storefront windows. He whistled a soft tune. The man was odd but, Vega was beginning to think, in a nonthreatening way, and she let the idea roll across her skin, smooth away her suspicious bristling. It didn't last. Zach had seemed nonthreatening, too, and look how wrong she'd been about that.

A fat raindrop hit the baby's tender skin, and he jerked. Sweat slid down the center of Vega's back. Once he started crying again, it was nearly impossible to get him to stop. And in the last week, if he was awake, he was crying. Sometimes she thought Riley cried because of all the bad in the world, like he was born knowing.

Heff moved quickly toward a small red door to the right of Eve's Place. "Would you like to see the apartment now? Get Baby out of the rain?" He opened the door. "I'll go ask Eve if she'd consider a one-night rental while you look around."

Just then, loud squeaking noises came from behind her. They were high pitched and rivaled the baby's. She turned to find two pigs, hair mottled white and brown, sauntering down the street, snouts pressed to the earth. Their hooves trampled the little garden outside the herb store where the woman, Jane, had stood moments ago. Their mouths turned the dirt, splattering soil across the yellow flowers.

"Kunekune," Heff said.

"Excuse me?" The pigs came to a rest at Vega's feet, literally falling onto their sides, their bellies jiggling under their wiry fur. She wrinkled her nose at the smell lifting up from their bodies.

"That's their breed. Kunekune. A local favorite. Supposed to be friendly, except they only seem to like Eve." His eyes crinkled. "And you, apparently. And also Betty. But who doesn't love Betty?"

Vega shrugged. Who was Betty? "You let them roam around town?" She bounced from foot to foot and rubbed circles on the baby's back.

Heff ran a hand through his hair. "Well, they don't hurt anybody except for Jane's flowers over there, so I'd say they're out of my jurisdiction."

She laughed and the sound surprised her and the baby. His little bow mouth opened wide, and he released a lusty cry, one she had learned by now meant irritation but mostly hunger. A lump thickened in her throat. Her entire twenty-four years, she'd never felt helpless. Her mother had made sure of that by teaching her how to survive. But after she died, Vega was a boat without a rudder. Stuck. And when she met Zach, he'd been so interested in her, so attractive, everything she'd dreamed about in a good man. She'd felt special. Riley had been unexpected, and early on, Zach had been upset, angry that her birth control had failed. She'd felt terrible, guilty at forcing him into something he didn't want. Because she'd wanted the baby from the very first second she saw the double lines on the pregnancy test. To her surprise, Zach had warmed quickly to the idea and invited Vega to move in. It was all so fast but also exciting. She was about to have everything she'd yearned so long for.

Heff cleared his throat, and Vega was yanked back to the present. In the two months since Riley had been born, the early warning signs that Zach wasn't what he seemed had grown into a screeching bell, but with an infant and no one other than Zach in her life, Vega had felt trapped.

"If you'd like, you can go up and check out the apartment on your own, maybe give you some privacy to feed Baby if you need to. No rush. When you're done, I'll be inside eating an ice-cream cone down here at Eve's. She makes her own ice cream too. Did I mention that?"

The way he implied that she might need to feed the infant—not embarrassed or flustered, like she supposed some men were at the mere mention of boobs and nipples. He said it with respect and the barest hint of awe. She briefly wondered if Heff was what her mother had called a good-enough man. It was how she described a man who didn't beat or try to control women. It had been her mother's opinion that even the best man would only ever be good enough because, at the end of the day, most men took more than they gave.

Vega thought of Zach and felt nauseous. Her mother had been right.

She gave Heff a curt smile. "Thank you. I won't be long."

CHAPTER FOUR

VEGA

The couch was small but soft, and after the hours Vega had spent in the stiff driver's seat of her van, it seemed to fold around her body like a cloud. But Riley was wailing now, his thin lips vibrating with the noise. The sight clamped around her heart, and she yanked open her bag, wanting to give him relief, wanting to fill his belly, wanting to do anything to ease his pain. She fumbled with a bottle, quickly warming water at the faucet, baby balanced in her left arm. He rooted around her bicep, searching for milk in her sleeve. Her throat clenched at his vulnerability, and she shook the bottle hard. He quickly latched on to the rubber nipple, letting out little moans with each gulp.

Vega breathed out and sank back into the couch, gazing outside the window. The view peeked over the rooftops of the buildings across the street and into the woods. Delicate green leaves unfolded from branches, and a flare of purple flowers and white petals dotted the depths. It was pretty. Different from the Rocky Mountain–spring brown that was punctured by dark-green pine trees and piles of snow. And remote, which made it an ideal place for her. It had been hard enough to find it on a map, and the one road sign for Crystal had been hit once or twice and leaned so far backward that all she'd been able to read was STAL.

For the moment, she felt far away from Colorado, and safe. It was peaceful, with the baby slurping at the bottle, the murmur of voices that floated up from the store below. Thin ceilings. One overhead light, missing a shade, the bulb spreading a garish white glow above her head. A musty smell in the apartment made it feel old and unused.

She wanted to lean back, close her eyes and rest, sleep for even a minute. It pulled at her with velvet fingers, and she almost gave in, but then she popped up, blinked, shook her head. She couldn't relax.

She was running low on diapers and formula; she had very few clothes except the ones she'd hurriedly packed for the two of them. When she'd moved in with Zach, they'd pooled her money into his, using a shared Venmo account to pay for nearly everything. Neither of them had much, so Vega had worked doing a few odd handy jobs right up until Riley was born, despite the fact that her belly had made some work more difficult.

She stared at her phone, afraid to turn it on. Her mother's words hung in the air: *If they can track you, they will.* She pulled her wallet from her bag, counted the cash she had left. A few hundred dollars. She bit her lip. For the first time in days, she was still, and with the stillness came a tornado of feelings that had no place to rest, whirling around her, stoking a panic that brought her to her feet.

She needed work.

She pulled a Chromebook from her bag. Her mother had bought it for her to use for her homeschool classes. It had not aged well and was often more glitchy than useful. But thank God she'd thought to grab it when she left yesterday. She often found work on the local sites for neighborhoods. She powered it on and waited for the several minutes it took to warm up, like an old car in the dead of winter. The screen lit up, and she clicked on the browser. Nothing.

She tried again. Same thing. No Wi-Fi? She looked around for a router, trying not to move while the baby ate. The bottle emptied, and she put him up on her shoulder, patting his back. If he burped or puked, it seemed to help. For a little bit, at least. She had never thought she'd ever want to be puked on. While she tried to coax a burp, she walked around the apartment, searching everywhere for a router. Seeing nothing, she gathered her bag, keeping the baby upright, and carefully navigated the steep stairs.

She hesitated outside, hand on the door, and tried to breathe. Riley wiggled against her, and she touched his head, thought of her mom. When Vega was little, Renee taught her how to ride a bike. *Every kid should know.* Later, it grew into mountain biking together, something Vega loved because it was time with her mom that wasn't work or rescuing women. It was normal. But on her very first attempt, the bike had wobbled and Vega was thrown to the ground, knees scraped bloody, tears hot on her cheeks. Renee had knelt beside her, let her cry. When she was done, her mom had pulled her to her feet and pointed her toward the bike. *When you fall, get back up. There's no sense in having a pity party.*

A wet breeze brushed over her skin and Vega looked down at Riley. She wouldn't go back. She'd made her decision, and even with nothing and nobody to help her but herself, she had to survive. For her son.

Her legs shook, tears building behind her eyes. Riley stared up at her, not crying, a lift of his lips. She wiped a hand across her eyes, smiled. "No sense in having a pity party now, is there, Riley?"

She opened the door.

Eve's Place smelled like coffee beans and firewood. Heff leaned against the bar, holding a chocolate-topped cake cone, his back to Vega and the baby. Beside him sat a woman drinking coffee from a tiny espresso cup. The store had wood floors that creaked under Vega's feet and a warmth in the air that feathered across her bare arms, comforting and welcoming after the cold sprinkles and unheated apartment. Riley sighed against her shoulder, and she pulled the blanket around his tiny body, keeping him upright. The peace he exuded at that moment with a full belly, gas expelled, rushed over her, too, and it was so unexpected tears pooled in her eyes.

She quickly wiped at her face. *No pity party.*

"We carry a few diapers but only in small packs that wouldn't last more than a couple days." The woman beside Heff stood and moved around behind the counter. She wore a leather cowboy hat over her long brown hair and at least four inches of silver and turquoise bracelets on both of her slender forearms. She smiled. "I'm Eve. And you must be Vega." Her voice was deep and hoarse, like a singer or a smoker. "Heff's already told the entire town about the beautiful new girl."

Heff turned, laughing. "I'm observant and I tell the truth, Eve."

Eve rolled her eyes. "You're an old man trapped in a young man's body." The two spoke like longtime friends.

Vega rocked her weight, the comforting press of the baby against her chest. She was socially awkward. A fact she'd realized after moving in with Zach, meeting his friends, having dinner with his family—her interactions stiff and uncomfortable. Always an eye on the door, ready to leave. But after two decades of living like a nomad, it wasn't surprising. Just painful. And it needled her. Made her question her mother's decision to raise Vega the way she had. Wish she could get answers for why. Resent her for not being more honest when she'd had the chance.

"I can order the bigger packs for you," Eve said to Vega. "If you're taking the apartment, that is." Her smile was easy and wide, and carried a youthfulness that reminded Vega of Renee, who, she guessed, would have been around Eve's age if she were still alive.

Vega felt the sting of tears again and bit the inside of her cheek in frustration over her unbridled emotion. "Is there Wi-Fi in the apartment?"

Eve studied her for a moment. "I only have Wi-Fi in the store, and it's spotty and slow, to say the least. The hollers around here make it nearly impossible for adequate internet access, and I'm a bit of a, well, a—"

"Eve's a traditionalist," Heff said. "She likes space to breathe and meditate and room to do—"

"Whatever the hell I want," finished Eve. "And, Vega, in case you're wondering how we function without fast Wi-Fi, well, I moved here to get away from the grind, and I've grown fond of removing most of that social media noise from my life."

Vega blinked. She was so tired her vision had started to blur. When had she last slept for more than a few hours at a time? She didn't understand why Eve was telling her all this. She didn't care if Eve wore Tibetan robes and had taken a vow of silence. That was her business. "You don't have to explain yourself to me," she said.

"Of course not, but if you're going to live here, you might as well get used to people sharing their business with you, good or bad. It's a small-town thing." Eve slid a package of diapers into a paper sack, along with a travel bag of wipes and a couple of wrapped sandwiches, and pushed it across the counter to Vega. "This should get you started," she said.

Her stomach twisted. It was generous but familiar. Like Eve knew she had no other options. She thought of the drive back to Columbus, and a cold, wet night in the van, shivering beside Riley. "I-I just need a place to stay for tonight. Is that a problem?" One night. It would give her time to gather her thoughts, maybe even sleep so she could have a clear-enough head to figure out her next steps. Get the van fixed up the way her mother had so she and Riley could stay in there if they had to. After that, Vega had no plans. She swallowed hard, tensed her biceps. All she'd wanted was a home, and she couldn't even give Riley that. The idea that she might fail gnawed at her stomach.

Fine lines spread from the corners of Eve's eyes. She exuded a maternal warmth that turned Vega's knees weak and made the store claustrophobic. "You hardly look like you're able to stand, and your eyes keep closing like you haven't slept in days. Stay the night. No charge."

"Um, no, I can pay. I don't need—"

"You can argue with Eve, but she usually wins." Heff handed her a paper cup of coffee. "I can get your things out of your van and take them upstairs for you."

The cup was hot in her hand but Vega froze. They seemed genuine, friendly, but she needed to do this on her own. It's what her mother had done. She thought of Zach punching her like she was nothing. The hardness in his eyes. Accusing her of kidnapping Riley. Making her out to be the bad guy. Anger swam circles in her belly. If Zach had reported her to the police, she couldn't stay in one place. And no matter how friendly they seemed, Heff and Eve were nothing more than strangers.

She tried to smile at Heff. "I don't have much, I . . . all I need is in my bag here. I'll just take the keys, if you don't mind." She set the coffee down and lifted the paper sack by the handles. "And thanks for this, Eve."

Eve smiled and crossed her arms; her bracelets thumped together, giving off a metallic tinkling. "Anytime."

The door opened then, bringing with it rain-soaked air. The coldness was a shot of adrenaline and Vega inhaled, letting it run through her body, wake her up. Riley moved his fist in her hair, still peering over her shoulder, and she was grateful that she'd removed the studs that rode up the curve of her ear. He'd almost yanked one out through her skin the day before.

Her exit was blocked by an older man who stood just inside the door, shaking the rain from his coat and hat. He narrowed his eyes. "Your gosh-darn pigs are tearing up Main Street like it's their own private mud pool. You need to control your animals, Eve."

"You're not kidding, Carl. Those pigs have minds of their own. I'll have to mend their fence, I suppose. Seems somebody thought it would be funny to run it over in the middle of the night again."

His forehead wrinkled, and for a moment he looked confused, like he'd been prepared for a fight and now couldn't figure out how to respond. "It happened again?"

"Sure did."

"Harrison boys?"

Eve laughed. "'Boys'? In their forties, some with grandkids, and we're still calling them *boys*?"

Carl folded his arms, and to Vega, he looked miserable. "It ain't right, what they're doing," he said, eyes on the floor, voice low and halting. "Betty and me . . . we don't agree with it, you know that. You're one of us, Eve, even if you don't look like it."

Heff made a noise and Vega thought he looked exasperated. The whole conversation felt played out, like everyone else had been here before. "Uh, well, Carl, that's not—"

Eve smiled at the older man. Vega wondered why the woman put up with it. Why someone like her wanted to live in a backwoods town in the first place.

But Eve didn't seem bothered. "How's Betty doing?"

Carl stuck his hands into his coat, appearing to have been disarmed for the moment. A pair of yellow suspenders made to look like two rulers running up and down his torso peeked out from under his coat. "Oh, she's doing real good, Eve. Said to tell you thank you for stopping by with your witch oils. They really did help her headache."

"My pleasure."

For the first time, Carl seemed to notice Vega, and she held in a groan. Crystal had seemed a perfect place to hide out and avoid people, and here it looked like she was on track to meet half the town.

His eyebrows shot up and his mustache wiggled when he noticed the baby. "My days, a littl'un. Ain't that just somethin'?"

"It surely is." Heff slid his hands into his pockets, rocked on his toes. "This is Vega, Carl," he said. "But she can tell you that herself, of course. She's going to give the apartment a trial run tonight, courtesy of Eve."

Vega fidgeted, guilt over not being completely honest about her financial situation a tick burrowing into her flesh. Her mother never took charity, always provided for the two of them on her own. Her mind searched for some way to turn this situation around. She thought of the warped floor in the kitchen upstairs, the hole in the drywall by the window, the radiator that hadn't turned on when she tried to adjust the heat. "I noticed that the apartment needed quite a bit of work. I can fix things for you—do some remodeling, light plumbing, a little bit of electrical work."

Carl's face lit up. "You're a handyman—er, woman, I mean. Sorry, Eve. Person?"

Eve smiled at the man, but to Vega it seemed indulgent, tired.

"I am," Vega said.

"Smart." Eve's eyes were soft. "Come to think of it, that apartment does need quite a bit of work."

"It surely does," Carl agreed.

"A trade, then?" Eve said.

An unfamiliar feeling spread across Vega's shoulders, straightening them out. She had found a way to provide for her son. Just like her mother had for her. "Yes, if that works for you."

"It's a deal."

Vega curled her hands into fists, would have punched the air in excitement if she'd been alone. Figured it was best to leave before they asked any more questions. "Baby here will need a nap soon."

Carl leaned down, smiling at Riley. "Betty'll be tickled pink to know there's a littl'un in town. What is he? Can't be more 'n two, three months?"

Vega's mouth went dry. She felt Zach's breath on her neck. An X on her back. If he wanted to find her, how hard would it be? Young girl with tattoos, an old van that made its own statement, a crying baby. How long could she stay anywhere? She turned to Heff. "Can I have the keys now?"

"Here, I'll walk you up. Let me at least take the bag for you."

"Okay," she relented. She wanted to get out of the store, away from their curious stares, and to someplace where she could smooth the panic that raced through her muscles. The need for sleep knocked around her head.

At the door, the man with the yellow suspenders reached out a finger and brushed it along the baby's delicate cheek. "You be careful around here, okay?"

Her skin turned cold. "What do you mean?"

"One time we had a girl show up in Crystal, and she went missing."

"And her daddy too. Right, Carl?" Heff said.

Carl gave him a look, shrugged. "That man ain't got no right to be missed." He leaned closer to Vega, his gruff expression melting into a grin when he looked at the baby. "There's other things you should take care about. Like the abandoned mines—dozens of 'em out in the woods. Wouldn't want to find yerself in the bottom of one." The baby grabbed on to his fingertip, and the older man's eyes opened wide, the corners raised in a delighted slant. "And haints. Plenty of those 'round here too." Vega got the sense that Carl enjoyed telling a few tall tales. "My Betty saw the girl once standing smack-dab in the middle of our kitchen. Turned her hair white, it did."

Eve let loose a loud laugh. "Betty's hair turned white because she's almost seventy, Carl." She sighed. "It's been twenty-five years, and this town still can't believe that Donna might have left because life was too hard for her here."

Carl slid his thumbs behind his suspenders. "Betty doesn't lie, Eve. And excuse me for living, but how would you know, anyways?"

The baby started to cry, and while the sound was a rock sinking into Vega's stomach, it also came as a relief to have a reason to leave right now. She had no idea what they were talking about, and frankly, she didn't care. Yet their back-and-forth made her wonder about her mother's connections to this town. Could any of these people have known her? A part of her wanted to ask, felt a twinge of hope. But she was on the run, and these people didn't owe her anything.

"Thanks for the tip. I'll be careful."

She hurried out the door, going past Heff, the baby crying, her eyes filling along with his, the rain heavy and pelting her neck, which she had craned to protect him. Heff opened the door and she moved inside, turning quickly to block him from coming any farther. "Thanks," she said, and closed the door behind her, grateful to be alone but dreading the sleepless night ahead and wondering why her mother had ever come to Crystal.

CHAPTER FIVE

EVE

When the door closed behind Heff and Vega, it took the crying of the baby with it, and the store felt preternaturally quiet to Eve. She tried to keep her movements natural, but the air was charged in a familiar way. The minute the tough-looking, tattooed blonde had walked into her store, something that had been tightly bound inside Eve unspooled, and she was dragged back to the night she died and the experience that came to shape and define the rest of her life.

Most people thought having a near-death experience took away the fear of dying. But it was dying that had finally taken away Eve's fear of living.

She'd met others like her in the years since it happened, a little club of people with NDEs. It bonded them, but it also set them apart, the experience changing something profound in their DNA and instilling in many of them a peace they struggled to share or adequately describe. Some people divorced; some quit their jobs; and some, like Eve herself, finally lived the way they were meant to since birth, even if it destroyed every relationship they'd ever had.

And then there were the few who were marked in not-so-subtle ways. Eve had a sense about things now, but it was frustratingly out of her control. Nothing like the mediums on television shows or the fortune-tellers who read cards. Things just came to her, whether she wanted them to or not, and once she understood the message or vision or whatever it was, it left her no choice but to say something. Like Carl. She knew Carl was going to have a heart attack. On the face of it, that wasn't shocking. With Carl's substantial weight, his red-veined nose, and his love of all meat red or purple, anyone could guess he'd be on a short list. But Eve knew down to the day, the hour, even the second. Not long after she'd moved back to Crystal, she was working on the far side of her property, building a fence line. Carl had pulled up in his old blue pickup truck; it groaned when he hefted his weight out.

He'd stood for a moment, observing, and Eve had gone on working. It had been decades since she'd last seen Carl, but he hadn't changed.

He cleared his throat and said at last, *Heard a gal bought the old Snyder farm.* His eyes took in the fence, his thumbs running under his yellow suspenders. *You gettin' animals?*

Eve had smiled and pulled the brim of her hat above her forehead so he could see her face. *I inherited it, although technically, it still belongs to the Shawnee.* When she had learned about the Native Americans as a kid, ten-year-old Eve had been confused and angry, and accused her parents of living on stolen land. Her father had told her it was God's land. She'd asked why God had let something so awful happen. So her father had grounded her. Eve had always been too willing to question for his taste. She'd been a disappointment long before she was an abomination.

Carl squinted at her and made a sound in his throat. *That sounds like our E—*

Eve laughed. *That's because it's me, Carl. And yes, sir, I'm planning on getting some ducks, maybe a few alpacas—even thinking about a couple of pigs to help with the garden. I've got big plans for this land.*

Confusion had twisted his features, and his mouth opened and closed. Eve felt bad for him but she was also guarded. It had been a gamble to come back, because either folks didn't know what to do with her or she stirred an anger so ancient and deep it was like throwing chum into a school of piranhas. Carl looked at a loss for words, his eyebrows moving up and down—not angry or affronted by her, she didn't think, just confused. He'd kicked at the dirt, mumbling, *Uh, think I heard somethin' 'bout all that from Betty.*

Eve had breathed in. It wasn't new; in fact, it was old and tiresome for people to be uncomfortable around her. But she still wanted to believe that there were some people who had the capacity to accept change, even if it was painful and slow and they said all the wrong things along the way. Like Carl.

Eve had smiled, thinking about how Carl and Betty had found her at the hospital after that terrible night. How they gave her money and an old car so she could leave Crystal forever. Carl was worth the wait. *Betty still making those buckeye cookies?*

Carl closed his mouth and seemed to relax the tiniest bit at the mention of his wife. *Every Saturday.* He'd pulled again at his suspenders, cleared his throat. *When you was a young'un, you'd sneak a handful of 'em. Betty never said nothin'. She didn't mind.* Carl met her gaze, and it was firm, no wavering in whatever he was going to say next. *We didn't think it was right, how your dad treated you, so you know, even if it was because* . . . He held his hands out as though that were explanation enough. *Well, you know.*

Eve nodded and patted his arm, and that's when she'd felt it. His heart quiet, the blood stagnant, his body cold and lifeless. The vision, this *knowing*, was an electric shock. But she didn't tell Carl. She waited until Saturday and paid Betty a visit, ate one of her buckeyes over coffee, and told her that Carl was going to die of a heart attack unless he made some changes. Being the kind of superstitious that had her knocking on wood, sprinkling salt on her doorstep, and dreaming about pigs, Betty had taken her at her word. *I had a dream about a pig in mud last night. Guess I shoulda seen that coming.* Eve had missed the superstition that ran deep in this part of the country. In many ways, with her NDE and her knowings, she fit more in her mountain hometown than she ever had.

It was easier to find a place where she belonged when she'd lived in cities like Cleveland, Chicago, and New York. But it had been lonely too. Her NDE had been a gift, allowing her to understand people in a deeper way. But it didn't change their hate. Didn't make it any more bearable to be the object of it either. Plus, she'd missed the clean air and open spaces of her childhood. The mountains were in her blood, and as the years away from home piled up, Eve felt like she straddled two places, never fully belonging anywhere.

Her move back hadn't been simple, pockmarked by hate and ignorance, so Eve had kept her head down and focused on what she wanted: a home, her farm, the store, and the few friends she did have. She didn't need much else.

Now she stood in her shop with Carl after Vega had left, absorbing the aftershocks of another knowing. This one powerful and confusing, spreading in her mind like a string of constellations.

Carl leaned against the bar, and Eve poured him a cup of coffee. "That girl seems scared of her own shadow. Don't she, Eve?"

"That she does," Eve agreed, and tried to focus on something else because the knowing made her hands shake just the tiniest bit. She'd been expecting Vega, she realized, without knowing her face or her name. Her dreams had intensified in the last few months, and Eve had felt something coming, like water pulling away from shore, building in intensity, growing higher and higher, rushing toward land. When Vega walked through the door, it had crashed.

Eve's skin tingled. All she knew was what she felt: an uneasiness that had settled in her stomach, the expectation of something unexpected but not surprising, and the realization that whoever she was, Vega would change everything Eve knew.

CHAPTER SIX

July 1995

The woods were dark, the air rank with rotting leaves and wet earth that sucked at Donna's tennis shoes. She ran, stumbled. The sharp edge of a branch whipped across her already-tender face, and she cried out. But she kept running because nothing would make her turn around. Nobody could ever make her go back home.

Her face was wet with blood and tears that had soaked the collar of her T-shirt. She couldn't hear her father hollering for her, chasing after her, anymore. He'd stumbled at some point and fallen behind. Her lungs burned, muscles ached. It was silent in the woods now, except for the swish of leaves under her feet, the hoot of an owl.

She tripped, tumbling forward, and it felt like her heels hit the back of her head when she fell. Her hip landed on a knotted root; it bit into the bone, and she gasped at the pain. Leaves clung to her hair and skin, slimy and wet. She shivered and part of her wanted to stop, wanted nothing more than to give up. Her father would find her. He always found her. When she was still small enough to crawl under her bed or into the cabinet in the kitchen, where she could squeeze between the stockpot and the baking sheets. Later, when she grew and tried the root cellar or the loft in the old barn, which had rats in the hay and holes in the walls. In the middle of the night, while her mother slept or covered her ears so she could pretend like it never happened. He always found her.

Donna hit the ground with her fist, the tang of soil filling her nose. A simmering rage seeped out of her. She pounded the earth. Tonight she'd fought back, bashed his head with a rock, screamed until her throat was raw, begged for her mother to help her. Something had finally broken in Donna. Nobody would ever help her but herself.

She'd run, and while her father was bigger and stronger than she'd ever be, Donna was faster and not sluggish from whiskey and muscles overgrown with fat. But she'd been running for miles now, through the woods in their secluded holler, past a town she didn't recognize. She wanted to get lost. To disappear and never be found again.

She pushed herself to her knees, ignoring the burning pain in her hip, the swelling that had closed her right eye, and she ran until she had nothing left, until she had no choice but to collapse and let him find her, because she'd given it everything she'd had. At least she'd tried.

And that was when she saw the school bus. A greenish yellow in the fractals of moonlight, black spray paint blocking out the school district name, replacing it with skulls and crossbones, f-bombs, and pentagrams. Most of the windows were gone, but curtains fluttered in and out of the holes, and it seemed to Donna as though the bus breathed.

She hesitated, staring at the bus, her chest heaving. It was out of place, here in the middle of the woods. Spooky and unearthly. From behind her, a rustling—leaves moving, branches tittering. It kick-started her adrenaline, rolled her fear into a ball and buried it deep inside. It didn't matter that the bus looked like a portal to the underworld; it was the only place she could hide. She picked her way toward the hulking piece of metal. Up close it looked worse. She tried to steady her breath and pushed open the folding door. The quiet night was broken by its soft creak.

She dragged mud and leaves up the steep steps, holding on to the handrail until she reached the top and looked down the dark aisle. Her parents were homesteaders, living off the grid, shunning everything modern, and spending their days preparing for the end. Donna had never ridden a bus to school, having been homeschooled her entire sixteen years. But she'd often imagined what school would have been like. The friends she would have made. The boys she might have liked. She reached the top step, level with the dark rows of seats that stretched long. She imagined it filled with kids, doing whatever teenagers did; she wondered what that was like.

The inside of the bus wasn't what she expected. It was hard to make out much in the dark, but the curved walls had been painted white. In the back, a few of the seats had been ripped out, leaving room for a desk with a mirror, a chair, and a lantern. She pushed a button on the lantern and nearly jumped when it turned on. The light swung around, sending shadows popping up from behind the seats at the front of the bus. She shivered, turning away from the dark recesses and toward the soothing light. There was a portable clothes rack at the back of the bus, packed with what looked like old dress-up clothes—sparkly costumes, furs, scarves, and hats. A selection of flats and shiny heels were neatly organized on the floor below the clothes. She smiled and winced at the sharp stab it sent through her jaw. *Must be some kid's fort or hiding spot,* she thought.

Beside the shoes was a mattress with a blanket and pillow. It looked soft and the idea that she could stop running, if only for the night, was the greatest gift anyone could have ever given to her. She silently thanked the little girl this bus belonged to and let her eyes close, pretending that this was her house, her bus, her clothes—and that her other life was the terrible nightmare.

CHAPTER SEVEN

VEGA

April 2021

Vega sat on the edge of the bed, still in her coat with her bag slung over her shoulder, Riley in her arms, crying. She stared down at him; a ball rolled tight in her throat. She was useless. Unable to ease her baby's pain. She rubbed his stomach with her fingertips, trying to iron out the gas bubbles. "I'm sorry," she whispered, kissing his scrunched-up face, her own eyes wet. She inhaled; a sourness rose from the folds of his skin. He needed a bath. In her hurry to run, she'd grabbed some onesies; his formula, which would last a few more days but was already running low; diapers; and a bottle of baby soap. But not the small things. Like the plastic bathtub at home—the one that fit across a sink—or the blue rubber duckie that floated in the warm water alongside him, or the velvet-soft washcloth she used to gently scrub his skin clean.

She let her bag fall to the floor, slid out of her coat, and looked around the apartment, deciding on the small bathroom sink. She removed Riley's clothes while he cried, warmed up the water, and held him with one arm while she squirted him with soap, rubbed it all over his skin with her free hand, using the rough washcloth only when necessary. He squirmed, his body so slippery she imagined him sliding out of her grip and bashing his head against the side of the hard porcelain. She winced at the image, her heart beating fast, so she splashed water over him and pulled him away from the sink, wrapped him in a towel, and held him tight to her chest.

Nightmare visions like that bloomed often in her head: accidentally dropping him, catching his head on a corner of a wall when she walked by, clipping his nails and cutting the skin instead. It haunted her, imagining any number of terrible things that could happen if she let her guard down for a second.

She zipped up a fresh onesie, made a bottle, and lay beside him on the bed while he ate, his quiet gulping filling up the spaces in her heart. When she was a teenager, she'd grown frustrated with the situations women found themselves in. Especially the ones with kids. *Why don't they just leave?* she'd asked her mom once. Her mother had given her a look that spoke of things Vega was too young to understand. It had cut right through Vega's chest; her cheeks warmed.

Don't judge what you can't understand.

The soreness in her belly had eased but not the memory of Zach's fist, his callous punch that had caused her bladder to leak, her pants wet and stinking of her fear. She understood now. It was scarier to realize she'd been living with the most dangerous thing that could happen to her baby.

Riley finished the bottle, and when she put him up on her shoulder, he let out a long and loud burp followed by a cooing sound that Vega had never heard him make before. She laughed and laid him back down, his tiny spine curled against her, blond hair damp and drying in soft curls against his scalp. She pulled a blanket over them both. The radiator had made a halfhearted attempt to heat the apartment, but away from the source, the bedroom was cold. Riley lay on his side, staring at the wall, big dark eyes that seemed to take in everything and nothing at all. Vega touched the tiny rolls that waterfalled down his neck, smiling at the funny pairing of newborn and triple chin. Her skin, marred by black vines that inked down the tops of her hands, looked alien against his untouched flesh. Renee had been alone too. Raised Vega on the road, nap times in the van. Vega's father was a ghost who inhabited her dreams or in the minutes before dawn when she lay curled against her mother. Vega wanted to believe he'd been different.

Do I have a dad? she'd whispered. The van's windows were small and covered by thin handmade paisley curtains. Milk-water light filtered through the space.

Renee had sighed; Vega felt its hum against her back. *Of course you do.*

Vega didn't want to ask, but she couldn't help herself. *Is he a bad one?*

Her mother had pulled her close, inhaled, and kissed the top of her head. *No, your father was good enough.*

Vega wasn't sure if she believed her, and she didn't ask again. She didn't want to know why her mother was alone, why they lived in the van, never settling down long enough to make friends or go to school. She'd started to dream about living in one place, asked her mom if they could stay longer. Renee's typical response: *Life is lived in motion.* And then they'd pack up and go. Vega didn't hate it—not all the time. There was so much she loved about their time together. She just wanted something more permanent than the van.

Riley tensed and his bottom lip began to quiver. Vega quickly picked him up and put him belly down against her chest. The position sometimes helped, and this time, he relaxed into her. Night had fallen hard outside, dark without streetlights, still and quiet. Her mother had said that Crystal was a nothing town full of nobodies and bullies. Vega couldn't help but wonder if her father had been one of those nobodies.

Riley's eyes fluttered closed and his breathing deepened. She carefully scooted up against the bed frame, the knot in her chest loosening. She should sleep—her body craved it, sand filling her legs—but now, when she had the chance, her eyes bugged wide. She was cocooned in a strange town, a thousand miles from Zach. But for how long? She felt every inch her youth in that moment and wished more than anything for one last chance to talk to her mom.

The baby scrunched up his legs and started to whimper. Vega stood, keeping him upright against her chest, and bounced from foot to foot, patting his back and praying that the moment would pass. His whimper became a cry, and his cry quickly morphed into a high-pitched wail. Vega breathed in. She knew what her mom would say. *Toughen up, V.* Her son needed her to be strong, and if her mother had managed it, so could she. Riley deserved nothing less.

Outside the rain had stopped and the night had cleared. Vega had been a fussy baby too; her mother used to tease her about it. But a walk in the cool night air always did the trick. Her mom had said she'd loved those moments the best.

Vega felt the familiar burn in her eyes and slid into her jacket, wrapped the baby in a blanket, and headed outside. Maybe the cool night air would work for Riley too.

∽

It wasn't even nine o'clock and the town was deserted, storefronts darkened, the stoplight and a lamppost outside of Eve's Place shedding the only light. It was a ghost town at this time of night, and Vega felt safe in the emptiness. The rain had left everything damp and smelling fresh, like grass and mud mixed with the perfume of budding flowers. She walked down the street, feeling the cool air on her cheeks, the soft thump of her shoes on the ground. The quiet soothed her, even if it was marred by the baby's cries, which never seemed to end. She wondered how such a tiny body had the energy to cry for so long and so loud. At least outside his cries were carried away by the breeze, absorbed by the trees and earth.

At the edge of town, forest replaced buildings, made the road appear small and lonely. She stood there, staring down the road, so tired the yellow lines wiggled—and hungry too. The sandwich that Eve had given her had been her first bit of food since yesterday morning in Denver. With formula and diapers to worry about, she hadn't had the money for a proper meal, and tonight she felt it in the fog behind her eyes. Riley's crying seemed to come from far away.

She turned around to head back toward the apartment and yelped, suddenly awake. The pair of pigs from earlier that day stood just behind her, snuffling at the ground. She must not have heard them above the baby's cries. Having lived on the road her entire life, she'd never had a pet and had hardly ever been around animals. Plus, well—pigs. Were they pets or livestock, anyway? She sidestepped around them and quickened her pace back to the apartment.

A pickup truck appeared around the corner, driving slowly down the street. Vega tensed, cursing her vulnerable position, and pulled a slim can of pepper spray from her pocket, gripping it in her hand. Her mother had always carried one, and once Vega was old enough to not accidentally spray herself, she carried one too. She hadn't seen the need for it after moving in with Zach but had kept it stored in the van just in case.

The truck pulled to a stop, and when the door opened, she relaxed her grip but didn't put the spray away. Heff.

"A nighttime walk?" He wore plaid pajama pants, a sweatshirt that read GIVE BLOOD, PLAY RUGBY, and moccasin slippers; his hair stuck out on the top like he'd been sleeping hard and had been suddenly woken up. "And with the Kunekunes, I see."

She jiggled the baby, whose crying had intensified. Her head ached. "Thought the cool air might calm him." She gave the pigs a glance over her shoulder. They were rolling in a muddy patch on the road. "And the pigs weren't invited."

Heff sighed. "They never are."

Her eyes narrowed and she squeezed the pepper spray. "What are you doing here, anyway?"

"Got a call about a disturbance. Carl said he heard a child being murdered or a ghost screaming on Main Street. He and Betty live just up that ridge, and sound travels when the trees are still bare." He pointed up into the hills above the town, and Vega could just make out a light shining through the branches.

She took in his pajamas and slippers. "And you came dressed like that?"

He slouched against his truck, crossed his arms, and yawned. "I heard Baby crying earlier and I know gas pains when I hear them, and Carl, well—Carl likes to get all riled up, so I don't put much stock in his assumptions. Plus, Eve said that until that radiator gets fixed, she's worried it might be a little bit cold in there tonight, so I thought I'd bring by a portable heater."

"Okay." She stood there, staring at the man. No way was she letting him inside.

His eyes were soft when he looked at the baby. "Is it colic?"

"I think so." She tried not to sound defensive, but it came through anyway. Her face heated. Their health insurance was minimal, and the C-section bill had been a shock to them both. Riley had been due for a checkup soon, and she was going to ask the doctor about his crying. But when she'd googled it on the road, colic was exactly what it said it could be.

He straightened, put his arms out. "May I?"

His offer surprised her, and she held the baby tighter; the pepper spray fell from her hands and landed on the ground at her feet. She scrambled to pick it up, but when she stood up, Heff hadn't moved.

"Smart," he said. "You know how to protect yourself. My mother moved here when I was just a baby. Single mom, worked her tail off to keep us both fed and warm. She always knew how to take care of herself too." He paused, seemed to be lost in thought.

Vega held tight to Riley. "Does she still live here?"

Heff's sunny demeanor dimmed. "Life can be hard, you know?"

Vega nodded, tense, sensing there was more. Not sure she was the right person to hear it.

"She was a good mom." He rubbed his chin, looked up at the sky. "But drugs don't care if you're a good person, and my mom—" The muscles in his jaw twitched. "Somehow she lost her way, got mixed up with the wrong people. I lost her going on ten years. So now I help out when our deputy isn't in town."

Vega felt a pang. Riley jerked his arms and legs, still crying, but the sound was softened by her empathy. "I lost my mom too. It's been . . ." She swallowed. "It's been really hard. I'm sorry for your loss."

He gave her a gentle smile, seemed touched. "And I'm sorry for yours."

Riley cried harder, and part of Vega wanted to lie down in the street and give up. Her nerves had fried. Exhaustion hung on her like an unwanted friend, and in the shadows hovered images of Zach, angry and threatening. She couldn't feel the ground beneath her feet, only an unending tiredness that inked through her bones. She realized that, since her mom died, she'd been drowning, and she hadn't known until her lungs had filled with water.

Heff's voice was measured and deep, like he was calming a spooked cat. "When I was a boy, we looked after kids in town to help other moms who needed a break. We also fostered a few kids over the years. As I got older, I helped, and as it turns out, I have a knack for soothing fussy babies."

Vega tried to interpret what he meant. "You want to soothe my fussy baby?"

He smiled, and combined with his pajamas and mussed hair, the effect was nonthreatening. "I'm not Rumpelstiltskin, if that's what you're implying."

It went against everything her mother had ever taught her about men, but at that moment—with Riley in pain, grief curling around her heart, fear twisting her insides—she was utterly lost. Something poked at her, an instinct that said Heff wasn't like Zach. Maybe it was their shared loss. Maybe she was just too drained to be scared, but she needed Riley to stop crying. She needed peace.

She held Riley out.

Shadows collected in his dimples. "Okay, then." He took him gently, looking more natural, more at ease, than she had ever felt. Her arms—empty, weightless—hung by her sides. To her surprise, he flipped the baby over, placing him belly down on his forearm so that Riley's legs and arms dangled, his head cradled in Heff's palm. Then he brought his arm close to his chest.

Heff looked down at the infant, a softness around his mouth. "We fostered a baby girl once who had terrible gas pains just like your little guy. Sometimes this worked." Heff looked up, raised an eyebrow, his voice a soft hum. "*Some*times. You must be exhausted." He hesitated. "It's hard work raising kids. The hardest."

She leaned heavily against the truck door, fighting to keep her eyes from closing, a small voice inside her calling her an idiot for letting this man hold her baby. But Riley was at peace, and she wanted that for him more than anything. It was an unexpected balm. Heff rocked from foot to foot, humming a song she didn't recognize and watching Riley, whose body lay limp over the man's arm, cheek squished in his palm, face relaxed.

After a few minutes, Heff placed him carefully into Vega's arms, and she settled the baby in the same manner across her forearm. Heff went back to his truck, pulled out an electric heater, and placed it outside the door. "Can I bring this up for you?" he whispered.

Her head was a bit clearer, and with Riley back in her arms, she couldn't believe she'd let this stranger hold him. She shook her head.

His smile deepened his dimples. "Yeah, I didn't think so. You seem like you prefer to do things yourself." He backed toward his truck, pantomiming taking big quiet steps. "You go on up. I'm afraid I'll wake him when I start my truck."

She went inside and navigated her way upstairs, locking her door behind her. Riley didn't wake up when she put him on the bed, placing pillows on one side of him in case he took to rolling in the middle of the night. Then she tiptoed to the front window—Heff's truck was gone—and hurried down the stairs to snatch the heater from outside. When the bedroom had warmed, she climbed into the bed and fell asleep with the spray under her pillow, Riley snug beside her, and dreamed about a walk outside with her mom.

CHAPTER EIGHT

VEGA

Sun streamed through the window above her bed. Vega pushed up on one elbow, hair stuck to her cheek, pillow wet from drool, and a crick in her neck. She swallowed and her mouth felt dry. For a moment she had no idea where she was, but the sheets were soft, the bed softer, and she lingered between wakefulness and sleep before it all came rushing back. She had left Zach. No, not just *left*—she had *run* from him, just like the women they'd helped. The women Vega thought had nothing in common with her.

Men hurt us. It was something her mother had told her often but Vega hadn't really believed until that day when she was ten. The day she brought the woman with the clogged drain a thick envelope.

That day, she'd rung the doorbell, chomping on a piece of strawberry-flavored gum, feeling the cool morning air evaporate with the heat of the sun. It was just another day, another job, as far as she'd been concerned. The woman would take the envelope, and then Vega and her mom would be on their way to a different city or the next state. But the woman didn't answer. A man did. He wore a work shirt with his name stitched across his chest—Lars—and he'd looked at Vega like she was nothing.

Who're you?

Vega's skin had prickled, and she backed away, hiding the envelope behind her back, but he followed her. *I-I'm just selling cookies. Girl Scouts, you know?* She turned, but when she did, he'd yanked the envelope from her hands. It had split open on the ground. Papers and money and a driver's license from Idaho had scattered across the cracked sidewalk. The man had grown bigger, his hands tightened into fists, and his face turned to stone in a way that scared Vega right down to her toes. From the house had come a sound, and in the doorway stood the woman with the clogged sink. Today, her hair was tangled, her bottom lip split and bleeding, a red-and-blue bruise on her jaw.

Vega had felt her body whip backward, and then she was behind the wide hips of her mother, Renee's hand on her arm in a protective grip. *You can leave him right now.* Her mother's voice was calm and even, and she'd spoken directly to the woman, as though the man were nothing but an annoying bug. *He won't hurt you outside like this. He's a coward. I can get you somewhere safe.*

The woman had wrapped her arms across her body, and Vega saw what giving up looked like if it were a person.

Please. Vega had flinched because she could hear something different in her mother's voice. A trembling, like she was scared, and Vega had never seen her mother scared. *He will kill you. I know the type.*

The man had charged. He took Renee by her shoulders and threw her to the ground. Her eyes met Vega's. *Run.* She did, hiding in the floor well of the passenger seat, hands over her ears, body shaking so badly her teeth rattled.

A few minutes later, her mother's door had flown open and Renee jumped in, her face white and strained. *Get your seat belt on, V.* She scrambled into her seat and did as she was told. The van's back end had fishtailed when her mother put her foot to the gas, and when Vega looked back, she saw that the woman with the clogged sink was gone. The man had stared after the van and then slammed the front door.

Renee had reached out and taken Vega's hand, squeezing gently, and Vega wanted to climb into her lap and close her eyes. *That's the kind of man we run from, V. Got that?*

Vega had nodded, the road ahead a blur of gray and yellow. She'd pulled her feet up onto the seat, squeezed her knees tight to her chest, and swallowed back the tears that wanted to run down her face. She swore to herself that she would never be that woman. But it had battled with an even deeper desire. To have a family of her own. A nice husband. A cat. Kids. How would she ever have what she dreamed if there were men out there like Lars?

Riley wiggled, bringing his arms and legs tight into his torso, eyes blinking open. The glow of the sun drifted across his body, veins blue beneath his translucent skin. Vega loved him so much it turned her heart inside out. She'd often wondered what had happened to the woman with the clogged drain. Her eyes caught the bruises across her own wrist, now an ugly blue green, and she swallowed hard, hoped the woman had found the courage to leave. Was out there somewhere living a life free from that man's abuse.

Vega touched Riley's nose and the corner of his mouth lifted; laughter bubbled up at his response. "Hey, buddy," she said. He turned his head toward her voice, and she held her breath, waited for the crying to start. Instead, his eyes searched the air, locked onto her face, and his body jerked, mouth wide in a grin. Riley wouldn't hurt people. He would be different and she would do whatever it took to give him a good life.

Being a mother herself had made Vega miss Renee even more. Vega would have liked more time to say goodbye. To absorb all her mother's advice, to apologize for the time she stole the van and blew a tire when she was sixteen and stupid, leaving Renee stranded at a KOA in Nevada. To ask more questions. If her mother had been alive, would Vega have seen Zach more clearly? Understood the kind of man he was from the beginning?

From below the apartment came the muffled sounds of people talking and the earthy smell of coffee sifting with the buttery scent of baking dough. Her stomach growled. If she thought too much about Zach, she felt paralyzed with indecision, torn apart by fear. Instead, she focused on what she needed to do to make some money.

She pushed herself out of bed, yawning, and pulled on a pair of jeans, a long-sleeve T-shirt, and Birkenstock sandals. Riley had slept for a couple of hours straight before waking up to eat and, for the moment, seemed content. She ran a brush through her spiky blonde hair, brushed her teeth, and checked again. Still peaceful. She bit her lip, hating to ruin the moment, but she had no choice. *Depend on no one but yourself.* Her mother had lived it and preached it. And for the first time in her life, Vega understood it. Nobody was coming to save her. It was up to her—and she needed to find work.

~

With the coming rain, it had been gloomy when she'd arrived yesterday, and she hadn't fully appreciated the natural beauty that surrounded the town. In the morning sunlight, it sparkled; drops of water on bright-green leaves caught minuscule rainbows of sunlight, wildflowers dotting the sides of the road and spreading up the hills. A handful of cars were parked along the side of the street, and the restaurant, J's Grill-n-Go, looked open this morning. A tiny woman with short gray hair walked out of the restaurant and waved. Vega looked behind her but nobody was there.

"Hi, Vega!" The woman approached her. "Welcome to Crystal! Carl told me all about you." Her eyes lit up when she spied Riley, tucked against Vega's chest in the front carrier. "Oh my, and there's the little one himself." She wore a bright-pink rain jacket and carried an open umbrella above her head, despite the blue sky, and she was the tiniest woman Vega had ever met, barely reaching Vega's chest. Her diminutive height brought her eye level with the baby. Under the woman's coat, Vega spied the edge of what appeared to be an apron and a dusting of flour across her cheek. She looked at Vega's hand, where the tips of vines poked through her sleeve, wrapping around her fingers. Eyed her neck and down to the tops of her feet. "Can't say I know anybody who's got so many pictures drawn into their skin."

Vega smiled, thought of the tattoos she'd grown up tracing along her mother's forearm, bicep, around her ankles. "Yeah, it kinda runs in the family."

The woman's eyes opened wide. "Ain't that something. So the baby was born with 'em too?"

Vega smiled, charmed. "That'll be his choice."

"Good answer. Best not to get your hopes up, though. Children like to do exactly the opposite of their parents." She took a step back. "Now, then, if you're looking for coffee, go to Eve's. J's does a good egg sandwich and some decent chicken and waffles, but that's about it."

"Okay."

"Heard Heff helped you with the baby last night."

Vega was speechless. The idea that so many people already knew about her didn't sit well, shrank the distance between Crystal and Denver. It made her antsy, unsure of herself, and she wondered if she should pack up her van and go somewhere she could disappear easier, like Columbus or Cincinnati.

"That boy's never been quite the same since he lost his momma. Shoulda been living in a big city by now. Went to college and every-thin'." Riley squirmed, gave a sharp cry, and Betty smiled at the baby. "Sweet littl'un." She looked up at Vega. "See here, Carl said you fix things. We got a lot of things need fixin' at our cabin. It's older'n we are. The Good Lord knows we could use some help."

"I could use the work," Vega said.

The woman squinted up at her. "'Course, the price better be good. We're old but we ain't stupid."

Vega nodded. "My work's good and my prices are always fair."

The woman smiled, seeming satisfied in some way. "When I saw Eve's pigs standing in my yard this morning, I just knew it was going to be a good day."

Vega had no idea how to respond, wondered if the woman was teasing her. Riley moved his fists along her body, still sleeping, still peaceful—and for that, she was willing to stand outside and talk about pigs for as long as it took. "You like pigs?"

The woman gave her a look like she was a marble or two short. "There's a lot you can learn from nature. Not just pigs, you know. My momma used to dream about cats, but I've always favored pigs."

Vega couldn't help her interest. This woman reminded her of Heff—chatty and friendly in the way of people reuniting. It warmed her. And was exactly how she'd imagined a hometown would feel. "Why?"

"People think they're dirty, that they symbolize all the bad things that God don't like. I think they're misunderstood. And since God loves an underdog, when I dream about 'em, I write it down because you never know when it might be a message. Like my dream last night. It's a good sign to see a pig standing far away."

"What does it mean?" Vega said.

"Means something good will happen in the future. Like meeting a handygirl like you." The umbrella shook with the woman's laugh. "Or you can just ask Eve. If she's got one of her knowings, she might tell you something about your future too. Crystal's full 'a omens, if you know where to look and who to listen to."

"Okay," she said, half expecting the woman to pull out tarot cards.

Instead, she gave her a wave and headed down the street, disappearing into the woods, where Vega could just make out a narrow trail leading up the hill and to the house she'd seen through the trees last night. *That must be Betty,* she thought. Vega sighed and turned toward Eve's. So much for hiding out. The town could put up a billboard with her face on it and it wouldn't broadcast her presence here any louder than the way their gossip spread. A shot of anxiety curled her fingers, but she breathed out and reminded herself that Zach knew nothing about Crystal.

Compared to the early-morning coolness outside, Eve's Place was warm and smelled like toasted coffee beans. Vega sat at the small bar and pulled out her Chromebook.

"Password is *Crystal*." Eve had appeared behind the bar. This morning, she wore a baseball hat, and her long brown hair was braided down her back. Silver bracelets moved along her wrists, and she wore skinny jeans and work boots. The whole effect was both glamorous and practical. It seemed out of place here, and yet Eve made it look natural and effortless. Vega's mother had been similar. Renee was never glamorous, but she'd had a confidence and a sureness in herself that Vega had loved. A lump grew in her throat. Memories of her mother were paintings in her mind that grief deepened in color and time faded the longer she was gone.

"Latte? Cappuccino? I don't do a lot of the Starbucks drinks because I'm morally opposed to all that sugar, but I've been known to make exceptions." Her smile was kind.

"Black coffee is fine."

Eve smiled. "My kind of girl." She set a WELCOME TO CRYSTAL! mug in front of her. The same picture from the postcard stretched across the curved ceramic. "Your baby seems more peaceful this morning. Heard Heff stopped by last night."

So much for Crystal being a nothing town full of nobodies. Seemed everybody here knew somebody's business. Vega ducked her head. And everyone also knew that she was the kind of mother who couldn't comfort her own baby. She searched for something to change the subject. "Heff told me about his mom." It hadn't felt like a secret; he'd told a complete stranger, after all. She guessed it must be common knowledge, especially in this town.

Eve leaned forward on the counter, her eyes dark but warm. "Such a tragedy. It happened before I moved back, but Heff wasn't much younger than you at the time. He blames himself, though."

"Why?"

Eve gave her a long look. "Because he wasn't here to see the signs. He was away at college. When he realized how bad things had gotten, he quit school and moved back home. But by then it was too late." She wiped the counter, shaking her head. "Now he thinks he can save everybody if he tries hard enough."

Vega tapped her coffee cup. Heff had seemed too good to be true, too upstanding, counter to everything her mother had warned her about. Her stomach still held on to Zach's assault, and a shiver ran down her legs. She couldn't imagine Heff punching a woman. She sipped her coffee, wanted to offer something in return for Eve's confidence. "He calmed my baby."

Eve smiled. "He's a natural."

Riley started to cry, and it was loud in the store, echoing off the wood floors, wriggling into Vega's ears. She looked down at him, feeling utterly useless, tears already filling her eyes.

"It's hard to be a mom." Eve's low voice fluttered over her, comforting, kind. "That's why you sometimes need a village to help."

Vega wiped her eyes with her sleeve, looked up to find Eve pointing to a wooden sign hung on the wall behind her with the same sentiment burned into the painted wood. She smiled and walked away, disappearing into the back of the store.

Vega stared at the sign. Renee had never had a village, and she'd done okay. The computer blinked on, and Vega easily connected to the Wi-Fi. Her hands hovered over the keyboard. She wanted to know what Zach was doing, if he'd called the cops or tried to reach out to her again. But she was afraid to check her phone, afraid he'd use it somehow to track where she was. Like her mother always said could happen.

She typed in a Denver news station, scrolled through the headlines: a spring snowstorm, a local marathon, a hit-and-run. Nothing about a woman kidnapping her own child. Nothing about Zach. She logged on to her Instagram account and inhaled sharply at the number of messages and posts she'd been tagged in. All from Zach. She clicked on his story. It was a reel of him holding a stack of poster boards with words scrawled on each one, dropping one by one to form a plea. *Bring. My. Baby. Home. @vega. #bringrileyhome.* Her arms tingled, anger-sharp pricks inside her skin. There were dozens of comments from people Vega hardly knew. Mostly Zach's coworkers and high school friends.

Dude, that's fucked up.

Bitch should be locked away.

She's trash.

Let's hunt her down.

She bit her lip so hard it bled tiny drops of copper into her mouth. Another post with a picture of Zach holding Riley, before he'd left for work one day in a button-up shirt. Followed by one of Vega in her favorite ratty jean shorts and tank top, tats on full display. The caption: **Please help me find Vega. She's sick and needs help. #mentalhealthawareness #bipolar #bringrileyhome**

She slammed her computer shut, looked down at Riley, who was still sleeping despite an angry twitching in her body. She wanted to throw the computer through a window. Scream until her throat turned raw. What gave him the right to make her out to be the bad guy? It was exactly what her mom had warned about—that men held the power, even when they were the abusers. It was why Renee told women to disappear.

As Vega grew older, she questioned her mother's black-and-white views. Challenged her. Ran away one night when she was sixteen, wound up in a King Soopers parking lot, drinking beer with a group of local kids. She'd been awkward, felt like she said all the wrong things, realized how odd she was compared to them. More mature than these kids but less experienced, naive all at the same time. A guy had kissed her, and she'd been so surprised and a little drunk that she'd thrown up all over his shoes. He hadn't been angry or violent, just disgusted. And she couldn't blame him—so had she. But it had fed Vega's growing suspicion that Renee didn't know everything when it came to men.

She stared at her computer, tried to calm her racing heart. Zach had proved Renee right.

She'd met him at the lowest point of her life. Her mom had died the month before, leaving Vega alone for the first time. She'd floundered, sleeping more than working, until the leads dried up and she slept through the day. When the van grew claustrophobic, she dragged herself out and mountain biked the trails not far from where she was camped. On her first ride, she cried the entire time, missing her mom's solid presence. On her second ride, she met Zach.

He'd been nothing like what she'd been taught to expect. He was generous, kind, funny. They'd started out as friends—mountain biking, hiking, or just hanging out and talking. He gave Vega something to look forward to, and in those dark days following her mother's death, she had desperately needed it. Apart from the boy in the King Soopers parking lot and a handful of other boys from various camp spots they'd frequented, Vega had little experience. A kiss, a few gropes, but nothing more. Zach gave her butterflies, and their gentle fluttering softened the emptiness left behind from her mother's death.

They'd drink instant coffee from water boiled in a hot pot in her van, served in metal cups that warmed their palms. Soon they were swapping stories about their childhoods, Zach having been born and raised in Lakewood, his working-class parents married for decades and still living in the same house he'd grown up in. He'd been fascinated by Vega's life on the road with her mom, thinking it adventurous and different. It made her exotic, unique, he'd told her, like finding a rare flower. She'd cried when she found out she was pregnant. Sure Zach would want nothing to do with her. It was what she knew to expect. But he surprised her eventually and had even seemed to get excited by the idea of becoming a dad.

She held her stomach, resting Riley's bottom on her forearms. Zach had invited her over for Sunday dinner at his parents' house. Vega was nervous. She'd never met parents before. Plus, she was still in the early stages of her pregnancy, nauseous for most of the day, sometimes well into the evening too. His dad had welcomed them at the door, bigger than Zach, who favored his mother's slimmer build, but with his same brown eyes. Dinner had been quiet, punctured by the scrape of forks on plates, the clink of ice in water glasses. His mother spoke softly, hardly meeting Vega's eyes. His father asked questions about Zach's job, the new place he'd rented, insurance. At some point Vega remembered the soft peal of alarm bells. Something was wrong. Zach's family seemed like actors in a charade put on for the benefit of someone else. That night, as she and Zach spooned, his hand on her belly, Vega told herself to grow up. Maybe sometimes what seemed too good to be true was just normal.

Eve's voice interrupted her thoughts. "Would you like a croissant with your coffee? It's on the house—day old."

"Sure, thanks."

Eve slid the pastry onto a small plate and refilled Vega's coffee. She looked at her from under the brim of her hat. "I have a small budget set aside for the apartment. Maybe we can talk about what you think needs done? I also have some odds-and-ends kind of work on my farm. If you're interested, let me know. I could use another set of hands."

Vega stiffened. It was the second offer in less than thirty minutes. Even when things were good, they were never that good. She got the feeling Eve pitied her. "I appreciate the offer, but you don't have to come up with work for me. I don't take charity."

"And I don't offer it. My farm is a lot to manage, and with the store and the other things I do, I don't have much time to repair busted drywall, or refresh the paint, or mend the fence for those damn pigs, cute as they are."

Riley squirmed, stretching his arms and legs. Vega noticed his eyes were open, and he wasn't crying. She tried to keep her breaths shallow, not wanting to ruin the moment. "Okay."

Eve leaned over the bar, and her long silver earrings brushed along her angular jaw. "You've had some bad luck, huh?"

"Is this the part where you predict my future?" Vega kept her voice casual. What could this woman really know?

Eve laughed. "I see that the rumors about me have made it to your ears already."

"It's pretty much the first thing people say to newcomers."

"Let me guess, Betty and Heff?"

Vega smiled into her coffee. "Not in that order, but wow, you are good."

Eve laughed again. "People here are their own brand of different."

"Sounds like dying made you a bit of a celebrity."

"That's not hard to do in Crystal. We're all a little off our rockers." She raised an eyebrow. "Maybe that's why you're here."

Vega stretched out her hands. One tattoo, an orange-and-brown snake, roped down her wrist, the tail wrapping around her pinkie. She curled her fingers into her palms, settled her hands back on her lap. Despite the wagging tongues, something about Crystal called to her. And the thought of leaving left her cold. Where would she go? At least here, she had offers of work—charity or not—and a place to stay. Nobody here knew about Zach. And Zach knew nothing about Crystal. There had been some things she'd kept to herself. She thought about the postcard and the picture of her mother by an old school bus. It might be her chance to learn more about her mother's past. "Actually, I came to Crystal because I think my mom grew up here."

"Really?"

"Her name was Renee Jones." A little cry erupted from Riley, and she felt the familiar scrunch of his body against her torso—the telltale sign that he was in pain. She stood, patting his back and rocking back and forth on her feet. "Did you know her?"

"No, I don't think so. But—" The animation had left Eve's face; she looked like a wax figure suspended in a moment.

"Eve?"

Eve blinked but didn't smile. She leaned closer to Vega, both hands flat on the counter, shook her head like she was trying to shake something loose. "But that's not why you're really here, is it?"

Riley cried harder and Vega unclipped the carrier, pulled him out so that she could lay him across her forearm like Heff had done last night. Her pulse raced. She didn't really believe in psychics; she thought it was a skill to be able to read people, so she stood her ground. This woman knew nothing about her, and it certainly wasn't hard to make a few guesses that might be close enough. "My mother died a year and a half ago." She lifted her chin, felt it tremble. "My son never knew her, and I thought coming here might help us both feel a little closer to her. So that's why I'm here." It was close to the truth. But the rest was her own business. With Riley's crying and the bewildering way Eve looked at her, Vega's nerves had unraveled.

Eve shook her head and something shattered behind her eyes. She smiled, radiating a deep warmth and empathy that Vega felt like a hug. Eve leaned over the counter; there was an unhurried manner in everything she did, as though she sipped moments, savored interactions like the coffee she sold. "I'm really sorry about your mother, Vega. That was incredibly rude of me." She released the steam from the espresso machine, and it was loud in the store. "I typically try to keep my knowings to myself. I'm not a psychic; I'm more of an Appalachian kook who thinks I know more than I do."

Vega rocked Riley, her failure to help him a frustrated twist in her stomach. She was taken off guard but grateful for Eve's apology. It chased away the anxious prickles that moved up and down her legs. She put Riley up on her shoulder and patted his back. Eve never seemed to register Riley's cries, smiling at him without the flicker of annoyance she'd caught on Zach's face. It calmed her.

She kept thinking about Zach's posts, his accusations. Tried to focus on something more concrete and started to make a list in her head. The familiar process helped her push those thoughts away. "The apartment needs quite a bit of work. There's a leak in the kitchen sink, the toilet isn't flushing well, and the radiator probably needs some maintenance—clean the pump, maybe bleed it for any trapped air. That's where I'd start, at least. Are you hoping to sell it or rent it?"

Eve's mouth softened; she looked amused. "Rent it."

"Then you might want to consider a fresh coat of paint, new plumbing in the bathroom, some tile work—there's quite a few cracked ones, and mold in the shower."

"Noted," Eve said, wiping the counter. "Put together an estimate when you can."

A lightness wiggled under Vega's feet, threatened to lift her off the ground. Eve's offer meant safety and the security of a job. She started to do the math in her head. If she worked to pay off the rent, would she have much left over for diapers and formula? Food? Her feet rooted back to the floor, her back bowing under the weight of reality. Probably not much if she couldn't find other jobs.

Behind her the door opened with a creak, and Heff's voice filled the store. "Best coffee, too, am I right?" The man seemed to always be in the middle of a conversation. "And then I found this in my garage, left over from my mother's fostering days, and I thought, I know exactly who could use it." He winked at Eve. "See now, Eve, either you're not the only one who knows things or maybe your powers are rubbing off on the rest of us." He set a long object on the ground at Vega's feet and tilted his head, his soft gaze on Riley, whose cries continued. "Poor little guy—and poor mom. Colic is just the worst. There's nothing you can do about it until Baby grows out of it."

Vega's cheeks burned. The man could see right through her. Was everyone in this town a psychic? "Thanks," she said, and she had to blink back tears when she saw what Heff had brought her. "Is that a pack 'n play?"

He smiled. "Sure is."

She nodded, touched and relieved. It was one of the many things she had left in her hurry to get out of there. "Thank you."

Eve frothed milk and added it to Heff's cappuccino. "Vega and I were just talking about all the work that the apartment needs."

Heff nodded. "It's in pretty abysmal shape, if you ask me, Eve. Couldn't believe you wanted to rent it out in the first place."

"Well, I had a feeling."

Heff looked at Vega. "Eve decided to rent out the old apartment last week. I helped her clear it and clean it, and then, boom—you show up looking for a place to stay."

Vega thought about what Heff said when she'd arrived yesterday. Something about Eve knowing she was coming. A chill raced across her shoulders.

"But now that I think about it, and after what Vega's pointed out, I really shouldn't be renting it out in the shape it's in," Eve said.

Vega stiffened. She didn't want Riley to have to sleep in the van. She wanted him warm and cozy inside. "I didn't mean—"

"It's probably against the law." Eve looked at Heff, who was already nodding.

"It definitely is," he said. "I'm just glad you brought it up first before I had to go put on my deputy hat." He smiled at Vega. "I prefer my art to policing."

71

Eve clapped her hands. "Then it's decided. Vega, you stay in the apartment—rent-free, of course, given the state it's in—while you work on fixing it up for me."

Vega's face felt stiff. It was exactly what she needed. "I don't take charity." It sounded halfhearted because Vega knew she couldn't turn her down. Not with Riley to take care of.

"Good," Eve said. "Neither do I. So please give me your estimate for the work by tomorrow."

Riley's crying, Eve's kindness, and Heff's thoughtfulness built an enormous pressure behind her eyes. She clipped Riley back into the front carrier, shouldered the pack 'n play, and tried to smile. Her lips wobbled. "I'll have that estimate to you as soon as possible, Eve. Um, thank you, and"—she looked at Heff—"you're right, you know. Eve does make the best coffee this side of the Appalachians."

He slouched against the counter, his smile touching every part of his face. "Told you."

CHAPTER NINE

EVE

Being around Vega was like having a word on the tip of her tongue and not being able to retrieve it. Vega was a total stranger, and yet there was something familiar about her too. It was in the lift of her chin and the hardness in her eyes. A determination that women like Eve and others she'd known in her forty-three years developed when life twisted into something monstrous and cruel. The girl was scared of something. Her fear was palpable; Eve had felt it in the squeeze of her own quad muscles and an overwhelming desire to run.

She busied herself with scrubbing the milk-steamer and took note of Heff watching the woman leave the store. He sighed when the door closed behind her.

Eve laughed. "You know, most men hide their feelings about a woman with bravado and machismo, not moon over her like a lovesick puppy."

Heff nodded. "I'm a romantic—you know that, Eve." He turned to look at her. "So what's her story?"

"Come on now, Heff. We've talked about that." She poured out Vega's coffee. "I have enough trouble in this town. And sometimes I get things wrong." Eve slid a chocolate croissant onto a plate and pushed it in front of him.

He'd moved to Crystal as a boy with his mother not long after Eve had left, so they hadn't known each other, but he was the first one to welcome her back. He'd stopped by the farm a month or so after she'd arrived, with a basket of cornbread muffins, a beautiful bunch of black-eyed Susans—stems tied with a pink ribbon—and a small painting of the mountains. *Welcome back!* he'd said. *I painted that, by the way. I'm a local artist.*

Eve had hesitated. Heff seemed friendly, but she'd learned to wait; true colors often came with time. It didn't take long, though, to see his, because although he looked like any other frat boy in America, Heff's heart was true gold.

Carl said you're planning on turning your parents' property into a small farm? He smiled when he talked—or rather, he talked around his smile.

That's my plan, she'd said, wondering how much Carl and Betty had told him about her, wondering, as she often did, what he saw when he looked at her.

A pickup had come down the road just then, spewing dust and rocks when it slammed to a stop. Levi Harrison opened the driver's-side door; his sons jumped from the bed, guns strapped to their thighs or slung around their waists like they were in a mountain gang. A couple of their teenage boys pulled up on ATVs. They stood behind their fathers and grandfather, except for one, a younger boy who seemed no more than ten. He half hid behind a tree.

Eve had straightened her spine and stood tall, noticing that Heff had turned and now stood shoulder to shoulder with her, hands on his hips. Levi approached. Time had not been kind to the man, settling deeply into the leathery lines across his forehead, leaving a pale hollowness in his cheeks. Eve's scalp had prickled. The man was ill, cancer eating into his bones. As soon as she'd felt it, another truth formed and she relaxed. It wasn't her job to tell; he already knew.

You died, he'd said.

Eve had retained a feeling since her NDE—a deep understanding for herself and for others, even for cruel and closed-minded Levi, and it had stopped the hatred from breaking her. She'd stuck her hands in her jeans pockets and smiled.

Guess it didn't take.

Levi spat black saliva onto the ground, the minty tang of his chewing tobacco pungent in the air. *Your dad wouldn't want somethin' like you livin' here.* His top lip had curled. *God don't neither.*

Eve brushed a strand of hair out of her face. *Dad is dead, Levi. And God cares a whole lot more than you think.*

Levi had stared, working his jaw, but couldn't seem to figure out how to respond. The boy behind the tree caught her eye, and damned if he hadn't given Eve a shy smile.

Heff had never said a word, but he stayed by her side on that day and in the days to come as Levi and others like him tried to make her leave. And Eve did what she'd done her entire life: she moved ahead with her plans regardless of what people thought and without needing anybody's help. She'd learned to stop expecting others to change. There were some exceptions, like Carl, but not many. So she'd kept her head down, and over time, whether they liked it or not, Eve had become part of Crystal.

Heff bit into the croissant, followed it with a sip of coffee. "Oh yeah, this one's a winner."

"You say that about every chocolate croissant."

"Do I?"

Eve laughed, remembering what had happened right after the altercation with Levi. She'd touched Heff's arm. *Thank you fo—* And frozen, locked into a knowing that burned bright in her vision. Of a phoenix, feathers brightly colored, beautiful, engulfed in flames. She'd spoken before thinking, before knowing how this man would react. *A phoenix will change your life.*

He'd looked confused, a little irritated but still smiling. *Listen here, Eve. I've heard about your supernatural powers from Betty, but you need to know something about me.*

Eve had pulled away, off-centered and unsure of herself. Ready for this man to do what most people in her life had done: disappoint her.

I don't want to know my future. I like the freedom to live as I please without worrying when I'll die or what good fortune will come my way. That sound like something we can agree on?

Eve had nodded, surprised because it wasn't what she expected to hear and relieved. Heff seemed like someone who might one day be a friend.

Someone banged on the glass. She looked up and sighed. Jane. Her store was next to Eve's. Jane had put up the biggest fight when Eve decided to buy the space a few years back. Picketing outside for three days straight, even gathering a handful of her friends to join her. Argued it wasn't wholesome. That Eve would bring sin, and evil would follow. All the Old Testament threats that Eve had heard for most of her life. It was tiresome.

Jane opened the door a crack. "When you roast your coffee beans, it stinks up my herb shop and drives my customers away."

Eve sighed. "Sorry about that, Jane. I'll roast them earlier in the morning before you open. How's that?"

Jane pursed her lips, disappointed, like she'd hoped for a fight. "It'll have to do."

Heff raised an eyebrow when she left. "Why do you let her talk to you like that?"

Eve shrugged. "Some people can't be changed. You know that, Heff."

"I know that those same people don't have a right to walk all over you either."

Eve smiled at the man. He had become a good friend, one of the best. "I'm happiest just living my life. I don't need to make trouble."

The bell above the door rang and Joshua Harrison, Levi's youngest grandson, walked in.

Eve felt the words grow stale on her tongue. Her pulse quickened. Joshua Harrison had come to ask her a question that would make the exact kind of trouble Eve wanted to avoid. But she couldn't say no. She knew firsthand what happened when family turned their backs on one of their own. After she'd left Crystal, she went to Cleveland, ended up on the street without options or a home to go back to. Her NDE the only source of comfort—but it wasn't enough to feed, shelter, or keep her warm.

"Hey there, Joshua," she said, heart thumping hard. Eventually, someone had found Eve sleeping in her car—dress torn, missing one of her shoes, face swollen from a recent beating—and they'd opened up their home to her and others like her. A safe space. A place where she could be herself without the constant threat of violence. It had saved her.

Joshua sat on a stool next to Heff, hunched his bony shoulders over the counter. He was a skinny kid with dark smudges under his eyes that made him look too old for his fifteen years, and he was quiet, too, in a sullen way. In the last few months, he'd taken to coming into the store in the early hours before school. Joshua's family, especially his grandfather, had lessened their vocal opposition to only the occasional property damage or spray-painted sign to indicate their intolerance, but they steered clear of Eve and her store. Joshua's appearance was surprising for everyone but Eve. She knew why he was coming and what he wanted to ask. And part of Eve wished he'd stop coming, because she could never tell him no.

She filled a glass of water and set it in front of the kid. His lips were dry and chapped, fingernails bitten into the nail bed. "How's your grandpa?" She put a banana muffin on a plate and added a small bowl of fruit.

Joshua shrugged, picked at the fruit. Eve felt something tug at her heart when she looked at the boy.

"Not good," he mumbled. "He can't get out of bed no more."

"That's rough," Heff said, and patted Joshua's shoulder. "Sorry, man."

Joshua shrugged again, looked at Eve. "He's an asshole, anyway."

Before her NDE, Eve would have readily agreed with him, but after, well . . . her experience had given her a deep and abiding empathy for people because they knew so little and thought all the wrong things were important. They worried about the small stuff, let the most absurd issues drive a wedge between them, elevated the inconsequential. "We all are at some point or another, right?"

Another shrug. "I guess." It had taken a few visits for Eve to realize Joshua had been the young boy who smiled at her all those years ago. "It was my brother that did that to your fence. Sorry."

"Oh, no bother. My pigs have enjoyed the vacation in town."

"Carl's planning on turning them into bacon if you don't do something about that, Eve," Heff said.

"I asked our newcomer if she'd like the work, so it'll be fixed shortly."

"Did you, now? I suppose I might plan on offering my assistance, then."

Eve shook her head. "This town is too small for two handypersons. Plus, I think our guest prefers solitude."

"I'll offer to help with the baby, of course. We all know my skills fall mostly on the maternal side of things."

Joshua smirked into his water and Eve laughed, picking up his empty coffee cup, but when she did, her vision dimmed and she smelled the acrid stink of a discharged gun, saw Heff facedown—blood pooling out from under his chest—and she dropped the coffee cup. It clattered off the counter, fell to the floor, and split in half. She pressed a hand to her chest, felt her heart beating against her palm.

Heff jumped to his feet, retrieved the broken mug pieces. Eve stood, frozen, and watched, trying desperately to regain her composure and erase what she had seen.

Joshua abruptly rose from his seat. She'd forgotten the boy was there. "Um, thanks for the water." He turned to go, stopped.

Eve's arms tingled and her heart sank. "Have something you want to ask me, Joshua?"

The boy looked at Eve, then at Heff, and the tingling intensified. Her skin was cold, clammy. Once he asked, she'd never say no, but what cycle of events would it start? And did it have anything to do with Heff getting shot?

Joshua shook his head. "Nah, nothing. Bye."

Heff stood. "I'm off too. Have a house to show in Nelsonville this morning—"

Eve reached out and grabbed his arm, felt the warmth of his flesh beneath his shirt. It was reassuring. "Wait, I have to tell you—"

Heff backed away, hands up like she was about to rob him. "I knew you had one of your knowings when you dropped that cup. No, thank you, Eve. The phoenix one slipped out before you knew me, but never again. I've told you before that if you ever have another one about me, I. Do. Not. Want. To. Know." He emphasized each word, still smiling but with a serious squint to his eyes. "I intend to live each day like it's my last, and if it happens to be, then so be it." He gave a quick wave and ducked out the door.

Eve stared after him, numb in the wake of her knowing. Heff could die within the month.

Pieces of knowings swirled in her head, possibly connected or completely unrelated. She didn't know. She rubbed her neck and leaned her weight against the counter, terrified that there was nothing she could do to stop it.

CHAPTER TEN

July 1995

Something touched her hair and Donna screamed. Eyes blurry from sleep. Fists out, flailing until they met flesh, and then she started pummeling as hard as she could.

"Ouch, hey, that hurts! Stop!"

The owner of the voice didn't punch her back, and she scrambled to the far edge of the mattress against the hard wall of the school bus and wiped the crud from her eyes. She winced and realized that one eyelid was swollen shut, but through the other eye, she could make out a boy about her age, maybe older, standing midway down the length of the bus, eyes bugged wide like he'd found a wild barn cat tearing up his living room.

Donna's heart beat fast and she kept her fists tight in front of her. Bounced from foot to foot, a boxer ready to attack. "I will fuck you up if you come any closer to me," she said. And she could; she knew just by looking at the way his clothes hung from his skinny frame.

The boy looked at her, his eyes soft, shoulders rounded like he was afraid to take up any space. A kid used to hiding. Like her.

She lowered her fists and tried to smile, but it split her scabbed lip right open, and blood ran into her mouth. She smiled anyway. "This your bus?"

"Nah. It doesn't belong to anybody."

Donna collapsed into the chair at the little makeup table, elbows propped on her knees to keep her upright. Her head hurt and the bus had begun to spin. "I bet it's some kid's hideout," she said. "I had one, too, when I was little, but it was in a busted-up old car, and a raccoon made a nest in it and kicked me out. Those animals are nasty mean. This is much nicer."

Donna used a tissue to wipe the blood from her face and picked up a brush from the table to pull the tangles out of her hair. She thought of her sister, three years old and quiet as a mouse. Donna had shown her sister a hideout spot in the back of their pantry and underneath the lowest shelf. Told her to hide there if she was ever scared. Pressure built behind her eyes, and fear for her sister clawed at her stomach. She shouldn't have left her. She gripped the brush, hit the table with it. Beth was the reason she hadn't run away before now; what if he went after her next? Flashes of the night before played on repeat in her head. Her mother, pointing the barrel of the rifle at her chest, when it was her father who deserved to be shot. Tears on her sister's face, her father cowering in a heap on the floor, his blood on her fingertips.

She pressed a hand to her chest and breathed against it. Her mother loved Beth more than anything in the world. She'd keep her safe. For now, at least.

"I won't steal nothin'," she said to the boy. "I just need a place to sleep and figure some shit out." She tried to sound tough, like she had some grand plan, because the truth was that she was terrified to leave the bus. Scared her father was waiting for her out in those woods to take her back home. Doubt had crept into her heart. She couldn't leave Beth to fend for herself, but she wouldn't ever go back home either.

"Your face looks really bad," the boy said. "Somebody hurt you?"

Donna turned to look in the small mirror on the desk; her face filled the oval. "No, dumbass, this is just my natural beauty." She flipped her long hair behind her shoulders and studied her reflection. He wasn't wrong—she did look awful. Besides her swollen eye, which had turned a nasty shade of blue black, she had scratches across her cheeks from running through the woods, her split lip, and the trail of blood drying on her chin.

In the mirror, she saw the boy slink down in a bus seat, turned backward so that he faced her, only his head rising above the vinyl. His eyes were sunken, the sweep of his cheekbones catching the light.

She picked up a makeup brush, swiped it along a peach-colored powder, and painted it across her cheeks. She'd never worn makeup before. Her mother didn't allow it. She leaned back from the mirror, studying the color against her tanned skin, and had no idea if it looked good or like a little girl playing dress-up. She wiped it off with her sleeve and turned to face the boy. "What're you hiding from?"

"Nothing." He'd slung his arms over the top of the seat.

"That's funny. You're funny."

"What are you hiding from?" he said.

She turned away, looked down at the table, and broke the makeup brush in half. "Nothing."

The boy went quiet then, and so did she. Her skin crawled when she thought of her father and his breath, hot and foul and in her face. She touched her lip and her fingers came away red. She'd rather take his fists, but she'd never had a choice.

"You hungry?"

Her stomach rumbled at the thought, loud enough to be heard.

The boy threw something at her, and it landed on the mattress. It didn't look like food, and it felt like a roll of tape when she picked it up. She frowned. "What is it?"

"You've never had a Fruit Roll-Up?"

She opened the package. It felt like rubber but smelled kinda like strawberry, and she was hungry enough to try it. She took a tiny bite and then a larger one, and then it was almost gone. "It's good."

"Yeah." He tossed her another.

It was quiet while they ate, except for the loud chirp of crickets.

"Where'd you come from?"

She threw the wrapper on the table, still hungry but now a little queasy too. The sun had risen, making everything outside brighter and gloomier at the same time. She had nowhere to go. "That way," she said, and pointed outside.

"What a coincidence. I came from that way too."

It wasn't funny, not really, but he was trying to make a joke—and after last night, and with her face feeling like it had swollen to the size of a watermelon, she started to laugh, even if it hurt. He smiled.

"Donna!" From somewhere outside came her father's muffled voice. It hit the trees and fell down on top of the bus like a grenade. She sprang to her feet, muscles electrified. She had to get out of there.

The boy had risen, still looking too skinny and unsubstantial, like he could be broken in two by the wind. But there was something in his eyes that calmed her the tiniest bit. He raised a finger to his lips and pointed to the very back seat, and she didn't hesitate, sliding to the floor and hiding half-under the seat, using the blanket from the mattress to cover her head. The bus moved and she heard the boy's footsteps go down the stairs and outside.

"Donna!" The *n*'s stuck together from too much whiskey. She knew the sound. "Boy! Have you seen my girl? Bitch ran off."

"Nah. Haven't seen nobody." The boy's voice wasn't loud but it carried.

The bus listed to the side, and the air glued itself to her lungs. "Donna!" Her body tingled, spiders crawling over her skin at the thought of his hands touching her one more time. She'd rather die than go back. He walked to the back of the bus, and from her hiding spot, she saw the toe of his boot come even with the seat she was hiding under. She'd grab a makeup brush, stab it into his eye, use her nails to claw at his face, take the clothes rack and jab it into the softest part of his belly. She tensed. Ready to fight. To kill him.

He sniffed. "What the hell?"

He'd seen the clothes and makeup, and she balled her hands into fists. She'd pummel his face into a pulp. But his feet disappeared and the bus rocked when he stepped out.

"Donna!" he yelled, and she couldn't believe her ears, but it sounded like he was walking away. "Donna!" Farther this time.

She stayed put until the bus rocked again. The boy sat on the floor across from her, pulled his knees up to his chest, and hugged his legs. His hair was dark and shaggy, falling down to cover one eye. She hadn't been around boys—or at least, not without her parents. This one was cute, she decided. And safe.

"He's gone."

She pulled the blanket from her head, felt the staticky trail it left behind. "Him," she said.

His eyebrows came together. "Huh?"

"That's what I'm hiding from."

"Yeah, I'd hide from him too. I'm Ethan."

"Donna."

"You can stay here as long as you'd like, Donna." He handed her another Fruit Roll-Up.

"You don't think the other girl will mind?"

He took out another roll-up, pulled it open with his teeth, and for the first time, he smiled. Donna thought it made him beautiful. "Not one bit."

CHAPTER ELEVEN

Vega

April 2021

Vega turned Riley so that he faced outward, and his cries grew softer. "Maybe you just wanted some fresh air, hey, bud?" She started walking. It felt good to move. The sun had risen higher, burning off the rainy mist that had clung to the ground, and the air skimmed warm across her arms. She started down Main Street and slowed when she came to the herb shop. The windows were packed with herbs, some creatively displayed in colored glass jars or ceramic pots, each neatly labeled. The small flower garden outside had been demolished yesterday by the pigs. Vega decided to hurry past, not wanting another run-in with the unpleasant woman.

When she got to the end of Main Street, she noticed a narrow trail hacked out of the weeds and following the road.

She walked, enjoying the feel of her leg muscles working, the uneven ground beneath the rugged soles of her sandals, the tickle of foliage across her toes. Vega was accustomed to manual labor, jobs that taxed her body, and the last few months without work had worn on her in a different way. The woods were quiet, with the occasional chirp and rustle of a forest body flying or skittering through branches and leaves.

The minutes turned into a half hour, and the path sometimes petered out, then picked back up, looking more like a trampled human-and-animal path than a planned trail. She came to an opening in the trees and noticed that the path split—one side following the road, the other going deeper into the woods. She chose the woods.

It was darker under the trees, the sun blocked by budding leaves and thick limbs, shadows smothering the light. But it was peaceful, too, and Vega breathed in the fresh air and the baby's rare state of contentment and kept walking. The trees moved closer, making her walk in zigzags around the trunks, moss below her feet muting her steps. Just as it occurred to her that she could easily get lost, an unnatural color glinted in the green and brown in front of her. She moved closer and her breath caught in her chest. It was a school bus—old, tires flat, grass and weeds growing up and around and through the wheels as if the vehicle itself had sprung up from below, a twisted yellow flower.

Riley kicked his legs, and it mirrored an excited twist in her chest. "I know this bus," she told the baby. She was sure it was the exact same one in the picture she'd found as a girl. The one that still hung in the van. A concrete reminder of her mother's life before Vega. She leaned her hand against a tree, legs suddenly weak. A deep sadness battled with twitches of resentment that she tried to smooth away. She hated to feel this way about Renee, especially now. But the truth tugged at her. Why had her mother kept so much hidden from her? Maybe Vega would have made better decisions if she'd understood what had driven Renee. What had made her so afraid to stop moving.

The moist earth absorbed her footsteps. It was quiet—a secret of the woods. She moved closer and her mother's youthful form materialized in the doorway of the bus, a laugh frozen forever on her face. Vega stopped and looked up at the yellow beast and breathed in a past she knew nothing about.

It looked different from the picture, a little more worn for the wear. All the windows in the bus had been broken; a few had tattered, weather-torn curtains, but most were empty eye sockets. It sat rusted and alone and completely out of place in the small clearing, surrounded on all sides by trees. Graffiti covered nearly the entire bus: big cartoon faces; pentagrams; some good artwork, including a decent Bart Simpson holding a can of spray paint. That one was new. The graffiti was what had caught her eye when she was a little girl. It had reminded her of her mother's tattoos.

The bus beckoned her, and without giving it much thought, she took a tentative step inside. Dark and musty, the air moved with her, dirt and leaves shuffling along the floorboards when she walked down the aisle.

In the front of the bus, the high-backed seats were torn, the padding spilling out. In the back the seats had been ripped out, leaving space for a table and chair. Oddly, this area had been swept clean—tidy, even—with a pallet on the floor neatly made up with what appeared to be clean sheets and a pillow. Suddenly, Vega felt like she was trespassing. The baby made a small noise, and she looked down to see that he was awake and staring, his eyes shifting as though he wanted to take it all in. She touched his soft head, ran a finger through his thin curls, smiled. A breeze from outside wormed through the windows, fluttering the curtain rags.

Vega sat down in the chair by the small table with an oval mirror on top. The baby's face reflected back—round cheeks, soft pink lips. The spitting image of his father. She kissed his head and looked around the bus. What had this place meant to her mother? It had to mean something for her to have kept a picture of it all these years.

It looked like a childhood hideout spot in the woods. Vega's hideout spot had been their lavender conversion van with the captain's chair that spun in circles and the ladder that she climbed to sit on the roof with her mother to watch sunsets. They'd lived everywhere, taking jobs up and down the West Coast, weaving their way through the Rocky Mountains and down to the deserts of Arizona. They stayed mostly west of the Continental Divide. Her mother never wanted to venture much farther east. Vega had, though, and had begged Renee to find work on the beaches of Florida or North Carolina. Later, it became anywhere they could stay and call home. It wasn't that she was unhappy—her mom was her best friend. She just couldn't help feeling the pull toward something more normal, more boring.

She started to cry. It came on so suddenly she hadn't even realized until a breeze swept cool over her wet cheeks. Maybe it was the loneliness of the bus that reflected her own or the realization that she knew so little about her mother. Or the still-tender skin around her wrist, the harsh truth that she'd stayed with a man like Zach because fear made him seem like her best option. Had her mother made a similar choice? Was that why she'd never speak about her past?

The bus shifted. "Oh, shit. What are you doing here?"

Vega sprang to her feet, one hand on the baby's back to keep him from jostling too much. A teenage boy had climbed into the bus, dark-brown hair greasy, his cheeks flushed. He breathed heavily, like he'd been running, and his eyes held a wildness nurtured by fear.

She reached for her pepper spray, held it ready in her palm, assessed the situation: in the middle of the woods, no cell service, infant strapped to her chest, the only exits through the windows or past the boy.

The boy retreated a step, surprise pulling his eyebrows up. "Sorry, it's—no one comes here, sorry." He backed all the way off the bus. She stayed put, watched him through the window. He wore a gray sweatshirt with worn jeans and old black Vans, and stood with one arm pressed across his chest. She climbed off the bus, giving him a wide berth, even if her instincts told her he might be more scared of her than she was of him. He was young, his cheeks clean of hair, soft peach fuzz on his upper lip.

"I was just out for a walk," she said. "Didn't realize I was trespassing. I'm heading back to town anyway."

He pulled a cigarette from his pocket, lit it. "Ain't you the one staying at Eve's?"

At this point, nothing surprised Vega. "I am."

He stuck a hand into his sweatshirt pocket. There was a hint of youthful sweetness about him and in the way he smoked, like he did it more for how it made him look than how it tasted. A quick glance over his shoulder and his jaw tensed. "What're you doing out here?"

She touched the baby's back. "We were out for a walk and I just . . . found the bus, I guess."

"Yeah, Betty says that happens." One side of his mouth lifted when he looked at Riley. "My sister was a mean baby. She bit me when she got mad."

"Oh." Vega didn't know how else to respond, her body stiff with uncertainty about the kid.

"Yeah, but she was sweet as candy all the other times. So it was okay. Lucky me, she stopped before she got too many teeth." He dragged on the cigarette, released the smoke from the side of his mouth, and smiled at the baby. "You're Vega, right? Heff's told everybody about you."

Vega's face turned to stone. That was the last thing she wanted. "What's your name?"

"Joshua."

A squirrel scurried across the clearing and clambered up one of the tires, disappearing under the bus.

Joshua exhaled smoke. Glanced into the woods behind him. "Some people think you take sides if you go to Eve's." He kicked at a rock on the ground, sent it flying at the bus. When it hit, something dropped from underneath the bus and ran through the dead leaves—probably the squirrel.

Vega considered what he was saying, toed a rock of her own. She suspected what he was getting at, but just as she didn't care if Eve wore

Tibetan robes or had taken a vow of silence, she also didn't care that Eve was a trans woman. That was a lesson Renee had taught her from a young age.

They'd been camped on the outskirts of Boise in a truck stop parking lot. Vega had drifted off to sleep, hair wet from the showers, snuggled beside her mother on the mattress. She awoke to a noise outside the van. The sickening thump of fists and boots on bone and flesh, cries of pain, and Renee's hand covering her mouth, eyes wide and pleading for her silence. They lay frozen until a car engine came to life, tires squealing, pitiful whimpers in the quiet night. Renee, through clenched teeth: *Stay here.*

The van door squeaked open, and the soft tones of her mother's voice tightened the bones of Vega's chest. She crawled to the door, peered outside. A thin man lay sprawled on the pavement, head cradled in Renee's lap. Blood on his face, scratches across his bare arms. A splash of greenish fluorescent light across his body highlighted a short skirt; torn stockings; black, shiny heels scattered by his feet. Vega's mother caught her eyes. *Get the first aid kit.*

Renee cleaned and disinfected his wounds, made him chicken noodle soup from a packet, gave him a set of her clothes. His name was Colleen. When he fell asleep, curled into a ball in the passenger seat, pure exhaustion carving deep lines along his face, Vega crawled into her mother's lap. She was only seven, but she wasn't shocked; she'd seen lots of things she hadn't understood. But she trusted her mother, and that made her feel safe when nothing else did. Renee had kissed the top of her head. *Colleen is all alone and she needs our help, okay?* Vega nodded into her mother's chest. The next day she made Colleen a beaded bracelet in bright pink and deep purple with C-O-L-L-E-E-N spelled out in white and black beads across the middle. Colleen had touched it, a sad smile lifting one side of her mouth. *Thanks.*

Vega breathed in the moist air of the forest, eyes wet from the visceral memory of Colleen's pain, her mother's gentleness. Colleen was the first trans woman they'd helped, but she hadn't been the last. So when Vega met Eve, she'd only been surprised that the woman had chosen to live in a town like Crystal, far from urban meccas of modern thought, and it pained her to wonder at the challenges Eve had faced to carve out a life here.

She tensed, wondered what side this kid was on. "Is that what you think?" she asked. "That I'm taking sides?"

His eyes opened wider; he seemed surprised by her question. "I'm a Harrison." Like it was explanation enough.

"That means nothing to me."

For the first time, he smiled. It was small, hardly more than a lift of his lips, but it revealed a deeper layer to the kid, made him more than a small-town teen who ditched school to smoke in the woods.

"Cool," he said, and squinted his eyes when he took another drag from his cigarette. "There's abandoned mines around here. You should be careful. Some are so deep people think they go straight to hell."

"Sounds scary."

Joshua stared at her. "You know what's scary? A girl and her father went missing in these woods. They say she murdered her own dad, so she was cursed to haunt this place forever. Some say she chases people outa the woods, and if she catches you"—he made a cut across his throat—"you're dead."

It was the kind of local tale that Vega could tell had been told and retold until it was one big exaggerated story molded to fit the storyteller. Vega tried to look shocked; she didn't want to take the fun out of it for the boy. Whenever they'd had a campfire, her mother used to read her traditional Native American folktales, and she'd loved listening to the stories. Joshua's tale was more of the ghost-story variety, but she got a kick out of his enthusiasm for trying to scare her with it.

"And a kid was beaten to a bloody pulp. Right here." He pointed to the ground as if the blood could still be seen. The silence lengthened.

"Wow," she said, amused. "I'm heading back to town. The bus is all yours, Joshua." She hesitated. "Shouldn't you be in school?"

"School's stupid."

She shrugged. She'd never gone, having been homeschooled by her mom, so who was she to argue? "See you around."

From somewhere in the woods came the sound of more male voices—deeper, older than Joshua. The boy crumpled, and he looked smaller than before. "Um, you should go now. My brother and cousin are out by the road." He pointed. "Maybe go that way." Sweat glistened his forehead, and his face had paled. "They're real assholes." He flicked the ash of his cigarette and disappeared inside the bus, taking the stink of tobacco with him.

The hair on the back of her neck stood straight, and Vega half jogged in the direction he'd pointed, pepper spray gripped tight in her hand. She knew a warning when she heard one.

～

She'd just made it to the road when she heard the squeals. It wasn't the same sound she'd heard yesterday or even last night, the curious grunt of pigs going about their business. These were pained and they stopped her in her tracks. The echo of the men's voices from the woods and the look on Joshua's face should have been enough to send her running back to town, not consider going to check on a couple of pigs. All her tattoos and piercings made her seem hard, but inside Vega was soft—sensitive, even—and she couldn't stand the thought of anyone or thing in pain.

The sound had come from somewhere just up the road. She walked, listening; the squeals had grown louder. Her heart thumped against her ribs. Clouds smothered the early-morning sunlight, turning the forest darker, the air thick with humidity. A truck had pulled half-off the road, like the driver had swerved to avoid hitting something or—she realized with a start—to run it down. Goose bumps pricked her skin.

Men's voices floated from behind the vehicle, and they set her pulse racing. Through the truck windows, she saw two men and froze. One arm pressed Riley closer to her chest, as if by keeping him glued to her, she could protect him from all the evil in the world. She knew better. Some of the kids she and her mother had helped had had bruises like their moms and a hunted slouch to their backs. Thoughts of Zach made her hold Riley even closer. She'd never let Zach hurt her son like that.

A laugh from one of the men raised goose bumps down her arms. Vega tried to walk away because the air felt dredged in testosterone and tobacco, and her baby wasn't safe here. But she couldn't move, couldn't bear to leave these animals to whatever fate the men had planned.

Run. Her mother's voice sifted through the trees, easier to ignore when the pig screamed again. Her legs moved first, shooting her toward the men.

"Hey!" she yelled, and hurried around to the other side of the truck, pulling up short when she saw what they were doing. The hooves of one of the pigs had been tied together, and the poor beast lay on his side, frantically scratching at the air. A man with a shaved head jumped out of the ditch. Holding a knife, the tip covered in blood. Red splattered across his fingertips. Something had been carved into the pig's flesh. A sourness filled her mouth.

The man with the knife took her in, his eyes running up from her legs, around the baby, and to her spiky blonde hair. Something animal-like flickered in his eyes, and Vega stepped back, skin cold.

"You must be that new girl." He wiped the blade on the edge of his shirt. "A little weird lookin', ain't she, JJ?"

The other man, JJ, had the same shaved head, a scar running along his jawline, a likeness to the boy from the bus. But only in looks. She shivered. Joshua had a kindness to him. JJ smiled, making a lump in his cheek that pocketed chew. "Kinda cute. Like a cat who ain't got no claws."

Her blood boiled, cooled only by a rational fear. Vega felt her isolation. The emptiness of the road behind her. The vastness of the woods surrounding them. She clenched her fists, felt the sharp bite of her nails in the skin of her palm. What had she been thinking?

The pig had quieted, but his stomach shuddered with his frantic breathing, and the marks in his skin seeped blood down his belly, mixing into black mud on the ground. Riley had started to cry—scared, she thought, by the men's voices and the pig's whimpering. Two words had been carved into the pig: *Queer Bitch*. Sloppy, crude, like the markings of a child. Vega's stomach turned. They were doing this to hurt Eve.

Anger gripped her, spewed acid into her throat at the cruelty that infected people. It made her think of Zach, and all of a sudden a wave of anger rose inside her, flooding her body, shorting out her reasoning. "What the fuck is wrong with you?" she said. The baby cried harder and she knew exactly why—because people like this still cared so damn much about something that had nothing to do with them.

Why don't we teach them to fight back? she'd asked her mom. *Why do they always have to be the ones to run?* As she grew older, it angered her to see a woman and her kids sneak away, as though they had done something wrong, not their abusers. The injustice of it ate away at her, made her question their approach.

Renee's answers had never satisfied her. *If they fight back, they could die.*

Vega thought it was weak, at odds with Renee, who was strong and didn't let anyone push her around. She'd punched her thigh with a fist. *Maybe they want to fight.*

Pain had flickered in Renee's eyes, and she brushed a finger across Vega's cheek. *Sometimes running is the only answer.* There had been a desperate tone to her voice. *You remember that, okay?*

Vega rocked from side to side. Patted Riley's small back. Told herself she should smile and apologize. Get the hell out of there. Felt an urgency in the twist of her stomach. But the pig struggled against the ropes, pitiful and scared, and Vega could not force herself to move. She stood tall, the way she might if she'd run up against a bear instead of men. Or against Zach—the way she should have from the very beginning. She was being reckless but she couldn't seem to stop herself.

The man, JJ, who at first glance had seemed much older but was probably around Vega's age, lost his smirk, annoyance in the slant of his eyebrows. "Ain't nothing wrong with me."

The other man slid the knife into a case on his belt and crossed his arms, his lips a thin line. "You a queer too?"

Vega's heart beat loud in her ears, and she felt the size difference in the chill that snaked down her spine. And in the tilt of her chin to meet JJ's steeled gaze. *Run,* her mother called to her, but her voice was a weak breeze that never left the trees. Vega didn't move. She wrapped an arm around her baby, held him tight against her, and slowly, slowly reached for her pepper spray.

A grunting sound from the woods turned the men's heads. The other pig had appeared, rooting and pawing at the ground.

JJ looked at Vega, his smirk back, something dangerous in his eyes. "Let's make some road bacon."

The other man laughed, reaching for more rope from the truck, and sauntered toward the other pig. "Here, piggy-piggy."

His cruelty and her helplessness blended with the memory of Zach's hand squeezing her wrist, punching her gut. A reminder of how weak she'd felt then and now. The rage from before boiled over and Vega reacted. She lunged toward JJ, covering the baby's face with her left arm, leaning him as far back as possible, and sprayed the man's eyes.

"Bitch!" he growled.

The other man sprang at her, holding the rope out like he intended to tie her instead. She screamed, sprayed again, and jumped away from the cloud, dropping the canister onto the ground. The men grunted, rubbing at their faces, strings of curse words as thick as the pepper spray. They stumbled blindly after her, and she ran as fast as she could, holding the baby's head between her hands, trying not to jiggle him too hard. Praying he didn't get any of the spray into his own tender eyes. Her heart lodged in her throat, and her legs burned with the effort. It had to be a mile back to town. She couldn't outrun them. Not with the baby. Panic wriggled inside her lungs. She couldn't breathe. How could she have been so stupid?

One of them caught up to her, hand grazing her shoulder. She screamed and lurched forward, tripping on her own feet, holding Riley tight and landing with a crunch onto her knees. Sharp pains raced up her thighs, but she stayed upright, didn't fall forward onto Riley. She pushed up with one hand, spun around. JJ was right behind her, his eyes hard, unflinching.

A crashing sounded from the woods, and out flew Joshua, who ran toward them, eyes on JJ, chest heaving. "Thought you was just gonna hurt the pig."

JJ's face was red, eyes weeping. "This bitch got in the way."

Joshua didn't acknowledge Vega. "Momma'll be pissed if she finds out you hurt some girl."

"Shut up, Josh." The other guy had reached them, gasping and holding his face like she'd shot him.

Vega started to back away, heart pushing against her ribs. With his skinny arms, Joshua was no match for his brother. The other guy eyed her, and Vega couldn't see how she was going to get away. She tensed her arms, prepared herself to run like she should have from the very beginning.

An old truck ambled down the road, and she waved, frantic—partly relieved, partly terrified it was another Harrison. The truck stopped and she almost sank to the ground. Carl, still wearing his yellow suspenders, jumped out and moved quickly to her side.

"Help, Carl! Please."

He took hold of her elbows because she must have looked like she was going to collapse. "Okay, now, missy. It's okay. What's—" His eyes narrowed behind his glasses, and he released her, moved so that he stood in front of her. "Damn those boys."

Vega groaned.

JJ and the other man stared at Carl. Joshua had moved so that he stood behind them. JJ spoke from behind a hand, rubbing at his eyes. "Move, Carl. This ain't none of your business."

Vega leaned into Carl. "They hurt Eve's pig," she whispered, the fear she'd quashed before having finally bloomed, her anger a deflated heap on the ground beside her, leaving her body shaking and cold.

Carl nodded but kept Vega behind him. Part of her wanted to push him aside, tell him she could handle this on her own. But the bigger part was relieved that someone wanted to help, that she wasn't alone.

"Go on," Carl said and walked toward the men, hands out like he was shooing a fly. "I'm guessing you boys destroyed Eve's fence too? And now you're after her pigs? That's not how we live up here. We help each other, even when we don't see eye to eye."

"He don't belong up here," JJ said.

Vega saw Carl's shoulders stiffen, and his mustache shook. "*She's* always belonged here."

Her throat tightened to hear Carl use the pronoun. From what she'd gathered, Carl had lived here longer than these two cavemen, but he couldn't be more different. The Harrison men were exactly what her mother had taught her to expect. It was men like Zach, the snakes who said one thing but did another, that Vega felt unprepared for. She thought of Heff, with his kind eyes and gentle way with the baby. Or even Carl, who said all the right things. How would she ever know who to trust?

"And I'm reportin' you to the deputy," Carl said.

JJ gave a bitter laugh. His skin looked mottled from the pepper spray, his eyes still red and weeping. "Heff? That man ain't got no right to do nothin' but sell a house."

"And he's not good at that neither," said the other man. He stomped the ground with the heel of his boot. "Goddamn, that stings!" He looked at Vega between his fingers. "You cu—"

"Son of a gun!" Carl said. "You can't talk to women like that."

"But she—"

"Even if she clawed your eyes. And especially when you deserved it anyways."

The man glared at her, and Vega tried to keep her chin lifted, to look braver than she felt.

"Go on, JJ," Carl said. "Get." Like he was a dog. Vega liked the image, wishing JJ had a tail he could tuck between his legs.

JJ hesitated. Vega shifted her weight, hugged the baby tight. Carl was old and in questionable shape, and Vega had just made the two men cry. What was stopping them from doing what they wanted?

"Your momma's a good woman," Carl said, his voice gentler, laced with respect. "Don't disappoint her."

JJ stared at them, then shrugged, his lazy smile from before returning. He looked at Vega over Carl's shoulder. "See you around, new girl."

A familiar spike of anger. And her mother's words: *A nothing town full of nobodies and bullies.* She thought of Zach. There were bullies everywhere.

JJ sauntered back to the truck, followed by the other man and Joshua, who walked hunched, staring at the ground. The tires spit rocks and dirt when the truck peeled out.

Vega hurried to the pig, who lay panting, like he'd given up. The blood had already dried, and she hoped that meant the wounds weren't too deep.

Carl followed her, and when he looked at the pig, his cheeks puffed in and out. "Dang them," he said, and moved into the ditch. In one quick movement, he pulled the loops of the knot outward and jumped back, scrambling to get out of the ditch. His belly heaved with the effort. The rope fell away, and the pig flung its sizable body to the side and jumped to its feet, running into the woods with a high-pitched squeal. Its companion followed and the pair disappeared, leaving Vega and Carl alone with the baby's now-hungry cries, which echoed a sad emptiness in Vega's chest.

"Why does Eve live here?"

Carl sighed and ran his thumbs up and down his suspenders. "It's her home."

Vega didn't know how to respond. She wasn't a stranger to hate. She and her mother had moved in the fringes, hung with the outcasts, identified with the misfits. But they'd never lived anywhere long enough to have to deal with the consequences of not fitting in, not belonging, or worse, experiencing the hate that comes from being different. They could just pack up and leave. Home was their van. And their community was each other. Thinking about the hate that drove those two men made her feet tingle, and for a moment she understood her mother's desire to pack up and move along. To leave behind the ugliness in favor of something new. Vega bounced the baby up and down, rubbed his back, panic writhing in her stomach. She had nowhere to go. And if she kept running, when would she ever stop? She was tired, heartbroken, angry that there were no safe refuges for someone like her.

She felt the air move through her body, calm the tumult inside her. She couldn't afford to panic or be sad. She had Riley now, and he needed her to be strong. "I need to feed my baby, Carl. Can I have a ride?"

Carl grunted, his face going all soft when he looked at Riley. "You bet. Let's get you back to town, missy."

CHAPTER TWELVE

Eve

Eve hefted a bag of dog food from the back and walked it to the small section of feed she kept in a corner of the store, letting it fall to the ground beside the other bags. She swatted at her ear, trying to scatter the remnants of pigs squealing inside her head—a knowing that made no sense. Her pigs weren't outside mucking around Main Street; she was sure because she'd checked several times. The sound echoed softly, so muffled that at first she thought it was because the store was too quiet, so she'd played some music. When that didn't work, she'd checked outside again to see if they'd made their way back to town through the busted fence. They tended to follow her. But no, no pigs. Eve figured it was her conscience getting on her to fix the fence before they ate more of Jane's flowers.

The store door opened.

"Eve." Vega, her voice breathy, like she'd been running.

Eve turned. Vega's hair stood up in blonde spikes, and her face was pale. The baby cried against her chest, and Vega rocked back and forth on her feet, one hand rubbing the infant's back—all of it robotic, like she'd forgotten how to do anything but try to calm her baby. Eve stepped toward her, sympathy stretching through the muscles in her arms. The poor woman looked exhausted, angry, and sad all at the same time, and it had settled in a line carved between her eyebrows. Carl came through the door next, standing just behind Vega. She focused on Vega. "What's wrong?" Eve said.

Vega lurched forward. "Someone—"

"Harrison's boys—" Carl said.

Eve started to remind Carl about the definition of *boy* when Vega piped up. "Excuse me, but they're grown-ass sociopaths who hurt animals."

Carl cleared his throat, thumbed his suspenders. "Well, now, I suppose there's some truth to that."

"They carved something horrible into that poor animal." Vega's eyes were an intense brown, fringed with dark brows that looked at odds against her white-blonde hair but also gave her a Marilyn Monroe quality—if Marilyn had favored leather jackets, tattoos, and a crying baby strapped to her chest.

Eve pulled in a deep breath, let it flutter over her, cooling her anger. There had been a time when she'd wanted everyone to see the truth the way she did. When she thought that the gift of death should have made her more capable of lifting the veil that covered the eyes of the living. To show them that death wasn't to be feared or that the afterlife wasn't a gift to be parceled out for only the chosen ones, a game of who deserved it more. That it was for all, a truth deeply threaded into the fabric of existence, and because of that they could let go of the very human need to make sense of death by deciding that it was only for those who behaved a certain way and believed in God the right way.

But words had failed her time and time again to convince anyone. And her gender was a barrier for so many. Eve had learned to move through life clinging to the remnants of her experience but letting the expectation that she could convince anyone to change fall away like rain flecking off an umbrella. The Harrisons' views were carved into granite, but she refused to let their small-mindedness change her. Her anger deflated. She lifted an eyebrow.

"Let me guess—*queer bitch*? *Die bitch*? Something *bitch*? Or something *queer*? They're not very creative and sometimes their spelling is questionable. But points for getting my pronouns correct." Eve shrugged. "Not that they realize it. They're mostly just angry. Aren't they, Carl?"

Carl raised his eyebrows, rocked on his heels. "With the world. Those boy—" He gave Vega a sheepish look. "Those *men*, well, they haven't been taught good—or, I mean, they don't understand Eve here, and Levi, well, he's a Bible man, see, and . . ." Carl looked like he was losing his way. "So am I, see, but Betty—well, we just don't think it's okay to hate what's different, is all. That's not what the Bible says."

"Amen," Eve said, and Carl's smile lifted his cheeks so they puffed under his eyes. She gave a glance out the window, and her shoulders tensed. A quick knowing fluttered in the grayness outside, flitting through the tree branches with the breeze, and Eve shivered, unsure what it meant. "Was the poor animal okay, Carl? Do you know which way he went?"

"He'll be fine. The cuts weren't deep. They headed in the direction of my property."

"Why do you put up with those men?" Vega said.

Eve took a moment, then smiled. "Put up with Carl? Good question. I'm not sure. Why do I put up with you, Carl?"

"For Betty's buckeye cookies, I think."

Vega breathed a frustrated sigh and Eve laughed. "I've known Carl and Betty my whole life. My father wasn't a Bible man in the Harrison way of things, but he had an intractable belief in the natural order of the world, and I fell way outside of the norm. Carl and Betty gave me a safe place to land when things got tough at home."

Carl's eyes shifted to the floor. He was not the kind of man who liked accolades or compliments, preferring to do what was right because right was right.

A delighted squealing inside her head and the pressing of something warm against her chest, the intoxicating scent of chocolate. Eve smiled. The pigs were just fine. "You're right, Carl. The Kunekunes went to see Betty, and she's probably already tending to his wounds. Smart animals." Eve felt at peace when her knowing ordered into something she understood. Betty was a natural caretaker.

Carl cleared his throat. He was always uncomfortable when Eve talked about her NDE gifts. He was a churchgoing Protestant whose beliefs fell firmly between heaven and hell, right and wrong, God and Satan. Somehow, though, despite all that, he had become a true friend to Eve. "Still need to fix that fence," he mumbled.

"I agree." She folded her arms, eyed Vega. "Can I add some fence work to your estimate? Seems I'll be needing that done first."

For the first time since she'd met her, Vega's smile was genuine, and she looked more energized than Eve had seen her. "Yes, absolutely. I could get started right away. I need to feed the baby first and then—" Her face clouded. "Well, I was hoping to put him down for a nap, but . . ." She bit her lip, looked unsure of herself, and Eve understood. The poor woman had no one but herself.

"You can just fit the work in around nap times. The pigs can wait. Or there are plenty of willing babysitters around here—"

"Betty's always loved looking after the young'uns," Carl said.

Vega seemed to shrink right in front of her eyes. Like she wanted to disappear. "I can't ask anyone—"

"For help?" Eve said.

Carl grunted. "Small-town folk help each other, as a matter of fact."

Vega narrowed her eyes. "Has anyone told that to the Harrisons?"

"Well, now, ain't that some truth," Carl agreed. "But folks like them are just louder than some." He looked at Vega, and Eve noticed the slight tremble in his mustache. "We all have to ask for help at some point or another, missy. If it's offered, take it. And return the favor when you can."

"We've all been there, Vega," Eve echoed, and noticed the woman's cheeks redden. Eve felt a pang. She remembered all too well what it had felt like to be alone in the world, when accepting help was the only way to survive. "Betty and Carl gave me a car once so I could leave this town for good. And when I was living in that car in Cleveland, someone else offered me a safe place where I belonged." Eve shrugged. "I wouldn't be here if I hadn't taken their help."

"But you came back to Crystal?" Vega looked mystified, and after her run-in with the Harrisons, Eve couldn't blame her.

"I was just as surprised as you are. But family is complicated, and home is a place we're always trying to find."

On the night Eve died, Betty had made a frantic call to Eve's father. He'd come to the hospital, racing through the hallways, pulling up short when he saw Eve's body on the cart in the emergency department. A long flat line across the monitor. Doctors and nurses working like a hive of ants around each other to save her. But it was the remnants of eye shadow above her swollen and bloodied cheeks, the black lines of mascara twisting down her face, that had carved a disgusted peak into his upper lip. And her favorite sundress cut in half to expose her chest—it had stopped her father in his tracks. A dust cloud of his fear and disgust had funneled upward to where she hovered above her body. It covered her in the excrement of humanness. She'd at once loved him for it and wanted to get away.

Her father had stared at her body for some time while her limbs flopped on the table. His hands worked into and out of fists; then he'd turned, and when he pushed his way out the hospital door, the cord connecting her to her body snapped and Eve was released.

Later, she'd woken up in an unfamiliar room to a heaviness in her arms and a deep ache that stretched from her skull, over her face and neck, worming deep into her chest and arms, cutting across her abdomen. Betty stood on one side of her bed, Carl on the other, his eyelids thickened and puffy from tears. She'd never seen Carl cry.

Eve had tried to shift in the bed, desperate to find a spot where everything didn't hurt. It didn't exist and she'd given up, let her own tears slide down her cheeks. She remembered everything and nothing. The tail end of a dream that flitted just out of her reach. *Did I stop him?*

Betty's lips had pressed together. Carl ran his fingers up and down his suspenders, looked out the window, then back at Betty. *He won't hurt anyone again,* he'd said. *But you can't come home. Folks are already talking, and you're an easy blame.*

They had an old car, a bag of clothes, some money—a meager amount to start over but more than they had to give. When she'd finally left the hospital, they waved goodbye, Betty with her arm around Carl, Carl with a tissue to his eyes.

Eve smiled at Vega, warmed by the memory. "All we're trying to say is, if you need some help, take it."

The baby had stopped crying, turning his head from Vega's chest to stare at Eve. His eyes were dark saucers ringed by a blue light. A feeling like fingers running up her spine and between the halves of her brain. Her senses fired. She smelled cold and damp, the tang of blood, the stink of fear, and another smell she remembered with such clarity her knees gave way and she leaned against the stack of dog food. Of Marlboro and Old Crow. Goose bumps pricked her skin. Why would she exhume those memories? Especially of that man? It was a message, some kind of message, and it came from Vega.

Eve studied Vega, trying to understand what she felt, what she saw, but it made no sense. "I'm sorry, but I . . . I'm a little—"

Vega stared at her like she'd grown an alien head, and the baby cried again. "Are you okay?"

"There's something wrong. Something about a father, your father? Or the baby's father?" Eve swallowed, a sour taste blooming in her mouth, and she rubbed a hand around her wrist, felt her eyes drawn to Vega, saw her doing the exact same thing. Realized that the ink around the woman's wrists wasn't part of a tattoo. It was a bruise of fingerprints. The idea that someone had done that to her a shock that ran cold, and Eve was so deep in the knowing she didn't think before asking, "Who's the baby's father?"

Carl made a noise in his throat. "Well, now, Eve, even I know that's an impolite thing to ask."

Vega's face drained of all color and she backed away. "What? Why would you—" Her face hardened. "I need to go. He's hungry." She was at the door.

Eve stretched out her hands. "I'm so sorry, Vega. Carl's right. I had no business asking that. Wait!" She ran a hand over her arms; an ancient chill swept across her skin, and a familiar image appeared in her mind. "Where were you this morning?"

Vega narrowed her eyes. "I went for a walk. Found some old school bus in the woods. Stopped those men from *killing* your pig." There was heat in her words, a coolness to her eyes.

Eve didn't blame her for being angry. She'd been inconsiderate, gripped by a knowing that wouldn't let go. "You confronted the Harrisons?"

Vega nodded, and the charred remnants of that encounter spun in the air around her.

"That was very brave of you."

"Or stupid."

Eve smiled, trying to gentle the intensity of her gaze, which she knew could be a bit much, wanting to put Vega at ease after her onslaught. The woman looked like a bird about to fly away, and the idea that she might leave Crystal forever gripped Eve with a deep sadness. There was something about her that dug right to the center of Eve's core. She didn't understand it, but she'd learned that she didn't always have to understand a feeling for it to affect her. "I'm really sorry for what

I said. When I died I was given an imperfect gift that's made my life and relationships more complicated. I often get wrong what I think I know."

Carl chuckled. "It's true. Few months back, Eve told one of our local pastors he was ruining Christians."

Eve gave him a look. "He left me no choice. That man's sermons are full of hate."

One side of Vega's mouth lifted.

"He'd spent an entire Sunday's lecture on me," she added. "It wasn't a knowing, Carl. I was just being honest. Christianity is not about hate and fear. It's about love. Seemed the good pastor had forgotten that. I just felt like I should remind him."

The baby cried, wiggling his arms and legs like he wanted to punch something. "Go," she said to Vega. "Go feed your baby. We'll talk about the work later. And forget what I said, okay? I'm a crazy bat. Ask Jane."

Vega hesitated in the doorway, holding Eve's gaze, and for a second Eve thought she was going to say something, but then she left, taking the crying of the baby with her.

"You okay?" Carl's mustache twitched; he sounded concerned and weary, no doubt, of what she had seen.

"I'm fine, Carl."

But she wasn't—not at all. Something about Vega had stirred Eve's own past, and she felt sick to her stomach, flooded by memories that still haunted her. Of a person who was scared of their own skin. Too timid to be brave. And of the girl who'd freed her.

CHAPTER THIRTEEN

July 1995

Donna liked waking up in the school bus. The floor had a stale rubbery smell that mixed together with the dead leaves and moist soil outside in a not-totally-unpleasant mixture. It wasn't the yeasty aroma of her mother's homemade biscuits that filled their small cabin on cool mornings. And it didn't come with her mother's humming. But that sound ground into her skin.

Sometimes, in the bus, she woke up in the middle of the night to the scratch of animal nails on the floor or scurrying across the roof, and when it rained the bus turned into a metal drum, the pelting so loud she covered her ears. Still, she slept more soundly than she ever had at home. Without her ears tuned to the creak of the floor outside her bedroom, the click of the handle when it turned, the shifting of the bed, the stink of his breath. And in the morning, like a song on repeat, her mother's biscuits, the humming, the blind eye.

She'd told her mother once. After their Bible devotions and before school. In a rare moment of tenderness, her mother had braided Donna's hair, told her that her auburn locks reminded her of her own when she was young. And the warmth of her mother's fingers gently dividing her hair, plaiting one piece over another, unlocked the box and the words hurtled out.

Dad d-does things he shouldn't.

Silence had followed. Heavy, dangerous. Her mother's hands pulled harder until her scalp burned. A kitchen drawer opened, and Donna felt the tug of blades on the strands, the snip of scissors. Her braids fell to the floor. Afterward, her mother had pulled out the math lesson and started school. That night, they did extra devotions before bed, one focused on promiscuity, and Donna had been made to kneel, praying, her knees digging into the cold wood floor for an hour before bed. After that, Donna stuffed the truth into a box, locked it, and buried it so deep she forgot where it was.

When Beth had come along, Donna thought the little baby brought with her a ray of hope. Maybe they could be a regular family now. Instead, the new infant slept beside her mother, never far from her arms, like Beth was her daughter do-over, and Donna's father started visiting Donna every night.

The bus door creaked open and Donna sat up, pulled the blanket to her chest, tried to keep her lungs from expanding.

"It's me." Ethan's voice floated down the aisle. He'd been bringing her food and water and some books to read—one about a hobbit, another by someone called Stephen King. She'd never read anything but the Bible.

Donna stood, letting the blanket fall to the ground. "You scare me every time. Maybe you should knock or somethin'—wait, what happened to you?"

Ethan held his side as he walked down the aisle, easing onto the floor across from the pallet. She joined him, crisscross, their knees just touching.

"Nothing," he said.

Donna had been at the bus for a week now, leaving only to go to the bathroom. She wasn't from Crystal, but it was the closest town to her parents' homestead, and it wouldn't be hard for her father to guess where she might have gone. She swallowed. "Did my dad do that?"

He looked at her, still holding his side like he'd been punched or kicked in the ribs. "You aren't the only one with a dad, you know."

"Oh." Her ears burned. There was so much she didn't know about people outside her family, but it seemed that men were all the same. Except for Ethan; he was different. She reached out and touched his side. "Why'd he do that to you?" The only kids she'd known before she ran off were the ones from church, but they weren't allowed to do anything more than go to Sunday school together. Ethan was her first real friend, and part of her had hoped that he had a different life. That hers was the exception.

Ethan shrugged. "Sometimes I can't keep my mouth shut. I'm not good."

"What do you mean? You kick animals? Mean to little kids? Forget to say your prayers?" She'd stopped saying her prayers a long time ago.

Ethan laughed even though it seemed to hurt him. "Nah, it's not like that. That's more like the Harrison boys. They're the kind who'd kick an animal and be mean to a kid at the same time."

Donna made a face. "Bullies, huh? Bunch of assholes, sounds like." Donna wasn't allowed to curse in front of her mother. But her father had always done what he'd wanted, and so she'd learned all the words from his filthy mouth. "What's not good about you?"

"I don't know." Ethan looked down. "I'm scared all the time. I hate it here. My dad hates me."

"Yeah, same here."

A lock of hair fell over one eye when he looked up at her. "Really?"

Donna sucked in her cheeks. "Hell yeah. I hate my parents, and I want to get as far away from here as I can get."

He nodded. "Me too."

Donna smiled, reached out her hand. "Let's shake on it, then."

Ethan stared at her, not understanding, so Donna grabbed his hand and pumped their arms up and down. "We agree to get the hell out of here first chance we get." He didn't say anything, but Donna thought he looked a tiny bit less sad. "Guess that makes us friends, then," she said.

"I don't really have any friends," he said.

"Me either."

He stood. "Come on. I want to show you something."

~

They walked side by side, and Donna liked the muffled thumps of their shoes on the ground, the crinkle of leaves, the early-morning breeze sweeping through her hair. Their elbows knocked against each other as they walked. It felt natural to be with Ethan, like breathing.

Not far from the bus, Ethan slowed and turned from the trail, climbing over some rocks. Donna followed, her heart beating faster from the exertion. From the rocks, the earth sloped down into a small meadow, and in the middle of it was a jagged hole. Ethan stopped and sat down by the hole. Donna stood and stared. It looked like a mouth—not huge but big enough to swallow a person whole, and it belched cold air.

"What is that?"

"It's a hole in the ground."

She kicked him lightly. "Duh. I mean what's down there?"

"I think it's an old mine. There's thousands of 'em in the state. They don't even know where most of them are. I guess it caved in or something and the ground opened up like a pimple."

"Ew. How far down does it go?"

Ethan shrugged. Donna picked up a stick and tossed it in. It hit something metal. "What was that?"

"Mine things." He sat with his knees drawn up, arms hugging his shins. His jaw worked, the tendons popping. Donna sat next to him, leaned into his side, felt the warmth of his body through her jacket.

111

Birds rustled in the trees, branches creaked. She rested her head against his shoulder. "I hate him," he said.

"Yeah."

"I shouldn't. It's not right."

She pulled back to look at him, and something stuck in her throat. His face was wet. She grabbed his hand and held it. "They're the ones who aren't right," she said.

Ethan squeezed her hand. "He hates me too."

"God doesn't."

"How do you know?" His words pricked her skin.

If she listened to the God her mother preached, she didn't know—not really. And she didn't really know Ethan. It had been only a week, but she was pretty sure that Ethan was the nicest person she'd ever met. He was funny and gentle, and he was her friend. She didn't know how to tell him why God didn't hate him, wasn't even sure if it was true, so she held his hand and stared into the dark hole with him.

After a few minutes, Ethan pulled something from his jacket pocket. A knife—its blade old, serrated, deadly. "This belongs to my dad, and to his dad before him and his dad before him. A family heirloom. My dad loves this stupid knife so much that when he's not using it, he puts it on a stand in my mom's china cabinet." In one quick move, Ethan hurled the knife into the hole. It fell without sound.

It seemed fitting to Donna. The hole was black and dank and unnatural, like fathers who hurt their kids. "I bet this goes all the way to hell."

Ethan was quiet.

Something opened up in her chest then, like the hole in the ground, and memories that she kept inside seeped out and covered her with dirt. She balled her hands into fists, wished she had something her father loved to throw in the hole too.

"He belongs down there," she whispered. "He belongs in hell."

CHAPTER FOURTEEN

VEGA

April 2021

Vega dragged the pack 'n play that she'd left by the door earlier into the apartment and hurried to the kitchen to make a bottle. Her mind spun; it was familiar to deal with numbers and estimates. A comfortable place for her brain to go. But the images of Zach on Instagram pleading with her to return Riley, shaming her to his friends with hashtags of mental health issues, kept pushing its way to the front, and she collapsed onto the sofa, exhausted from worry. She kept imagining the police coming to Crystal, hauling her away in handcuffs, Riley screaming and being handed to his father. How long could she keep him safe?

She wanted to turn her phone on. Wanted to respond to his accusations, his lies. But it was pointless. All their friends had been Zach's friends. Vega's vagabond life had kept her isolated from everyone except her mother. She had no one to defend herself to but her baby.

Riley ate heartily, gulping the formula down. She let her head settle against the couch and thought of Eve and her questions about Riley's father. Was the woman for real? The bottle emptied and Vega put the baby up on her shoulder, patted his back to coerce a burp. After a few moments he went still, and Vega realized with a start that he'd fallen asleep instead of crying. She eyed the pack 'n play, still folded up by the door. *Damn it.* With the baby, she always seemed to be one or two steps behind.

She took him into the tiny back bedroom and carefully leaned over until his back was on the mattress; then she quietly and gently released him, lingering a moment with her chest still pressed to his, waiting for his sharp intake of breath, the wail that would follow. But nothing. The enormity of keeping him alive reverberated through her bones, the realization that she alone was responsible for him a weight she didn't feel strong enough to carry.

She backed out of the room, leaving the door open a crack, and picked up her hastily packed bag from where she'd dropped it on the floor when she came in yesterday. She pulled out the few items she'd thought to pack and made a pile on the small kitchen table. Inside was a journal where she'd kept the postcard of Crystal and the picture of her mother by the bus. Her eyelids felt weighted down and she collapsed onto the couch, head resting on the arm, picture held up so she could study it. The photo had been taken on an overcast day, making the picture grainy. Vega had studied this picture so often she could probably draw it from memory. The tilt of her mother's head, the youthful slope of her shoulders, the stained tips of her fingers—black from the discarded can of spray paint at her feet.

She stared at it until her eyes crossed, and she let them close, intending to rest for only a minute. When her eyes opened again, late-afternoon sunlight flooded the apartment. She jumped up, disoriented, panicked. How long had she slept? She ran into the bedroom, heart squeezing into her throat at the thought of the baby alone this entire time. She pushed the door open and stopped short. Tiny fists wagged in the air. She moved closer, hand pressed to her chest. He stared up at the ceiling, dark eyes filled with a peaceful kind of wonder.

"Hey, buddy," she said, and lay beside him on the bed, her face just inches from his. His eyes tracked over to the sound of her voice and latched on to her face. She smiled, touched his fist, and it opened long enough to grab on to her finger. "So strong," she said, and felt her mouth relax, the edges move easily upward. He made soft gurgling sounds in his throat, his body jerking as his limbs explored the space around him. "Are you talking?" He smiled at her, and it was such a beautiful and unexpected sight that she laughed.

She still felt the shock of Zach's violence. Thought again of the terrible things he was saying about her. She needed to make money because if he did try to come after her, she'd do what her mother always told her to do. Run. And she'd keep doing it for as long as it took to keep Riley safe.

She found a pad of paper in a drawer in the kitchen and put together a rough estimate for the apartment job, leaving room to add the fence once she saw how much work was needed. Then she wrapped Riley in a blanket and headed down the stairs, her steps a bit lighter at the prospect of work.

$\sim$

Eve was ringing up a customer when Vega walked in, so she picked up a basket, baby in one arm, and started down the aisle, sliding instant soups, canned meat, and anything else she could afford on her minuscule budget into the basket. It was a laborious process with the baby taking up one arm, and she cursed herself for not putting him in the carrier.

"This might help."

Eve wheeled a small but sturdy-looking stroller with thick wheels that looked like they belonged on a mountain bike. Vega's mouth went dry. She didn't like how everyone seemed to notice what she was lacking. "Heff bring that by too?"

Eve laughed. "A couple of weeks ago, I went garage-saling and picked this up from a family in Chauncy."

"Why?"

The woman shrugged. "For you, I suppose."

Vega took a step back.

Eve left the stroller in the middle of the aisle and returned to the counter.

"I can't pay you for it," Vega called down the empty aisle, hating the hardness in her voice.

"Then pass it on to someone who needs it more than you," Eve replied.

Vega shifted her weight, felt the pull of the baby's body in her lower back. He weighed hardly anything, but carrying around an extra fifteen pounds had its toll, she supposed. She slid him into the seat, fumbled with the adjustments until the harness looked right and he could recline a bit. When she was done shopping, she pushed the stroller up to the register, placed her basket on the counter. "Thank you," she said.

There was warmth in Eve's smile. "You're welcome."

"Is your pig okay?"

Vega had been replaying the scene with the pigs from that morning, still in disbelief at what the men had been doing. Wondering how Eve put up with people like that.

"Yes, he'll be fine. Betty took good care of him. Sooner the fence goes up, the better, I suppose."

"Doesn't it make you angry what those men did? What they said?"

Eve leaned over the counter, steepled her long fingers under her chin. Her irises were a deep brown that blended in with the black centers. "Their hate is shallow and without reason. It comes from a place of fear. All hate and anger does—and jealousy and greed and most negative emotions, when you think about it."

Vega didn't buy it for a minute. "That's very zen of you."

"Dying has its advantages. It gave me perspective. We make life here far too hard on ourselves. We strive for all the wrong things—perfection, success, money—when all we really need is love."

Vega smirked. "You went to the other side and brought back a Beatles song?"

Eve's face brightened. "I knew there was a reason I liked you."

"My mother loved that band." She'd played their music on the ancient cassette player in the van.

"Your mother had good taste." Eve tilted her head to the side. "She loved you." Her face clouded. "She loved—oh, wait . . . the Ouroboros?" Her eyes opened wide. "She had a tattoo of one around her neck?"

Vega tightened her grip on the stroller's handles. Her head swirled. There was no way. "Yes." Was she guessing? Making assumptions based on the tattoos that painted Vega's own skin?

"Why?" Eve said.

Vega shifted her weight. If she answered, she gave her more information. Vega was skeptical, yet Eve didn't exude swindler vibes. She seemed genuinely perplexed with her own questions. Vega touched her hip, where her own smaller version of the serpent lived. The Ouroboros was a symbol of destruction and rebirth, depicted by a serpent devouring its own tail. "She said she liked the idea of rebirth." Her mother had had one around her neck, and she'd touched it often, especially upon waking from one of her frequent nightmares, as though it were a talisman that protected her. Vega rocked on her toes, breathed in Riley's sweet scent, the familiar ache spreading through her chest whenever she thought of her mother.

Renee had been dead for more than a year, but talking about her brushed away the dust. Vega wasn't the kind of person who opened up easily to strangers, but something about Eve was new and comfortable at the same time. Like finding a pair of shoes that fit just right. "We-we helped women in abusive situations. We helped them to start over." When she died, Vega hadn't continued that part of her mother's work.

It wasn't that she hadn't loved helping women escape terrible situations; it was more that Vega didn't feel capable of doing it as well as Renee. She was afraid she'd fail.

She blinked hard, flattened her lips to keep the tears at bay. It had been the right decision anyway. Because then she'd met Zach and realized she knew nothing about men.

Eve's eyes glistened. "What a brave thing to do."

"We didn't have much. I think it was a way for her to give to others."

"And she's passed. I'm so sorry, Vega."

Vega swallowed. "How did you know all of that?"

For the first time, Eve looked uncomfortable. "I really don't know. I wish it was more straightforward, but it just comes to me like a sudden rainstorm. Your mother loved you—that's as clear as a sunny day."

Vega didn't need to ask how she knew that. It was a fact she'd never doubted. From her pocket, she pulled the paper with her estimate and handed it to Eve, nervous for some reason. She'd given estimates hundreds of times, and she knew her work was good and her prices fair. But she was gripped by a sudden worry that Eve would reject it and that she'd have no job, no place to stay, and would have to sleep in the van. She thought of the bus in the woods and her mother living here as a teenager. Vega didn't want to leave Crystal. Not yet.

But Eve glanced at the estimate, nodding, and slid it into a drawer under the register.

Vega pushed the stroller back and forth. "I'm ready to start on your fence."

Eve smiled. "Perfect timing. Heff said he could watch the baby this afternoon at the farm."

Vega shifted her feet. "I appreciate the offer, but I don't have money for a babysitter."

Eve laughed. "I don't think Heff would take it anyway. C'mon. You can follow me to the farm."

~

The road to the farm was a dirt lane, well maintained but rutted from the recent rain. It opened into a clearing around a decent-size cabin with a covered front porch and a magazine-style outdoor sectional surrounding a clay kiva. Beyond the cabin Vega could see a barn, a fenced-in garden, and a few outbuildings, including a yurt. There were chickens and ducks; a long-haired white dog; and within a larger fenced area by the barn, some goats and even a couple of alpacas. It was homey and inviting and felt like a peaceful haven with the clucks and mews of the animals. Vega breathed in; the air tasted clean and natural.

Heff walked out of the yurt, carrying a basket of folded laundry with a small kitten on top. "Found that kitten we thought the fox had gotten."

"Housekeeping?" Vega said.

Eve laughed. "If I had the money for such a luxury, Heff would be top of the list. But no, the yurt is my laundry room. The main house was built in the 1850s, and while I love authenticity, I do like some modern conveniences, like a washer and dryer."

Heff set the basket onto the ground, and the kitten jumped out, then scurried back toward the yurt. "My washer just broke, so Eve's letting me do my laundry here until I fix the one I've got or buy a new one."

"It's payback," Eve said. "Heff helps me with the animals."

"I love animals."

"And babies?" Vega mused.

"I'm a modern man." Heff's smile was effortless, charming. "Speaking of, where's your little guy? I'm ready to work."

She nodded toward the van. "Sleeping." He'd fallen asleep on the dirt road, and Vega hadn't had the heart to wake him. He'd lost as much sleep as she had in his short little life. She ran her fingers up her arm, suddenly nervous. She'd never had a babysitter before. "Are you staying here?"

"I'll be inside the house. Don't worry about us. You go and fix Eve's fence before the Kunekunes meet an unnatural end." His face turned serious. "Heard you had a run-in with JJ."

She stiffened, ready to defend herself. "He was hurting that poor pig."

Sun lines cracked the skin around his eyes when he smiled. "Rumor has it you bested those two by cursing them with some kind of spell."

Vega almost smiled. "Because I stopped two grown men from hurting a defenseless animal, I must be a witch?"

"Seems that way."

"Join the club," Eve said.

Vega laughed and the lightness of the moment freed something inside her. "It's an honor," she said, and Eve and Heff both laughed.

Heff picked up the laundry basket and put it in the back of his truck before heading to the van.

She followed Eve to a small off-road vehicle loaded with wood and wire in the back. "It's my perimeter fence that's the problem." Eve turned to look at her. "Fixed a fence before?"

"Once, in Colorado with my mom."

The vehicle lurched forward. "You sound qualified to me."

Eve dropped her off with the materials and left to go back to the store. Vega was grateful to be alone and set to work immediately. She surveyed the damage. It looked like someone had run the fence down, and she could picture the exact truck that did, along with the faces of the driver and his cousin, eyes red-rimmed and weeping. Had it just been that morning when she'd pepper-sprayed the two lowlifes? She eyed the dense forest that crowded the road, felt a prickle across her shoulder blades. Surely they wouldn't come back? Or come looking for her?

She pulled on a pair of heavy work gloves and started ripping out the ruined wire, cutting off the pieces of splintered wood, digging out the bases of the damaged posts, and keeping an eye out for a silver truck and two assholes the entire time. The exertion felt good: the soreness in her legs, the spread of muscles across her back, the feel of using her hands. It was nice to remember what she'd been good at before she struggled with motherhood. Sweat trickled down the side of her face. It was cool but humid, a combination Vega didn't realize could exist together. She'd reached a good stopping point and put on a headlamp to collect the last of her tools.

Dusk had blanketed the sunlight, turning the tree trunks a dark brown, the woods into an impenetrable fortress that caught the sweep of headlights. A loud grumble of an engine, and Vega looked up, her headlamp swallowed by a truck's roof lights that momentarily blinded her.

The truck slid to a stop on the side of the road so that Vega was bathed in its bright white lights. She brought a hand up to shade her eyes. "Hey!" she called. "Turn your lights off!" The engine revved. Vega's heart thumped against her chest bones. She was alone out here on the edge of Eve's property.

The engine revved again and the headlights shifted to bright, and she thought she heard a man laughing. The hairs on her head stood on end. She turned from the glare, red shapes floating in the darkness, and backed away, pulse racing, her thoughts only of her son.

"Is that you, bitch?" A man's voice from the road.

She stumbled, feeling for the pepper spray she kept in her bag, remembering she'd dropped it after spraying the two men. She picked up her toolbox, tight grip on the handle. Ready to swing it at a head or a groin. The slam of a door. Outline of a tall figure in the headlights. Vega's throat tightened; a scream stuck in her chest. Was that JJ? Or the other man from this morning? Their faces loomed in the dark: angry, vengeful. They weren't the type of men who forgave, especially a woman who'd humiliated them. Her leg muscles tensed. She'd sprint deep into the woods, find her way back to Eve's farmhouse and to Riley.

Another set of headlights down the road from Eve's—the shape of Eve's two-seater vehicle moving nimbly over the unpaved lane. Her lungs expanded and she released a shaky breath. Heff pulled to a stop, Riley strapped to his chest. The baby stared at her from above the slobbery edge of his carrier, and Vega's heart compressed. She didn't want her baby anywhere near JJ. She started to say something when Heff's jaw tightened.

"JJ bothering you?"

The truck's engine revved again. Riley cried at the sound, and Vega saw anger flash in Heff's eyes. He turned abruptly, taking long strides up the hill toward the truck, bringing Riley with him. Vega lurched forward, heart in her throat. She stumbled, arms outstretched.

"Heff!" she screamed. "No, stop, please!" Overcome by a feeling of having no control, of another man doing what he wanted regardless of who it might hurt. Her face heated. "Heff! Stop!" Her voice sounded shrill.

Heff froze, his tall form outlined in the bright headlights.

JJ's laugh. "Yeah, Heff, listen to the little bitch."

Vega caught up to him, and on the slope she felt shorter than normal. Insignificant against either one of the men. But Heff had already unbuckled the carrier and was holding Riley out to her. His face looked pasty white in the glare of the lights. "I'm so sorry."

She held Riley close to her chest and retreated down the small hill, heart pumping. Heff stayed where he was, produced a Maglite, and shined it on JJ's face. The man squinted, looking young and irritated and maybe even a little bit nervous to be confronted by Heff. Vega hummed in Riley's ear to calm him, bouncing on her toes, throat tight.

"Harassing women? Destruction of property?" Heff said. "You know I can arrest you, right?"

"You can try." JJ's voice sounded young, unsure.

"And then there's the matter of Eve's pigs. You want animal cruelty on your record too? Those two charges combined will get you five, probably six years up in a federal prison. You ready to join your daddy in Columbus, JJ?"

"Five years for some queer's pig? That ain't right."

Heff balled his hand into a fist. "Call her that one more time and let's find out."

JJ glared into the Maglite's beam, kicked the ground with his boot. "Fuck this." He turned and lumbered back to his truck. The tires squealed across the pavement when he gunned the engine.

Heff half jogged down the hill, stopped when he reached Vega and Riley. His eyes were dark, serious. "I was out of line, Vega. Going after JJ like that with your baby. I wasn't thinking. I'm so sorry."

She lifted her chin. She'd heard apologies before. "Riley could have been hurt."

His shoulders rounded. "I know. I drove up and saw JJ about to do I-didn't-know-what, and I let my anger get the best of me. I hope you can forgive me."

Vega stiffened. Zach was always so sorry. She sucked on her lip. The difference was that Heff actually sounded sincere. When she thought back, Zach had just said the words, but he'd never really acted that way. And he'd never—not once—asked for her forgiveness. She recalled what Eve had said, that Heff tried to help others because he believed he'd failed his mother.

She let the silence build, testing her instincts. She believed him. "Can you grab my toolbox?"

Without her headlamp pointed at his face, she couldn't see his smile, but she could hear it in his voice. "You bet."

They settled into the off-road vehicle, Riley nestled safely in her arms. She turned to Heff. "Six years in prison? You sure about that?"

In her headlamp, Heff smiled, shrugged. "I have no idea—but more important, neither does JJ."

She wiped a hand across her forehead, a good tiredness sinking into her muscles, melting into the jittery aftershocks of another run-in with JJ. "I'm guessing the Harrisons are the type to hold a grudge?"

Heff sighed. "I'm afraid they are." His hands gripped the steering wheel, but he didn't press the gas. "I'm truly sorry. Sometimes I act before I think. Eve says it's my one true downfall."

Vega flipped off her headlamp, smiled. "Only one?"

He started the engine. "Yep, just the one. If Eve thinks so, it must be true."

She laughed, feeling the last of the tension from earlier melt from her shoulders.

"Oh, here." He held something out to her, and when she reached for it, the shape was familiar in her palm. It was a can of pepper spray. "Heard you might have left yours at the scene of the crime earlier. Imagine you don't want to be without."

Vega slid it into her bag, touched and surprised and unable to meet his gaze. "Thank you."

He slipped a pacifier from his pocket, handed it to Vega. "Baby and I had a good afternoon, didn't we? Even petted the kitten."

The night air was cool but with a velvety warmth that whispered of summer days to come. With JJ gone, Riley safe in her arms, and after Heff's sincere apology, a calmness settled over Vega. In two days her entire life had been hurled into the air, and as it landed, pieces of it were forming into this odd community that was at once foreign and familiar. And without seeming to expect anything in return, people had helped her. It made her hands feel empty because she had no way to repay anyone.

"Riley."

From the driver's seat, Heff looked at her. "Excuse me?"

"Baby's name is Riley."

"Your name is Riley. That's a good name." He spoke gently to the baby. "You sure are lucky to have such a hardworking momma, Riley."

The dark surrounded Vega, suffocating her. All she could see was the look on Zach's face, like she was nothing. "Don't call me that," she said between her teeth. *Momma* was what she'd called her own mother when she was little. It was someone who was strong and capable, smart and unafraid. It was someone who would never have found themselves with a man like Zach.

Heff hadn't driven yet and the two of them sat in the off-road vehicle in the dark, the hum of crickets moving around them like ghosts. Riley was quiet, listening, it seemed, to the insects. Heff turned to look at her, the light too dim to see his expression but his voice soft, unhurried. "Okay. But it's what you are even if you struggle. No one is born knowing how to care for babies. It's a learn-as-you-go job." He reached out and touched the baby's chin; Riley gurgled, smiled, and the sweetness in it nearly broke Vega's heart. Heff spoke to the baby. "You can call her mom or mommy, gorilla or cucumber." His voice was higher pitched, and Riley seemed to love it, his eyes moving over Heff's face, minuscule dimples forming in his cheeks. "It doesn't really matter, because a momma is a momma, no matter what."

Heff's words broke something in her, breached the wall she'd been barely holding up. "Can you take me to my van now?" Her tone was rude and she hated it, but his kindness, his easygoing patience, got under her skin. It was too familiar, and Heff didn't know her well enough to assume that tone.

"Yes, ma'am," he said.

When they got to her van, Heff jumped out and slid open the van door, standing back while she buckled Riley into his seat. When she turned, there was a crinkle in the skin of his forehead. He reached out and lifted her fingers, and for a split second, Vega thought he was going to kiss her hand like he was some knight in shining armor. It was a ridiculous gesture. Instead, he brought her wrist up into the light from Eve's barn, turning it gently one way, then another. "I thought it was a tattoo." Heff looked at her and something changed in his eyes. "Do you need help or anything?"

She recoiled, yanking her hand away, crossing both arms across her chest.

"Or do you want to talk about it?" Heff said.

"No, I do not." She turned from the man and slid into the driver's seat. Her hands shook.

Heff stood beside the driver's window, tapped on the glass. "Vega?"

"I have to go," she said through the glass.

He shoved his hands into his pockets, nodded, and backed away from the window. "If you need anything, I'm here."

She backed out and drove away, leaving the man standing in the dark, watching her go. Riley started to cry.

CHAPTER FIFTEEN

EVE

Eve washed her face, taking extra care to apply a thick cream under her eyes. Her nights of restless sleep showed. She wasn't a vain woman, but she wasn't immune to how time tiptoed around her face, sharpened the angles, a tiny trowel of lines across her forehead. She pulled the sheets from her bed and slipped under the covers. It was quiet on her farm; the animals had settled down for the night, and she lay on her back, soaking in the silence. She'd come home to Crystal seeking the peace that came from the mountains' embrace; the solitude in being surrounded by trees, not buildings and exhaust; the privacy to live life on her terms.

In New York, Crystal had called to her, invaded her waking moments, and Eve had felt anxious, like something was missing from her life. She'd started dreaming of a monstrous snake, slithering its scaled form through her tiny apartment, its grotesque body entangled in furniture and hallways, until it found its tail and began to devour it. An Ouroboros. Destruction and rebirth. A symbol fitting for anyone who'd experienced trauma. Like Vega and her mother. Like Eve herself. Her own symbol of death and transformation.

The dream woke her night after night, in tears for the snake: its pain, its confusion, and its fear. She hadn't understood why it plagued her, but it had something to do with Crystal, and it would make sense in time. Her feet had itched with the need to go home. To be there for when it all came together.

Her friends were in disbelief that she was moving back. But once Eve had felt the pull, the desire to breathe in her beloved mountain air, she knew it was where she was meant to be. And with her parents gone, her moving home had caused no one pain. Except for people like the Harrisons, but those kind of people lived everywhere, even in progressive cities. At least in Crystal, they had faces and names and couldn't spew their hate and violence in anonymity. There were some who she assumed disapproved of her, like the small group of Catholic nuns who ran a local charity, and she'd done her best to avoid them. Or any number of other folks—like Jane, who believed that *normal* meant sticking with your born gender no matter what your heart said.

Eve had kept her head down and focused on building up her farm. When she opened the store, it had caused a stir, but by that point people had grown used to her. Tolerant. Eve hadn't come back to make waves, but she also had no intention of ever pretending to be someone different. She was Eve, and if she'd learned anything from her NDE, it was this: that everyone dies and if she could get to the end of her life still loving herself and others, then it was worth every minute of her journey.

So, while she'd made some friendships along the way—Heff, Carl, and Betty, to be precise—she minded her own business, kept to herself, and didn't expect anything more. It could be lonely, but her life up to this point had always been a little bit so. Anyone who chose to go against the tide found themselves fighting it alone at some point or another.

But a wind was blowing that brought with it the stink of the snake from her dreams. In the last few nights, it had woken her in a sweat, sheets twisted around her ankles.

The dog growled, barked, waking the pigs, who snorted, the poor one from before squealing—probably scared of his own shadow now.

Eve shot straight up in bed and sprang to her feet. She thought about the old rifle stuffed above her winter sweaters in the back of the closet. It had belonged to her father. When she'd moved back, there had been moments when she'd considered keeping it close by and loaded. Heff had suggested it more than once. But since her NDE, Eve hated guns and violence of any kind, couldn't bear the thought of being the cause of pain or death for anyone, so she'd stored the gun in the closet and taken her chances. Death would find her again, one way or another.

She tiptoed to the kitchen window, peered through the curtains. A thin shadow slunk across the yard, crouched low and staying just outside of the floodlight. Eve watched the figure sneak onto her property and listened to her heartbeat calm, her skin dry, not clammy with fear, because she already knew who it was. She opened the door and spoke through the screen. "Have something to ask me, Joshua?" He reached the lights strung under the awning of her porch, and the glow skidded across the hollows of his cheeks.

He wore a winter hat over his head, and at his feet was a small backpack. "I-I'm the one that drove over your fence." He wiped a hand across his eyes, sniffed, and his voice broke when he said, "I'm sorry." He lit a cigarette, hands shaking, inhaled. "I was driving and JJ—he just hates you, and he kept tellin' me to do it." Another inhale, and in the dim light his eyes looked dark and watery. "He's testing me or somethin', and I'm such a pussy I just did it." Inhale, exhale, embers red in the dark. "I'm . . ." He swallowed, his Adam's apple moving up and down his skinny neck. "I'm gay, you know, and JJ'll kill me if he finds out."

"I know." And she had known, like she knew the sky was blue, she was a woman, and Joshua was a gay kid in a family that couldn't accept him.

"I just—I fuckin' hate my life." Another crack in his voice, and Eve felt a sharp pain in her chest; she knew his pain, had lived with its visceral effects as a kid. Had let it soak into her soul. Grow limbs and a voice that whispered she wasn't good enough, that nobody loved her, that she was a freak of nature who belonged nowhere.

"I was thinkin' of going to Cincinnati or somethin', but I just—I don't have nothing, you know?" He wiped a hand across his nose. "I don't even know where the fuck to start." He pulled hard on the last of his cigarette, tossed it to the ground, and smothered it with the toe of his shoe.

She pushed open the screen door. "You'll start by making that your last cigarette and then move on to cleaning up your language. There's really no need to use all the four-letter words at once."

For the first time he met her eyes, and she flinched. He'd never planned on going to Cincinnati. "You were going to hurt yourself." She didn't ask because she knew. "But you came here instead."

"My grandpa will kill you if he finds me here. So will JJ."

Eve shrugged. "I've died before and it didn't take, so."

Joshua grinned, ear to ear, his shoulders finally relaxing away from their hunched position by his ears.

She hesitated. The smart thing to do would be to call his mom. Once upon a time, Tera had been Eve's friend. Until she saw Eve for what she truly was and never spoke to her again. Or Eve could work with social services, find someone who could legally help Joshua. The last thing she should do was offer him safe refuge here. If the wrong Harrisons found out, it could justify all the anger they were barely containing over Eve living in Crystal. But Joshua deserved to feel safe. And she couldn't turn him away. "Would you like to stay here?"

"Yes, ma'am."

She stood to the side. "Then come on in. I'll make up the couch." She'd seen it coming and knew she'd never turn him away. She remembered all too well what it had been like to grow up different. The disgust in her father's eyes, the sad pinch of her mother's lips. She'd tried to be who they wanted her to be, tried to live the way they hoped she would, but in the end, she couldn't. *You'll go to hell.* Something she'd heard more than once. And the funny thing was, when she'd died, she had not, in fact, gone to hell. But by then it was too late because the people who should have loved her no matter what had already decided she was dead to them.

Joshua helped her pull the fitted sheet over the couch cushions, quiet—but for the first time since she'd known him, he moved more like the teenager he was. He flopped onto the couch and kicked his shoes off one by one. "Thanks, Eve."

At first she couldn't speak, feeling the past lap the shoreline of her present. Then she smiled. She had no idea what the fallout would be, but helping Joshua was the only right thing to do. She felt the whip of the snake's tail, the warmth of its body pass through the house, and she shivered. She'd have to face the Harrisons, something she'd been avoiding all this time. But she couldn't harbor a minor forever, no matter how good her intentions.

"Good night, Joshua."

It took her hours to fall asleep, and when she did, she didn't dream of the snake slithering around her house. She dreamed of it racing through town, swallowing all of them whole.

CHAPTER SIXTEEN

Vega

Vega woke the next morning to the sound of rocks hitting her window. She sprang from bed, heart pounding, hand clutching a frying pan from the kitchen, and crept over to the window, crouching low. A small pebble flew up from below and tapped the glass before falling away. She straightened enough to catch a glimpse of a woman on the street below. Betty, still wearing the bright-pink raincoat from yesterday, an umbrella perched above her head, tipped back just enough for her to crane her neck and look up.

Vega waited for her pulse to slow before pulling on a sweatshirt and opening the narrow door that led to the tiny balcony. She rubbed sleep from her eyes, ran a tongue over her teeth. She'd slept hard.

From below, Betty waved. "You're awake!"

Vega yawned, brushed her hair from her face. "Wasn't that the point of the rocks?"

The woman looked genuinely perplexed; then her eyes widened and she laughed. "Funny girl! Yes, I guess it was. But now that you're awake, would you like a job?"

From inside, she heard Riley stir, a cry stuck in his throat. She could just see him, face scrunched up, hands in fists, tongue vibrating and ready to let loose a wail. She almost smiled. He was hungry, and the sooner she fed and changed him, it was possible he might cry a little less. Maybe. The normalcy of her thoughts caught her off guard. A few days ago she'd disappeared from Zach's life. She replayed that morning in her head. He was wrong. That was a truth that curled around her heart. But should she have called the cops? Her mother never advised women to do that. Renee had believed that to survive, women needed to learn how to do it by themselves first. And this was Vega surviving.

"What work do you need done?" she said.

"I'd like my kitchen painted—bought a pretty pale yellow—but see here, my knees bark at me and Carl worries about me on the ladder. I have all the supplies, so just bring yourself. And you'll need to bring your baby, what with there being nobody else to watch him. Heff has a showing this morning," Betty said, still craning her neck to look up. "Carl and I love being around young'uns. Makes our souls lighter."

The thought of more work, more money for Riley, shoved thoughts of Zach aside. "I'll be over in thirty minutes."

She pushed Riley in the stroller and stopped in at Eve's to grab a coffee. The boy from the school bus—JJ's brother—stood behind the counter, arms crossed, awkward, and looking out of place next to Eve. "Good morning, Joshua," she said. "You work here?"

"Yeah, guess so."

Eve smiled at the boy. "It's his first day, I've been—"

A pounding on the door interrupted her. Vega turned to see a young teen girl, thin brown hair in a ponytail, glaring at them. She opened the door. "What the hell you doing, Josh?" she hissed. "Uncle Joe noticed you gone missing. Momma lied for you. You can't be here." The girl's eyebrows wiggled together when she took in Vega. But Vega noticed how she didn't look at Eve. As though she didn't exist. Vega felt an urge to take the girl by the ponytail, fought it, squeezed the stroller handles so hard her palms burned. Eve never flinched, and Vega hated even more that it didn't seem to affect her. She deserved better.

Joshua kicked at something under the counter that made a loud thump. "I'm not going home, Casey. Don't tell Momma you saw me, okay? I'll figure somethin' out."

Casey shot him a long glare before storming out and slamming the door.

"Sorry 'bout that, Eve," Joshua said quietly.

Eve patted his shoulder and shook her head. "That's nothing at all. Besides, Casey won't be that way forever. She'll learn to be a bit more open than you might think."

"Do you *know* that?"

Eve just laughed, shrugged. "I know because your mother would lie for me when I was running from your uncles. Hid me in the girls' bathroom at school more than once."

Joshua looked surprised but didn't say anything, instead leaning over to pick up whatever it was he'd kicked. Then he walked into the back. Eve handed Vega a black coffee in a to-go mug.

"Is he staying with you?"

Eve nodded.

"Is that—do you think that's safe? For you, I mean?" Vega thought of JJ from last night, the blood on the ground from the pigs yesterday morning. This would definitely ignite even more of their hate. "You need to be careful."

Eve studied her for a moment. "Thank you, Vega. I will. But I couldn't turn him away. You understand, don't you?"

"More than you think. It's exactly what my mother would have done."

"Sounds like my kind of person. What was she like?"

The question caught her off guard. Hit her right in the heart. "She was my best friend." Renee had been strong, both physically and emotionally, with just enough softness to give the women they helped and Vega a place to land, arms to fall into. She'd never judged, instead allowing anyone who knew her the space to be vulnerable. "I-I think she was hurting too. But I don't know why. She never really talked about her past."

"And that's why you came here?"

"Yep." Vega felt her cheeks warm, wondered if Eve could sense a lie too. "She didn't love it here, but it's the only place she ever talked about." It was more than she'd ever shared. Loving her mom was personal, not something she opened up to critique. Renee had been far from perfect; she'd never graduated high school, had a roughness that extended to her choice of clothes and her demeanor, she wasn't refined or easygoing, and she didn't suffer fools. But talking about her made Vega wish that Eve were a psychic and could tell her something about her mom she didn't know. "Um, how did you know about her tattoo . . ." She trailed off, unsure how to ask about a *knowing*, not sure if she even believed Eve. People could fool themselves into believing just about anything if it was what they wanted.

"I just had a sense about her, a strong one—I'll say that. But nothing more." She touched Vega's elbow and Vega felt herself soften almost immediately. Eve exuded her own kind of peace, and being around her felt like settling into a big comfortable chair, easy and familiar. "But her love for you is overwhelming. It kind of floats around you."

Vega blinked, gripping the coffee cup.

"And there's something else." Eve seemed undecided, as though she waffled between speaking or not, but her eyes kept flicking to Vega's wrist. "Are you in danger?"

Vega went cold, crossed her arms to hide the bruising. Zach was a thousand miles away. She was safe. Riley was safe. She tipped her chin up. "Not anymore, unless you count JJ Harrison."

Eve's face remained serious, not touched by Vega's attempt at lightness. "I do count him. Is everything okay, Vega?"

Her chest hurt and the air gummed in her lungs. Nobody had cared enough to ask her since her mom died, until Heff and Eve. It made her realize how alone she'd been. Feel the blinders she'd worn when it had come to Zach. The truth was that she was very much not okay. But Eve wasn't her friend. She was a stranger in a town that would likely be no more than a blip in Vega's and Riley's lives. She pulled the Chromebook from the storage basket under the stroller, settled in at the counter, and opened the cover. "I have an infant who cries most of the time, a van that is on the cusp of breaking down, an apartment I can't afford, a couple of small-town hicks I maced, and work I can only do if someone babysits for me. So, no, I'm not okay, but I'm surviving."

Eve refilled her coffee, doubt lingering in her gaze. "That is quite a list."

Vega typed in her password and gave Eve a soft smile. "It is. But I'm managing. My mother did; so can I."

The door to the store opened, and a couple in their late twenties came in, dressed in brand-new outdoor gear, sporting thick backpacks and rubber-soled hiking shoes. Eve wandered over to tend to her customers, and Vega was happy to be left alone. The computer whirred to life, and she opened Instagram. Anxiety burrowed into the small of her back. There was a message from Zach.

> I saw you viewed my story. You're sick. I'm going to find you.

Zach had posted more images that made him out to be some kind of saint, her a tatted-up liar with mental health problems. Comments from his friends and strangers had piled up, supporting him, tearing her to shreds. She dug her nails into her thighs. They didn't even know her. Hadn't even bothered to get to know her either.

She'd moved in with Zach shortly after finding out she was pregnant. The nausea had been constant, and when he'd offered, she'd known it was too soon—they'd been dating only a few months—but the idea of a real bed and a bathroom was a luxury she couldn't refuse. He'd thrown a party shortly after she moved in. Said he wanted her to meet his friends. She made burgers; he bought a few cases of beer. She'd gone to bed at ten, while they stayed up until three. Some had spent the night, snoring on the couch or the floor the next morning. One had been in the bathroom, asleep beside the toilet. She'd had to run outside and throw up in the bushes by the front door. When she'd made light of it later that day, Zach had been on the couch, watching the Broncos, drinking a beer to nurse his hangover. He'd given her a look. *Or you can find your own house to live in and stop bitching about mine.*

It had left a rawness in the pit of her stomach. She gave a nervous laugh and went to their room, closed the door, and lay on the bed with her palm flat against her stomach, breathing in and out. Back then, she'd tried to explain it away. He'd wanted to provide a home for her and the baby. They were still getting used to living together, but it was all so new for them. She'd made mistakes too.

Hindsight made her feel the fool. And now she shuddered to realize how blind she'd been to the cracks.

She sipped her coffee, let the bitterness of the brew wash away the memories. There had been soft moments, too, that smoothed over her suspicions, made her feel unfair. Like when he'd make her breakfast in bed or took her to a doctor's appointment, the time he brought home a rocking chair he'd found at a garage sale. Each one had reeled her back in with promises of the life she'd always wanted. She stared at his message, fingertips hovering over the keyboard. How could she respond? What could she say to someone like Zach?

You know what you did. Leave us alone.

She shut the computer, hands shaking. Riley cried out and she got up from the stool, started to push the stroller back and forth. Eve came back, leaned over the stroller, and pushed Riley's pacifier into his mouth. He quieted. Eve's natural way with Riley put Vega at ease.

"Betty asked me to paint her kitchen, and I thought afterward I'd head over to finish the fence later on this afternoon. Is that okay?"

Eve smiled. "Perfect. You can stay for dinner."

Before Vega could say no, Eve added, "If Betty's got any leftover buckeye cookies, bring them for dessert."

"Okay," she said, surprising herself. Maybe it was because she'd talked to Eve about her mother or simply the woman's overall warmth, but Vega didn't want to be alone tonight.

～

Steep, uneven stairs led up to the couple's cabin, so Vega left the stroller at the bottom and climbed with the baby to the top. A deep porch wrapped around the structure, with an outdoor stone fireplace, a couple of rocking chairs, and an old yellow-and-gray dog sleeping on a bed. Through the branches and unfolding spring leaves, the town below was nothing more than a dirt road with a few buildings. The earth undulated, rolling high above the road into deep and unending woods, stretching for miles in every direction.

The front door opened and Betty walked out; her raincoat had been replaced by a thick and brightly patterned sweater. She held out a small knitted blanket. "I'll take the baby. It's cold up in the woods. Sun don't hit us till later in the day, and even then, only for a bit."

Vega handed Riley over; today he'd been awake more than asleep and peaceful more than crying. It was a minute change but one she felt in the smoothness of the skin across her forehead.

Betty disappeared inside the cabin and Vega followed. It was dark, the only glow coming from lamps that cast more shadow than light. The walls were wooden beams. A quilt stretched across one; others held small framed photos.

Betty cooed at the baby, hummed something soft. "Oh, yes, you sure are a handsome one, aren't you?"

Vega pointed at a picture of a boy, the exposure in the photo old, grainy like it had been taken before everything became digital. He stood in front of Betty's cabin beside a girl with shiny blonde hair that tickled her waist. "Are these your kids?"

When Betty didn't answer, Vega turned. The woman stared down at Riley, one of her fingers squeezed by his tiny hand. "Well, now, see—me and Carl weren't blessed with any young'uns of our own. But we did right by the kids in this town and kept our door open for any one of them that might need a little somethin' extra."

She looked back at the picture. The girl wore a sullen frown, and her eyes looked up at the bunny ears the boy held above her head. In the background was Carl, sitting on the porch, dog at his feet, smile under his mustache. "Who were they?"

"That were Ethan and Tera."

She wondered why there weren't any recent pictures of the two, thought about Heff's mom and felt a sad twinge. "It must be hard growing up here."

Betty nodded. "There's good and there's bad. Like any place, I reckon. Some of the kids 'round here are born into a life they can't escape. Others escape by runnin' and some by dyin'. Then there's the ones like Heff and Eve who come back and make it better. Me and Carl, we're just blessed to have helped any of 'em we could."

Vega chewed on the inside of her cheek, touched and thinking about her own mother. "My mom died about a year ago." She swallowed, unsure why she was telling Betty but unable to stop. "It's been hard. I don't think I'll ever stop missing her."

Betty's head tilted to the side. "That's because she's still with you. 'Least, that's what I believe. I got all my babies I lost around me." She looked down at Riley. "That's why you're so comfortable with me, ain't it? You hear my babies? Tell them Momma loves them."

Tears pricked Vega's eyes at the woman's loss, and she let a silence build between them. Since losing her mother, she'd learned that silence was where she felt the most at peace. It was regular living that seemed a farce when someone she loved was gone. She studied the rest of the pictures, felt her pulse speed up when she saw one of the bus. "I've been to this bus," she said. "It's out in the woods."

Betty smiled. "That it is. It's right close to the edge of our property line." Her cabin wasn't big, just a small sitting room with a woodburning stove, a two-seater dining room table, chairs with hand-sewn pads on the seats, and a galley kitchen. But it was comfortable and homey, and Vega felt a drowsy sense of belonging. "That bus is there for those who need it."

Vega sat down in an old rocking chair across from Betty and Riley, pushed herself back and forth. "I met Joshua Harrison when I was out there."

Betty gently rocked her arms, and Riley's eyes were wide open and staring up at the underside of the woman's chin. "Makes sense. That boy needs it, all right."

Vega thought about the gaunt teen with the slouched shoulders. "Eve's helping him."

Betty's arms stopped rocking. "That so?"

She felt a twinge of doubt. Maybe she shouldn't have said anything. "I mean, he's just working at the store." She wanted to change the subject, feeling like she'd just betrayed Eve. "He told me about the girl whose ghost roams the woods."

Betty *pfffff*ed. "There's real ghost stories, and then there's the made-up ones. Like my aunt Millie. Died right there in that old rockin' chair, and sometimes when it starts to rock all on its own, I know she's just come back for a visit."

Vega fidgeted, gave a look behind her, let out a breath at the empty space, and almost laughed.

"Oh, don't you worry. She's not here right now, God rest her soul. It don't bother me none to have her here, though. I just tell Carl to watch his step so he don't smash her toes. See here, that's a real ghost story.

Nothing too excitin', just a matter 'a fact." She leaned forward. Her features were all small: eyes, mouth, nose. And she had them pinched together like she was sizing Vega up. "Now, this business with Donna—that's the girl who disappeared. That's nothin' but a made-up tall tale meant to scare the young'uns from making out in the woods."

Vega smiled. Betty was a character. It was the most abnormally normal conversation she'd had in days, and she didn't want it to end. "Carl said you saw her ghost in your kitchen."

Amusement stretched out in lines from her eyes. "Carl shore does love to tell a good ghost story." Riley had grabbed on to her finger, and Betty smiled down at him, tugged back. "The girl weren't a ghost, see. She were as alive as you are, standing right by my fireplace."

The cabin was chilly, and in her sweatshirt, Vega shivered. "You knew her?"

"'Course I did. Carl and me knows most of the young'uns 'round here."

Vega liked being distracted by their local lore. It kept her mind off the very real threat of Zach. "Joshua told me she murdered her dad."

Betty held her gaze. "No one knows what happened to that man. That's between him and the good Lord."

"But she came here to see you?"

Betty blinked several times, as though the memory dug up old feelings. "'Course she did. Carl and me helped her on occasion."

Vega felt a pressure build in her chest. She'd lived such an isolated life that she thought of her mother as a one-of-a-kind superhero who lived her life to help others. But here in tiny Crystal, there was Eve giving Joshua a safe place, Betty and Carl helping kids in need, Heff and his mom fostering children. People like her mom, taking care of each other. "My mom helped others too," she said.

"Sounds like your momma would have fit right in, just like you."

Vega was so touched all she could do was rock a little harder. "My mom grew up here, I think—or I mean, she visited at least." She swallowed hard. "I—when I was little, I found a picture of her at your school bus."

A smile lifted Betty's entire face. "Is that so? I thought your pretty face seemed familiar. What was her name?"

The thought that Betty might have known her mother sent a bolt of energy racing to her fingertips. She moved to the edge of the chair so that the rockers tilted up. "Renee Jones. Did you know her, Betty?" Her heart raced; she'd carried a deep yearning to know more about her mother since her death, hoping it would make losing her even the tiniest bit easier to bear.

But Betty's face clouded. "Renee Jones? Well, now, I remember all the kids we helped, because Carl and me think of them as family, even if we only knew them for a minute. Most of them still write us letters—'course, now it's email, but mostly texts, if you can believe it." She dipped her chin, sympathy in the slant of her eyes. "Kids find the bus all the time. It's the ones who need it that find us too. Maybe your momma just spent the day there? Added to the spray paint art? Kids do that all the time just for fun. Between me and you, I love it, even if I have been known to chase a few off from time to time."

Vega's heart deflated when she thought of the black tips on her mom's fingers, the discarded can of spray paint on the ground by her feet. Betty was right.

Riley scrunched up his legs, then shot them out from his body with a loud cry. Betty laughed, her attention back to the baby. "There now, sweet baby." She put him up against her shoulder, patted his back, her frame so small that Riley's body nearly dwarfed her.

From outside came the now-familiar squeal of pigs. Betty's eyes lit up at the sound. "You know what it means when you hear a pig squeal?"

Vega shook her head.

"It's their way of sayin', 'I love you.'" Riley jerked his body and made a gurgling sound in his throat. Betty smiled and said to him, as though sharing a secret, "I heard tell your momma did a very brave and stupid thing yesterday."

Vega shivered, thinking about JJ and the knife. "I couldn't stand back and let them hurt that poor animal. I had no choice."

Betty met her gaze and her green eyes glistened with tears. "We all have choices, and you chose to do a good thing, Vega." She sniffed, wiped a hand across her eyes. "But steer clear of JJ. His father was a bad seed, and JJ don't seem to want to take a different trail." Betty stood. "Come on now. I'll show you what needs painting. And before you leave, I'm gonna wrap up some of my buckeye cookies for you. I have a feeling you'll need them."

Was everyone in this town psychic? "Eve just asked me to bring some to dinner. How did you—"

Betty laughed. "I'm just having fun with you. Eve sent me a snappy chat. I like making pictures with those filter thingies. They're fun."

Vega felt the heaviness from before lifting. Betty was a natural mood booster. She spent the rest of the morning painting the kitchen and listening to Betty's many, many ghost stories. When she was done, she collected Riley, her payment—Betty paid in cash, which Vega thought might have come from under her mattress—and hurried back to the apartment to get ready for the afternoon at Eve's.

CHAPTER SEVENTEEN

July 1995

Donna sat on the bus stairs, waiting. Ethan had said he'd be late tonight, something about youth group after dinner. He came every night, even if it was only for a few minutes—just to give her some company, she knew.

Her toes tingled with a desire to put more trees and dirt between her father and her. But the thought of leaving the safety of the bus and Ethan behind curdled in her stomach. He brought her food, made her laugh, gave her something to look forward to every day. How could she and Beth survive out there?

She leaned back, the edge of the stair biting into her hips, and looked up. Stars winked at her from above the trees. The woods were peaceful, quiet, safe, and when she was awake, she was happy—reading the books Ethan had brought, sewing up a hole in her sock with a needle and thread he'd left behind last week, listening to the creaks of the trees when the wind blew through, playing solitaire.

It was when she slept that the memories crept under the blanket, slithered across her skin, and poisoned her dreams. Then she would wake up in the middle of the night to the screams of a fox mingling with her own, and in the morning, she'd be ready to go, forming a plan. By afternoon, the desire to leave had faded with the impossibility of it, the world beyond the bus too big to comprehend.

Something rustled in the trees, and she shot the flashlight out, its beam sticking to branches and knotted trunks. The woods were thick around the bus, and she often marveled at how anyone had driven it in here in the first place. She swung the light around. Raccoons came out around this time, and those buggers were mean. Something flashed white and blue, and she jumped to her feet, adrenaline pumping through her muscles. She thought of the flimsy plastic butter knife Ethan had brought with her dinner two nights ago. It was sturdy enough to go into her father's soft eye tissue. Her foot moved backward, feeling for the step behind and above her, but the heel of her shoe hit it and she stumbled, dropped the flashlight.

She scrambled to the aisle, crouched low, fists tight, testing the length of her nails against her palms. She'd claw his eyes out, scratch his face, draw so much blood he couldn't see her run.

"Hello?"

A woman's voice and not her mother's. Her fists softened a fraction but she stayed crouched.

A head poked up from the stairs, features hidden in the dark, a flashing reflection against what she assumed were glasses. "Don't you look like a bobcat 'bout ready to attack." The woman sounded amused, her voice high pitched. "Come on out. I ain't gonna hurt you." She backed down the stairs.

Donna hesitated. What if it was a trap? What if this woman tried to drag her back to her dad? She felt cornered, without options.

"Ethan's told me and Carl all about you. I just come down here to talk."

Donna pushed to her feet, walking hunched, ready to fight, even against this woman if she had to. But when she stepped outside, arms tensed for a confrontation, she almost laughed. The woman's body was an outline in the dark, but it was a small one, more like a tall child than a small adult.

"What do you want?"

A click, and light shone in the space between them, painting shadows into the woman's cheeks, around her glasses, under her chin. "See now, I been hearing things 'round town 'bout the girl who's gone missing up Mount Kinley way? Pastor announced it at church for your daddy. He's all over town, carryin' on about his lost little girl." She tilted her head. "You don't look so lost to me."

Donna crossed her arms, enjoyed the bit of power she felt at being so much taller. "You can't make me go home."

"Yeah, I figured, and I weren't gonna make ya."

Donna felt a sting of betrayal thinking about Ethan. "Why'd Ethan tell you 'bout me?"

"We've known Ethan his whole life. More like a son to us, you could say."

"Do you know why his dad hates him so much?"

An owl hooted in the distance. The woman shifted, making the light jiggle. "That's a whole other story, ain't it? Like yours, I guess." She stepped closer. "I'm Betty, and this here bus is on my property."

Donna flinched, feeling like the earth had pulled away from her feet. "I don't have anywhere to go."

"I know, I know," she said, and Donna nearly teared up at the softness in it. "Here." She held something out. It was covered in foil. "Those are some of my buckeye cookies. Ethan loves 'em and I figured you would too. Most everyone does, if I'm telling the truth."

Donna took the paper plate. The woman's kindness tugged at her heart, and Donna suddenly felt like glass, easy to break. "Thank you."

"How long you thinkin' 'bout holing up out here?"

Donna shrugged, tried to sound calm when she said, "I'm just figuring stuff out right now; then I'm heading west."

Betty was quiet and Donna felt foolish, could hear how flimsy her plan sounded.

"I got you an extra blanket too." Betty handed her a small bag. "And a few other things for comfort. You can stay as long as you like. But if you're leaving, you need a plan. Can't survive without one. And don't leave the woods till then. Your daddy wants you home, and I'm guessing that ain't the best place for you."

"No, ma'am, it's not." It had taken her years to be brave enough to leave, but now that she had, she would never go back.

"Be careful at night."

"Yes, ma'am."

After Betty disappeared into the woods, Donna hurried inside the bus and closed the door behind her. With the extra blanket wrapped around her shoulders, she sat on the pallet, eating buckeye cookies until her stomach hurt. She slept hard that night, dreaming about mountains so tall she couldn't see the tops, sunsets so pretty she cried.

~

A dog's bark woke her the next morning. She sat up, drool sticking her hair to her face. She rose to her knees, peeked out the window, rubbed sleep from her eyes. A brown-and-white dog bounded into the clearing, nose to the ground, long ears flopping. From the woods behind the dog came a man wearing yellow suspenders that looked like rulers, brown work pants, and boots. A brown-and-white mustache covered his upper lip, and he wore wire-rimmed glasses that looked too small for his face. He stopped at the edge of the trees, thumbs stuck under his suspenders.

"Hey there, missy!" he called. "Betty sent me to talk to you 'bout your plans." He held a plate in his hand. "Got some scrambled eggs and bacon too."

She pulled on her sweater, kept the blanket around her shoulders, and stepped out of the bus. Her stomach growled at the thought of food. "Are you Betty's Carl?"

"I do belong to her—that's the truth."

She took the plate, ate the eggs and bacon fast. Most of what Ethan had been able to bring was packaged food, peanut butter and bread some mornings. This tasted like dinner at a fancy restaurant.

Carl sat on a tree stump, the dog by his side. He rubbed the dog's long ears. "So, you plan on headin' west?"

Donna nodded.

"You got people out that way?"

"No, sir."

His mustache moved when his eyes squinted. "How you gonna pay for yerself?"

Donna shrugged. "Work, I guess." It seemed like the right answer because the truth was she had no idea.

He rubbed his chin, crossed his arms. "My daddy taught me how to use my hands. If you can use your hands, you can near always make some money off it."

"Okay." She'd been taught how to make dinner, clean the cabin, tend to the chickens. "How do I learn?"

He breathed in and it sounded muffled, like his nose was stuffed up, or his big stomach blocked his lungs a bit. Then he hefted himself from the stump; the dog sprang to his feet, eyes never leaving the man. "I suppose I can teach you a bit of woodworking, repairing things, painting—that sorta thing. Not hard to learn, just takes some time and a want to work. That sound like something you can do, missy?"

She thought of Ethan. Would he come with her? Could they move out there together? Pinpricks of hope danced across her skin. Why not? What could possibly make him want to stay here? Plus, it sounded like something an adult would do, and if she was going to be taking care of her sister from now on, she'd better start figuring out how to be one. "It's something I have to do."

"I'll be 'round later today with some tools and probably some lunch fixins from Betty." The dog bounded after him when he left.

Donna returned to the bus, picked up a book, and tried to read, but she couldn't focus on the story. Her stomach fluttered with excitement at the idea of her and Ethan and Beth starting a whole new life together. She couldn't wait to tell him.

CHAPTER EIGHTEEN

Eve

April 2021

Eve tossed a handful of feed out to the chickens and watched them madly pecking at the ground. Something about their frantic movements soothed her with thoughts of the hectic life she'd left behind in the city, and their gentle clucking, the dance of their claws on the dirt, symbols of the peaceful country that surrounded her now.

She breathed in the sweet air perfumed with budding leaves and newly plowed earth. She'd left New York yearning for open space, driven by a dream and a need to be back in the town she'd thought she'd never see again. The pigs found her, snuffled around her feet; one leaned into her leg. She rubbed its head and it grunted in pleasure.

"I finished mucking the barn." Joshua emerged from the building, his forehead dotted with sweat and pimples. In the last day and a half, he'd relaxed, smiling a bit more with each passing hour away from his family. It brought back, in stark contrast, what she had been like at his age—an unfinished sculpture of who she would become, stunted by a fear of who she was. Back then, Betty and Carl had been her escape, and

Betty's kitchen, with its aromas of buttery dough and melting chocolate, made her feel safe, even today.

"Want me to take a look at that old tractor of yours?" The sun touched the tip of his nose, drifted over his dimples. "I learned some things before Dad went to prison." He crossed his arms, looked unsure of himself. "Not the drug-running part, just the fixing-engines part."

Eve laughed. "I figured." Joshua had come from a chaotic home, and Eve knew he'd brought it with him to her farm. At some point she'd pay the price for letting him stay. "That would be great. Thanks, Joshua." She knew she needed to talk to someone for him, that staying with her long-term wasn't an option.

She should have reached out to his mom, but Tera hadn't spoken to Eve since she moved back. Time had eroded whatever friendship they'd once shared. The last time they'd seen each other, they were planning on leaving town together, starting over somewhere far away. And then everything had fallen apart. When she came back to Crystal, Eve had tried to reach out through Betty, inviting Tera to lunch. She never responded, and after a few more attempts, Eve had decided to let it be, dousing her last bit of hope that the girl she remembered—the one who had protected her, the one who had been her friend before anyone else—hadn't been changed by her withered dreams.

The thought of seeing her old friend, face-to-face, made Eve's heart flutter with uncertainty.

The sound of tires on dirt came from the drive, and she turned to see Vega's van picking its way down the lane. Dust swirled in the air where it stopped. "Sorry I'm late," Vega said when she got out. "Riley slept later this afternoon." She waved to the boy, who'd made his way to the tractor by the garage. "Hi, Joshua!"

"Hey, Vega!"

Eve joined her at the van. Something about Vega struck a chord in Eve, made her nostalgic—for what, she wasn't sure. But the girl's presence brought out a protectiveness in her, and she scanned the area, squinted into the woods, looking to make sure she hadn't been followed. She didn't trust JJ Harrison.

Eve opened the van's side door, pulled out the car seat with an awake and gurgling Riley.

"You don't have to—oh, okay, thanks," Vega said, shifting her weight, hands out like she wanted to stop her.

"Find it hard to accept help, do you?" Eve said.

Vega stuffed her hands into her leather coat. "Sometimes."

Eve smiled at Riley. If it was possible, he seemed to have changed in the last few days—cheeks slightly rounder, eyes a lighter blue. "Aren't you a handsome fella?" He stared up at her and smiled back, arms jerking like he hadn't figured out what to do with the space around him yet. "I can watch him while you work."

Vega sucked in her bottom lip. "If that's okay with you. Shouldn't take me too long, but he might need a diaper change and a bottle—"

"Well then, I'll take munchkin here inside and get started. Heff brought over another pack 'n play to keep here too."

Vega blew air from her lips. "Does he always think of everything?"

Eve laughed. "Most of the time. But don't ask that man to be on time. That is the one thing he can't do."

~

Eve set a salad on the table, listening to the coos of the baby, who smiled at Vega around the nipple of a bottle. She checked the clock. "Late, as usual. At least Riley doesn't have to wait for that man to eat."

"He's really hungry today," Vega said. She talked about the baby as though he constantly surprised her. "I guess his gas is better?"

"I guess," Eve said, picking up the bowl of spaghetti and setting it on the table alongside the eggplant Parmesan. "I've raised a lot of animals but not a single human." At one point in her life, it had been what Eve wanted—a partner, kids, a family. She wanted a chance to make right what her parents had not. But time had passed too quickly, and now Eve found herself in her forties, living in a town with a dating pool that didn't celebrate diversity and a sense that her moment had ebbed.

Vega's cheeks reddened. She looked at her baby when she spoke. "I have no idea what I'm doing."

Eve pressed a hand into her chest. The girl sounded so lost. While she'd never been a young single mother, Eve could relate to feeling lost. She touched Vega's shoulder.

"My mom was a single mom, too, and younger than I am." Vega looked up. "She always seemed to know what she was doing."

"I suspect Riley will feel the same about you," Eve said, and filled Vega's glass with water from a ceramic pitcher. The kitchen was warm from the oven, smelling of cheese and garlic. And Vega looked like she belonged here with Riley in her arms, like the house hadn't been whole until now.

Vega smiled. "You seem pretty wise for someone who lives in a town without reliable internet."

"Yes, well, death turned me into a trans Yoda. I have much knowledge to share."

They both laughed and it shocked the baby, whose eyes opened wide, and he reached a hand around the bottle and snagged Vega's shirt with his tiny fingers. She looked down at him, touched his cheek, seemed to be lost in thought. Eve was gripped by a knowing that fluttered around her, soft as butterfly wings. Vega missed her mother. Eve breathed in, feeling the woman's loss in the fibers of her soul. And prepared herself for the question she sensed was coming.

"What was it like to die?" Vega's voice was a whisper, like she didn't want to put the idea of death so close to the infant.

Eve's mind flashed with memory. Over two decades and the experience was still as sharp as though it had happened yesterday. She could tell Vega about the warmth that had infused her, the figures that held her—neither male nor female but beings she felt she'd known down to a molecular level for her entire existence. And the love. That had been overwhelming, all encompassing, and there were no words that could ever bring to life what she had felt. She breathed in the calm that always came when she recalled her NDE. No matter what had happened in the years since, when she thought back to her experience, it encased her heart—her armor against a world that could be so heartless and cruel.

The baby gulped his milk; Vega waited for her answer. Eve knew her question was personal. She wanted to know that her mom was okay. Eve's kitchen felt suddenly crowded, and her skin itched.

"At first, I was terrified." She started slow. Her story, more often than not, made people uncomfortable. She'd had one or two friends who loved to hear about it, but most of the time the listener's eyes glazed over; it was just too much for most people, too out there. "But that was because I was still in my body and scared I'd go to hell like everyone had said."

Vega leaned forward. "Was there a tunnel?"

"No tunnel. Although I have spoken to others like me who did experience a tunnel and a review of their life. For me, it felt like coming home. I'd spent my whole life at war with my body, ashamed of my true self because it didn't meet everyone's expectations, especially God's." She pulled her fingers through her long brown waves, smiled at the silky feeling against her skin. She loved her hair. "When I was free of my body, when I was reduced to my true self, I felt the weight of those expectations slide off me like they'd been chains. And then I saw who I really was."

"Who are you?"

Eve smiled, memory warming her from the inside out. "I'm beautiful." She ran her hands down both arms. "Our bodies are shells. Our true selves are here"—she pointed to her head—"and here." She pointed to her heart. "When I decided to come back—"

"You *decided* to live?"

Eve looked at her, saw something dim in her eyes, and understood. She reached out, covered the woman's hand with her own. "I think it was your mother's time to go, Vega. I-I think that we each have a purpose, and once we've served it, we move on."

Vega flinched, removed her hand. She dropped her gaze to the baby. "Maybe." She sipped her water. "What made you want to live?"

Eve took her time, wanting to focus on Vega, be sensitive to her pain. "I'm not sure, but I just knew it wasn't my time."

There had been one part of her experience that she'd kept to herself. Before the light and the figures and the love, she'd found herself locked in a dark room, hiding under a bed, her heart pulsing against the cold wood floor. Beside her was a girl, also on her stomach, head lying in her hands and breathing so hard she blew dust across Eve's face. The girl's terror shot out of her skin, arrows of fear puncturing everything around her.

The vision was the only negative part of her NDE. She didn't like to think about it, but in the years since, it came to her unbidden. She'd close her eyes until it faded. She'd looked for meaning in the vision, finding nothing. But when she'd died, it had been like an umbilical cord, connecting her to her body, to the living. When it was time, she chose to go back. Even with the hardship and the pain and the loss that would come. The only thing she knew for sure was that she still had purpose. And the girl under the bed had something to do with that.

Over time, she'd hoped that it would make sense. But it never had, and sometimes Eve doubted herself, wondered if it meant something more sinister.

"Are you okay, Eve? You look pale."

Eve shook her head and smiled. "Sorry about that. My NDE is as clear today as if it just happened."

The tense lines between Vega's eyes softened. "I get it. Sometimes I can't believe it's been over a year since my mom died. It feels like yesterday."

Eve touched Vega's shoulder. "I'm so sorry, Vega."

Vega set the empty bottle on the table, perched Riley on her shoulder, and gently patted his back. "Thanks." The baby let out a long, loud, and very wet burp, and Vega jumped to her feet with a squeal. "Right down my shirt!"

The door opened and Heff walked into the kitchen, seeming even taller under Eve's short ceilings, hair always a bit out of place, a look of amusement lifting the corners of his mouth. "That's the worst!" And talking like he'd been there all along. He grabbed a hand towel from a kitchen drawer and gave it to Vega. At first, the woman seemed reluctant to take it, her body curving into itself as though she wanted to protect something. Vega was a dichotomy of soft and hard, fragile and unbreakable. Eve didn't have to know her well to see it. And her presence felt like two puzzle pieces fitting together, the rest of the picture scattered around her, frustratingly unclear.

Heff placed a basket of bread on the table, melted butter glistening on the toasted slices.

Vega cleaned up and put Riley in the portable crib that Eve had set up in the kitchen. Her motherly love threaded through her every action, and her tenderness gave Eve a pang.

They filled their plates and sat down. Joshua slunk inside, bringing with him the scent of rust, oil, and cigarette smoke. He washed his hands, gave Eve a sheepish look. "Sorry. It's damn hard to quit." His face reddened. "Oh, sorry for that too."

Eve tried not to smile, but his attempts to quit smoking and cussing had been heartfelt, even if he sneaked cigarettes every chance he got and let cuss words slip out like they were old friends. He'd asked if he could stay in the yurt, and she agreed and put an air mattress out there this morning. He was happier here, more relaxed, already losing the dark smudges under his eyes, but Eve felt uneasy. Word would get around to his family eventually.

He was earnest when he said, "I only had three today. Promise. Maybe four—but I'm trying. It's addicting, you know?"

Heff laughed. "On the side of every pack."

They started eating, the clink of glasses on the table, squeak of forks on plates. "Sell a property today, Heff?" Eve said.

Heff speared a tomato. "I did not. Seems the market for a fixer-upper in economically challenged ex–coal mining towns is not, in fact, booming. But I did convince the owner to consider renting it instead. You remember Tamara Mason? She's got herself two little ones and a good job at the Resource Center, and now she's the proud renter of a three-bedroom fixer-upper in Millville. And I got the landlord to agree to paint and replace the flooring and install a new boiler."

"Seems you just negotiated yourself out of a commission," Eve said.

Heff smiled, chewing on a piece of bread. "You know my true passion is my yard art, anyway."

A buzz and Joshua pulled out his phone, looked at the screen, and his face turned to stone. A tremor ran down Eve's back, across her thighs. Someone would find out he was here, and the minute they did, they were going to come for him.

Heff laughed at something Riley did, and Eve was overcome by her vision of him dying. She wanted to reach out and take the man's face between her hands, force him to listen to what she knew. Her hands trembled. She was muzzled by his stubbornness. But if his death was connected to her helping Joshua, Eve refused to let her friend die because of it. She'd have to find a way to warn him.

CHAPTER NINETEEN

Vega

Joshua sat beside her, reading a text. He'd been at Eve's for only a day, but the change from the kid she'd met at the school bus had been immediate. It reminded her of a woman her mom had helped in Albuquerque—successful, smart, accomplished, lived in a house with five bedrooms and an infinity pool in the backyard. But the woman had kept her movements small, hands fluttering around her, nervous, like she was afraid to be noticed. She'd heard about Renee through a friend. All she'd needed was some painting done in the foyer. Vega remembered how the woman had pulled at her hair; there was a bald spot, like she did it often. Vega had stayed quiet, wondered how someone with so much could be so lost. Renee had reached out, captured the woman's shaking hand, and held it between her own. *You can leave. I can help you.* It was never that easy. But by the time most women came to her mother, it was a last resort. The only way out.

This woman had collapsed under her mother's kindness. *He's going to kill me.*

Her mother had nodded. *Then let's get you out.*

They'd run into the woman again, months later, at a gas station outside Santa Fe; the change in her had been dramatic, like she'd been a bird who couldn't see her cage, and now she flew anywhere she wanted. Vega clasped her hands in her lap, overcome. She wished it had been her mother's hands that had led her away from Zach and not his fist in her stomach.

Joshua's phone made a thump when he put it facedown on the table. Vega looked up. The boy sat with his shoulders hunched, looking smaller than before.

"You okay?" she said.

He took a sip of his soda, shrugged. "Yeah."

Heff and Eve had gone quiet, studying the boy but neither saying anything. From behind Eve, came a *drip, drip, drip* that tickled Vega's ears and made her fingers twitch. A leaky faucet. She stood, put her napkin on the table, and went over to the sink. She turned on the flow of water, then turned it off again. After looking underneath the sink— no leak there—she turned to find everyone staring at her. "It's probably the cartridge. Pretty easy fix."

"Add it to your list," Eve said. "I probably have enough work in this old cabin alone to keep you in a job for decades."

"My momma does the fixin' at our house too," Joshua said. Vega noticed that his plate of food was largely untouched, wondered about his text message. She wished she could help.

She rejoined the table, smiling at the boy. "Same here. I grew up watching my mom, and then one day I was doing it too."

"Best way to learn," Heff said, sounding genuinely interested. "Your mother must have been a pioneer."

She was, but for Vega, it wasn't anything out of the ordinary; it had just been her childhood, and her mother was no more unusual than the next female tradesperson. Except as Vega grew older, she'd realized it *was* out of the ordinary, even now. Maybe not as much as when her mother had been a girl, but still. She'd grown used to the skeptical looks, the insinuation that a woman couldn't possibly fix things or at least do it as well as a man.

"Carl's always been willing to teach anyone how to use their hands," Eve said. "Taught a few of us girls in town over the years how to change the oil in our cars, build a table—you name it."

In a decent Carl impression, Heff said, "'If you can use your hands, you can near always make some money off it.'"

Joshua laughed. "You sound just like him."

"I wonder if Carl ever taught your mom when she lived here," Eve said, and Vega felt her body lighten, touched by the idea. "When was she here?"

Vega did the math in her head. "Midnineties, I think." Her heart expanded; could Carl have taught Renee? The thought linked Vega to a past that felt concrete, and she shifted in her chair, wanting it to be true, wanting to know she was connected to good people.

But if Carl and Betty had known her mother, why wouldn't Renee have talked about them? Or wanted Vega to know they existed?

The warmth from before faded, and Vega's head filled with the tortured cries from Renee's nightmares. She shivered. Whatever had caused her mother to live like a fugitive was something she'd kept locked away for a reason. Maybe Vega should stop asking about Renee before she found something out she couldn't forget.

"She was mostly self-taught, though." The kitchen light blinked, and outside a dark, moonless night had descended on the farm. Vega shivered, thought of the unlit drive down the curving dirt lane, the dark recesses between the trees, the quiet that came when the crickets stopped their chirping. Her dark apartment in town with the bare walls and the empty closets. This wasn't her home. Her mind drifted to Zach, and she wrapped her arms across her stomach. She didn't belong here any more than her mother had. Her stomach churned at thoughts of raising Riley on the road, drifting. She'd never wanted that for her child.

"Yeah, my mom finds a lot of videos on YouTube," Joshua said, picking at his food again.

Vega smiled. "There were no videos back when my mom was starting out. She had this thick book—it was like the bible for home repair—that she used in the beginning." Vega had loved flipping through the book with her mom, smelling the musty pages, staring at the glossy images of faucet cartridges and drywall repair. She still had the book, tucked away in one of the storage bins in the van.

"She was always running from something, wasn't she?" Eve's words flowed from her like a valve had been turned. She dropped her gaze, looked uncomfortable. "I'm sorry. That wasn't okay."

Heff leaned forward and looked at Vega. "You don't have to answer, and you don't have to know anything, if you don't want to." He crossed his arms, sat back in his chair, seemed ready to shush Eve if Vega wanted him to. Vega liked him a tiny bit more for it. "Eve keeps trying to tell me when I'm going to die, after I've told her a dozen times I'd rather live my present and see where it takes me. I've found walking away from her helps."

"I never said that." Eve had gone a shade white.

"You don't have to. It's written all over your face when you look at me like it's my last day on Earth."

Joshua laughed as only a teenager could at something so macabre. "You could make some dough telling people that stuff."

Oddly, Eve mentioning her mother didn't upset Vega. She liked that someone knew something about her mom, even if it was other-worldly and strange. Renee might not have been forthcoming, but Vega had always suspected that their nomadic life came because she'd been running from someone or something. A deep longing tugged at her chest. "Do you—can you see her?" It ended in a whisper, and her face burned at how impossible, how stupid it sounded.

"Oh, honey," Eve said, and the kindness in her voice nearly broke Vega. She shrank in her chair. "It doesn't work that way. I don't see souls or anything like that. Bits and pieces come to me but never in order—and often I can't ever make heads or tails of it. I'm so sorry."

Vega tried to play it off. "Yeah, I was kidding anyway. I'm like Heff in that way. I wouldn't really want to know anything."

Eve stood, picking up her plate, stacking the others on top, and when she got to Vega, she lingered, kindness radiating from her. "I'll try to keep my knowings to myself until I understand them better. Deal?"

Vega nodded, her throat tight.

Eve set the plates down by the sink, playfully knocked Heff upside the head. "And you, know-it-all—it's not all written in stone, and sometimes information is power, you know."

Heff laughed, deep and rich, the kind that comes from years of friendship. It stretched around Vega like a thick winter coat.

The table buzzed and Joshua picked up his cell phone, stared at the screen, and his body seemed to deflate, shadows sliding back under his eyes. He put his phone screen down on the table.

"Joshua?" Eve's voice was firm.

He slugged his water.

"Was it your brother again?"

He shrugged, shrank a little more in his seat.

Eve's hand hovered in the air. "May I see?"

Joshua's fingers shot out, and he slid the phone off the table, pressed it against his stomach.

Eve let her hand drop, glanced at Vega, then Heff. "I'm going to talk to your mom."

Joshua sat straight up at the same time Heff said, "Tera? You think that's a good idea?"

"It's not," Joshua said. "My dad might be gone, but my brother's just like him."

"Your mom is a good woman, Joshua, and she loves you very much. I'll be careful."

Vega thought of the pigs and felt a little sick at the thought of Eve going to speak with one of the Harrisons. "Can I come with you?" Her heart raced thinking of going anywhere near JJ and his family. But it was instinct to help someone. And Joshua deserved to have people on his side. Plus, she didn't want Eve to go alone.

Eve leaned her elbows on the table, nodding like she'd consulted with someone else. "Yes, I think that's a good idea."

"I don't." Heff ran a hand through his mop of blond hair, making it stick out on top, and cleared his throat. "JJ's still smarting from that pepper spray incident, and I don't trust him. I'll go."

Eve gave Heff a look. "No offense, Heff, but you might escalate things, especially if JJ's around. This is really between me and Tera. Why don't you help by making sure JJ is away from home for a few hours?"

Heff seemed like he wanted to disagree, but Eve leaned forward, touched his hand, and smiled when she said, "Some things are best left to women."

Vega ducked her head, coughed to cover a laugh.

Heff leaned back, relaxed and seeming amused himself. "Fair enough. I can keep JJ occupied. But are you comfortable going there, Vega?" The way he asked, considerate to her feelings, how he looked at her, concerned like she was breakable. Vega covered her bruised wrist with her palm, lifted her chin. "Just let JJ know that if he comes near me again, I'll spray him *and* kick him in the balls."

One side of Heff's mouth lifted, and he smiled, shaking his head. "10-4."

Joshua pulled at a cuticle, looking sick to his stomach. "You don't have to do that for me. It ain't safe and my momma's taking care of Grandpa now, and he's just, well—"

"He's old and he's dying," Eve said. "It's something I have to do, Joshua. I won't let this town destroy another kid."

There was a fiery light in Eve's eyes, a determined angle to her jaw, and Vega felt her heart twist, reminded of her mother. It's exactly what she would have done: help someone in need. It was so familiar it felt like coming home. She wished her mother had known Betty and Carl, Eve and Heff. It might have changed her life. They might have had a place where they belonged.

CHAPTER TWENTY

July 1995

Donna couldn't stand to look at the inside of the bus a minute longer. Two weeks of being cooped up and she'd begun to feel like a feral cat. Her nightmares were getting worse too—fuzzy ones that woke her in the early hours of the morning, had her clawing at her throat, thrashing against something that wanted to hold her down. Guilt was an animal lurking, ready to pounce the minute she thought about her sister. Her eyes felt swollen, and more than anything she wanted a cigarette. She'd been smoking them secretly at home, sneaking them from her mother's stash inside the flour tin.

Ethan tugged at her hand, splayed her fingers out in front of him. She'd bitten all her nails down to the quick; some were red and inflamed. "Gross. You gonna start on your toes next?"

They sat outside the bus on the blanket Betty had given her. She'd brought more stuff since her first visit: clothes, underwear, a brush and ponytail holders—even a huge yellow sweatshirt that Donna guessed had once belonged to Carl.

She sat with her legs out in front of her, sweat running down her back from the extra heat in the air. Above them, wind played in the tips of the trees, danced through the leaves. She stretched her face up, willing the air to brush over her skin, and tapped her feet against the grass, impatient. The breeze floated high, taunting her, and she stood, frustrated and so damn hot. "I gotta get out of here." She chewed on another nail, her skin feeling the hot press of her dad's hands, a mounting fear that if she didn't leave soon, he'd find a way to drag her back and nobody would stop him.

Ethan jumped to his feet. "You're leaving?"

She almost laughed at the look on his face, all sad and mopey like her bulldog at home. "One day, yeah, I'm leaving. Soon, but not yet." Since she'd told Betty her plan to head west, the idea had grown like a water stain, and Donna had decided that it wasn't a stupid idea at all. If she'd survived her father, what were a few bears and strangers? She needed money, a plan, a way to get out there, and maybe some warmer clothes. And she needed her sister. She bit her lip, hopped up and down on her toes, flapping her arms to move the stagnant air around her. "Let's go into town. I need cigarettes." She had a little bit of money she'd taken from a cookie tin her mother hid behind the pots and pans. It wasn't stealing, she'd reasoned—more like what her mother owed for pretending that Donna was the bad one.

"I don't think that's a good idea."

Donna blew air through her lips, annoyed. Ethan hemmed and hawed about everything. The boy was scared of his own shadow most days, preferring to spend his time at the bus too. Hiding from his dad and other kids who knew prey when they saw it. Donna welcomed his company, but she worried about Ethan. She was the strong one, even if he was the one who'd been taking care of her all this time.

"Don't be such a wimp." She took his hands, spun him in a circle with her, laughing, both of them with their heads flung back. The leaves smeared green across the gray sky, and when everything blurred together, they both tumbled into a heap to the ground. She landed on top of him, their faces inches apart. His breath smelled minty. His lips were red, soft-looking. Donna breathed hard, her chest pushing into his, and it happened fast. Before she knew what she was doing, she kissed him. Quick, light, nothing more than lips touching, but it sent an electric jolt through her stomach and down her legs. The sensation shocked and scared her, and she rolled off him, curled into a side position with her hands a pillow under her head.

She stared at the dirt and grass that stretched to the edge of the meadow, to where the ring of trees began and then beyond into green shadows. Her stomach curdled as she thought of the words her mother had flung at her. *Whore. Harlot. Slut.* They bounced off her skull, and she covered her ears, tried to smother her voice. The things her father did—she didn't want it, she hated it, hated him. It confused her to feel desire, to want to touch Ethan in that way. It was disgusting. What was wrong with her?

She didn't realize she was crying until Ethan's arms were around her, pulling her up to sitting, her back to him. She wiped at her face, cheeks burning. She'd run away and never look back. Then she felt the brush, pulling gently through the tangles in her hair until it went smooth. Another stroke, bristles massaging her scalp. A breeze fell through the leaves, its feathery caress across her wet face. With her head tilted back, neck exposed, she was vulnerable and weak, and Ethan was the strong one.

When he was done, they sat in silence, her back slouched against his shins, listening to the squirrels clack from branches, rodents scurry through weeds, the air a blend of rotten vegetation and sweet summer wildflowers.

"I dream about killing him."

Ethan didn't say anything, just squeezed his legs that cradled her back.

"The night I ran away, I tried to."

She heard Ethan's breath stutter.

That night, like all nights, her door had creaked open, her father's boots scraping the wood when he walked inside, the musky stink of whiskey in the air. She'd been hiding underneath the bed, shaking but determined.

"I didn't want it to happen again." The words felt blocky on her tongue, and her cheeks burned; she was grateful that she was facing away from Ethan. It was humiliating and she wondered what he thought of her now.

The tips of her father's boots had come even with her face, smelling of dirt and dog shit. He'd cursed, thrown the covers to the floor. She'd held the air inside her lungs. Their bulldog came into the room, sniffing the floor. Her heart pushed against the wood planks, and she'd tried to squish herself farther under the bed. Her father's knee appeared, followed by the side of his face.

"I was hiding." The walls of her throat stuck together, and she swallowed, felt Ethan's hand touch her shoulder. "He yanked me out from under the bed." She'd hit her head on the bed railing, seen stars. "Then he punched me. I screamed for my momma."

Donna hung her head, focused on the dirt under her fingernails. "She never came. She never does." Her body had reacted before her mind caught up, and she found herself staring at a rock in her hand, the one she'd pulled from the dirt outside the barn the week before. It had pretty threads of glittery white that ran through the stone. "I bashed his head with a rock." She'd stood above her father, rock tightly gripped in her palm. Blood shiny in streaks down his cheek. The side of her head ached and her eye swelled shut, making everything blurry and dark. She'd raised the rock high above her head; she'd bash his head all the way in, keep going until his brains spilled out. He'd never hurt her again. He'd never touch her sister. Bright light had flooded her bedroom, and Donna looked up to see her mother standing in the doorway in her robe, pointing her father's shotgun directly at her. Beth hid behind her, peeking around her hip and staring at her big sister. Tears ran down her sweet face. *No, Donna,* Beth had said, and the rock fell from Donna's hand, thumping hard on the carpet.

"My mother told me to leave, but I couldn't move 'cause I couldn't leave my little sister." Donna was finding it harder to breathe, her lungs too small for the air she needed. "She fired a warning shot out my bedroom window." Her hands shook. Had it been a warning shot or had she missed? Her father had pushed to his feet, barking at his wife to go back to bed because he'd take care of it. Her mother had shifted her grip to the barrel of the shotgun, grabbed Beth's hand, and left. Donna had nearly given up right then, but her father reached out, tenderly touching her cheek where he'd just punched her, and Donna's mouth filled with bile. She screamed, pushing him with every bit of strength she could find, and with the help of the whiskey floating around his body, he stumbled backward, falling into her closet. "I ran as fast as I could." She felt cold, even in the heat. "And then I found this bus."

The air thickened, humidity coating her throat with moisture. Where her back made contact with Ethan's legs had gone sweaty from the added body heat, adding to the droplets that ran from her armpits. But the human contact settled her. And telling Ethan felt like spitting up a rotten bite of apple.

"Yeah, I woulda tried to kill him too," Ethan said at last.

Donna laughed—not because it was funny but because it was exactly what she needed to hear. That she wasn't crazy. That she wasn't alone.

"Want to get those cigarettes now?" he said.

She turned and finally met his gaze. He was smiling, even if it didn't reach his eyes. "Never heard of a better idea in my life."

~

She followed him through the woods, dodging animal scat and dead logs teeming with termites, ducking spiderwebs that stretched sparkling and delicate between trees. The farther they got from the bus, the more she felt it pull her back. She looked behind them, and the trees seemed to close ranks around their prize. Flashes of yellow between the trunks and then it was gone—her safe place, her fort, swallowed whole. The air felt raw in her throat, and Ethan must have heard because he looked back, eyebrows meeting, concerned. He took her hand and together they emerged from the woods and onto a curved two-lane road. They walked side by side, the only sound that of their feet crunching tiny rocks and dirt on the asphalt.

Town was a few buildings, most with windows broken, FOR SALE signs on the doors. There was a dusty store at the end with old gas pumps out front and a picture in the window of an ice-cream cone. They walked inside. A man was buying chew at the register, hacking up a lung while he dug money from his pocket. Ethan pulled her to the rear of the store, where a short cabinet stood against the wall. He slid the door open and leaned over, pulling out two Drumsticks. "Ice cream?"

Donna's eyes widened—vanilla, topped with chocolate, nuts, and caramel. Her mouth watered and she grabbed the cone from him, smiling. "Perfect."

They walked up to the register, stood behind the man who was counting out pennies and nickels. The employee slid each coin off the counter and into the open tray, looking bored; another day at work. Donna's nose burned at the tobacco stink filling the air from the man's clothes—probably his skin too. It was familiar. Like how the tips of her dad's fingers smelled. She held her stomach, wanting to throw up, needing air. She put a hand to her mouth and hurried to the door.

"Hey, wait!" the guy behind the counter yelled. "That's stealing!"

Donna didn't get far because someone grabbed her arm, and she was spun around until she faced the man with the chewing tobacco. "Get back here," he growled, the skin around his lips creased with hundreds of tiny lines—a smoker's mouth.

"Don't touch me," Donna said, yanking her arm out of his grip. "I wasn't stealin'. I thought I was gonna be sick." She threw her Drumstick onto the counter, took Ethan's from his hand, and tossed it alongside hers. Then pulled a few dollars from her pocket and put them on top. Glanced at the old man. "See?"

"Careful," Ethan whispered.

Donna ignored Ethan and glared at the man, who stood by the door, staring at her. It made the hairs on the back of her neck stand on end. She should have shut up, but Donna was tired of feeling small, so dang sick of being scared all the time. She turned back to the counter. "And, uh, a pack of, um . . ." She'd never bought cigarettes, just stolen them from her mom. "The ones with the camel on them."

The clerk tossed a pack onto the counter; her change felt cool against her palm. When she turned to leave, the man had left and she felt a relieved whoosh of air escape her. "Creep," she said.

Ethan was quiet when they left the store, timid, like a dog with its tail tucked. She ripped off the paper wrapping and bit into the ice cream; the hard chocolate splintered and a chunk fell to the ground. "Shoot," she said, but didn't pay it too much mind because the ice cream was salty and sweet and cold in her mouth. Delicious. She licked it, this time careful to catch any falling chocolate. The sugar gave her a rush of optimism, the thought of a cigarette a boost of calm.

"You know, you can't let everyone push you around all the time, Ethan." Away from home, out from under the control of her mother, the obsession of her father, Donna felt like she'd been asleep and was just now waking up. The way the man in the store had grabbed her arm, touched her like he had some right to put his hands on her, burned in her gut. The way she had to hide from her father, like she was the one who'd done something wrong. The way Ethan made himself invisible. "Some people like to kick an animal when it's down, you know?" Donna felt an urge to help the boy, wisdom growing in the quiet moments since she'd left home. Fear a rope bridge with frayed knots. She elbowed him in the side. "You should come with me."

"What?" He'd barely touched his ice cream.

"Out west. You should come with me. I'm taking my little sister with me, too, so you have to be okay with kids. But she's the best. You'll love her. We could go to California. Have you been there?"

He shook his head.

"See the ocean. Have you ever seen that much water?"

"Went to Lake Cumberland once when I was a kid."

"Oh, well, I've never seen anything bigger than our pond." She finished the cone. "Yeah, you should come with me. We could go wherever we want, do whatever we want, and never have to worry about people trying to hurt us ever again."

Ice cream and chocolate had melted down the sides of Ethan's cone, running over his fingers.

She eyed the dessert. "If you're not gonna eat that, I will." He handed it to her. "Come on, Ethan, what do you say?"

"There's awful people everywhere, Donna." He gave her a look that made the tips of her ears burn. "There's good here too."

Donna laughed then; now she knew he must be kidding. Before she could say anything, a truck pulled up alongside them on the road. It was the man from the store.

"Shit," Ethan murmured, and Donna tensed.

"Just keep walking," she said, and slid her hand into his, squeezed.

But the man gunned the truck, pulled it diagonal so that it cut them off. Donna's heart thundered against her chest bones. He opened his door and got out, the stink of tobacco drifting out from the cab. "You that girl I heard 'bout at church? Yer daddy lives up Mount Kinley way, that right?"

She froze and her bravado from minutes ago wriggled out of her skin. Thoughts of her dad exorcised her confidence. She felt the man's hands on her arms from earlier—small but with a wiry strength she knew would be hard to fight off. Ethan squeezed her hand, reminding her that she wasn't alone, easing the shaking in her legs. She would not go home. She'd pick up a rock and bash this guy's head in too. Take a stick and stab anywhere soft, punch his tobacco-yellow teeth out. Nothing would make her go back.

"Mary's my cousin from Portsmouth, Mr. Harrison."

The man dragged his eyes from Donna to look at Ethan. His upper lip curled.

"Betty heard that other girl took off for Cincinnati," Ethan said. "Thought maybe she'd followed a boy."

The man sucked air in through his nose, then spat a fat glob of something gross on the dirt not far from Ethan's feet. Anger scurried up Donna's spine and her fingers curled, but Ethan, who seemed able to read her every emotion, moved so that he stood partially blocking her.

"Girl deserves whatever happens to her, then," the man said, rubbing a hand across his mouth. "Running off from her daddy like that. God don't suffer fools."

"Yes, sir," Ethan said, and Donna wanted to stomp on his foot for how obedient he sounded.

The man gave Donna one last look, then turned and climbed into his truck, taking his stink with him. When the truck was gone, she breathed in the clean mountain air before turning to Ethan. "Why'd you let him talk to you like that?"

"What, Levi Harrison?" Ethan looked at her like she'd lost a screw or two, and then something hardened in his eyes. "Why're you so convinced that life's better somewhere else?" He stepped away from her.

Her arms were stick straight by her side, and she stomped her foot into the dirt, her belly hot with anger. "I don't know. But anything's better than acting like a whipped dog and letting these assholes think they're better than you."

The fight leaked from his eyes and he looked sad, disappointed, like she'd said all the wrong things. "You don't know anything, Donna." He turned then and walked down the road, missing the trail into the woods that led to the bus and leaving Donna standing on the road alone.

She hacked her way through the woods back to the bus, spider-webs sticking to her hair, tripping over a stupid stump. Angry tears slid down her cheeks. When the bus came into view, she felt a brief sense of relief that she pushed away, stoking the flames of her decision. She didn't need the bus, or Ethan, or Betty with her cookies. All she needed was herself, and the sooner she moved on, the better. Tomorrow, she'd find a way to sneak Beth away from home, and she'd leave Crystal and never, ever look back.

CHAPTER TWENTY-ONE

VEGA

May 2021

Vega climbed the steep stairs up to Betty and Carl's cabin, sweat clinging to her back by the time she reached the top. It was warmer, mug-
gier today, and her skin soaked in the moisture, so different from the
dry climate out west. Carl sat on the porch in a weatherworn rocker,
drinking from a tin mug; the golden retriever, muzzle a snow-white,
snoozed at his feet. Carl's eyes lit up and his mustache twitched above
a smile when he saw Vega.

"Well, good morning, missy." He stood, stepping over the dog,
and raised his voice an octave when he spoke to the baby. "Hey there,
little fella."

Vega and Eve were headed over to see Tera that morning, and she
didn't want to bring Riley. With half the town offering to babysit, Vega
decided she'd put their hospitality to the test. But without her phone,
her only option was to walk over and ask.

"I suppose you're lookin' for a babysitter," Carl said.

Vega sighed. Either she was extremely predictable or everyone in this town was a psychic. "I'm running an errand with Eve and I'd appreciate it, if you don't mind."

The door opened and Betty walked out, wiping her hands on a dish towel. "I just finished putting a pot roast on for supper, and I ain't got nothin' better to do now except watch this sweet baby boy."

"Hey now, Betty, I was here first," Carl said.

Riley jerked his legs, tiny fists punching the air, and Betty laughed. "Oh, look. Little guy's excited to see us, Carl. Ain't that something?"

"Who wouldn't be excited to see you? You smell like sugar."

Betty playfully punched Carl's shoulder. "Stop, you old man."

Their banter draped her in the warmth of their friendship and Vega smiled, unbuckling Riley and handing him over to Betty. "I just changed him, and he's eaten. I don't think we should be long, but there's formula in the bag and more diapers. He usually naps in the morning—sometimes but not always." She sucked in her lip, unsure. "He can be pretty fussy."

Betty gave her a look and Carl laughed. "'Course he's fussy," he said. "Little guy just started livin' and it's confusing. We don't mind it one bit. Woulda filled this cabin with fussy young'uns if we'd been so blessed."

"We did in a different way, didn't we, Carl?"

He nodded, seeming suddenly choked. "Yes, we did." He turned to Vega. "Heard your momma used to roam these parts."

Vega tried to keep her expectations low. Nobody here seemed to have known her mom. She thought of the picture of her mom by the school bus that she'd left in the apartment, the paint staining her fingers, and gave Betty an apologetic look. "I think she was one of the kids who added to the graffiti on your bus."

Betty bounced Riley, smiled. "Oh, that's no matter. Not really my bus, anyhow."

Carl pursed his lips, making his mustache dance. "Hmm, now. Betty, who was that young gal who camped out by the chickens?" He sipped his coffee. "Stayed a couple 'a nights."

Betty shook her head. "Roxie from Coolville. Had a boyfriend she was hidin' from, if I recall."

Carl rubbed his chin. "Maybe that were your momma?"

Vega's pulse quickened. If Renee had been running from someone, it was possible she'd have lied to keep herself safe. It's certainly what she'd told the women they helped to do.

"Blonde hair like yours, too, Vega. A wisp of a thing." Betty laughed. "And not much taller than me. I recall tellin' her I liked having someone around my own size."

Vega tried not to feel a crush of disappointment. Her mother had been tall and strong, tan and dark-haired. Not a wisp. She inhaled and tried to smile. Crystal had been a temporary stop for her mother, nothing more. From below came a short and faint honk. She looked down through the trees to see Eve's truck on the road. "Thank you again. I won't be long."

"Take as long as you need, missy."

Eve's truck bounced over the rutted road that ribboned up a steep hill. Vega held on to the handrail above the window to keep from hitting her head on the glass. This part of the country was beautiful and rural—small towns hidden in the hollers, homes scaling mountainsides. They passed a stone memorial for a mine disaster that happened in 1930.

"Killed eighty-two men," Eve said.

"Do their ghosts wander the woods too?" Vega said half-jokingly.

Eve smiled. "No, but sometimes if you press your ear to the ground, you can hear their last thoughts."

"Ha ha." Vega knew Eve was kidding, but the thought of being trapped underground spread goose bumps across her back.

They reached the top of the road and Vega breathed out. "It's beautiful." The trees opened up to a view that spread out below in a carpet of bright green.

"The Harrisons own quite a bit of property." Eve maneuvered the truck onto a narrower lane, deep indentations filled with mud. "This one goes back to Tera's house."

"You knew her when you were a kid?"

"I did." Eve drove slowly, keeping her tires straddling the ruts, Vega supposed, so they didn't get sucked into the mud. She wore her hair in long waves over her shoulders; it shone a walnut brown, and on her wrists were stacked beaded bracelets, turquoise rings on three fingers, long roped leather earrings with a turquoise bead swinging from the end. Her makeup was flawless, natural.

Vega pulled at the ends of her hair, touched her cheeks, feeling very plain next to the woman. She hadn't worn makeup since Riley was born, and hardly any before that. "Tera stuck up for you?" She wondered about Eve's childhood, tried to imagine what it would have been like for her here. Marveled at how warm and kind she was despite what must have been a very difficult time.

Eve chewed on her lip, seemed to be thinking. "Tera did what she could, given how she was raised. Life's been hard for her. Her father was always more interested in his sons, her husband's a criminal serving time in federal prison, and she lost her job last year after a terrible car accident had her missing multiple days at work. She's a survivor."

The trees parted to reveal a double-wide trailer with a built-on deck without railings, a chicken coop over to the side, and deeper into the woods, an outhouse. Everything was neat and tidy, given the amount of stuff in the yard: old bikes leaning against a ramshackle barn, car parts rusted in a heap, a burned-out shell of an old sedan. But empty of JJ's truck. Vega unfurled her fingers, relaxed, and followed Eve to the front door. Eve paused before knocking, glanced at Vega. "Tera is tough, sometimes unfair, but she cares."

Eve knocked and a howling came from inside, followed by the click of nails on the floor and another bark. "Git back, Romeo. Git!" A shuffling from inside and then the door opened a crack. At first, nothing—and then a hiss: "What the hell you doing here?"

"I need to talk to you about Joshua." Eve's voice was smooth and kind.

A snout pushed through the opening, bringing with it a large droopy-eared hound, followed by Tera, who had lost her grip on the collar. Romeo sprang forward, jumping up in one smooth motion, paws on Vega's shoulders, big brown eyes even with hers. It was so unexpected she laughed, and it calmed her nerves. He released her and jumped off the deck and started sniffing the ground. Tera pulled the door shut behind her, leaned her back against it, and crossed her arms. She was Eve's age, but the years had worn harder, pulling the corners of her eyes into deep grooves that cracked outward in an expanding semicircle. Deep wrinkles digging into the skin around her mouth. An unhealthy pallor in her cheeks. But Vega could see Joshua in the woman's eyes, guarded but not unkind.

From her jeans pocket, Tera pulled out a pack of cigarettes, popped one out, and lit it in a smooth and well-practiced motion. She inhaled, breathed smoke into the space between them. "Joshua's staying with a friend for a few days," she said.

"Yes, of course he is. I just want to make sure you're okay with that—or if not, if there's something that his friend could do to help."

Tera ashed her cigarette on the grass below the deck, held the burning tip away from them. Her blonde hair hung limp across her shoulders. "Daddy's inside," she whispered.

"I know."

Her eyes left Eve and moved to Vega. "You that girl who pepper-sprayed my boy?"

Vega nodded. "I'm sorr—" She shook her head, dismissing the idea. "No, I'm not sorry. He was doing something terrible to Eve's pig, and I didn't see another way to make him quit." Without Riley strapped to her chest, Vega didn't know what to do with her hands, so she folded her arms, tried to look less defensive than she felt.

Tera inhaled, studying her. Vega fidgeted. "It's a he-said-she-said." Pointed the lit end of her cigarette at Vega to emphasize her point. "But you spray him again and I'll come for you."

Vega nodded, wondering why she was here. She certainly hadn't made things calmer. "Yes, ma'am." The word felt wrong on her tongue, a nicety she'd never adopted but that fit the situation.

One side of Tera's mouth lifted, and she turned back to Eve. Vega noticed the dent in Tera's chin tremble. "He's not safe here. I-I think he's tried to hurt himself." Her voice sounded like it had gotten stuck in her throat. "I need to know he's okay."

"He's okay. He's safe. But I think JJ's harassing him over text, and that's been upsetting him. I just wanted to make sure you knew where he was. He's a good kid, Tera." There was an innate genuineness to Eve that Vega admired.

Tera nodded, pulled hard on her cigarette, then whistled for her dog, who jumped on the deck, muddy paws and all. His tongue swiped across Vega's hand, leaving a trail of slobbery dirt. She wiped it on her pant leg, tried to pretend it didn't bother her. Tera reached down to grab his collar, and Vega noticed a tattoo that looped around her wrist.

She had to fight the urge to grab the woman's wrist in her hand so she could take a closer look. Her mother had had the same one in the same spot, an old stick-and-poke tattoo she'd said had been her very first. One she'd refreshed herself every few years. As a kid, Vega would sit on her knees and watch her mother's fingers holding the needle, burying the ink into her flesh one small dot at a time. Tera had the same cheesy design—barbed wire circling her wrist, more permanent looking than the one her mother had had. "My mom had that same tattoo," she said, pointing to Tera's wrist.

The woman stared at it, turned it one way, then another, as though it brought to the surface memories from somewhere she'd forgotten. "Everyone had one of these," she said. "Thought I was a tattoo artist 'cause I had a needle and ink. I used to stick anyone who'd stand still long enough." She exhaled smoke through her nose, laughed, and it stirred up mucus, making her cough instead. Smiled at Eve. "You remember when I gave you that flower one on your ankle?"

Eve laughed too. "It was a dot, not a flower."

"Yeah, because you wouldn't let me finish. You were such a girl, even then." She smiled, and there was depth to it that hinted at something shared.

Eve shrugged. "What can I say. I don't do pain."

Tera looked surprised. "Unless it's the kind that kills you, huh?" She turned to Vega, eyes open a bit wider. "You've got some good ones."

Vega rubbed her arms. Her tats were such a part of her she often forgot how different they made her look. Not to Tera, probably, who had quite a few of her own. "Yeah, my mom kinda got me hooked. It was a hobby for us, I guess." Her chest tightened. They'd had a tattoo fund, one they added pennies to whenever they could. As soon as it could fund two tattoos, they'd make an appointment. "I haven't added to mine since she died. I just can't."

Eve made a sound in her throat and Vega stiffened. Tera was a complete stranger. What was she doing reminiscing about her mom in front of this woman? She tried to smile. "Sorry about that."

Tera stared at her. She had light-green eyes with tiny specks of golden brown circling the pupils. And for a moment Vega glimpsed the girl she'd been, fair haired and pretty and born into a life that had made the uphill even steeper. "My momma died when I was ten. She was a good woman. Never apologize for talkin' 'bout those who loved you. You keepin' her alive by remembering her."

A lump hardened in Vega's throat and she nodded, touched by Tera's unexpected softness. "Thank you."

From inside came a voice, yelling but not making much sound, as though the volume had already been used up just by trying. "Tera, who're you yammering on to? Get inside. I'm thirsty."

Tera inhaled one last time, tossed the cigarette to the ground below; the ember grew red, then smoked out. She gave Eve a look. "Don't nobody here want you around. Git off my property." The screen slammed shut on useless hinges, and once inside, the dog ran to the window, pushing aside the curtain, nose on the smeared glass, growling and barking like he'd never met them.

Vega followed Eve, who'd been particularly quiet, back to the truck. Once inside, she sat with her hands on the wheel, staring at the trailer.

"Are you okay, Eve?"

"That went well," she said.

Vega raised her eyebrows. "It did?"

Eve turned to her. The sun was high, streamers of light falling through the trees and hitting the ground in patches. "It's the first time she's spoken to me since I died. So yes, that went exceedingly well." She started the engine, turned to look over her shoulder, and backed the truck until the front end faced away from the house.

Just as they were driving away, the trailer's door opened and an old man stood in the doorway, bent heavily over a walker, his skin a grayish white, mouth creased into an ugly frown. His eyes met Vega's, and he swiveled his head like he wanted to see who was driving. Instinctively, she leaned forward to block his view, and the trailer slipped from sight when the truck crested the hill and began a bumpy descent back to the main road.

"Who was that man?" she said.

"Old-man Levi? He's the patriarch of the Harrison clan. And the reason JJ is the way he is." Eve pulled a bag of jerky from the center console and offered it to Vega, who took one piece, held it in her hand. "You said your mom had a tattoo like Tera's?"

"Yeah, but Mom's looked like a kid had drawn it. Tera's was professional."

"She's had it redone."

"Oh." Not sure how else to respond. It wasn't an unusual tattoo for someone to have—a bit cheesy, but it was cool when her mom had gotten it as a girl. Or so she'd told Vega. That's how Vega thought of her own artwork: as a visual timeline of her life, reminding her of her past. There was the smaller Ouroboros she had on her hip; her mother had gone big with the one around her neck. Vega had been eighteen and it was her first tattoo. Renee had said she'd never forget her first one. They'd been lying on the tables, Vega on her side, facing her mom, the sting of the needle in her flesh, the buzzing of the drill like the distant humming of bees. She'd reached out and touched the barbed wire around her mother's wrist. *Is that why you keep this one? Because it was your first?* Renee had run her fingers around her wrist, smiling, but her eyes were serious. *Yes, and because it reminds me that there's good people in the world. Few and far between, but they do exist.* "It was my mom's first tattoo. It was special to her."

Eve was nodding. "Makes sense. I'm glad you came with me today."

"Really?" Vega hadn't felt like her presence added anything to the interaction. "She's a little scary."

Eve laughed. "She's tough—then again, so was your mom."

Silence mushroomed between them and Vega's breath caught. "H-how would you know?" Suspicion fluttered against her chest. Either she believed that Eve had some kind of psychic intuition or the woman was lying about not knowing her mom. And neither option made sense.

The truck lurched into a deep hole, climbed out, black mud splattering across the passenger-side window. Eve's eyes never left the road. "I'm not sure how I know these things, Vega. I'm sorry. Dying changed me in ways I can't fully understand. For some reason, your mom is very clear to me."

Vega looked down at her lap. It didn't seem like Eve was trying to mislead her, and Vega couldn't figure out what the woman had to gain by lying about her mom. She breathed in, went with her gut. "You're right. She was tough. I wish—" She was going to say she wished she were as strong as her mother, but she stopped herself.

Eve pulled the truck onto the main road, and the smooth asphalt made everything too quiet. "You don't think you're strong like she was?"

Vega blew air into her cheeks, at once amused and annoyed. "Do you read minds too?"

"Some things aren't hard to guess. You remind me of someone I knew once."

"Really? Another bleached-blonde tatted woman with an infant and no clue what she's doing?"

Eve laughed. "No, but she was strong-willed like you are—determined too. And, honey, let me tell you, from what I understand, nobody knows what they're doing when it comes to kids. My parents are prime examples of that. But you're off to a good start."

"How would you know?"

Eve looked over. "Because you love him."

Vega looked down at her lap, overcome. She'd doubted herself since the moment she brought Riley home. Zach's mood swings had made her world unpredictable, shattered her confidence. And without her mother, Vega realized how much she'd been drifting, hoping that her life with Zach would be the stability she'd always wanted. Turning a blind eye to everything that screamed it wasn't. Eve's words struck something deep inside her, and Vega's vision clouded.

"Riley's father, he, uh . . ." The words were coming out, and Vega was powerless to stop them. "He punched me and I-I just left, and I kept driving and the only place I could think to go was Crystal because of this postcard that my mom kept. It reminds me of her, and I thought that if I was here, I might feel closer to her or something." She tugged at the ends of her hair. "But nobody here knows her, and Zach is trying to find me, and I can't afford to pay the bills." Her face was wet. "And I don't know what to do." She stared at her hands. It was more than she'd told anyone. More honest than she'd been to herself in the days since it happened.

Eve slammed on her brakes, and Vega's head jerked up, the seat belt straining against her chest. The Kunekunes stood on the side of the road, noses stuck to the earth, oblivious to the truck.

"Damn pigs," Eve said.

Vega felt pulled, like she was attached to strings holding a hot-air balloon, and suddenly she was weightless and laughing. "Escape artists!" she said.

Eve smiled. "I'm used to it." And together they pulled a foldable metal ramp from the bed of her truck and hooked it to the back. One by one, they corralled the Kunekunes into the truck and started back toward Eve's.

"Why do you put up with those pigs?" Vega said.

Eve kept her eyes on the road, but her mouth softened. "Because they make me feel closer to my mother too."

"Oh." Vega blinked hard, and looked at the pigs in a whole different light.

CHAPTER TWENTY-TWO

EVE

Eve wiped her hands on her jeans, digging dirt out from under her fingernails. Vega latched the tailgate on the truck, stood back to look at the pigs, who were safely—for now, at least—locked in the smaller pen.

"How do they keep escaping?"

Eve shook her head. "I have no idea."

Vega laughed, and Eve marveled at the change in her since she had told her about Zach. Like it had been a creature feeding on her little bits at a time, and it had jerked back to let her breathe. After Tera's dog and then the pigs, Vega looked a little worse for the wear—smudges across her jeans where the dog had rubbed his muddy fur, streaks of dirt along her cheek from helping push the pigs up the ramp, her hair a spiky blonde mess. Eve's heart compressed. The woman was barely in her twenties, but she bore the weight of loss and trauma in the slope of her back. Eve wished she knew how to make things right for her.

There was the rustle of a breeze through the trees; then the clucks and mews of the animals suddenly muted, cotton filling her ears, and a loud whooshing replaced all sound. Eve grabbed on to the side mirror of her truck, the ground wriggling, thousands of worms moving under her soles. She felt herself pulled back to the vision from her NDE. On her stomach, in the cramped space beneath a bed, with a girl by her side. Nestled in Eve's palms, a baby, impossibly small and crying. *Take care of my baby.* Feet approached the bed, and the girl was gone. But the baby remained, crying and crying and crying.

A hand touched her arm. Vega stood in front of her, a worried slant to her eyes.

She blinked and the vision lurked, the sunny day a gauzy curtain that barely hid the girl under the bed, the baby in Eve's hands. Eve focused on what was real—Vega, the pigs snorting in the pen, the breeze on her face—and the vision disappeared entirely.

Vega gripped her elbow, like she alone could keep Eve's knees from buckling. She felt the strength return to her thigh muscles, and she let go of the mirror.

"Whoa, what happened to you?" Vega said.

"I don't really know." She thought of Vega sharing with her about Zach and decided to do the same. "When I had my near-death experience, I had a vision about a girl and a baby. I've never been able to figure out what it means."

Vega leaned against the truck, chewed on her cheek. "Do you know the girl?"

Eve had never seen the girl's face. "No, but she's familiar, I think."

"Do you know many women with babies?" Vega asked lightly, like it was a joke.

Eve stared at the young woman. A knowing wrapped itself around her torso. She'd been expecting Vega and Riley. Did her vision have something to do with the baby? "Does Zach know where you are?"

Vega's body seemed to grow smaller at the mention of the man. "No."

"And he doesn't know anything about Crystal?"

"I never told him. Why, Eve? What does it have to do with me?"

Eve softened her voice. "I think it has to do with Riley." It felt nearly right, and her heart thumped faster.

"What are you saying?" Fear etched into the lines across Vega's forehead.

"I'm not sure. Somehow, I knew you were coming into my life, but I still don't understand what it has to do with Riley or my vision. But if it's to keep you safe, you have nearly half a town that wants to do that."

Vega wrapped her arms around herself, gave her a weak smile. "It's not funny to joke about it, you know."

Eve wasn't surprised at her reaction. People doubted her. It was normal. "I know this is all hard to believe, Vega, but it's not a joke, and I'd never make light of what's happened to you."

Vega nodded. "You think I should be worried?"

Eve thought about it, tried to force herself to understand it better. It had gone cold. "I think you should be careful."

Vega looked sick. "I need to get Riley. Can you take me back to Carl and Betty's now?"

The woman was scared. Eve understood why and what haunted her thoughts. She curled her hands into fists, frustrated by her half visions and wishing she could give her something more than empty promises.

~

Eve opened the door to her store, flipped the BACK SOON sign over to OPEN. Vega had gone up to the apartment, saying she needed to head to the hardware store for a few supplies. Eve had paid her half of her estimate so she could get started. She'd been quiet on the way to town, and Eve couldn't blame her. She wished she'd kept her vision to herself, afraid she'd needlessly worried Vega or, worse, pushed her away with her unreliable second sight. Vega had been in Crystal only a week, but it seemed longer, like she'd always been part of the community.

Once inside, Eve noticed an unfamiliar old car parked along the street. Someone was in the driver's seat, their head back like they were sleeping. She hesitated, thought of Vega and Riley, an uneasy prickling across her neck. Would Riley's father come after them?

Jane pushed through the door and tossed a ruined purple iris onto the counter, its flower wilted, stem broken.

"Oh dear," Eve said, joining the woman at the counter. "But now it makes sense why I picked these up yesterday." From the shelves behind the cash register, she pulled down a six-pack of purple irises.

Jane stared at the flowers. The apples of her rounded cheeks were pink, and she clasped her purse like she was ready for Eve to run her out of the store or cast an evil spell. Jane did not approve of Eve.

"Your pigs are a nuisance."

"I know, I know." And she did—they were. "But this time there's no way they'll get out." The pigs were smart and had been escaping long before the fence was mowed down. She had no idea how, but sometimes she thought they had their own portal. It was more likely that they'd shimmied under the pen fencing and walked down the driveway and straight through the open gate, but she liked to imagine they were a little bit more special than the average pigs.

Jane's lips pinched together, and she held her body upright, leaning away from the counter and Eve as if transgender were catching. The woman focused on Eve's chin or neck, hardly ever meeting her gaze.

"Anything else I can help you with, Jane?"

"I'm not the only one fed up with your pigs." She wore glasses that made her eyes appear larger than normal, and with how wide open they were in admonishment of Eve and her pigs, they looked inhuman. "Heard they tore through the nuns' vegetable garden too."

Eve breathed air in through her teeth. Sometimes it seemed she could do nothing right. It would do her no good to upset the nuns. While they were friendly enough, she suspected she knew exactly what they thought of her. Eve flattened her lips, her patience a little thinner than normal today. "You know, Jane, underneath my gorgeous hair and flawless skin, I'm just a regular person, like you." She'd put up with Jane's disapproval, ignored it for the most part. It wasn't Eve's job to change the world. But she couldn't seem to keep her thoughts to herself today.

Jane opened and closed her mouth, held her purse to her chest. "I never said—" She seemed flustered, maybe even embarrassed to be challenged. "God loves you, of course, but he's, well . . . he made you perfect when you were born."

Eve smiled. "Something we can finally agree on, Jane. I am exactly as he made me."

Jane's forehead wrinkled; her cheeks wobbled. She seemed confused and speechless.

"Thanks for stopping by." Eve handed her the flowers, and Jane took them and left. Eve shook her head, pleased. Sometimes she felt like a bystander in her own life, choosing more often than not to ignore the underhanded comments or half-veiled insinuations that there was something wrong with her. She didn't believe she should have to fight all the battles. But today, she'd felt a shift inside her, a desire to stand up, to say something back, even if it was only words and the chance of it changing Jane's opinion was no greater than it had been the day before. She smiled to herself. It had felt good to go toe to toe with Jane.

Her thoughts turned fondly to the pigs. Sometimes she was grateful they'd become such a nuisance to others in town. They'd almost caused her more issues than her being trans. Almost. She kinda loved them for it. They had been one of her first additions after she'd cleaned out the old barn and scrubbed the cabin. Her parents had lived their entire married lives on the farm, her mother dying first, followed by her father years later. He'd wanted nothing to do with Eve, but her mother . . . Eve had always believed that had her mother been a stronger woman, she would have found a way to love Eve as she was.

She pressed the heels of her hands to her eyes. It still hurt to remember the way her mother's eyes had hardened when she saw Eve for the first time, after the hospital and before she left Crystal for good. Against Carl and Betty's insistence that she leave, Eve had gone home, convinced that her mother's love was strong enough to accept her for who she was. Instead, her mother had gone cold, and it felt like a hatchet to the bond that was supposed to be unbreakable, that of mother and child, hacked to pieces by her mother's biblical submission, her father's staunch beliefs. If her mother had always been cold, if she'd favored the rod over love, then maybe it wouldn't have felt like a fresh wound when she walked away from Eve. But Eve's childhood had been sepia-toned moments: tightly bound in her mother's arms, reading *Curious George*; crickets loud in the inky black night; running through the tall grass in the pasture; riding in front of her mother on a horse, the animal muscled and sweaty beneath her legs, her mother soft against her back. The pig her mother had brought home from the state fair that Eve helped bottle-feed, letting him sleep in a warm pen in the kitchen when he was little, moving him to the barn when he grew too big for the house. He was meant to be bacon, but her mother had grown too attached, couldn't bear the thought. Her father had laughed—they'd all laughed—and he'd called her Fern and nicknamed the pig Wilbur. But in the end, he'd relented, let her mother keep the pig as a pet. And she'd loved that pig. So had Eve.

Those were the memories that had given Eve a false courage, a belief that while she might lose her father's love, she'd never lose her mother's. She poured beans into the grinder, and it was loud in the store, drowning out her memories and taking with them the nips of pain she still felt at her mother's rejection.

The sound of something brushing against the shop window; she looked up and moaned. Speaking of. The pigs were outside, sitting with their backs pressed against the door. Maybe they did have their own portal. Maybe she liked that they followed her around. Maybe she knew about the loose bit of wire.

She opened the door, and they shot to their feet. "Go home! Get!" The car from earlier was still parked on the street, the driver either asleep or watching Eve's store. A knowing crept from the ground, tugging at her shins, crawling up her arms until it settled on her shoulder and whispered in her ear. They had come to Crystal to see Eve. She walked out of the store and directly over to the car. The person had a hoodie pulled up and cinched, arms crossed, head back, sleeping. Old food wrappers scattered across the passenger seat, a big plastic cup of soda, pillow, blankets and clothes spread across the back. Homeless and living out of their car. Eve swallowed hard and rapped on the window.

The person inside shot forward, yanking back their hood and exposing a short black Afro, a thick sweatshirt, and cargo shorts. A kid. He cranked down the window and stared up at Eve, dark eyes wary.

Eve stood back, crossed her arms, and studied him. "I saw you parked out here. Is everything okay?"

The kid opened the car door; the unoiled metal squealed as loud as her pigs. He stood with his arms wrapped tight across his front, as though hiding something, and Eve knew—maybe because of her enhanced intuition, maybe because she was trans and she knew a young person in pain when she saw herself reflected in their slumped shoulders and lowered gaze—this kid had come for help.

"I just needed to sleep for a bit. Can't I park here?"

Eve shook her head. "I don't mind, but Jane over there—" Jane stood at her shop window, staring and, Eve had no doubt, about to call Heff to order him to give this kid a ticket. Or she'd call her pastor to pray the intruder out of town. Jane was convinced that most strangers were liberal city folk spreading their godless beliefs throughout small God-fearing towns.

"Are you Eve?"

"I am." It made complete sense, like she'd been building up to this moment for her entire life and now all she had to do was say yes. It gave clarity to the bigger picture, why she'd left her life and friends to move back to her parents' farm, but also swirled everything into a confusing heap. She was halfway down a path she could never turn back from, and it was dangerous as much as it was the right thing to do. She thought of what she knew about Heff, and it sat heavy across her shoulders. "How can I help you?"

"I'm—" He stopped, kicked at the ground—frustrated, it seemed. "I'm Antonne," he said, and when he did, he stood a tiny bit straighter and met Eve's gaze.

Eve nodded. "How can I help you, Antonne?"

He swayed, his courage from seconds earlier already seeming to melt away. "I know Joshua, or, well, we've never met, just from Instagram, and, um, he told me he'd left home. He seems—" He slid his hands into his sweatshirt pocket. "Will you help me too?"

It was all happening so fast, and yet she'd lived a lifetime seeing others in pain, feeling it herself. The hateful words thrown at her because she was different, the rage it evoked in others, the fear of the unknown that led to violence. She'd felt the pull to come home, the urge to create her own safe space. She thought of the girl under the bed. *Keep my baby safe.* Something clicked. Maybe the point of coming back from the dead was exactly this. To provide a safe space for people like her. It set her pulse racing in the way that meant she was onto something true. She smiled. "Where are you from?"

"Portsmouth."

The town was a few hours down the road, much bigger than Crystal. "What you want to do, Antonne? You know, it won't be easy. Leaving your family, your home—any of it."

Antonne's eyes hardened. "Nothin's been easy, so what's the difference? Besides, I don't live at home no more." He wilted then, chin trembling, his utter exhaustion evident in the swollen skin under his eyes, the slump of his back.

There were stains down his sweatshirt, skin greasy. She wondered how long he'd been homeless. A pressure built inside her chest. So many trans kids were forced into homelessness, and the suicide rate among them was staggering. If she could offer a safe place to even one or two kids, what was stopping her?

She dug her fingers into her palms. Other than the legality of it, of course. The wind had kicked up outside, swirling leaves in the air, dust scratching at the windshield. The iron sting of blood crept into her nose, reminding her of the knowing she'd had about Heff's death. She felt the pull of an invisible thread, blind to what it connected, desperate to understand, frustration a thorny tangle in her gut. She felt as though saying yes would seal Heff's fate. But looking at the desperate loneliness in Antonne's eyes, the knowledge that she was more than likely his last chance, she reminded herself that sometimes life took a turn at the last moment. She'd never considered herself psychic, because she believed in free will. There were many choices a person could make that led them on different paths. And in this moment, the only right choice was to open her home.

"Joshua didn't invite me or nothin'." His hands shook; he looked vulnerable and alone, and Eve wanted to do anything in her power to help. "I ain't got nowhere else to go." His voice broke at the end, and he wiped a fist across his eyes.

She touched the boy's arm, and when he jerked back, tears stung her eyes. He was so used to hate he didn't know what to do with kindness. "You can stay with me, Antonne."

He croaked out a sob, nodding and still hugging himself, like he'd been suffocating and she'd reminded him there was air. "I'm a good worker. I cook good and I'll learn anything. I drive." He pointed toward the old heap of a car—one window busted and covered with a trash bag, the paint thin and rusted, tires bald.

Eve wondered how the old thing still drove and if it would make it down the dirt road to her farm. She smiled at Antonne. "How about you help in the store today; then you can follow me to the farm after work? But first, lunch. Okay?"

Antonne nodded and followed her to the store. Jane stared from her window, lips creased into a frown. Eve twirled her fingers in the air, brought them together, and flicked them at the woman. She flinched and jumped away from the window, letting the curtain fall back into place.

"What was that all about?" Antonne said.

"Jane has herself convinced that I'm a witch."

"Are you?"

"Of course not. But sometimes I like to have a little fun."

Antonne snorted.

Inside the store, Eve gave Antonne two croissants and a muffin, wished she had a stove so she could whip up some eggs. Soon his plate was empty, crumbs nesting in the folds of his sweatshirt. She filled a glass of water and set it beside a cup of coffee. Her arms tingled. Antonne's coming here was right; she felt it in her bones. She smiled. "I have some boxes to unpack in the back. Want to help?"

For the first time, he smiled, showing yellowed teeth and something else—the thinnest sheen of hope in his brown eyes. Eve felt a pang for the boy, and the space between them wavered with a slithering blackness, and the knowing grew stronger until she saw Heff, chest caving inward, body twisting unnaturally until flesh and bone had been ground into dust and there was nothing left. What did Heff have to do with Antonne? A rock sank deep into her stomach. It must be connected.

Her skin went cold, and her hands started to shake; she shoved them into her pockets. Her mother had thought that when Eve died, she'd go to hell. But kids like Joshua and Antonne were living through their own private hells right here on Earth. Eve would help—there was no turning back—but at what cost to the people she loved?

CHAPTER TWENTY-THREE

VEGA

Vega sat on the floor by the radiator, turning the key to open the valve, cloth beneath to catch any spurting water. It hissed, the escaping air a sure sign that it had been trapped inside. When she was done, she turned the heat back on and waited for the unit to warm up. It was midmorning and Riley had been hanging out in his pack 'n play, fingers grasping the pink cloth pigs that hung below a mobile. She sat back on her heels, pleased with the work, making a mental list of other items she might need for the projects lined up.

Downstairs, she heard Eve moving around the store, the hum of voices, and the slam of the door when people left. The portable crib jiggled, and Riley started to cry in little fits and starts, until he let loose with a loud wail. She picked him up, rocked him gently. "I know, buddy. Carl's right—life's just hard sometimes, isn't it?"

His fists grabbed at her skin and hair, and she quickly made him a bottle, sat down on the couch while he ate, and stared out the window, chewing on her lip. When she left Denver, she'd imagined coming here to regroup, see what she could find out about her mother before leaving for a different town. Staying in one place felt dangerous. But she'd rapidly grown comfortable, the faces familiar, a routine of work and having others help her with Riley making her feel like she belonged. Did she really want to be on the run forever?

The bottle emptied and Vega put Riley up on her shoulder to coax a burp. Since Riley was born, Zach had become distant, rolling over in bed when Riley cried, handing her a diaper and the baby if he thought he needed to be changed. Complaining about the noise, the smell, the cost of diapers and formula. Irritated that Vega had failed at breastfeeding, bringing it up often enough until Vega, too, felt like she'd fallen short. Did Zach really want his son back? Or was it only bluster, a show put on to make him look like a victim to his friends and family? Maybe she'd check her phone one more time, read his messages.

There had been an intimate moment just before Riley was born. They didn't have many of those. Zach worked late and often hung with friends, staying out until after Vega had gone to bed. She knew something was wrong, but she didn't have the words to say what it was. Or anything normal to compare it to.

But on this night, he'd come home early and suggested they watch a movie together. She'd felt her heart jump; small overtures like this were all it took to make her think she was happy.

They'd been spooning on the couch, watching a movie, Zach's hand on her protruding belly. She felt his chest shaking behind her, and she'd turned to see his eyes glistening. *I don't think I'll be a good dad.*

She'd pushed to sitting, turned to face him, empathy in every beat of her heart. *Same. My mom was such a good mom, and I don't think I'll ever measure up.* She'd touched his cheek. *I know how much you love your dad, and you'll be just like him. I know it.*

The vulnerable light in his eyes extinguished, and he sat up, pushing her hand off him. *Are you stupid? My dad is a piece of shit who makes everyone around him feel like a piece of shit too. I don't want to be anything like him.*

She hadn't known what to say, so she moved to the other end of the couch and tucked her feet under her, pushed play on the movie. He'd walked out of the room, slammed their bedroom door shut. It had happened before, the way he pivoted from adoration to hateful words and actions. Her face felt like stone, but inside she'd been an animal trapped in a cage, and she'd had no idea how to unlock the door.

She hadn't turned her phone back on, afraid of what she might find. Afraid he'd find her. But she couldn't help wanting to see if he'd written to her, maybe come to his senses, maybe even apologized and owned up to what he'd done. In her heart she knew it was a foolish wish. But she couldn't quash the small part of her that wanted to believe he was the guy she'd met on a trail. The one who'd seemed kind and funny. Not the kind of guy who would punch his girlfriend in the stomach.

A few minutes later she left the apartment with Riley strapped to her chest in the carrier, feeling a grim determination in the squeeze of her palm around the phone. A kid stood behind the counter, taking fishing gear out of a box. He looked up when Vega walked in, face guarded, and Vega noticed how his body curved inward, like he was already protecting himself from a blow. Eve appeared from the back room, smiling when she saw Vega. "This is Antonne; he's my new employee."

Vega took in Antonne's wrinkled, ill-fitting, and dirty clothes. He looked like he'd just come in off the street. Another misfit that Eve had taken in. A collector of lost souls. The thought brought on a rush of tenderness toward the woman. Like her mother, although Renee had been more like a guardian of lost souls. She and Eve would have made a formidable team. Vega's chest ached to feel her mother's arms strong around her, the impossibility of it breaking off a piece of her every time.

Eve set a coffee mug on the counter, filled it to the brim. Vega noticed black liquid trickling down the side of the cup. Eve's cheeks were pale, her normal confidence, her easygoing manner today a mask.

She thought about their conversation yesterday, Eve's belief that her vision had to do with Riley. Did Vega believe her? She wasn't sure.

While Eve showed her new employee how to take inventory, Vega powered on her phone and connected to Eve's Wi-Fi. Her hands shook, nervous of what she might find. She looked up. Antonne and Eve were in the back. Before she had time to let her nerves win, she opened Snapchat. There were hundreds of messages from Zach. Her heart thumped against Riley's body. The phone buzzed repeatedly in her palm, texts and Instagram messages downloading. Vega's throat went dry, the assault of messages a visceral reminder that nothing had changed—she was just hiding from the truth.

She pulled up a Denver news site, waited for it to load. She'd turned Riley so that he faced outward; he sucked on the edge of the carrier, his toothless gums soaking the cloth. She kissed the top of his head, inhaled. He smelled sweet with a hint of sour from the formula.

The site finally popped up. A hit-and-run, an overnight murder, a house fire, an Amber Alert. Her heart stopped, face turned numb, and the screen shook so badly she almost couldn't read it.

> A statewide Amber Alert has been issued on behalf of the Lakewood Police Department for Riley Jones. Riley is a 2-month-old white male with brown hair and blue eyes. Riley was last seen wearing blue zip-up pajamas with elephants. Riley was last known to be in the area of Goodland, Kan., with his mother, Vega Jones. If you have seen Riley or have information regarding his whereabouts . . .

Vega dropped the phone; it clattered onto the counter. She couldn't breathe.

The door burst open and two men barged inside, guns strapped to their thighs. Vega froze, her mind spinning with the Amber Alert, Zach's messages, and now these men. Her throat went dry. She stood, arms wrapped around her son, and felt her heart thump against Riley's back.

From the back of the store, Eve appeared, her face a mask of calm, as though she'd been expecting the armed men. A man with a cane hobbled in after them, and behind him strode JJ and his cousin. It was too much at once, and Vega felt her vision dim like she might pass out. She filled her lungs, balled her hands into fists, and willed herself to keep it together.

Oxygen tubing ran from the old man's nose to a metal canister slung around his shoulder. His skin was papery white. "Where's my grandson, Ethan?" he said.

Vega's body tensed. She stared at Eve. Ethan? Was this Betty's Ethan? The boy from the picture?

Eve sighed, stepped around the counter, giving Vega a quick glance before turning to face the men. Vega pressed her lips together, angry at the man for talking to Eve like that, empathy for the woman spreading through her chest. Fragments of information pulled together. Eve's near-death experience had happened when she was a kid. Vega pressed a palm against her cheek, thinking of all that Eve had been through alone. It swirled together with the idea that Zach had put out an Amber Alert after what he'd done. She pressed her teeth into her tongue, eyed the guns, and tried to balance a rising sense of panic against her stinging anger.

The tip of the old man's cane wobbled on the floor. She looked at him closer, recognized him as the man who'd stood in Tera's doorway. Levi Harrison. JJ and his cousin flanked the old man, knives fastened to belt loops on their jeans. JJ grinned at her, and Vega pressed her lips into a thin line, her heart racing, hating how vulnerable she felt. She measured the distance between her and the safety outside the store, desperate to get her son away from even more violence.

Her eyes burned with anger and fear and a helplessness that froze her in place. Zach got to be the good guy, the pained parent who'd lost his baby. And these men the righteous vigilantes convinced of their own moral high ground. The unfairness, the injustice, of it raced across her skin, pounded against her chest, and she stood, one arm around Riley in a protective grip, the other one reaching for her pepper spray. A seething rage spread like black ink over everything.

She'd stop them. Or at least she'd try.

CHAPTER TWENTY-FOUR

July 1995

The sun burned through the leaves, hot, humid, turning the bus into a sauna. Donna sat in the very front seat, hair stuck to the back of her neck, T-shirt damp with sweat. Flies buzzed loud in the grass outside. She stared straight ahead, a few things stuffed into a small cloth bag in her hands—everything that Betty had given her because Donna had nothing.

She wiped a hand across her forehead. Dry sobs bubbled up from her chest every time she thought about Ethan. She shouldn't have said those things. Shouldn't have pushed him away like that. He'd only been nice to her. But anger grew like a weed inside her heart, sprouting tendrils that twisted through her body. Toward men like her father and men like Levi Harrison, who hurt people because they were stronger and thought they had some God-given right. She felt it like a steel cage around her heart, and she'd let it rile her up, say mean things to Ethan.

There was no going back home now. Not when she'd experienced kindness, a glimpse of a different kind of life. Not that Ethan's was picture-book, but he wasn't what she'd expected. Same with Betty. It was enough for Donna to dream that she could choose her own future.

Her sneakers tapped the bus floor, crunching dead leaves, fingers doing the same on the cracked seat. She was ready to go. And now would be a good time because it was a Wednesday. Her dad should be out working, her momma getting supper ready, and Beth playing quietly by herself in her room. After watching her beat their father over the head with a rock, Beth might not want to go with Donna at first, but when she was old enough, she'd understand what Donna had saved her from.

In her head, it was all planned out, but Donna didn't move. The bus, while hot as heck, felt safe. Beyond this enclave—out where people like her father roamed free, hurting whoever he pleased—Donna was nothing. Where would she go? How would she survive alone? And with a little kid?

She started to cry. But the coolness on her cheeks was a traitor to her strength, and she rubbed hard at her eyes. *Stop it.* She hit the bus wall with the side of her fist; a sting lanced her skin. She hit it again, harder this time. Over and over until her hand went numb.

"Donna?"

Her fist stopped in midair. Ethan stood at the top of the steps, looking at her like she was a pathetic lost dog. She hit the bus wall again, noticed a warmth running down her wrist. Hit it again and heard Ethan make a noise. Then he was sliding into the seat next to her, putting his arm around her while she cradled her throbbing hand against her chest and cried.

"It's okay," he said, his voice low and soothing against her hair. "It's okay."

It helped. Her tears dried and she sat up and away from him. He grabbed an old rag and wound it around her fist. "You really messed that up. We should go see Betty. She'll take care of it, make sure it doesn't get infected."

Donna nodded and together they left the bus, taking a trail away from the road and farther into the woods. Her tennis shoes slipped on the soft ground, and sweat from the steep incline clung to the backs of her knees. Just when she started to think that Ethan had gotten them both lost, a cabin appeared. They approached it from the back, where there was a small garden with a chicken coop and a couple of goats. Wind chimes hung from the back porch, and mirrors in the garden caught the sunshine; hundreds of floating reflections danced among the plants.

The screen door opened and Betty walked out, wiping her hands on the bright-pink apron she wore over her shirt and jeans. "A visit from the wayward young'uns. What a pleasure."

Ethan laughed. "It's Saturday."

"Buckeye day, of course." Betty frowned at Donna's hand. "Come on in. Looks like your hand needs tending to. Carl's down at the market, sellin' his paintings." She shook her head. "That man might look like a coal miner, but he's an artist at heart."

From the yard came the sound of metal slamming against metal. Donna turned to see a girl about her age with silky blonde hair that hung to her waist and long tanned legs spilling from ragged jean shorts. She stood in front of a two-door car, wiping her hands on an oil-stained cloth. She eyed Donna, chewing gum, her face guarded, suspicious. "Who's she?"

Donna broadened her shoulders, stood closer to Ethan until their arms touched. "Who're you?" she said.

Ethan sighed and Betty laughed. "When you girls get done showing off your feathers, come inside." The screen door closed behind her.

The girl with the blonde hair threw the rag into a basket of similar-looking scraps and approached. Her light-green eyes glowed inside thick black eyeliner. She wore a pink tank top that showed her long muscular arms and ample chest. Donna crossed her arms, suddenly embarrassed by her nonexistent boobs. The girl's face softened when she looked at Ethan. The tips of Donna's ears burned; was this Ethan's girlfriend?

"She that girl I been hearing 'bout at church?"

"Yeah, but don't you say anything," Ethan said.

"Your daddy's got all 'a Crystal lookin' for you," the girl said. She lifted one side of her mouth in a sneer. "You must be a real daddy's girl, huh?"

Donna's injured fist shot out, and she punched the girl in the face. It wasn't a hard hit; she lost some momentum in her swing, and the shock of her knuckles hitting the girl's bony jaw lessened the impact.

The girl's eyes went wide, and she turned into a wildcat. She pounced on Donna, so fast she hardly saw the girl move. Donna was flat on her back, the girl straddling her and punching her hard in the face. Ethan grabbed the girl with both arms around her waist, somehow lifting her off Donna. She kicked her legs in the air like she'd go back for more the moment Ethan released her. Donna scrambled to her feet, fists out, injured hand burning, hoping to God the girl wouldn't pounce again.

She jerked out of Ethan's grip, wiped grass from her knees and hands, sneered at Donna. "You punch like a girl."

Donna worked her jaw, which had grown stiff from the fresh assault. "And you don't hit hard enough to tickle."

Ethan stepped between the two of them, held a hand out to either girl like he'd tackle them himself if they made a move toward the other. "Done?"

Donna nodded; so did the other girl.

She gave Donna a side smile. "I'm Tera."

"Donna."

Ethan lowered his hands, turned to Tera. "Working on Betty's car?"

"Just changing the oil."

"How's your car coming along?"

"Good. Soon as it's done, I'm driving as fast as I can away from this hellhole."

"Amen," Donna said, and Tera grinned at her.

Inside, Betty sat Donna at the table, disinfected and bandaged her hand. Wrapped ice in dishcloths for their faces. Then she set a mixing bowl in front of them and walked them through each step of her buckeye-cookie recipe. Donna's favorite part was dipping the peanut-buttery dough into the melted chocolate, because afterward she got to lick her fingers. Tera dabbed chocolate on Ethan's nose, and when Donna accidentally dropped a ball of dough onto the floor, Betty's dog zoomed over and snagged it before she could pick it back up. They laughed. It all felt so normal, like something she should have experienced before now. With the richness of chocolate in the air, the cozy warmth of Betty's kitchen, and Ethan and Tera sneaking dough when Betty wasn't looking, it was exactly how Donna had pictured a family.

Tera had tattoos up and down her arms, and Donna secretly tried to study them, fascinated that someone her age had done that to their body. She liked the idea of ink in her skin, erasing the imprints of her father's fingertips. "Your tattoos are cool." There was a tribal band around one bicep and what looked like a flower but was more of a blob spreading across her forearm.

Tera held out both arms. "I know, it's awesome, ain't it? My cousin wants to be a tattoo artist, so I let her practice on me and I get free tattoos." She touched a barbed-wire bracelet circling her wrist. "Did this one on my own."

Donna's eyes widened. "Really? That's so cool."

"Or dangerous and prone to infection," Ethan said.

Both girls rolled their eyes.

"I can give you one, too, if you want." She flipped her blonde hair behind one shoulder, seeming years older than Donna, who felt young and inexperienced around the girl. "It's just a sewing needle and ink—nothing big. But if you want one, I'll do it."

"Really?" She pictured her wrist with the ink permanently embedded in her skin. She felt like a badass just imagining it. "Yeah, totally."

"Cool. You staying at the bus?"

Donna looked at Ethan, who just nodded. If he trusted Tera, then so could she. "Yeah, me and some nasty raccoon."

Betty slid the cookies into the refrigerator to cool. Tera popped out of her chair. "I gotta go."

"Don't you want a cookie?" Donna said.

"Nah, I get them whenever I want. I'm here all the time. You eat 'em."

The lightness from the afternoon faded, and Donna felt cold, reminded that this wasn't her home. These weren't her friends. Tera waved and left. The goats bleated at her when she crossed the yard, and then she was gone, disappearing into the woods.

Betty poured them both a glass of milk. "Heard you had a run-in with Levi yesterday."

"Yes, ma'am," Ethan said.

"Heard I tole you 'bout some girl who ran off to Cincinnati after a boy." Betty gave Donna a sideways glance. "Seems I was mistaken."

Ethan ducked his head. "Levi had us in a spot. Sorry for lying."

"Oh, no matter." Betty started washing out one of the bowls. "You be careful. Levi's got it in his head he's the king of morals when it comes to Crystal." She looked at Donna. "Your daddy's convincing everyone in town that he's just all broke up over you running off. Says your momma can't leave the house, given her broken heart." Betty stood on her tiptoes to return the clean bowl to a shelf above the counter. Donna jumped to her feet, took it from her, and set it on the shelf, nesting the other one inside. "Thank you," Betty said.

"I'll be careful," Donna said.

Betty eyed her. "You still planning on headin' west?"

"Yes, ma'am."

"Carl talk to you 'bout workin' with your hands?"

"Yes, ma'am."

"Good. You got to have a plan if you're gonna make it on your own."

Donna blinked, overcome with how much Betty cared.

When they left, Betty waved goodbye from the house, and something tugged at Donna's chest. If she could choose her family, she'd choose them.

But staying wasn't a choice, and her sister needed her.

CHAPTER TWENTY-FIVE

Eve

May 2021

"Where's my grandson, Ethan?" Levi Harrison repeated the question.

Eve took a moment before answering Levi to let her heartbeat slow. She glanced at Vega; Riley sucked on the edge of his carrier, making a ring of darker black with his slobber. He stared in Levi's direction, no fear or awareness of the danger reflected on his sweet face. Eve's throat tightened and she felt the danger in her bones; the room had gone electric, and Levi was the powder keg.

The man had one way of looking at the world, one view of what was right and wrong, and Eve knew that he would die very soon having never really experienced what it meant to be alive. The thing that struck her was that the man was genuinely worried about his grandson, and that gave Eve pause. As did his two sons and grandsons, who stood like goon bookends on either side of the patriarch, fingers tapping their holstered guns.

Eve was at a loss. Joshua deserved the chance to choose his own future, not be forced back to his old life at gunpoint. She pressed her fingernails into her palms. Could she get Vega and the baby and Antonne out of harm's way? Try to deal with Levi on her own? The way JJ stared at Vega raised goose bumps along Eve's arms. She had to get them to safety, but she had no idea how she was going to do it.

From behind Levi, the door opened again; Tera walked inside and the air immediately changed, like her presence dampened the spark of violence. Eve felt it in the way her lungs inflated and in a knowing that wrapped itself around her. It was good that her old friend was here.

Tera spared Eve a quick glance. It had been a shock to see her the other day with Vega. The years had not worn kindly on the woman, turning her once-beautiful blonde hair a brassy shade of yellow, roots a solid inch of white. A lifetime of smoking had taken her youthful smile, compressed it into thin lips and wrinkled skin. She might look different, but a familiar warmth had returned the minute Eve saw her. For all her faults, Tera had been a good friend.

"Daddy, what're you doin' here?" she said, not looking at Eve.

Levi turned. "What *you* should be doing. Lookin' for Joshua."

There was a time when Tera had been terrified of her father. She'd told Eve, back when they were just kids and playing hide-and-go-seek in the woods. She'd been the one to show Eve the underground mine, said it was the place she went to when things at home were bad. She'd scream everything she hated about her family into the mine. But Tera was here now, and that could only mean she wanted to help.

"I told you that Joshua went to stay with a friend." Her eyes blazed and Eve loved seeing the fire in her. It had been smothered by her criminal husband, quashed by poverty and missed opportunity, but it wasn't gone. "He ain't missin'."

"That's not what his brother thinks." His lip curled when he looked at her. "You have a soft spot for faggots, and you coddled him into thinking he was one. Boy needs a man in his life."

"Yeah, Momma, you baby him," JJ added.

Tera reached up and slapped JJ upside the head. "Don't you back talk me, son. I don't care how old you are."

JJ ducked his head, took a step back.

A stool scraped across the wood floor. "What the hell is wrong with you?" Vega's voice from behind her, shaking with an unleashed anger.

Eve made a soothing noise in her throat like she might with one of her animals, hoping it would work on the woman. But Vega didn't spare her a glance, her eyes glued to Levi.

Eve wished she had the luxury to let her anger out like that. She thought of how the woman had pepper-sprayed JJ to get him to stop hurting her pigs, and she suspected that reaction came from the same fiery place as this. She marveled at how Vega seemed incapable of keeping quiet when she saw something wrong. Eve respected her for it, even if she sensed it simmered underneath, stoked by her situation, fed by regret of being with someone who had tried to intimidate her.

Tera glared at Vega like she wanted to throttle the girl, and Eve stiffened at the tension rebuilding in the space around them.

"What's wrong with *me*, girlie?" Levi said, using his cane to take a shaking step toward her. His face turned red. "This ain't none of your business."

It seemed to be all he had left, because his cane skittered across the floor and he started to tumble forward. His sons' hands retreated from their guns long enough to grab Levi's skinny forearms. As soon as he was righted, he shook them off and locked eyes with Eve. She kept her gaze steady, even if her insides had turned to Jell-O. She didn't want this to go sideways, didn't want anybody to get hurt.

"If I find out you had anything to do with my boy leaving, you're a dead man, Ethan." Spittle shot from his mouth, landing on his chin, where it caught the overhead light.

"Wrong, Levi," Eve said, a voice inside screaming at her to shut up. "I'll be a dead woman. But I've been there and back, so what's left, huh?"

From behind her, Vega erupted, laughing darkly, and it seemed to startle the baby, because he gave a loud wail that tingled Eve's eardrums. She stepped toward Vega and Riley, ready to do whatever she needed to protect them. Tera's nostrils flared and she flung her hands out like she might drag her father from the store herself.

Levi pressed his lips together so tight they went gray. His pant legs trembled, and Eve wondered how he kept himself upright. If he had the strength, she had no doubt he'd have punched her by now. As it was, he was a pathetic shadow of the man who used to haunt her dreams.

One of his boys reached for his gun, unclipping it from its holster.

Eve's arm shot out to cover Riley and Vega, the way her mom would do when she had to slam on the brakes. As though her mother could keep Eve's head from bashing against the dashboard. As if Eve's arm could stop a bullet.

Tera stared at Eve, unsmiling, tough as ever, but something softened in her eyes, and for a second Eve glimpsed the blonde girl who'd hidden Eve in the bathroom when her brothers were out for blood. The girl who'd learned how to fix an engine so she could drive far away. The girl who'd gotten stuck and never left. "Daddy, this is a family matter. Please tell my idiot brother to put his gun away before he does something stupider than him."

Her request was met with silence, and the air thickened with the threat of their guns. Eve stood in front of Vega. Riley's cries bounced off the tile floors, growing louder in volume, and it seemed to be the only thing to break the moment.

Levi blinked, as if just now realizing there was a baby in the store. "Put the gun away, boy." The man did as he was told.

Tension leaked from the room and Eve's shoulders slumped with relief. She felt Vega's hand touch the back of her arm.

"I'll find out one way or another if you've stolen my grandson. You're a sick man, Ethan. I'll come for you."

Blackness, like a thick blanket, settled across Levi's shoulders, swallowing him whole. She could have told him that he'd be dead before that happened. But she wasn't cruel, and very soon Levi would understand everything. In some ways, she envied him. Death had made sense of all the pain and anguish, the love and hope, squishing everything into a ball that she could hold in her hand. The details were still brightly colored and clear, but the feeling of death was something that slipped away, hard to grasp, always just out of reach.

They left, taking the air in the store with them, and Eve sank onto one of the barstools. Vega was by her side, hand on her back. "Are you okay?"

She waited for the oxygen to inflate her lungs, nodded.

"I'll go check on Antonne," Vega said, and disappeared into the back of the store.

The boy must have hidden when the Harrisons came in. Smart kid.

The door banged open and Eve tensed, but it was just Heff, eyes wide, hair sticking up like he'd been caught in a gust of wind. He came straight to her. "I heard the Harrisons are out for blood. That's it. I'm tired of them thinking they run this town." His hands were in fists and he looked ready to chase after them.

Eve leaned over the counter, assaulted by information, panic tangling it all into a knot. The Harrisons would find out. They would come for her. And Heff would stand in their way. She grasped his arm. She would never go back on her word; these kids deserved a place where they could feel safe, a place where they could be themselves away from the judgment, the opinions, the fear of the rest of the world. If there was some purpose she was meant to fill, she knew in her heart it was this.

But she wouldn't let Heff be a sacrifice for her plans. "Don't you dare go after them, Heff. Tera's got more control over JJ than you might think. Going after him will only make this worse."

Heff relaxed his hands, crossed his arms. "I don't like it, Eve."

"I know. You're a good friend, Heff." A pressure built inside her chest, and she couldn't keep it inside any longer. "I've started something I can't stop, Heff, and because of it something bad is going to happen," she said. "You're going to—"

"Eve!" He held his hands over his ears like a toddler. "Isn't there some kind of HIPAA law about this?" he said loudly. "How many times do I have to tell you? I don't want to know." Anger soaked his words, and that stopped Eve. In all the time she'd known him, anger wasn't an emotion Heff displayed much.

She took his hands from his ears. "You're a ridiculous man."

"Because I want to die on my own terms?"

"But what if I know something that can help you avoid an unnecessary death?"

Heff looked at her. "When you died, did you want to come back?"

"Not at first."

"Then why did you?" He could be a very annoying man.

"Because it wasn't my time yet."

Heff wagged a finger at her. "Exactly. If it's not my time, I'll come back, and you and I can form a 'We Died This One Time' club. If it's my time, then it's my time, and I don't want to mess with it. Got it?" She nodded. "Besides, what if I go out in a blaze of glory? What if it's doing something amazing, saving someone, or standing up for someone who needs it? That sounds like a great way to die, if you ask me."

She slumped over the counter, tired and feeling a tad more emotional than usual.

"Eve?" There was concern in Heff's voice.

"I'm fine."

"Are you sure?" This time it was Vega. She patted Eve's back. "That guy's a real jerk, huh?"

"Heff?" Eve said. "Always has been."

Heff snorted.

The woman was staring at Eve, and Eve thought she looked pale, unsettled. "So you're, um, you're the kid, Ethan? Betty told me a little bit about you. And Joshua too. Are you the one who was beaten to a pulp out by the bus?"

"The one and only."

"Wow." Vega leaned against the counter, and Riley smiled at Eve over the rim of his carrier.

Eve couldn't help but smile at him, touch the dimples across the back of his little hand with her finger.

"Was it Levi who did that to you?" There was anger in the woman's voice.

Eve felt her smile droop, the tension from the last few minutes wobbling above them, and she couldn't shake the feeling that everything was about to fall on top of her. Like a movie on repeat, her vision of the girl under the bed played in the back of her mind, taunting her with answers that made no sense. She dug her fingernails into her thighs. What good were these gifts if she couldn't use them to help the people important to her? "No, Levi didn't kill me. But he certainly never helped me either."

A buzzing sounded from Vega's bag, and the girl pulled a phone out, looked at the screen, stiffened. "I-I have to go." She hurried from the store, head down and focused on her phone.

Goose bumps scurried up Eve's arms and her breath stuck in her chest. She felt the crack of fists against her skull, the squish of her flesh beneath knuckles, the last memories Eve held of her life before, and they scurried after Vega. She shook her head to clear the dark thoughts, watched the girl disappear outside. "Heff, I promise I won't tell you anything you don't want to hear."

"Okay."

"But I'm going to tell you something I shouldn't. She's in even more danger than the rest of us."

Heff rubbed his chin with one hand, worry in the lines around his mouth. "It's a good thing she's here, then."

Eve nodded. "There's a reason she's here."

Keep my baby safe. The words echoed in her head. Eve wanted to keep everyone safe. But if death had shown her nothing else, it had taught her that it was impossible to keep bad things from happening.

CHAPTER TWENTY-SIX

VEGA

She closed her apartment door, locking it behind her, and leaned her back against it with her arms around her son, legs trembling. In Riley's short life, it seemed all she'd done was put him in one dangerous situation after another. She pressed the heels of her hands against her eyes. And talking to Levi like that? What was wrong with her? She put Riley in the pack 'n play and sat on the floor, phone in her hand. It taunted her, somehow holding on to a weak connection to Eve's Wi-Fi in the store, and Zach's messages littered the screen, a ping-pong of conflicting sentiments.

Don't hurt my son.

You fucking bitch.

Come home, babe, please. We can work this out.

I'm sorry, I really am. It'll never happen again.

Is Riley okay? Are you?

Her hands shook. The thought of someone taking Riley so she'd never see him again made her stomach cramp. She sank to the floor. Zach had called the cops. Reported his child missing. Riley cooed and she peered into the pack 'n play. He had rolled to his side, arms straight out in front of him. He needed to see a pediatrician, probably needed more shots. She touched the netting where his foot pushed against it. What kind of mother was she really? Her mother had always told women to leave. She didn't think staying was safe. But Vega had often wondered if a bad situation could be fixed. Had argued about it with her mom once. *Don't you think people can change?* Renee had gone quiet, and Vega recoiled at the pain in her mother's eyes.

I don't know.

It had surprised her to hear Renee's uncertainty. Her acknowledgment was the first time Vega realized there was a lot Renee didn't know about people.

And now Vega realized how little she knew too. Could Zach change? The past few days away made her question herself, her decision to run. Should she have tried harder with Zach? Suggested counseling? Gotten help for the both of them?

Guilt battled with her anger, made it soft and less substantial. She grabbed her phone and snapped a picture of Riley; he stared right at the camera, eyes a bottomless blue, toothless grin, skin pink and flawless. And sent it to Zach. He's fine.

Immediately she powered the phone off and tossed it into her bag. Had she done the right thing by leaving, or was she the bad guy? The bruises on her wrist were healing, her stomach less tender, but the cruel twist of his lips, the flash of cold rage in his eyes before he assaulted her remained. Her mother's voice: *There are some men you run from.* And Vega shook her head. There was no way she'd stay with someone who could do that to her. And no way she'd let Riley be raised by him either.

She thought of everything Eve had gone through. Dying because of hate; coming back and having to endure the stares, the opinions, the judgments because her choice to live life on her own terms scared and angered people. Vega felt Eve's strength like a gravitational pull that tugged at her, made her want to know the woman, to be around her more.

She wiped her face, tried to smile at Riley, who cooed at the mobile, laughed at the tiny stuffed piglets. She'd drive out to the bigger hardware store in Athens, get what she needed to fix Eve's faucet, and repair the drywall in the apartment. Staying busy was the key to keeping her mind off the things she couldn't control. Like Zach.

~

It was dark by the time she headed back to Crystal from the hardware store. The van rounded the curves like a cement box on wheels, so she took her time, despite the darkness of the night that blurred the woods and made her want to get home faster. Riley had gone quiet in his car seat, the turns and pitted road lulling him to sleep. Her hands squeezed the steering wheel, and thoughts of her mother joined her in the van.

The night bled into a Colorado fall day, Renee beside her in the passenger seat, framed by flaming red and gold aspens. They were going to the mountains to see the fall color. Vega had suggested it; at first, Renee had resisted, saying they should either land another job or move on to New Mexico for a few weeks, not go sightseeing. But Vega had insisted. All they ever did was work, and she was nineteen, young, desperate to experience a life that wasn't always on wheels.

Vega had tried to get Renee to see her point, tried to win her over to the idea of staying put for a while. She hadn't wanted to do it alone. Maybe she was codependent, scared of what the world looked like without her mother, but Vega had hoped Renee would take to the idea and join her. So she kept trying, even if Renee's response was always the same.

I think we should stay here for a while, Mom.

Renee had stared out the window without responding. She wasn't a woman prone to emotional outbursts. She was a strong boat that never wavered, regardless of how rough the seas. But when she slept, she had nightmares. Ones that woke Vega with her screams and tortured cries and had her crawling out of the tent she'd bought with her own money when she was seventeen and into the van, where her mother slept. She'd brush sweat-dampened hair from Renee's face and stay by her side until she quieted and the dream had passed.

Renee had sighed and spoken to the trees moving past: *Life is best lived in motion.*

It was the same thing she'd said every time Vega brought up the idea of staying in one place for longer than a month or two. But Renee never opened it up to discussion. She'd had a confidence and determination in everything she did. She never doubted that getting women away from men was always the right choice. Hers had been a dogged belief that left no room for questioning. Then again, they never stayed around long enough to know for sure. These women hadn't been friends; they'd been part of a job. Vega hadn't known the emotion that came through connection and friendships, or understood the nuances of a relationship that sprouted doubt and an irrational hope that love would make everything right.

The van's tires hit a pothole, jerking the vehicle to the right. Vega gripped the wheel.

There had been one time when Renee hadn't been so certain. After the woman with the clogged drain and Lars. She'd been quiet after that and drove the farthest east they'd ever been, to a farmhouse in Iowa that was surrounded by cornfields and a red barn, where they were serenaded by the clucks of chickens, the moos of dairy cows. It had felt like something out of a storybook.

A woman with straight brown hair and kind eyes pushed through the screen door, a smile spreading slowly. *Good Lord in Heaven, is that you, Renee? This far east of the Continental Divide? Must be the end of days.*

Renee had gone right up to the woman, whose smile faded slowly. She reached out, touched Renee's cheek, tilted her head to the side. *I'll put some coffee on.*

It was Gwynne. The one who helped women too. Vega had sat in the wood-paneled family room, watching cartoons while her mother and Gwynne drank coffee beyond the swinging door that led to the kitchen. There were pictures on the walls of Gwynne and her kids, later ones of Gwynne's grandkids—two babies and a toddler. The carpet was thick and brown. Vega squished it between her toes. The air smelled like vanilla and hay. She'd sneaked over and sat close to the door, arms around her shins, listening.

Her mother's voice, thick, shaky. *I don't think I can do this anymore. Then don't.*

They'd sat in silence, and Vega chewed on her lip, a swell of excitement rising in her chest. They could live here, in Iowa with Gwynne and all her family. Renee could raise animals; Vega would milk the cows. She'd get up super early, do anything if it meant staying in one place. If it meant having a real home.

Then her mother spoke, and it rained cold over Vega. *You know I won't ever quit. Too many lost souls out there to help.*

Like you?

Renee had sighed, laughed, and the next morning they were on the road by five, and Renee never spoke of it again. For a while, Vega nurtured a tiny bit of hope that they'd return to the farm and stay just like she'd dreamed. But they never did, and months later, when Vega asked when they'd visit Gwynne again, Renee shook her head and said what she always said: *Life is best lived in motion, V.*

The road curved sharply, and Vega took it too fast, felt the wheels kiss the pavement. She slowed, tears glued into the corners of her eyes.

Then her mother had died, leaving Vega alone, with no idea how to do it by herself. After letting Gwynne and the others know about her mother's passing, Vega had kept to herself instead of reaching out for help or support.

Sometimes she wished Renee had taught her more about living. Sometimes she wondered if her mother had ever actually lived herself.

A handful of lights sparkled inside the trees. She was getting close to Crystal, and it struck her with an unfamiliar feeling. Like she was coming home. In her short time here, she'd met people who easily accepted her into their community. She felt a pull to stay, but it battled with her uneasiness about Zach and gnawing questions about her mother: What had happened to make her want to keep moving her entire life? Was Vega making the same mistakes?

When she got to the edge of town, Vega saw Heff's truck parked in front of Eve's Place. He sat in the bed, long legs slung over the lowered tailgate—waiting in the dark, she realized, for her. Her stomach flip-flopped when she noticed the police car stopped on the road beside it. The police officer stood with his back to Vega's van, speaking to Heff. The air cemented in her lungs, and she didn't know if she should jerk the vehicle into a U-turn and floor it or park like it was an average night and she was just a normal girl coming back from the hardware store.

Her decision was made for her when the cop turned and watched her van roll down the road toward them. Vega cursed under her breath and parked beside Heff's truck, pulse hammering in her neck. She got out, left Riley buckled inside. He was asleep, anyway.

"You the one got mixed up with JJ?" The deputy was on the other side of middle-aged, gray hair with just a little bit of pepper left behind.

Vega lifted her chin, tried to get her heartbeat to calm. She felt like he'd just shined a giant spotlight on her. "'Mixed up'? The man was torturing an animal, and I stopped him."

The deputy squinted at her; then a smile cut through his serious demeanor, and he clapped his hands together. "Wish I could have been there to see the look on his face. Carl said you looked like some kind of avenging angel, but you're nothing but a wisp of a thing. And taking on JJ like that . . ." He shook his head, smiling, then looked back at Heff. "You keeping an eye on him? Can't imagine he'll let this type of thing go."

"Yes, sir."

Vega shifted her weight, surprised and touched that Heff had been helping her, uneasy that she was the focus of so much attention.

"Heard his momma's not happy with JJ's behavior," Heff said.

"Tera's been through some things, but she's a good woman," the deputy said. "Tough too. I'm sure she'll keep him in line as much as she can." He turned back to Vega. "Where's the baby I keep hearing all about? Carl tells me he's a real rascal."

Vega froze, thought of the Amber Alert. Was that something that would spread easily to Ohio? Could he have already seen it? A desire to run raced through her calves; Vega forced herself to smile. "He's sleeping in the van."

"Best not to wake a sleeping baby." He walked over to his car. "Be careful round here, okay? Have a good night, you two."

When his taillights disappeared, Vega felt the strength run out of her, and she leaned heavily against Heff's truck. "What are you—" She swallowed, tried to sound casual. "What're you doing here?"

"Just making my nightly rounds through town and thought I'd check in on you, see how you were after that scene at the store."

The day had become a blur with most of her thoughts on Zach. "I'm okay. I just can't understand why Eve would want to live around people like Levi and JJ." She hugged herself. JJ made Crystal dangerous in a way that worried her.

Heff leaned forward on his hands, swung his legs. "It's not easy, but people like that are fewer in number than you might think. Just louder than most."

Vega rubbed her arms. "Yeah, I guess."

There was a beat of silence, and she looked up to find Heff staring at her. "Is everything all right, Vega?"

Her immediate answer—to say yes, of course, everything was fine—stuck on her tongue. Heff was easygoing, friendly, willing to stick up and watch out for his friends and even a stranger like her. It made her want to tell him the truth. Sharing it with Eve had lifted a heaviness from her back, made her feel lighter than she had in months. She'd held so much inside, not even realizing herself the weight of the truth about Zach. That he was an abusive, manipulative, and controlling man who didn't love her the way he was supposed to. She pressed her arms into her stomach. She hadn't realized how heavy secrets could be. The thought burned her eyes with memories of her mom—the nightmares, the constant moving, her refusal to talk about her past. How heavy had her secrets been?

It felt like she'd approached a fork in the road. Vega could go down the path her mom had taken and spend her life letting the scars Zach had left behind drive all her decisions. Or she could forgive herself and move on, let herself trust others. Live.

She breathed in. "No," she said. "Everything's not okay."

The silence lengthened, but Vega didn't mind. It was comfortable. Her face warmed. Heff was nothing like Zach. The more she was around these people, the more she trusted her instincts.

From the van, Riley cried, and Vega brushed a piece of hair from her eye, smiled.

Heff held out a couple of silver cans. "Want to talk about it?"

"What's in the cans?"

He grinned. "Beer. It's just a hobby."

"You make your own?" She didn't wait for his answer. "Of course you do." She slid open the van door and picked up Riley's car seat.

"Is that a yes?"

Vega thought about it. The empty apartment, this quiet town, fear nipping at her heels with thoughts of the Amber Alert compounded by threats of JJ. A nagging sense that this was all temporary and soon she'd have to pack up and leave, keep on running just like her mother. She rubbed at her neck, felt uncertainty in the prickles across her skin, and waited for the feeling to ebb. For now, she could use a friend. "Come on up."

He picked up the beers and waited for her to lead the way to the apartment.

~

She left the door to her bedroom cracked open so she could hear Riley if he cried. Heff sat on a chair by the window; Vega chose the sofa. He'd opened one of the beers and poured the thick, dark liquid into two glasses. The mug was cool in her hand, and the beer smelled like oatmeal and whiskey. She took a sip—smoky but sweet. "That's good."

He raised his glass, took a long swallow. "Thanks. It's a new recipe. More like a stout-slash-spirits kind of beer, what with the whiskey flavor."

She hid her smile behind another sip.

Heff set his glass on the coffee table, leaned forward with his elbows on his knees. "You can talk to me, Vega. I know we hardly know each other, but I'm a good listener. And you seem like you need someone to listen."

She pulled at her fingers, head spinning with reasons she should keep her mouth shut. "Why were you at my apartment?"

He scratched his head. "Eve told me that you might be in a bit of trouble. And as the volunteer deputy of Crystal, I wanted to make sure you're safe. Town's pretty deserted after all the shops close."

She shifted on the couch, kicked off her shoes, and curled her feet up on the cushion, wary of his intentions yet touched that he cared enough to check up on her.

"Plus, I have a housewarming gift for you." From a small paper bag at his feet, he pulled a stack of what looked like coasters tied together with brown twine and handed it to Vega.

"Oh, thanks," she said, the tops of her cheeks warming.

"It's nothing, just a little something I give my clients when they close on a home." He ran a hand through his hair. "And as that hasn't happened yet, I've decided to give a set to any of my clients renting too."

She untied the twine, laid the coasters out side by side. Each one had been carved with the image of a phoenix rising from the ashes. She smiled at the familiar picture, impressed with the artistry of his carving. "These are really good."

Heff leaned forward in his chair. He seemed pleased. "It symbolizes new life. Fitting for someone starting out in a new home, isn't it?"

"I know about the phoenix." Her mother had had the image drawn onto one of her thighs, and Vega had loved the rich colors of the bird, the symbolism behind the image. It was what they gave the people they helped—a chance at a new life. "It was one of my first tattoos." She stood, lifting one side of her shirt to reveal the bird that wrapped around her side, ashes in blacks and grays along her hip. She let it fall quickly back into place, face burning, and slunk back onto the sofa. She was too comfortable with Heff. Too trusting. Had she learned nothing?

Heff sat back in his chair, unspeaking. "Oh," he said.

She sipped the beer. "What?"

"Before I understood that Eve had her future-predicting abilities, she told me that a phoenix would change my life. When I got into real estate, I thought it made sense because I'm all about helping folks start over."

Vega fidgeted, regretting inviting the man up. She was so naive, repeating the same pattern, trusting too quickly. She started to search for words to stop Heff from saying anything more. "It's a pretty common tattoo."

Heff just smiled. "Ever since you got into town, it feels like things are speeding up, coming together. I know how I sound, and I've probably just spent too much time with Eve. But the woman is right, most of the time. Maybe you're my phoenix."

"Oh, um." He looked so hopeful—happy, even—like she'd been the answer to a question on a game show. She squirmed, having no idea what to say. "I'm in no place to start anything." There was no denying that she found him attractive, and even sensed a spark of something between them, but she had so little experience outside of Zach, and she didn't trust herself. "I'm just—I'm sorry, you seem like a good man, but—" She tried to soften her words. "I just need to take care of Riley now." She tensed, already thinking of the exit behind Heff, the pepper spray in her bag, worried she'd offended him, hurt his feelings, angered him with her rejection.

He smiled. "We're friends, right?"

Heff and Eve were two of her first true friends. They knew more about her than even Zach had known. "Yes," she said.

"Then that's something."

She blinked, eyes burning at the simplicity of his kindness.

They sipped the dark liquid; Heff refilled both glasses, and in the quiet moments that followed, Vega emptied her glass. She suspected he could drink beer in silence with a person and never seem uncomfortable, but her stomach swam with indecision. The beer helped, a weighted blanket over her nervous energy. She ran a finger along the fading bruise on her wrist. "I took Riley from his father."

A few moments passed before Heff responded. Vega didn't mind the silence. "Seems to me like you had a good reason to do so," he said.

"He doesn't think that way."

"You did the right thing."

"How would you know?"

"Because men don't hurt women."

She thought of Riley, nodded. She'd make sure he would be nothing like Zach.

Heff took her glass, brought them both over to the sink, rinsed them out. Then he opened the other beer; this time, a hazy-orange liquid spilled out. He handed her a glass. "A hazy IPA. I bet you've had a taste of one of these before."

She nodded.

"Listen, Vega, I may not have magical powers like Eve, but I do know a thing or two about people. I can tell the good ones when I meet them."

She stayed silent, looked at her hands.

"So whatever mess you're in right now, I believe it was all for the right reasons. But around here, we like to help each other out. So let us help you, when you're ready or when you need it."

She thought of how her mother had turned to Gwynne when she'd been at her lowest point. Vega had always imagined her adult life would be full of friends. She'd never wanted to be as alone as her mom had been. And here, Heff and Eve, even Betty and Carl, offered her friendship and community. She sipped the beer, overwhelmed. "Thank you."

"Of course—but full disclosure, I'm also being a little bit selfish."

"How so?"

"Well, my friend," he said, "Crystal sparkles a bit more with you here."

It was sincere, said without a bit of sarcasm or self-serving swagger. She looked down at the beer, rolled the glass between her palms. "That's a nice thing to say." It sounded lame, but she was afraid anything else might lead him to think something more.

He washed out the glasses and threw away the cans while Vega stood in the middle of the apartment. What would her mother have thought about this man? She felt a pang wishing she could ask her. Maybe she would have liked him. Maybe not. Zach had certainly proved her mother right, but Vega couldn't help wanting to believe that there were good men too.

Heff stood. "I'd better get going."

He crossed the room to the door, his arm brushing her shoulder ever so lightly. Her stomach felt queasy in the good kind of way. Heff pulled a folded baseball hat from his pocket; it flattened his hair so that it stuck out over his ears. Then he smiled, saluted her with one finger from the brim of his hat.

Vega repeated the action, feeling ridiculous. Heff threw his head back and laughed like she was the funniest person in the room, then whistled all the way down the stairs and out the door to his truck.

Vega lay awake for hours that night—not because of Riley, who, for the first time, slept through most of the night. Because, she realized, she felt content. Like she could belong here. She thought of the bus in the woods and her mother, wishing she could have felt this way when she was here. Wondering what had made her miserable enough to leave.

CHAPTER TWENTY-SEVEN

July 1995

Donna dragged the mattress outside and lay down on it, staring up at the patches of blue sky. Flies buzzed a few feet above her head, moving the stagnant air with their tiny wings but not enough for her to feel it on her damp skin. She lay still, waiting for a breeze, a puff of air—anything that might cool her, if even for a second. The leaves were a deep green, thick and doing their part to keep the heat of the sun from drifting down to the bottom of the forest floor but also forcing the humidity to lie on top of her like an electric blanket. She fanned herself with an old church bulletin she'd found underneath one of the seats. It moved the air but didn't cool it.

She was bored. And so hot. And underneath it all grew an anxious fluttering in her stomach whenever she thought about Beth. When her sister was born, Donna knew she'd make everything better. She didn't know why, but something about a new life had seemed like a chance at a do-over. Maybe her dad would realize how sick and twisted and *wrong* he was. Maybe her mom would finally protect her.

She'd wake up early, sneak into the nursery, and hold Beth in the dark hours of the early morning. Her skin was pink and soft, her eyes round and alert, and Donna would sing her soft lullabies with lyrics that escaped her, so she'd hum or make up her own words. In those stolen moments—after her father's nightly visit, before the smell of her mother's homemade biscuits made the night before seem like a bad dream—Donna had pretended that Beth was her baby. She'd kiss her chubby cheeks, inhale her baby scent of lavender. *I'll never let him hurt you.*

Her plans to go out west were growing into a dream with edges and weight. She couldn't leave Beth, but the fear of going back home to take her crawled up and down her spine while she slept. It seemed impossible.

A thrashing sounded from the woods, and Donna scrambled to her feet, heart beating so fast it almost made a breeze of its own. Ethan wasn't coming today because he had some church thing to do with his parents, and Betty and Carl's dog bounded ahead of them, so she always knew when they were coming. She grabbed a stick, held it out in front of her like a sword. It was flimsy and light and would easily break, but it was something. Truth sank into the pit of her stomach. It was her father. He'd come for her. She searched the clearing, looking for something deadlier than a twig, another rock, a sharp piece of metal from the old bus. Her hand holding the stick shook.

"I'll kill you," she screamed into the woods.

A girlish cackle, then Tera jumped out of a copse of trees, hands curled into claws like she was an animal. "Boo!" she said.

Donna screamed and threw the stick at the girl, who looked like a wild animal with her hair in tangled knots, leaves stuck in the strands, white tank top grimy.

"Did you crawl all the way here?"

Tera brushed her hair with her fingers; it turned into shiny gold threads. "I'm not a half-asser." She laughed. "Oh my God, you shoulda seen your face." She returned to the trees, brought out a black shoulder bag. "And I stick to my word. I came to give you your first tattoo."

Nervous energy from Tera's unexpected visit pumped through Donna's thigh muscles. "That wasn't funny." She tried to sound tough.

Tera put a hand on her hip. "You want one or not?"

A jolt of excitement raced from Donna's heart and through her fingertips and toes. A tattoo meant she got to choose what she did with her body. It felt like she was taking a stand. "Hell yeah."

They sat outside the bus on a blanket. Tera opened the bag, took out a dish towel, and laid it on the ground between them; she added a sewing needle, a small vial of ink, and a container of petroleum jelly. "My cousin gave me the ink. I didn't steal it or nothing."

Donna didn't care one way or another, but it seemed important to Tera. "Okay," she said.

Tera took Donna's hand, turned it this way and that, as though surveying a canvas. Her blonde hair tented around her face, brushing along her tan thighs. It smelled like coconuts and soil. She opened the vial, poured some ink into the cap, and spread a bit of the jelly across the top of Donna's wrist. There was dirt in the creases of her palms. She held the needle in her right hand, placed Donna's wrist across her knee, met her gaze. "It's gonna take a long time, and it stings, but then your skin gets numb and it's not so bad. Ready?"

She thought of the number of times her father had touched her, the gentle caresses that curdled her stomach, the marks that were invisible to everyone except her. And she yearned to feel the sting of the needle sliding into her flesh, see the ink stain her skin black. Wanted to feel the pain and let it erase the dark memories of her father. Suddenly desperate to have every inch of her skin covered in ink, pictures of her own choosing.

"Hell yeah," she said again, and Tera smiled, dipping the tip of the needle into the ink. Two lines furrowed into the skin between her eyes.

The first poke felt like a tiny bite, but it was the beginning of her new life. It took hours and many sticks of the needle. Tera talked while she worked and Donna listened, enjoying the distraction.

"I've been workin' on an old car. Got a good frame, solid engine, even a workin' transmission. Just changing out some hoses, spark plugs, that kinda thing. Soon as it's solid I'm leaving."

Donna sucked in one side of her cheek. "Where you going?"

Tera shrugged. "Don't know yet. Just far away from this hellhole."

They were quiet for a while. Tera focused on working the needle in and out of Donna's skin. "I got a boyfriend now and we're having sex, so I better not get pregnant 'cause that'll screw up all my plans."

"Yeah," Donna said, looking down at her hands. "Um, how would you know you're pregnant, anyhow?" She liked to think she knew more than she did. But the truth was that she knew only what her mother had taught her and what her father did. She bit her lip—it was wrong, she knew that, but it didn't change how it made her feel. Like she was made of dirt.

Tera stopped her sticking, looked up. "You serious?" Donna didn't say anything, and Tera shifted position. "You have your Aunt Flo, right?"

"Huh?"

"Your period."

Donna smiled, thought the name was funny. "Oh yeah."

"Okay, so if that goes missing, you're pregnant."

"Oh."

Tera tugged at her hand, making Donna look up. "Has it gone missin'?"

Donna hadn't spoken to anyone this freely about anything to do with her body. Her mother had told her some things and then never spoken to her again. Mostly Donna had figured that what her body did was something to be ashamed of. But Tera didn't talk that way, and it made Donna relax. She wrinkled her forehead, tried to remember the last time she'd bled. "I don't think so."

"Good. You wanna keep it that way, else you'll end up like my cousin Sara."

"What happened to her?"

"Five kids and a lazy-ass husband who can't keep a job."

"Oh."

Tera kept working. The sun moved through the leaves, heating the ground wherever it touched. When Tera was finished, a breeze had kicked up, running sweet and cool over their sweat-stained bodies. Donna studied her wrist; the skin was red and irritated in places, the barbed-wire artwork crooked and blurred in spots, sloppy. She brought her wrist to her heart. "I love it."

Tera put away her supplies, leaned back on her hands with her chin tipped up to let the air flow across her face and neck. "It's addicting. Before you know it, you'll be covered in 'em. My cousin is." She crossed one leg over the other, jiggled her foot up and down. "It's so dang hot."

Donna was still staring at her tattoo. She already felt stronger, braver. She was going to take Beth and leave Ohio. And Donna would make sure that nothing bad ever happened to her sister. Her fingers twitched and a nervous energy crawled through her legs. "I need a cigarette," she said.

Tera rummaged through her bag. "I'm out."

"Shoot."

Tera hopped to her feet, started to pace. "I got some at home. Come on. I can show you that car I been workin' on. Maybe I'll drive us both outa this hellhole."

Donna wanted to roll into a ball when she thought of Levi—thin lips, cruel eyes, grabbing her arm at the store. She shook her head. "I don't think so. Your daddy—"

"—is an asshole. Yeah, I know. I live with him. But he ain't home today."

Donna still hesitated. The safe thing to do was to stay put. But she was restless, and she couldn't stay here forever. Tera and her car might be the only way she'd ever get out of Ohio.

Tera blew air through her lips. "You gonna live at the bus forever?"

Donna shook her head. A voice inside her heart gave a mean little laugh. She had no clue how she was actually going to leave. Deep down she was a coward. "Do we have to go through town?" She stared at her wrist as though the tattoo could give her strength. She'd never come into Crystal before she'd run off; her parents preferred their isolated homestead to town. It had seemed so far away, like another world.

Tera pulled her long blonde hair into a ponytail, making her biceps wriggle under her skin. "You afraid of your daddy?"

Donna nodded.

Tera's mouth softened. "We can go through some backyards, stay off Main Street." She stood. "I know how to avoid bullies."

Donna folded her arms across her stomach, tried to soak up some of Tera's bullheaded confidence. If she was going to get Beth away from her parents, she needed it. "Let's go."

~

She sat on the back of the bicycle with her legs sticking straight out, holding on to Tera's waist to balance and not fall off. Tera stood and pedaled; the bike wobbled and Donna laughed, her face cooled by the moving air. The sunlight filtered green through the leaves. When they got closer to town, they got off the bike and walked it through the grassy sections behind the buildings and before the ground sloped upward. It felt good to be out of the bus, and it buoyed her mood.

Tera talked, telling Donna tales about her grandma Harriet, who died three years earlier and haunted Tera's bedroom.

"Why you?"

"'Cause she don't want me having sex before I'm married."

"Oh. But aren't you?"

Tera gave her a look. "Ain't everyone? This place is so boring, what else we got to do?"

Voices drifted in from town and between the buildings. Donna noticed more people than usual, a few canopies and tables lining the road. Her feet stuck to the ground. "What's going on?"

Tera squinted. "That's nothin'," she said. "Just a market Carl started last year to sell his paintings and some food. Least, that's what Betty says. Guess other people are sellin' stuff now too."

With all the people around, Donna felt stupid. What had she been thinking? She turned around, stumbled.

"Where you goin'?" Tera called.

"I-I'm a dumbass for leaving the bus."

She walked quickly, heart pounding, and had almost reached the edge of town when she heard the voices. Cruel laughter, taunting words. The safe thing to do was ignore it and keep walking. Get back to the bus and away from so many people. She looked anyway, and her heart jumped into her throat. By the main street, on the side of one of the buildings, Ethan stood with his back pressed against the wall, two boys throwing rocks at him. One had hit his head, blood bright against his skin. Rage exploded in Donna's belly, and she wasn't thinking about herself anymore. She raced through the weeds, pulled up short when she reached the boys. Ethan stared at her, eyes wide, shaking his head like he wanted her to leave.

"Hey!" she yelled. "Leave him alone, you assholes!"

Tera caught up with her, blonde hair catching the sun when it swung around her shoulders, staring at the boys.

One boy turned, smiled when he took in Donna. She shivered. She recognized the look in his eyes—the hunger, the violence that knew no boundaries.

"Hey there, sweet thing. This ain't none of yo—"

She knelt down, scooped up a handful of dirt, and hurled it at the kid's face. "Run, Ethan!" she screamed and took off, the heavy footsteps of the boys on the pavement behind her. She hurtled down Main Street, past a woman selling cucumbers and tomatoes, past Carl and his paintings. No idea where she was going, already cursing herself for being so stupid. Her legs felt heavy, goose bumps rippling across her back. She was waiting for the boy to grab her shoulder, pull her down, hurt her.

"Donna!"

Her father's voice shrank her world to the size of the space beneath her bed. Fear fingered into her muscles, and the ground sucked at her feet, made it impossible to run. *Stupid, stupid Donna.*

"Stop, girl!" It was another man's voice.

A hand squeezed her arm, and Levi Harrison dragged her backward, spinning her around. His wrinkled mouth spread thin into a gloating smile. "Got her!"

Her father stood beside Levi with his feet planted, face hardly masking his rage. He grabbed her arm and started to yank her toward his car. The feel of him turned Donna's skin cold, and her body went limp. The woman with the tomatoes watched; a man walked by, eyes averted. She saw Carl in his uniform yellow suspenders walking toward them. "Hey!" he yelled, mustache twitching underneath round gold glasses. "Listen, Dan, I know she's your daughter, but let's sit down and talk. How about that?"

Her father ignored him and opened the car door, pushed her inside; she smashed her head on the frame, and a sharp pain bloomed in her skull. She bucked against her father. "No!" she screamed. "Help!" She gulped in air, heart racing so fast it left her squeezing air out of her lungs. She scanned the crowd. Saw Tera lingering back, head hanging, arms across her chest, looking small and scared.

Her father's face turned red, and his hand squeezed into a fist. But before she felt it crush the space between her cheekbone and jaw, a figure hurtled through the air and landed in front of her. Ethan. Her father's fist connected with Ethan's face instead, and Ethan crumpled to the ground. Her heart turned in on itself. Ethan was too skinny, too delicate to take on her dad. But he scrambled to his feet, fists up in front of his face, back hunched, feet planted, nothing of a boxer's wiry strength and agility—every inch her hero. "Leave her alone," he said.

Her father seemed taken off guard, his thick eyebrows raised—surprised, she knew, by the wisp of a boy standing between him and his daughter. Donna's chest hurt. Ethan was trying to protect her even if her father could break him in half.

Her face warmed. Nobody had ever stood up for her.

She dug her fingernails into her palms, lifted her chin, and met her father's eyes. She didn't want Ethan to get hurt again. Several people had gathered now, forming a loose semicircle around them. Carl stared at Ethan, hands out in front of him like he wanted to push the boy out of the way.

Her father lunged for Ethan, fists out, and Donna knew that he'd beat the crap out of him and not stop until someone pulled him off.

"My dad hurts me!"

Her voice shook, lost steam, and her body wilted, but it halted his attack. And when he looked at her, she saw something she'd never seen before: fear. Everyone was staring. She crossed her arms; she didn't want these people to know. Didn't want to expose herself to their judgment. But she couldn't let Ethan get hurt because of her.

"He-he does things he shouldn't. He touches me. He's b-bad."

Murmurs from the few people who were watching, disgust flickering in the eyes of Levi and everyone else. Tera had moved to the back of the crowd, hair covering her face.

Ethan craned his head to look at her, sympathy warm in his eyes.

Carl moved closer to her father, who stared at her, face slack from shock, she figured, because his daughter had dared to speak so publicly against him. It gave her a weak sense of power. "You'd better git, Dan," Carl said, and nobody disagreed.

Ethan pushed to his feet, blood red and dripping from his nose, over his lips, falling from his chin. He put his arm around her, moved her away from her father, who made no move to stop them. Together they walked away from the crowd, Carl behind them like a watchdog. Tera had disappeared. Donna's father slunk away, sliding into his car, and with a swish of the tail, drove off.

She leaned her weight into Ethan, and together they walked back to the bus.

CHAPTER TWENTY-EIGHT

EVE

May 2021

Eve was leaving for the day—a little earlier than normal, but with Antonne and Joshua at the farm, she felt a pull to go home. Antonne was, in fact, a very good cook, making hamburgers for the three of them last night with corn on the cob and potato crisps he made on the fire. He was quiet. Eve had no idea what kind of trauma the boy had experienced, so she'd given him one of the small spare bedrooms in the cabin with a door that locked. After dinner last night, he'd gone straight to his room and was still sleeping when she left this morning.

From upstairs came Riley's now-familiar cry; it was sharp and high and penetrated drywall and two-by-fours. She worried about the two of them—alone, traumatized, and scared—and touched a hand to her chest. Poor Vega. Trying to do it all by herself. A tough one.

She started toward her truck, but a tight rubber band slipped over her shoulders, tugging her backward and craning her neck. Vega's window was lit with a soft glow. A tickle at the base of Eve's skull.

Something waited for her inside. She started up the stairs to Vega's apartment. Riley's cries grew louder. She knocked. Her hands shook.

From inside, she heard something fall, Vega curse; then the door was unlocked, and Vega stood on the other side, hair mussed, bags under her eyes, Riley screaming in the pack 'n play. She wore a tool belt and held a putty knife in her hand. "I'm so sorry, he's just—he's crying so much today and I've done everything, and I was hoping to get the walls prepped and primed so I could paint in the next couple of days. But he's just miserable and I'm—" She stopped, bit her lip.

Eve forced herself to sound calm, despite the anxious swirling inside her. "What crying? I just stopped by to check on your progress."

Vega lifted one side of her mouth. "Right."

Eve came inside, dropped her bag, and picked up Riley. "How about I walk him around a bit so you can finish."

The woman's shoulders rounded. "Thank you. I'm almost done."

Riley squirmed in her arms, so she turned him around, belly down on her forearm the way she'd seen both Heff and Vega do it. After a while, he relaxed into her, and beneath her arm she felt the bubbles in his stomach shift. Poor little guy. Vega returned to her spackling, so Eve walked around the apartment, gently jiggling her arm while she moved and looked around the small space. What was she looking for? "Any visitors today?"

Vega looked at her, white mud across her forehead. "I don't do much entertaining. Crying baby really kills the mood."

Eve smiled. "Funny." Felt something on the tip of her tongue—a literal weight, like she knew something and couldn't say it. She shook her head, moved her jaw from side to side, confused and annoyed by the sensation. Riley gave a little mewl, and she jiggled him some more and walked. The apartment was sparse, no decorations from Vega, nothing homey or a reflection of who she was. Then again, she'd fled her home, taking only the most important things. Eve raised an eyebrow. There was something—a picture, edges curled, stuck to the refrigerator with a Hello From Crystal magnet that matched the postcard. She leaned in. The photo was grainy, dark, the kind taken with actual film and not digital. Her heartbeat slowed, thumping hard with each pulse.

The girl in the photo smirked at the camera, cigarette smoke curling in the air, spray paint black on her fingertips, middle finger extended. The air pressed against Eve, squeezing out a memory, and Donna appeared beside her, heartbreakingly young, thick auburn hair that had made her neck extra sweaty in the summer humidity. Green eyes that flashed fear and a false courage. Her face the last thing Eve remembered. Above the squish of her bones. Or the unbearable pain in her head from being dragged down the bus steps before everything went black and Eve never saw her friend again.

Her breathing grew shallow, and she looked at Vega, who was cleaning off the tool with a paper towel. Eve could see Donna now in the straight line of her jaw, the upturned end of her nose, the determined pinch of her lips. Details swirled around her, clues on torn-up bits of paper. She grabbed one, smoothed it out. Donna's baby sister. Her mouth went dry. Vega was the little girl Donna said she'd never leave behind. Eve was overcome, leaned a hand against the refrigerator. Donna had done it.

Eve cleared her throat, feeling betrayed by the unpredictability of her gift. How could she not have known this before now? "Vega?"

"Hmm?" Vega looked up from her work, eyebrows raised.

Eve pointed to the picture. "This is Donna."

Vega stood, brushing speckles of white from her pants, looking confused. "That's my mom. Renee. I asked you about her before."

Eve's stomach danced, the paper swirling into a funnel that skipped around the apartment, her knowing an elusive guessing game. "I know her as Donna."

Vega's hands froze in the air. "The girl who disappeared?"

"Yes," Eve said. There were rumors, guesses about what had happened to her, but it seemed nobody actually knew anything. Afterward,

Eve had tried to find her friend, but she'd disappeared, like she'd never even existed.

The woman seemed to melt, swaying away from Eve like she was almost afraid of her. "You were friends with Donna."

"I was."

"And you think Donna was my mom?" She sounded doubtful, and Eve couldn't blame her.

Eve took the picture from the refrigerator. "This was taken after she got her tattoo. See, you can kinda see it right here." It was hard to see, but Eve remembered the day like it had just happened. "Tera gave her that tattoo."

"Joshua's mom?"

Eve nodded and suddenly Vega sank to the ground, like her legs had given out on her.

"I don't understand. You all knew my mom?" She pressed a hand to her chest. "But her name was Donna?"

Riley had calmed, and Eve looked down to see that his eyes had closed. She carefully laid him down, then went over to Vega, sat cross-legged opposite the girl, who looked like she'd seen a ghost.

"I met Donna at the school bus. She'd run away from home because her father—" Eve hesitated, unsure how much was too much for Vega to hear right now. "Her father was horribly abusive to her, and her mother did nothing to help. We were friends. I loved your mother, Vega." Red thread flung itself from one end of the room to the other, touching the picture, Vega, Eve, and Riley.

The vision spread in her mind. The girl under the bed. *I won't let him hurt you. I won't let him hurt you.* The girl spoke to something nestled in the palms of her hands. Men's boots moved even with the bed, so close Eve saw granules of dirt stuck into the tread. She held her breath. The girl whimpered, seemed to finally notice Eve, hiding beside her. It was Donna, hair glinting red in the light from the door. She held out her cupped hands. *Keep her safe.* A tiny infant nestled inside her palms, minuscule, perfect. Eve took the infant—it weighed nothing—and she trembled. A pair of hands reached under the bed, grabbed Donna by her armpits, and pulled. She was gone, her screams becoming whimpers, and when Eve looked down at her hands, the baby was gone too.

She breathed in a knowing that spread through her limbs. It wasn't about Riley. It was about Beth, Donna's baby sister. She rubbed her neck. How could Eve tell her that her mother had lied to her? She ached to comfort Vega, but the woman was tough, and Eve knew that it might be too much, might push her over the edge. So she sat with her hands on her knees, waiting.

Vega didn't speak until Riley woke up and started making gurgling noises from the crib. She pushed to her feet, picked him up, cradled his head to her chest, and bounced gently up and down on her toes.

Eve smiled at an image in her head. "Did your mother favor overalls?"

Vega nodded, chin trembling.

"If it helps, Vega, she's with you. I don't think she's ever left your side."

"But why did she lie to me?"

Eve wanted to tell her everything, hesitated. It was too much and it didn't feel right, like a half-finished Scrabble word. The red strings disappeared, the scraps of paper fell to the floor, and Eve was left with what she knew. "I think she wanted to start over. What her father did, what he took from her, the only way she could survive was by leaving." She touched Vega's arm. "She did that for you."

"But then, if Donna was my mother, who's my father?"

Eve's throat closed. She didn't want to hurt Vega. Hated that she'd exposed Donna's lie. But she couldn't bear to tell her that her father had been a monster.

CHAPTER TWENTY-NINE

VEGA

Vega rubbed Riley's back, soothed by his warmth, his need for her care. Her mother was Donna, the girl who'd disappeared. The girl who'd murdered her own father. Tears stung her eyes. It hurt to hear. But it made sense too. She'd changed her name, dyed her hair, and raised Vega on an endless run from the truth. Vega shivered, bits and pieces from her past gluing themselves together. Her stomach turned. It made sense. Her mother's nightmares, the endless life on the road. Running from her father. Had she murdered him like everyone in Crystal thought? She rubbed her arms, chilled. If she had, Vega didn't want to know why.

She'd gotten a tattoo when Renee was in the hospital. Nothing fancy, just plain black lettering across her wrist. She held it up, stared at it over Riley's small shoulder. *Renee.* She rubbed at it like she could erase the ink from her skin. A lie. Her name had been Donna. And Vega knew so little about her.

Eve reached out, took Vega's hand, and read the name. Then she smiled. "Oh, I see now. Clever."

Vega took her hand back. "What?"

"Renee." Eve's eyes were wet, and Vega softened when she realized it was for her mother. "It means *reborn*. That's exactly what she did for herself and for you. Donna had no one, Vega, but she was a survivor, and what doesn't surprise me is that she raised you to be one too."

Conflicting emotions at being lied to all these years, desperate to know why. "I don't understand."

Eve waited, like she already knew.

Sprouts of irritation grew in her chest. "How could you not have *known* this when you first met me?" She felt like she'd been played; everyone in town had known the minute she arrived, and nobody had said a thing.

"I wish I had an answer for that. I'm sorry, Vega. But what I can tell you is that I've felt very connected to you from the first moment I met you. Maybe in some way, I did know. I just didn't recognize it."

Riley moved his head, trying to look around. Vega moved him until he faced forward. He jerked his hands and feet and gave a happy shriek that made Eve smile. Vega swallowed. "I'm sorry. That wasn't fair of me," she said. "I'm just so confused." For her entire life, she'd wanted to understand her mother better, to know more about her, and now she could. Eve had known Renee when she was just a girl. Had been her friend.

Vega dug her fingers into her thighs. A part of her wanted to throw her arms around Eve and hold on tight. The other part felt a creeping shame. She likely knew less about Renee than Eve. Vega tried not to resent Renee, but it pricked at her. Why had she kept them so isolated? So alone? No wonder Vega had drifted into the arms of someone like Zach. Her mother had kept her sheltered and ignorant, too scared to share her past with her own daughter. As soon as Vega felt it, though, the resentment faded, replaced by an aching in her heart.

Eve opened her mouth, seemed about to say something, then stopped, shook her head like she was having a debate with herself. "You came here for a reason, and I think part of that reason was because your mom wanted you to know. You belong here, Vega."

Vega kissed the top of Riley's head, felt her terror from a week ago tickle the back of her neck, a reminder of what she'd left behind. The Amber Alert for Riley drifting out from Colorado, painting a giant target on her back. She'd run to Crystal just like her mom. Except Vega had found a home. The realization hit her hard. She wanted so much more for Riley than a life on the run.

Joshua's words about the girl murdering her own father mixed with her thoughts. "Joshua said something about . . ." She swallowed. Did she really want to know? "About Donna murdering her own father?"

Eve sucked in her bottom lip, gave her a long look. "I'm so sorry, Vega. Nobody knows what happened to Donna's father. I've always assumed he took off. Everyone here, well . . ." Sympathy in the lines around her eyes. "Her family lived off the grid up in the mountains. Mostly kept to themselves. And afterward, he wasn't a good man, and when he disappeared, I think everyone assumed he'd holed up somewhere on his own and took matters into his own hands."

Vega shuddered. So much sadness littered her mother's past. "Did you ever talk to her after she left here?"

Eve's face clouded and she looked at Riley, reached out and touched his cheek. "I tried, Vega, but I had no way of knowing where she went. And back then, well, it wasn't as easy to find someone as it is now. I should have tried harder, though. She was very special to me. I'm sorry I didn't. I was caught up in my own survival."

Vega shook her head. "You wouldn't have found her even if you'd tried. My mom didn't want to be found, Eve."

Eve nodded, touched the back of Vega's hand, and smiled. "Still, it would have been nice to have known you before now." A moment of silence between them. Vega let the truth sink in and so, it seemed, did Eve.

"Why don't you come to dinner tonight?" Eve said. "Antonne is making Cincinnati chili, and that's best eaten with friends."

"Cincinnati chili?" She'd never heard of it.

Eve laughed. "It's like nothing you've ever had. Pasta, ground beef cooked in cinnamon, dark chocolate and other spices, onions, beans, and cheese. You have to try it to understand."

Vega didn't think it sounded particularly appetizing, but the idea of being with others folded a warmth around her heart. She didn't want to be alone. She wanted to hear what Eve remembered about Renee, wanted to try to forget about Zach, pretend he'd never existed. "Okay."

"Great, and I'll tell you about the time your mom found a raccoon sleeping next to her in the bus."

Vega laughed; she felt lighter just talking to someone about her mom. "She hated raccoons. Said they were mean little buggers."

"They were, but so was she."

She was right—her mom had been strong and bullheaded, opinionated, but also reserved and private. She wished she'd known her the way Eve had. Wished she'd understood why her mom had spent the rest of her life running. But the news had also filled her with a strange sort of contentment. Against all odds, Vega had found her way to Crystal and discovered a piece of her mother's past. Zach still had no idea where she was and had no way to find her either. She just needed to be careful. She'd keep her head down, keep working, and learn as much about Renee as possible. An excited beat of her heart. She'd stop by Carl and Betty's tomorrow. She smiled, thinking of Renee as one of their "kids."

~

The next morning, she pushed the stroller down the road, her step lighter. She passed Eve's Place just as the door opened and Heff walked out, paper cup of coffee in one hand, hair tousled and unruly as ever. "Good morning, Vega," he said, his deep voice comforting—familiar, even, after only a week. It's how she imagined summer camp would have felt if she'd ever gone. Instant connections and an easy sense of belonging. "Morning walk?"

"I'm heading over to see Carl and Betty." She was smiling and it felt genuine, and the truth bubbled out before she had time to think about it. "I found out that the girl who disappeared from here was my mother. Donna, or Renee—um, I mean Renee was Donna."

Heff's eyebrows rose. "No kidding? You're one of us!"

Riley cooed and they both laughed. "I guess I am." Heff started to walk with her to the path that led to the couple's cabin. "You don't have to be my personal bodyguard, you know," she said lightly.

He sipped his coffee, looked behind them on the road. "I don't trust JJ, Vega. He's nothing like Joshua or his momma. He's more like his daddy, and there's a reason that man's in prison." His tone was serious, and it made the hair on the back of her neck pull away from the skin. They came to the path and Vega unbuckled Riley, held him to her chest, grateful for Heff's protectiveness, hoping it was overblown. She didn't need one more man to worry about.

She smiled. "Thanks for the escort."

He dipped his head. "It's the most official police action I've seen all day." He stuck his thumb into a pocket, saluted her with the other. "Stay safe, ma'am."

She laughed, climbed to the top of the steep stairs, and when she looked back, noticed that Heff had waited until she'd reached the top. Her face warmed at his concern.

Betty met her on the porch, Carl not far behind. The tiny woman looked up at her, squinting into the sun. "So you're Donna's girl? Ain't that something, Carl?"

Carl shook his head back and forth, a smile peeking out from under his mustache. Behind his glasses, his eyes looked wet. "Oh, it is, Betty."

It did not surprise Vega one bit to find that word had traveled fast. She didn't mind. If anything, it made it seem more real.

"Come on and sit down here." Betty patted one of the chairs on the porch. "I put coffee on and made us some biscuits and gravy too. Turkey gravy, if you'll excuse me, but it's for Carl's heart. Now, I'm bettin' you'd like to hear some stories 'bout your momma."

Vega bounced Riley. "Eve tell you?"

Betty shook her head. "Heff did."

"But I just told—" She gestured down the stairs, at a loss.

Betty laughed. "The boy called me while you was walkin' up. Guess he wanted to make sure we welcomed you right."

Vega laughed and handed Riley to Carl, who already had his arms out and waiting, and they all sat down, Betty and Carl taking a seat on either side of her.

Vega rubbed her hands along her arms, asked the questions that bothered her the most. She figured if anyone would know, it would be Betty. "Do you know why she left? Or what happened to her dad?" She sounded desperate, but finding people who knew her mother brought all her questions to the surface.

Carl held Riley so that the baby leaned against him like he was a cozy recliner.

Betty rocked her chair. "Donna left because she couldn't stay. What happened to that man is one of God's mysteries."

Sadness cradled Vega's heart when she thought of why her mother had kept running—fear that if she stopped, he'd find her. Chills raced down her spine, and her admiration grew. Her mother had done the best she could, and in the end, she'd given Vega as normal a childhood as she could. She swallowed past a lump. "Did she ever write to you? Or call?"

Betty blinked a few times. "She never wrote to me, but I worried about her." She patted Vega's hand. "It shore does my heart good to know she raised a fine young'un such as yourself. Now"—her eyes brightened—"I taught Donna how to make my buckeye cookies. She ever fix those for you?"

Vega searched her memory for a time when her mother might have made the sweet treat. Her enthusiasm deflated. "I don't think so."

Betty slapped her knee. "Good. I'd like to be the one to teach you."

They rocked for a while on the porch, drinking Carl's strong coffee. Betty told her about the catfight between Donna and Joshua's mom the first time they met. Vega laughed, imagining Renee in a fight with the scrawny woman she'd met a few days ago. "But then they were fast friends." A shadow seemed to pass over Betty's features, and she looked down at her lap, quiet. "But that's well in the past now." She stood. "Come on in. I hear Carl's stomach growling at me from all the way over here."

Vega spent the entire morning with the couple and didn't leave until it was time to put Riley down for a nap. She smiled all the way back to her apartment, imagining what it had felt like to be one of their "kids." And happy that, for however short a time, her mother had been part of their family.

CHAPTER THIRTY

Eve

Eve set the last cleaned plate on the drying rack, listening to the sounds of Antonne and Joshua outside around the fire, playing guitars, singing. It was late May, and the days had warmed considerably—spring temperatures dreaming of summer. It was peaceful too; Joshua had heard that JJ had gone to Portsmouth for some concrete work.

From outside, she heard Riley squeal, and she smiled. Vega was out there with them. She'd been coming over regularly since finding out about her mom a couple of weeks ago. To work, but also to join them for dinner, hang, dig for any bits of memory Eve had about Donna. She asked questions, trying, Eve suspected, to match up the girl, Donna, with the woman Vega had known. It brought up memories for Eve, too, dark ones that filled her with empathy for the teenage kids from her past. Made her wish she'd known the woman, Renee, the way Vega had.

The door banged open and Heff came in, carrying water glasses from where they'd eaten dinner outside at the picnic table. He brought with him the heady aroma of burning wood.

"Still can't believe Vega solved the mystery of the girl who disappeared," he said, dunking the glasses into the sink of soapy water. "But we've lost our ghost story. How do we scare the kids now?"

Eve laughed. "There's still the mystery of what happened to her dad."

Heff shook his head. "Something tells me we'll never find that out."

Eve shrugged. She'd never spared many thoughts for that man. "Maybe not."

He returned outside, and through the window Eve saw him sit on a stump next to Vega and Riley, the glow of the fire slipping in and out of his dimples.

Eve had to ignore a tight ball of uneasiness rolling around her stomach. Her suspicion that Vega was Beth, Donna's baby sister, had grown teeth that tugged at her with doubt. But she couldn't bring herself to voice it to Vega. The woman seemed to find solace in people who'd known her mother, as though they brought her closer to her own memories, and Eve worried that telling her might hurt more than help.

Betty came back into the house, pulling on a pink jacket. "I'm going on home, Eve. Carl should be back from Columbus tonight."

Eve handed her a foil-covered plate of leftovers and tried to be nonchalant when she said, "Did you ever find out what happened to Donna's mother and sister after everything happened?"

Betty held the plate between her two hands, looked up at Eve. "That's an out-of-the-blue question, ain't it, Eve? And you don't ask out-of-the-blue questions, now, do you?"

Eve sighed. If anyone had a sixth sense, it was Betty. "No, I do not."

"Then what're you gettin' at?"

"Donna's plan was always to bring her sister with her when she left. Do you know if that happened?"

Betty tilted her head. "I know they don't live there no more. Few years back, Jane and I brought some produce up thataways to check in on a few folks. Donna's old cabin was deserted, looked like it had been for years too." Her eyes widened. "You think Donna stole her baby sister from her own momma?"

Eve cringed to hear her concern voiced. "I don't know, Betty. But keep it to yourself until we know for sure. I don't want to tell Vega until we have to."

"Truth's always better—don't you think, Eve." Betty said it not as a question and left without waiting for a response, which was good because Eve didn't know what she would have said.

After the kitchen was clean, she sat on her porch in the waning light of dusk, glass of red wine in one hand, a bitter square of chocolate in the other, savoring both. A set of headlights bounced down her road, stopping at the end of the driveway. Tera's old TransAm. She got out.

"Hey there," Eve said, surprised but also relaxed, like she'd been expecting Tera. It seemed right. A new beginning of sorts.

Tera climbed the stairs, duffel bag slung over her shoulder, and sat in a rocking chair next to Eve. "Wasn't you expectin' me? Didn't you dream I was coming or somethin'?" She snickered, and it was an echo of the girl Eve remembered, who smoked cigarettes, worked on cars, and was the prettiest girl in Crystal.

"'Course I did. Except in my dream, you came to give me a tattoo. It was a nightmare."

Tera laughed and Eve sighed, feeling a pang at the familiar cackle. She looked at the bag. "You moving in too?" She was joking but also prepared to make up a bed. Eve was settling into her role of helping others, and it felt good, like she'd been waiting to do it her entire life.

"Nah, just brought Joshua a few summertime clothes. Couple pictures, nothin' much." They rocked in silence, watching the fire, where Antonne and Joshua played their guitars, Heff and Vega listening. Crickets chirped from the grass, the sound of animal feet scurrying across the porch. "Daddy's dying."

Eve stared at the fire, let it burn red flames in her vision. "I'm sorry," she said.

"Yeah. Thing is, I've wished him dead most of my life, and now that it's finally happening—I don't know. It's sad, you know? He made my life miserable, couldn't stand the sight of me for most of it, and here I am gettin' teary eyed over the old bastard."

Eve reached out and touched Tera's arm resting on the chair. They'd been friends once, and Eve remembered Tera always being rough on the outside but tenderhearted to her core. A good person. And she was hurting. But people had disappointed Eve over and over again when it came to her being trans, so she always protected a part of her soul just in case.

But Tera didn't move; instead, she brought her other hand over, covering Eve's with it. She patted twice, then released her, and Eve slid her arm back to her side, warmed by the moment.

"Thank you," Tera said, sniffing, her voice thick. "Your daddy was a bastard, too, weren't he?"

Eve rocked, listened to the young people laugh, sing, the baby crying; she felt a piece inside her let loose and float to the top. "He never spoke to me again after that night, and I still cried when he died. So I understand. When someone dies, it's the end of something, good or bad."

"Yeah, bunch of bastards." After a little while, Eve heard the click of a lighter, the crackle of an inhale, ashes red in the dark. "You know, Eve, I didn't know back then—well, I still don't—but you being like you are, I didn't know how to be your friend. I'm sorry I was such a pussy."

Eve smiled in the dark. Tera was a proud woman, and Eve had never expected to hear her apologize. "I forgive you for being a pussy," she said, and Tera laughed so hard it mixed with her smoker's phlegm and turned into a cough.

"So Joshua told me that the new girl is Donna's daughter." The cigarette crackled. "What do you think about that?"

The smoke mixed in with Eve's hair. Tera had been close with Donna back then, too, but Eve had no idea how much she might know. "I think it's good she's come home."

"Maybe it's what Donna had planned all along."

Eve blinked against a wetness in her eyes. She'd known Donna for only a few weeks, and in the large scheme of her life, it was a minute. But it was as impactful as her NDE, as clear in her memory, and having Vega here was like welcoming Donna home where she'd always belonged. She thought of her vision, the baby, and looked out at Vega by the fire—smiling, relaxed, happy. Eve settled back into the rocker. The baby from her vision was here and in her safekeeping.

CHAPTER THIRTY-ONE

VEGA

Vega stepped into the clearing around the old school bus. It was late May, warm enough to be called middle of the summer in Colorado, where spring snowstorms were common. She swatted at a bug. They seemed to rise from the forest floor, biting her ankles whenever she stood still. Wildflowers dotted the clearing, sprays of color that added to the bus, making it homey and inviting.

It had been almost a month since the morning she'd left Colorado. A month since she'd first stepped foot in Crystal. In that time, she'd turned another year older, and she'd celebrated by thanking herself for leaving Zach. The time had both flown and stood still, but the longer she was away, the more unreal it became, and the more she worked on forgiving herself for being with Zach in the first place. If nothing else, it had given her Riley, and she'd never regret that. She'd kept her phone turned off, stopped checking Instagram on her computer too. Allowed the idea that Zach was firmly in her past to root into her present.

Eve and the others had become people she might have known for years. Their link to her mother gave her an instant connection, and the feeling that Crystal was home deepened with each passing day. Riley was growing like a weed; his crying had suddenly stopped a week ago. He still cried, of course, just not in the constant and pained way he had before. Vega had slept more in the last week than she had since he was born. The work at the apartment and farm kept her busy, with the occasional job elsewhere. The nuns had even had her out to take a look at their boiler. They were a friendly group who were curious about Vega and impressed with her know-how.

But the bus called to her, and she found herself coming out to the woods, picturing her mom living here as a teenager—sleeping inside. It didn't surprise her, not based on the woman she'd known her entire life. That woman knew how to survive. She hefted her backpack inside. Last week, she'd built a proper frame for the mattress in the back, wanting to give the lost souls who found their way to this bus a more comfortable spot to rest. Ripped out a couple more of the seats and added a built-in couch with pillows she'd purchased at the dollar store. Today, she was going to repaint the inside, give it a fresh new layer of crisp white. It was a way for her to give something back to her mom and to people who needed it like she had.

The bus creaked when she climbed inside. After sweeping and cleaning the inside and with the couches in back, it was welcoming and cozy; a honey-dipped breeze fluttered the curtains. She'd replaced a few of the windows and boarded up most of the others to keep the elements outside. Today, she'd dropped Riley off with Betty and Carl before heading out this way. They invited her over for breakfast at least a couple of mornings each week and offered to watch Riley whenever she had a job. Vega soaked it up, letting her memory of Renee deepen with the images of Donna here at the bus—a teenage girl who'd gotten herself out of a nightmare and raised her own daughter in the process. She blinked against the tears it brought to her eyes. Her mom had been a badass.

She sat down on the couch in back. There were whispers of doubt that woke her up at night. Nobody wanted to talk about her grandfather, and Vega felt a sickening twist in her stomach when she thought about him. He was the reason her mother had left. He was the reason she'd had nightmares. She squeezed her thighs, overcome by a suspicion that twisted its ugliness through her chest. Could her grandfather also be her— She clamped her eyes shut and felt a wave of nausea take hold. Shook her head and pushed the thought away. *No,* she told herself. *No.*

A wind blew through the trees, lifting the leaves that had bloomed a light green, and rushed through the bus. She had one more stop to make at Eve's before picking up Riley. She'd promised Antonne and Joshua that she'd show them how to change out the light fixture above Eve's kitchen table.

She stepped outside, breathed in, and let the heaviness of missing her mom move around her, readjust its weight. It never left her, but being here made it something that didn't feel like it would break her.

At the edge of the meadow, she turned; the bus sat quiet and alone, full of secrets. The air a mix of rotting leaves and spring growth. A cloud passed over the sun, turning the metal a flat yellow, making the graffiti artwork darker, more sinister in the shade. Goose bumps pricked Vega's skin, and her thoughts were pulled backward. To the question of her father. To something unfathomable. It wriggled holes through her chest, made her feel weaker than she had seconds earlier, made her wish for ignorance. She thought of Riley. He was the only thing that mattered now. She rolled her shoulders and turned away from the bus. Not all questions had to be answered.

～

She drove with the windows down, the Beatles playing from the speakers. It was a beautiful day—blue sky, new life in the woods making it all a colorful landscape. At some point a truck appeared behind her.

Vega's pulse sped up. It looked like JJ's truck. She pulled into Eve's farm, silently praying that she was wrong and the truck would keep driving. Her heart sank. It followed.

She parked by the barn; the truck stopped directly behind her. She squeezed the wheel, breathed in and out. JJ could not know that Joshua was here. But a sinking feeling made her think he already did. By habit, she reached for her phone to call for help, forgetting that she never carried it with her anymore. Panic twisted her stomach. She could not leave Joshua alone to fend for himself. In her rearview mirror, she saw JJ loping toward her, toothpick in his mouth, hair nearly all shaved off. She hopped out of the van, turned to face him.

JJ stopped within inches of her, sporting a new tattoo on his neck. Trembles ran through Vega's body, but she kept her chin lifted, eyes hard.

She touched the slim can of pepper spray in her back pocket, the one Heff had given to her. "You here to see Eve?"

He leaned against her van, chewing on the toothpick. "You know I ain't. I came to see if the rumors I been hearing is true."

Vega tensed. From the barn, she heard something fall hard to the ground. JJ's eyes darted behind her, narrowed, and he took off in the direction of the barn. She hurried after him, ignoring the panic that made her legs feel like jelly. Her mother's voice, which screamed at her to run.

It was dark inside the barn, the air musty and sweet with the scent of hay. A cat meowed from the loft above. Joshua stood in the center of the space, a bucket of feed spilled at his feet, a twitch in his chin. Vega's hands curled into fists at the look in his eyes. He was terrified.

JJ advanced on the boy. "It's true? You living with a faggot, Josh?"

Joshua's jaw tightened. "Shut up, JJ, and leave me alone. Momma knows I'm here." His voice shook, but Vega heard strength in it too.

JJ's fist shot forward, landing hard on the side of Joshua's head. Vega cringed when she heard the crack of his knuckles meeting skull. Joshua fought back, scrappy, slipping out of the bigger man's grip, jumping behind him and punching him in the side. JJ seemed more annoyed than hurt, like his younger brother was a fly. "You ain't staying here, Josh."

Joshua lunged, landing a punch square on JJ's nose. Vega heard a pop, and then blood poured from the man's nostrils.

"Son of a bitch," JJ growled, and lunged at the boy.

Vega ignored the voice that screamed at her that she was no match for this man, slipped the pepper spray from her pocket, and jumped between the brothers. She sprayed JJ in the eyes. Again. Grabbed Joshua by the arm and ran from the barn. She pushed him inside the van and started the engine. JJ stood in the doorway to the barn, chest heaving, hand over his eyes. With his truck parked close behind her, Vega had little room to turn around. She squeezed the steering wheel, reversed hard into JJ's truck. Metal crunched, giving her just enough space to turn around. "Where's Antonne?" she said, breathless.

"Out." Joshua held the side of his face, which had already started to bruise. "Hurry, Vega, he'll kill you for trashing his truck."

Vega felt trapped. She couldn't breathe.

JJ had reached her van. His meaty fist pounded the passenger window by Joshua. "You fucking bitch!"

Joshua jerked away from the window, looking small and scared and bruised.

It kindled her anger, and Vega pressed the gas, heart racing, leaving JJ covered in a cloud of dust. She drove without braking all the way to Eve's store, and when she got there, Eve was already outside, pacing, face white. When she saw them, she collapsed forward, hands on knees. Relieved, like she'd been expecting them.

Vega hurried to her side and Eve hugged her.

"You're okay? Joshua?"

Vega nodded. Joshua had gotten out of the van. "I've made things worse, Eve. JJ was going to take Joshua. I had to stop him."

Eve nodded. "Not your fault. But I don't think he's going to let any of this go now."

From Eve's pocket came the ring of a cell phone. Her eyes clouded, body stiffened. "Do you smell that?"

"What?"

"The burning."

Vega inhaled, smelled nothing, but the rage on JJ's face filled her vision. She'd put nothing past him.

A TransAm skidded to a stop, and Tera jumped out, stopped short when she saw Joshua. "You're here." She hugged him hard and he winced. She pulled back, touched his jaw. "Damn." Turned to face Eve. "JJ's home."

"I maced him again," Vega said, wishing she hadn't when Tera's attention focused on her.

"If you're defending my son, I don't have no problem with it."

Joshua's phone rang. "It's Antonne." He answered and his eyes widened. "Eve," he whispered.

Eve nodded like she already knew. "The barn's on fire."

CHAPTER THIRTY-TWO

July 1995

At the edge of town, Ethan turned and started to climb up a steep set of stairs to Betty and Carl's cabin. Donna followed, her thigh muscles burning. Carl labored up behind them, and when he reached the top, he sat down on a stump to catch his breath. Donna kept seeing the look on her dad's face when she'd told everyone what he did. Her whole body shook.

Ethan took her hands between his. Her face felt stiff, and the tips of her ears burned. She pulled her hands away and slid them inside her pockets. She looked down at the road below; nobody had followed them.

"I thought we'd walk to the bus this way instead of the road, just in case . . . well, you know." Ethan spoke softly, like he was afraid she'd bolt at any minute.

"In case he comes back?" She picked at a nail, scraped a line of dirt from underneath it. "Oh, he'll come back." Blood had dried on Ethan's face, giving him a red mustache and goatee that struck Donna as hilarious. She started to laugh, but her chest felt too heavy for something so light. She stopped.

Carl hefted his weight from the stump. "Come on inside, missy. Let Betty make you some hot tea. You're shaking like a leaf." He lightly clapped Ethan on the back. "And let's clean you up, Rocky. Didn't know you were such a fighter."

Ethan touched his face, cringed at the specks of blood. "I'm not."

Inside, Betty cleaned up Ethan's face, served hot tea in delicate floral cups.

Donna stared into the brown liquid. "He won't stop lookin' for me," she said softly.

Nobody spoke. Then Carl cleared his throat, got up, and pulled a book from a bookshelf, set it beside her teacup. "This has just about everything you need to know to get you started."

It was a hardcover, thick, with detailed steps and pictures on how to fix things. She flipped through it, felt a spark that quickly died. Leaving felt like a wall she didn't want to climb over.

Carl pulled up a chair. "Listen here, missy. That man ain't no father. And what he did—well, that ain't your fault. You understand?"

Donna stared at the book, shrugged.

Betty and Ethan seemed to hardly move.

"I'm scared."

"'Course you are," Carl said. "But you're a smart girl, know that? And listen here, I'll teach you some of the basics from that manual. Show you how to use the book and how to teach yourself. First, you learn how to survive on your own, and you'll make it through 'bout everything life's gonna toss at you."

She raised her gaze to find Carl's cheeks mottled, his eyes wet, and something broke a little inside her at the kindness of his offer, his own emotional response. She swallowed hard. "What about my dad?"

"He won't have much help from the pastor or any other church folk after what just happened. And I've a mind to call the police about him. What he done, that's what the law is for."

"The police can stop him?" She didn't know they'd do something like that. Where they lived, the police didn't come around much. Her father was the law.

Betty made a noise in her throat. Carl blinked, stared at her. Then he took off his glasses, cleaned them on his shirt. When he looked at her, Donna tensed at the pity in his eyes. "What he done is wrong, Donna. You remember that."

She hugged her arms across her chest, stared at her brand-new tattoo, scraps of her earlier optimism twirling around her. If the police told him he had to stop, would Beth be safe? Donna didn't think so. At least not forever. Her mom would have to call the police like Carl, and Donna knew she'd never do that. She gritted her teeth. Maybe it would scare her dad off long enough to give her time to make a real plan before she left. And when it was time to go, she'd sneak in through Beth's bedroom window, take her when everyone was sleeping. It floated a small reservoir of hope she kept tied down. Carl believed in her. Betty and Ethan too. "Can we start tomorrow?"

Carl nodded. "You bet, bright and early."

She nodded, finished the rest of her tea, and stood. "Can you show me how to get to the bus from here, Ethan?"

He took their cups to the sink. "Thanks for cleaning me up, Betty."

Betty nodded. "You two be careful." She puffed out her cheeks, seemed unsure of herself. "Sure you don't want to stay here instead? I can make up the couch."

The idea of sleeping inside their cabin sounded nice, but Donna had grown used to the bus; it was her cocoon and the only place she felt safe. "Nah, I'm good. I like the bus." She thought of the humiliation on her father's face. The way everyone else had stepped back from him like he was a dog who got sprayed by a skunk. How he'd slunk away without a word. Something heavy slid from her shoulders. He was the bad one. Not her. "See you in the morning, Carl. Thanks for the tea, Betty." She joined Ethan at the back door.

"Wait!" Betty hurried toward her, took Donna's hands between her small ones, her eyes crinkled at the corners. "You come to me if you ever need help, you hear?"

Donna swallowed past a lump. "Yes, ma'am."

~

Dusk was falling by the time they got back to the bus, the dim light turning Donna's tattoo into a blob of black lines. Ethan grabbed her hand. A campfire burned just outside the bus. Her heart thumped against her rib bones. He'd found her.

Tera popped up from where she'd been camouflaged by the bright glow of the fire, hidden in the bluish light. "Hey, losers, what took you so long?" She walked toward them with a bottle of brown liquid in one hand, taking a swig before holding it out to Donna.

Donna breathed out, relieved to see Tera. After she'd disappeared, Donna had deflated, feeling grimy for telling the truth, wondering if Tera would ever speak to her again. "What is it?"

"Hot Damn, and it's exactly what you need after that shit show in town." She took another swig. "Your daddy's an even bigger asshole than mine. Bigger than yours, too, huh, Ethan?"

Ethan took the bottle, tilted it back. "Yeah." He handed it to Donna, and she held it to her nose, sniffed. Cinnamon and spice. Took a sip. It burned and tasted like candy at the same time. She took another sip, felt the sting of the liquor on her tongue, down her throat, growing warm in her belly. She took another sip, felt her feet lift out of her shoes, and handed it back to Tera.

They sat around the fire, changing spots whenever the thick smoke found one of them. Tera added a log; it sparked, sending ash and bits of flame into the sky. The tang of smoke, heat of the fire, trees sprawling overhead. Donna felt like she belonged. But the image of her dad coming for her bled the warmth and turned her cold. She couldn't stay.

She sneaked a look at Ethan. The fire lit up his face, played along his full lips and strong jaw, and Donna tapped her feet, suddenly nervous. Ethan had protected her. She stuck her hands under her thighs, rounded forward in her seat, overwhelmed. How could she ever thank him?

"I got my car running today," Tera said. The liquor splashed inside the almost-empty bottle when she drank.

"What's your plan?" Ethan said, taking the bottle from her.

Tera shrugged. "Don't know. Maybe go south, somewhere with a beach. Or maybe—" She looked at Donna, seemed shy. "Maybe I'll tag along with Donna and her sister. See what all the fuss is out west."

It might have been the smoothness of the alcohol, but it took Donna a moment to process what Tera had said. When she did, a smile spread across her face. The idea that Tera might come, that she didn't have to be alone, a beacon of light. "You want to come with me?"

Tera took the liquor from Ethan, leaned back, crossed her legs. Her skin reflected the fire; her hair absorbed the color, glowing blonder. "I need someone to practice my tattoo skills on, and you need more tattoos." She pointed the tip of the bottle at Ethan. "You comin' too?"

Ethan stared up at the sky, quiet.

"C'mon, your daddy's a dipstick," Tera said. "Why would you stay?"

The alcohol had sloshed around her body, and Donna followed everywhere it went—her hips, thighs, chest, lips. She felt bolder, confident, unstoppable. She scooted closer to Ethan, reached out, and grabbed his hand. He didn't resist, and she leaned her head against his shoulder. "Come with us, Ethan. We can be our own family."

"Yeah." Tera jumped to her feet, stood with her hands on her hips. "Better to choose our own than get stuck with the assholes who made us."

Ethan sighed and Donna tensed, sure he was going to say no.

"Yeah, okay," he said, and she thought her heart might jump right out of her chest.

She didn't have to do this alone. She had friends now, her chosen family, and they'd get Beth and leave Ohio forever. Her body hovered above the earth, her mind already making plans, an excitement building for a different kind of future.

They finished the bottle; then Tera brought out a joint. It was the first time Donna had tasted alcohol or smoked weed. Her body buzzed, lips numb, and she relaxed into Ethan. Time passed. They all quieted, watched the flames licking the night. The fire died slowly, the air cooler without the heat. Goose bumps ran up and down the bare flesh of Donna's arms, and Ethan put his arm around her, held her tight to his side. Her head spun, mind replaying Ethan taking on her dad. For her. She touched his leg with her fingers, moved until her entire hand rested on his thigh, his wiry muscles tight beneath her palm.

An overwhelming desire to thank him rose up inside her, but she didn't know how, and words felt too weak, pointless. She wanted to show him.

"I gotta piss." Tera wobbled away from the fire and into the woods.

Alone with Ethan, Donna moved her hand farther up his thigh. He jumped. "Donna?"

She half stood, turned to face him, kneeling. Her feelings for him, mixed with the alcohol and the weed, slid into her lower belly. She wanted to show him how grateful she was, how thankful that he was brave enough to protect her. But all she knew about men was limited to her father and the disgusting things he'd done to her. And it messed with her, battled with her teenage self, the piece of her fueled by a desire she'd never known. She leaned forward until their noses nearly touched. His breath smelled like cinnamon candy and skunk. She heard the air stick in his throat, and she took that as her cue, leaning forward until their lips met. His were soft and opened easily against hers.

It was awkward but simple, too, and kissing Ethan didn't make her feel dirty or gross or wrong. It felt right and good, and her body sang. She took his hand and led him to the bus and to the very back, where he lay down on the mattress and she climbed on top of him. It was different and embarrassing, and afterward he quickly put his clothes back on and so did she. But he held her tight in his arms all night, and she'd never felt so safe.

~

The sun had risen high, warming the bus, the chill from the night before evaporated in the light of day. Donna pushed away from the heat of Ethan's body, annoyed and wanting space to cool her sweaty skin. Her head ached, like someone had clamped a metal claw around her skull and was slowly, slowly squeezing her brains out. The bus door opened, footsteps down the aisle.

"Well, shit fire and save the matches." Tera's voice.

Donna groaned and opened her eyes, hand over her brow to keep out any extra light. Waves of pain across her forehead.

"You and Ethan did it?" Tera stood above them, hair tangled and twisted, mascara smudged in black circles under her eyes, looking the worse for wear but still beautiful.

Donna ran her tongue over her teeth, fuzzy, the taste in her mouth sour, musty. She pushed up on her elbows, waited for the bus to stop spinning, fell back, hand over her eyes. "What did you do to me? I can't see straight."

Tera plopped onto the mattress, grabbed Ethan's calf, and shook it. "Wake up, sleepyhead."

Ethan moaned but didn't open his eyes.

Tera smiled. "You better treat him good. I'll kill you if you don't."

Donna believed her.

Tera lay down beside Donna, lit a cigarette, blew smoke into the air above their heads. "I figure that car should be road-ready any day now."

She offered the cigarette to Donna; she took it, filled her lungs, then let it out, coughing. Last night, she'd been ready to take her new family and hit the road. This morning, as usual, with her head pounding and the light of day making everything bigger and more impossible, she wasn't sure anymore. Here she had Ethan and Betty, Carl and Tera. More friends and people who really cared about her than she'd ever had. When she thought of home, she felt lonely and scared. But here, she felt alive. She wished there were another option, another way for her to stay.

"You ready to leave?" Tera said.

"Yeah, sure." It wouldn't give her much time to learn from Carl, but she figured the sooner, the better. Ethan moved beside her, his leg touching hers, and her face warmed, thinking about the night before. Was it good? Had he enjoyed it? It was all a little hazy, but the parts she remembered that didn't make her fidget made her smile.

Tera sat up on one elbow, reached over, and flicked Ethan in the temple. "Wake up! We got plans to make."

Ethan's eyes blinked open and he stared at the ceiling for a minute before turning his head and locking eyes with Donna.

"Me and Donna already planned our escape from this shit town while you been sleeping, princess." Tera sat all the way up, finished the cigarette, and ground it out on the floor. She stood. "We leave in a few days." She held her head, leaned forward onto her knees. "Oh man, I'm hurtin'!" She smirked down at them. "I gotta get, but I'll leave you two lovebirds to do it again if you want. Good thing I passed out by the fire, 'cause gross." Her laugh sounded like a cackle. "See ya, losers." She skipped down the aisle and left.

A nervous tremor ran through Donna's legs, and she couldn't bring herself to look at Ethan, who had moved over in the bed so that he was closer to the wall, not one part of him touching her. The silence grew, becoming so heavy it added to the humidity of the morning. She sat up, her back to him, rubbed at her neck. "If it was bad, you can just say it. Not be such a dick about it."

He cleared his throat. "It wasn't bad—"

Donna turned around, relieved to hear him say it, excitement a feathery brush across her skin. He'd pushed himself up, leaning his back against the bus wall.

"It wasn't?" Her voice was small.

He looked at her from under his curly bangs, seeming unsure, like he was nervous. "No."

She breathed out, smiled; her future had her people in it. Not just Donna against the world. She'd talked a big game to everyone, but the idea of leaving had paralyzed her. For the first time it felt possible to leave, and the idea saturated her with optimism. She scooted across the mattress, affection running hot just under her skin. She put her arms around his neck, kissed his cheek. "I love you, Ethan." It came out easy as breathing—a fact, a truth that she felt all the way down to her toes. She'd known him for only a few weeks, but in that time he'd been her friend, her protector, and now someone who'd shown her that she could be loved.

But something went wrong. Ethan stiffened, turning his face away from her and sliding out from under her arms. Donna's entire body went cold. She wrapped her arms across her chest, felt his rejection fill the spaces in her throat until she thought she might throw up.

He stood, moved to the aisle, hesitated, and Donna felt hope flare. Maybe he was just nervous, or it was his first time; maybe she'd been too forward. She chewed on her lip, ready to apologize—anything to keep Ethan as her friend. She needed his friendship above everything else.

"I'm . . . I'm not who you think I am."

She rose to her knees. "What does that mean?"

"I can't go with you, Donna. I'm sorry." He hung his head.

Tears stung her eyes. She didn't understand why he'd changed overnight, why he wanted nothing to do with her anymore. But one thing did make sense: what her father had done to her was disgusting, and Ethan was embarrassed to have been with her. Donna turned from him and faced the wall, shame slipping back over her soul.

"Get out," she said, her face already wet.

"Donna, I'm sor—" His voice cracked.

"Get out!" she screamed so loud it echoed in her head, bounced around the inside of the school bus, reviving her Hot Damn hangover. It was even quieter afterward, and when she heard his footsteps move down the aisle, she crawled to the window and watched him hurry through the meadow and into the woods, never looking back.

CHAPTER THIRTY-THREE

EVE

May 2021

Eve could hear the animals screaming. "Drive faster," she said to Tera, hands clenched in her lap. Tera did, the back end of her ancient TransAm skidding on the country road.

Eve was a mess of emotions: disbelief, heartache. And anger. It spread out from her core, unregulated. Her NDE had been a gift that left her with a larger capacity to forgive and empathize. But she had her limits. It was tiresome to repeatedly witness hatred for what was different. She thought of the message it gave kids like Joshua and Antonne—that fear would always win. Eve pressed her lips into a line. She would never let fear win, but it was exhausting how hard she had to keep fighting to make that true.

Tera tore down Eve's dirt lane, but even before she saw the flames consuming her barn, Eve felt it in the prickle of knowledge, the scent of burned wood, the silence of the animals. Smoke played thick in the trees, black and foul. The barn came into view, and even though she'd expected it, it was a shock to see. Antonne ran from the house to the barn, full bucket grasped in his hands, water spilling on the ground. He tossed it onto the closest flames, a drop against the torrent, then ran back to the hose to fill it again.

Eve and Tera jumped out of the car; Vega's van tore down the road, followed by Heff's truck. Nobody spoke but everyone ran to grab a bucket and each filled one, throwing the liquid one by one onto the fire. Nothing happened, of course. Eve knew it was useless, but doing something felt better than standing by and watching it burn to the ground. She felt the negative ripples that shot out from her choices, the ones that had led to this fire. Even knowing this outcome, she wouldn't have changed anything.

There was soot smeared across Vega's cheeks, her blonde hair darkened with grime. Everyone moved like ants, scurrying around, faces lined with exhaustion, backs slumped from the full buckets. She was overwhelmed by their determination and the fruitlessness of their efforts. The smoke settled in Eve's lungs, made her cough. She felt sick. There were no animals to be seen.

Heff, holding his arm in front of his face, moved closer to the inferno, trying—Eve knew—to see if the animals were trapped inside. Panic unfurled. The knowing that Heff was going to die had not dissipated; it had plagued her since she first saw it.

Eve screamed, "Stop!"

Heff paused, bucket in midthrow. Joshua was leaned over, breathing heavily, Tera rubbing his back. Antonne sat on the ground, knees up, rocking back and forth. But Vega didn't stop. She raced to the fire, back for more water, a determined frown on her face. They watched her, everyone a little stunned. Finally, Eve approached her, took her by the arm, and relieved her of the bucket. Vega looked shocked. "What? Are you giving up? We can't stop. The animals!" Tears ran through the black ash on her cheeks.

"It's too late, Vega."

Vega tried to rip her arm away. "I can't. It's my fault. I can't stop."

"Your fault?"

"He was going after Joshua, and I just didn't know how else to stop him and then I smashed into his truck and I've already maced him once before and that made him angry as hell. It's my fault."

"So you think JJ torched the barn because a woman maced him and wrecked his truck?"

Vega nodded.

"And not because JJ's a homophobic, transphobic cisgender male who still believes that gay is catching and AIDS was a plague sent by God?"

Vega stared at her; then the side of her mouth lifted, and Eve hugged her, grateful that this girl, who only weeks ago had been a total stranger, now felt like part of Eve's life.

They moved as far away from the intense heat as possible, sat down on the ground, and watched the flames eat at the wood, shedding tears for the lost animals. It was devastating to think they were all just gone. Even the pigs.

A fire truck sped down the road, but by then it was far too late. They sprayed until all that was left was a smoldering hunk of collapsed and burned wood.

Heff touched Eve's shoulder. "We can rebuild a barn."

Eve nodded. "I know."

"Not everyone feels this way," he added softly.

"I know."

Carl's truck bounced down the road. He got out, eyes wide, taking in the empty space where the barn had stood, running his thumbs along the inside of his suspenders. He walked over to Eve, mustache twitching, with a look in his eyes that Eve didn't often see in the easygoing man. "Someone do this to you, Eve?"

"Looks that way," she said. "Lost all the animals too."

Carl shook his head. "That's the thing. Betty and I was watching the young'un when we heard a racket outside the cabin. I got my rifle." He rubbed his fingers across his upper lip, and he was smiling. "It was your pigs, trampling through Betty's vegetable garden."

She hung her head, relieved. "Oh, that's such good news, Carl—not about Betty's garden, but that they're alive."

Carl was shaking his head. "But that's not all of it. It weren't just the pigs; it was all your animals, Eve, even those kittens you thought had gone missing again. Scattered all through the woods, but seems they'd followed the darn pigs. Ain't that somethin'?" He seemed delighted to be the first to break the news. "'Course, Betty said she dreamed about a good-luck pig last night, so she wanted you to know she saw it before you."

"She gets full credit." Eve leaned back on her hands, stared at the space where the barn had been only that morning. "You know, Carl, I think it was time I rebuilt the barn anyway. It was getting a bit small for my needs." It was terrible to lose a piece of the past, but no one had died, and for that, Eve was beyond grateful. She looked at Heff, shivered, had for a second believed this was the end she'd seen. But he hadn't died, and Eve tried to push away her doubts, to ignore the feeling that something worse was coming. After all, she didn't know everything. She never saw the barn burning down, so how likely could it be that Heff was going to die?

CHAPTER THIRTY-FOUR

Vega

She stood in the shower, letting the water run over her skin, whisking away the soot and ash that clung to her, going over everything that had happened. Eve was right—JJ had it out for her, and finding out that Joshua was living there had been the only spark he'd needed to let loose his violence. Still, could Vega have reacted differently, said something to defuse the situation?

Her heart ached for Eve. The fire was a symbol of the hate that divided people, and it hurt to see that directed at the woman. She'd never met anyone like Eve. She was genuine and forgiving, and she'd known Vega's mother. If only her mom had stayed in Crystal. If only she'd kept in touch with Eve. What little Vega had learned about Donna, it sounded like she'd done the right thing by leaving. The knowledge that her grandfather had abused his own daughter ran slimy and cold across her skin. Her mother had escaped something horrible and survived, despite him. Her eyes stung when she thought of all Renee had gone through. But it helped Vega to see their life together in a different light and pained her to think of how alone her mother had been.

She stepped out from the shower, wrapped herself in a towel, and sat down on the lid of the toilet. Her phone was perched on the edge of the sink, screen blank. The fire had made her feel off-kilter, wondering what Zach was doing. What he was saying. She turned on the phone, which found the store's Wi-Fi and buzzed in her palm. She held her breath, watched the messages downloading. She scrunched her eyebrows. They'd stopped a few days ago. Nothing new since. His last Instagram post was one of him with Riley, a call of support for #mentalhealth and #vega. Fortunately, his following was small, so it had only gotten traction with his old high school friends and work people—most of whom were too young or too caught up in their own lives to care more than to like or add a strong-arm emoji to the comments. But that had also been a couple of weeks ago. And now nothing. It was a little eerie. Like walking into a dark room and expecting a jump scare.

She breathed out a sigh. Or maybe it was the end. She felt buoyed by a tiny bud of hope. Zach didn't care enough to come after her or Riley.

She walked out of the bathroom, bringing the hot, moist air with her, and hurried to her bedroom. There were no curtains on the french doors that faced the street, and it was dark outside, making her feel like a fish in a bowl. She pulled on sweatpants and a T-shirt and slid her feet into her Birkenstocks. She made herself a salad and ate alone at the table. After the excitement with the fire, Betty had offered to keep Riley for the entire day, telling Vega to go home and rest; she'd bring him by later. Exhaustion hit her and she sat on the couch, laid her head on the arm, and promised herself she'd rest for only a minute.

She sat at a long table set for a party. In front of her was a large platter, and in her hand a butcher's knife, its blade reflecting the light, blinding her. She blinked and a pig appeared on the platter, its head severed cleanly from its body, the blade of the knife, her hand, up to her elbow, drenched in blood. She screamed and screamed, and when her eyes fluttered open, her throat felt raw. She pushed up, hand to her chest, heart pumping. It had been horrible and grotesque. Her window was lit from the glow of headlights. She stood, letting the last of the dream fall away, and peered out the window. Must be Betty returning Riley.

She frowned. No truck on the road below, no headlights. She looked left, then right. She froze. Parked along the side of the road by Jane's herb shop was a white sedan, headlights dark except for the orange glow of the parking lights. She swallowed, rubbed the back of her neck. It wasn't JJ's truck. Then the lights came on, and the car started, gliding past her apartment. She pulled back from the window, pulse racing.

Someone knocked on her door and Vega jumped, hand to chest. She peered through the peephole and breathed out. Betty.

She opened the door. "I didn't see your truck."

"It's a nice night, so Riley and me decided to walk. Carl's waitin' outside."

Riley squirmed in Betty's arms, and Vega smiled and took him. His weight felt solid, the smell of him a comfort. "He looks bigger. Is he bigger?" He cooed at her, reaching a hand up, grabbing for her ear.

"He does have an appetite. But I think you just missed your little man."

She kissed his forehead. "I did. Thank you, Betty. It was a long day."

Betty sighed. "Poor Eve. Heard JJ hightailed it outa town."

"He left? Just like that?"

"Well, he mighta gotten wind that Heff were comin' for him. Didn't want to face Heff when he's angry. That boy might seem like a gentle giant, but he's a fighter for the right cause."

Vega thought of the night when she was fixing Eve's fence—his clenched fists, the unleashed anger in his voice. She didn't doubt it. But she still couldn't quash the uneasy feeling from her dream, and Betty seemed like the perfect person to talk to about it. "I had a dream about a pig," she said.

Betty's eyebrows shot skyward. "Did you now? Were you cooking it, killing it, or selling it? Those are all very good omens and seem fit for your situation."

"I cut off its head." Goose bumps spread down her arms at the look in Betty's eyes.

"Oh. Well, now, okay. Was this at night or in the morning?"

"I'm not sure. Does it matter?"

Betty shook her head. "Nope." She touched her chin, seemed to be thinking.

"What does it mean?" Part of her couldn't believe she was asking. It was only a dream.

Betty blew air into her cheeks. "Listen here. It's just a dream. Half the time I make mine up to see if I can rile Eve. Never can. You get some sleep—that's what you need. It was a long day." She turned to leave, looked back. "And lock up your door real good, okay?"

Vega tensed, wanting to push Betty harder, but she was already halfway down the stairs, surprisingly fast for someone with such short legs.

"How bad is it?" she called.

Betty stopped, turned. "It means that someone's coming for you."

Vega held Riley tighter; her scalp prickled. She thought of the look in JJ's eyes. "JJ's gone, right?"

"Right."

"Okay." Her voice had gotten small, and all she could think about was Zach.

Betty's eyes softened. "You're in Crystal now, Vega. We'll take care of you."

~

The next day, Vega woke up smelling the stink of burned wood and smoke toasted into the air from the pile of clothes on the floor. Eve had lost so much, put up with so much. Last night, Betty had said they'd take care of Vega. She pushed the covers to the side, felt the smooth wood floor beneath her feet. Today, she was going to do something for Eve. She was going to make sure that Eve knew how much people here cared about her.

And she'd start with the nuns.

CHAPTER
THIRTY-FIVE

August 1995

Ethan had tried a couple of times to come back to the bus; Donna threw sticks and rocks at him—small rocks, but they got her message across. Her heart hurt badly, and she squeezed her skin between her fingers whenever she thought about how she'd told him she loved him. His silence in return. The humiliation that ran loops in her stomach. She was stupid and naive. Of course he didn't love her. She was gross, and he was an asshole. Seemed all men were. Except for Carl, maybe.

She yawned, rubbed at her eyes. With her father out there some-where, sleep was impossible, and she woke up easily to the swish of leaves or the crack of a twig. Carl said the police hadn't been able to find him, that they figured he'd taken off. Maybe. But she knew he'd be back for her.

Donna thought that she and Tera would have left by now, but Tera kept putting it off, needing to fix this or that on the car. It had been almost two weeks, and the delay was eating at Donna's nerves, keeping her awake with worry for Beth and herself. Betty had assured her that no one had seen her father and that if he showed up in town, he'd get a mountain welcome. For the moment, Donna had no choice but to wait for Tera. Leaving in a car sounded better than walking for miles with her little sister to a bus station. Besides, she was using the extra time to learn whatever she could from Carl.

Today, he was going to teach her how to install a light fixture. She took the trail that avoided the road and twisted through the woods. The first time she'd gone alone, she had been afraid she'd get lost, but when she paid attention, she noticed the trampled path along the forest floor and followed it straight to their cabin.

Betty was working in her garden, pruning leaves and pulling ripe cucumbers and putting them into a basket of other harvested vegetables and fruits. She smiled when she saw Donna. "Well, if it ain't the action-hero girl who lives in the woods. Look at you and your muscles! I didn't know girls could look so strong as that."

Donna grinned, flexed her bicep. She woke up before the sun, and the first thing she saw was the look on Ethan's face after they'd been together: disgust and embarrassment. It spun a nervous energy through her muscles that had her doing jumping jacks, push-ups—anything to make the memory go away.

"Tera get that car a hers fixed yet?"

Donna shrugged. "Don't know."

Betty wiped dirt across her cheek. "Listen here. I think it's a good thing you girls get out of here, and soon. Carl heard that when the police showed up at your cabin, your momma called you a liar."

Donna's stomach turned. "They believed her?"

Betty stood, a sad look in her eyes. "I believe you. It ain't fair, but sometimes adults get the benefit of the doubt."

The air stuck in her chest. "Guess we better be leaving soon."

Betty nodded, wiped her hands across her apron. "There's some bacon inside—pancakes too. Fill your belly." She pointed a small hand shovel at her. "You been on my mind, Donna. Even had a dream about cookin' a pig last night."

"Okay." Betty talked a lot about pigs, but most of it slipped in and out of Donna's ears. It was only a mountain superstition.

"I think it was for you. Means you've learned all you need to move on."

Goose bumps pricked her skin despite the heat. The idea of moving on turned her stomach inside out. She talked a big game, but there was a part of her that had thought maybe her dad would disappear and she could just live in the bus. She left Betty in the garden and went inside to the coolness of the dark cabin. When her eyes adjusted to the light, she crossed her arms and tried to look mean. Ethan sat at the table, eating.

"What're you doing here?" she said.

Pancakes filled his cheeks. He drank orange juice, wiped his mouth. "You don't own Crystal, you know."

She kicked the floor with her toe. "I know."

"Listen, Donna, I'm sor—"

Tera burst in through the door, a tornado of energy that upended the room. "I did it!" Her eyes got big and she walked to the table, stuffed a piece of bacon into her mouth, followed by another. "Damn, I love pig." She turned to Donna, still chewing. "My car's ready. I broke up with asshole. Let's get the hell out of here." Still standing, she spread a pancake with butter, poured syrup on it, then folded it like a taco and ate it. "Leave tomorrow morning? Daddy's looking at me all suspicious. Sooner the better, I think. When you want to get your sister?"

Donna couldn't speak. Ethan's eyes met hers, and she had to look away, sure he could see the fear in her eyes. "Um, on our way out of town?" Panic spreading like the butter on Tera's pancake at the thought of going back home. She pictured her father waiting for her, rifle in his hands; the disgusted flick of her mother's eyes, ignoring everything. The idea that she could be trapped back there with no one to help her. She pressed her teeth into her tongue, tried to find a shred of courage. She would not leave her sister behind. Betty thought she was ready. Tera seemed ready. And Ethan was nobody to her anymore. She ate a piece of bacon and tried to ignore the anxious fluttering in her bones. It was time to go.

Ethan stood. His face looked paler, eyes dark and full of doubt. "Tomorrow morning? Don't you think that's too soon?"

Tera pressed a hand flat against his chest. "Us girls are leaving. You lost your chance, lover boy, when you walked away from my girl here." She turned to Donna. "C'mon, let's get back to the bus and start plannin'."

Donna made fists with her hands, told herself she was brave. "Bye, Ethan," she said with a smirk. "Have a nice life."

~

Tera bounced ahead of her on the road, the frayed ends of her jean shorts brushing across the backs of her thighs. "Ain't a single thing I'm gonna miss," she called back to Donna. "'Cept maybe Betty's buck-eyes—but other than that, nothin'."

Donna tried to be as carefree, but the future was a black hole that ate away at her excitement. How would she keep Beth safe? She shuddered. Her father wasn't the only horrible man in the world.

And she couldn't stop thinking about Ethan. Hard as she tried. She already missed him. Wished he'd been different. She'd thought there was something between them, something special, and it hurt like a slap to the face to know that it had all been in her head. A part of her had dreamed up an apology from him, imagined him coming back to the bus one more time, flowers and chocolates and whatever else sounded like a scene from a movie, and getting down on one knee and— Her dreaming ended there because she didn't want to marry him. That was stupid. It just seemed like the most romantic kind of thing he could do.

Tera stopped, waiting for her, blonde hair hanging to her waist, lifted by the breeze. "You walkin' in mud or something?"

She didn't know how to tell her she was scared. "Nah, just thinking about everything." Her stomach cramped. She tasted bacon grease, and she pressed a palm against her mouth; it filled with saliva, and she ran to a tree, leaned against it.

"You gonna be sick?"

One hand on the tree, the other pressed against her stomach, she croaked back to Tera, "Just give me a minute." She swallowed, tried to focus on anything else, but the heat and the moist vegetation in the air tipped the scales, and suddenly her stomach convulsed and she was throwing up all over the mossy ground.

"Gross!" Tera said from behind her.

Donna felt the girl's hands take hold of her hair, rub her neck, and the maternal comfort and the sickness in her belly turned into hot tears. She pushed away from the tree and Tera, slid to the ground, her back to a different tree, sucking in hot air and trying to calm down.

Tera joined her, long legs crossed at the ankles, toes swinging back and forth like Donna's puking hadn't even fazed her. She felt Donna's forehead; her hands were cool and a little clammy. "Don't feel like a fever."

Donna wiped her eyes with the back of her arm, felt her stomach settle along with her heartbeat. "I think I'm just nervous."

"Yeah, me too."

Donna turned to stare at the girl. Tera didn't seem afraid of anything. "You're nervous?"

"'Course I am. I'm not stupid."

Tera pulled a pack of cigarettes from her pocket, offered one to Donna, whose stomach roiled in response. She shook her head.

"I figure we leave, or we turn into my momma."

"What happened to her?"

"She died, stuck with a bunch of kids, no pot to piss in, and married to my daddy." She pulled in the smoke, blew it out above their heads. The familiar smell calmed Donna's stomach, and it lifted her mood enough to dry the last of her tears.

"I'm never gonna marry, ever." She felt the weight of her decision. "Men are scum, and I don't want anything to do with 'em."

Tera gave her a half smile, smoke drifting from the lifted part of her lips. "'Cept maybe sleep with 'em. They have some uses."

They both laughed, and when Tera finished her cigarette, she flicked it toward the road, stood with her hand held out. Donna took it and Tera pulled her to her feet. "C'mon, let's get—"

A truck came barreling down the road, and Donna's whole body tensed. She recognized it.

"Oh shit," Tera said, sounding small and nothing like the girl from a few seconds ago.

The driver saw them and pulled over. Levi Harrison got out. A boy followed, hair blond like Tera's. "Girl, I tole you to stop runnin' around with her." Levi's eyes flicked to Donna, disgust in the tent of his lips. "Get your ass in the truck, now." He spat a glob of black stuff onto the ground.

Donna stood with her arms crossed, chin lifted, trying to look as tough as she could. The boy's eyes drifted over her; she made her hands into fists. Beside her, Tera wilted like a flower on a hot day, the girl from before gone, replaced by someone smaller. She kept her eyes on the ground when she walked to the truck and climbed inside, spine rounded forward like she wanted to disappear.

Levi gave Donna one last hard look before getting behind the wheel and peeling out.

CHAPTER THIRTY-SIX

EVE

May 2021

It was dark under the bed. So dark that Eve couldn't see the floor that rubbed against the tip of her nose. She heard the frantic breathing of the girl beside her, the scratch of clothing across the wood planks, the smell of cigarettes lingering in the confined space. She'd been here before. Her heart thumped against her ribs, adrenaline skittering through her muscles.

The door opened, a sliver of yellow inching toward where they hid, the scuff of boots. Eve trembled. So hard her teeth scraped against each other. The girl beside her whimpered. The door opened all the way, and the light spread until it touched the girl's face. Eve pulled back. It wasn't the girl from her vision—it was a woman; the silver clips of overall straps across her shoulders; hair shorter than she remembered, darker; her face broader, older. Vega's mother, Renee, but also Eve's friend Donna.

Her past collided with the present, and Eve's cheeks were wet. They'd never said goodbye. Eve had died and Donna had disappeared forever. Eve reached out, touched her cheek. Everything had gone so horribly wrong that night.

Donna smiled, covered Eve's hand with her own. The man approached the bed, knelt down to look underneath. Eve scrambled backward, her body remembering the assault of fists on her skin, absorbing the kicks of his steel-toed boots, the crack of bones. Donna squeezed Eve's hand. *Keep my baby safe.* Then she shimmied herself out from under the bed and threw herself onto the man.

Eve woke up on her side, hands over her ears, the dream as clear as the blue sky outside her window. *Keep my baby safe.* She pushed herself to sitting, pressed a hand over her heart. Eve had tried to find her friend, never succeeded, stopped when she realized that some people don't want to be found.

She heard a baby crying; it came from outside. Eve got out of bed, dressed quickly, and followed the sound.

Vega stood outside her door, hand raised like she'd been about to knock, Riley strapped to her chest—the source of the crying. The minute he saw Eve, he stopped and Eve couldn't help but smile at him, charmed and happy to see them. The dream whipped around her like the tail of a snake.

"Good morning," Vega said, smiling. She'd changed in the last month, more prone to laugh, at ease around everyone. "How are you after yesterday?"

Eve leaned against the doorframe, the morning sun bright in her eyes. She hadn't slept well, the stink of burned wood permeating her pillow, and she couldn't help but feel defeated. Sometimes it seemed that life had a giant leaky drain somewhere that sucked all the good out way faster than the bad. "I'm okay. Relieved about the animals."

"About that," Vega said. "I came by to build them some temporary fencing, at least until we rebuild the barn and the pen. Nothing fancy, just enough to get us by and keep Jane from suing you."

Us. The way she said it, so casually, as though she saw herself as part of Eve's family. Eve blinked, touched. But the warmth didn't last. A mushroom-cloud sensation ballooned over her head, some kind of threat lingering in the shadows. She frowned, staring at Riley and thinking about Donna. "Are you sure everything's okay with Riley's dad?"

Vega turned serious, put one arm around the baby as though she alone could protect him. "He stopped posting about me a few days ago."

"And you think that means he's done looking for you?"

"I hope so." She said it without conviction.

The hum of engines from outside. Eve shaded her eyes and stepped out onto the porch. A line of cars and trucks, beds loaded down with wood and other materials, driving toward her house. "What's this?"

Vega elbowed her. "Help."

The lead car was Tera's TransAm. She got out, a red bandanna tied around her hair, cigarette hanging from her lips. Her daughter stood beside her, sullen like a teenager but with a flicker of interest in her eyes. She glanced at Eve, lifted her lips, then let them settle into a frown. Others followed, one a van full of the Catholic nuns who provided food and spiritual counseling to people in the area.

Tera ground her cigarette into the gravel drive. "Got the nuns to help. You believe that shit?"

More cars kept arriving: Carl and Betty; Heff; another van from the Presbyterian church; even Jane, her mouth pinched into her familiar look of distaste, but wearing work clothes and carrying two shovels.

A burning in her eyes, Eve had to sit down on one of the porch chairs. "For me?"

Vega sat beside her. "They've come to clear out this mess so we can build you a new barn."

Tera smirked. "It don't make up for years of being assholes to you, but it's a start."

Betty stood at the bottom of her porch stairs wearing a bright-pink sun hat. "Crystal ain't the city, but we help our neighbors. That's a country thing."

Eve nodded. She'd grown up here, but until this moment, she'd always been an outsider, never one of them. Tera was right—it didn't make up for everything, but it was a start. "It's amazing. Thank you."

Betty sighed. "You didn't see this coming, Eve? Seems your knowing don't work when it comes to your own life."

Eve laughed. "Maybe." She pulled her hair into a ponytail and grabbed a ball cap from the rack by her door. Her dream lingered; the feeling that something was off persisted. But for the moment, Eve wanted to focus on what was concrete and build herself a new barn. "Let's get started."

~

Eve wiped the back of her neck with a hand towel. It was hot for late May, and combined with the warmth still emanating from the burned wood, sweat poured down her back. It had taken more than three full days of work to clear the area of all the old wood and prep the ground for a new foundation. What had surprised Eve was how everyone had kept coming after that first day. The cynical part of her had expected them to peter out, but they'd all surprised her. Even Jane.

She wiped her hands on her jeans and headed to the house. She was making dinner for the crew tonight: chili, with enough cornbread to feed an army. Betty was already inside, cutting up onions and garlic. Vega came out of the back den, where Joshua's sister, Casey, and a friend were babysitting Riley.

"I'll be back." Vega sighed, smiled. "They ran out of diapers. Think they might have changed him every time he tooted. Need me to pick up anything?"

The room suddenly grew smaller, and Eve had to grip the counter. "Where are you going?"

Vega gave her a look. "Just to my apartment."

"You're leaving Riley here?"

Vega's eyes narrowed. "Yes. Is everything okay, Eve?"

Take care of my baby. It played on repeat in her head. "You'll be back for dinner?"

Heff came inside, smiling. "I need to run into town on official deputy business."

"Hey," Vega said. "Those pigs are safely inside their pen. Built it myself, and those suckers aren't going anywhere."

Heff laughed. "The pigs have been behaving, thanks to you. This is more traffic-slash-police business. Jane's made a formal complaint about a car that's been parked in front of her store for the last few days. Says it's driving customers away and she's convinced it belongs to college kids from Athens. Thinks they've gone camping in the woods."

"What customers?" Betty said.

Heff nodded. "Exactly. But Jane's here helping, and I figured I could look into it for her this one time."

"Can I catch a ride with you?" Vega said. "I think my van is blocked in."

Heff's eyes crinkled. "It would be my pleasure." He opened the door, held it out for Vega, who ducked her head, smiled. "Eve, we'll be back in time to help you serve this hungry crew." The door closed behind them, and Eve was left feeling like she was moving in slow motion and everyone else at regular speed.

"That boy can't take his eyes off Vega. Have you noticed that, Eve?" Betty said. Onions and garlic sizzled on the stove. "I think he's sweet on her."

Eve sat down at the table, spread her fingers wide on the surface. "Something's wrong, Betty."

Betty wiped her hands on her apron and sat down across from Eve. "You looked a little funny just then. Tell me."

"I'm not sure. It's all twisted up in my head, but I can't get rid of this feeling that something else is happening."

Betty frowned, looked up like she thought the answer might fall from the ceiling. "Have you told Vega about her momma and her daddy yet?"

"No." Eve felt ashamed that she'd held it back, but it worried her. She didn't want to ruin the new memories Vega was forming of her mom by telling her it was all a lie. Or by exposing her to the painful truth of who Eve thought her father might be. It left a sour taste in her mouth. "But I don't want to hurt her."

"'Hurt her'?" Tera's voice from the door. She stood half-inside, like something had stopped her. "I been wondering why you ain't said nothin' to her." She cackled. "I thought you were a modern woman, Eve. And she's taken to you—anybody can see that. Why would the truth hurt her?" Tera went to the stove, stirred the onions and garlic. The smell clung to Eve's hair, played on her tongue. "I always figured you for the maternal type, anyhow. Even back before I knew 'bout you."

Eve was losing touch with reality. Tera wavered, Betty had gone dark; tiny ants ran up her legs, across her skin. She heard a baby crying, and the sound made Eve race down the hallway and bust open the door to the den.

"Oh shit! You scared me!" Casey had leaped to her feet, breathing hard and staring at Eve like she was crazy.

Was she? She felt that way, untethered, overcome by a desire to find the baby and to find him soon. "Where's Riley?"

Casey pointed to the pack 'n play, and through the netting, Eve saw Riley, slobbery chin, big blue eyes, holding his feet with his hands and rocking back and forth.

Take care of my baby. Donna's voice in her head, insistent, growing louder.

"Eve?" Betty stood in the hallway, concern pasted into the creases lining her mouth.

She leaned her hand on the wall and walked back to the kitchen. Tera looked at her funny. "You look like you seen a haint," she said.

Eve focused on her old friend. What had she said? She shook her head, locked eyes with Tera. "What did you mean by 'maternal type'?"

Tera's mouth dropped open, and she tossed the spatula onto the counter. "Oh my Lord in heaven. Are you telling me you don't know?" Her eyes had gone wide. "Donna knew. She was shore of it."

"Knew what, Tera?" A crescendo of noise in her head drowned out the baby and Tera's voice so that when she answered, Eve couldn't hear her. "What did you say?"

Betty was rubbing her arm, tears in her eyes. "Oh, don't that make the most sense. I dreamed about feeding a bunch of pigs last night, and now I know it was about you."

"I don't understand," Eve said.

Betty put an arm around her; the woman was so short it rested across her midback. "Just because you came back special, don't mean you got to know everything. God does love a mystery."

Tera reached out, took Eve's hand. "Donna never got her little sister that night. Her momma wouldn't let her. You're her daddy."

Betty cleared her throat, gave Tera a stern look. "Don't you mean she's her momma?"

Tera nodded. "Yes, ma'am, I do."

A wave crashed on top of her, washing her clean, bringing back memories she'd left behind in her other life. The smoky taste of cigarettes mixing with the cinnamon spice on their tongues. Donna's long hair brushing across Eve's face, the warmth of her body in Eve's arms, the crushing weight of loving Donna, and the truth that she couldn't possibly love Eve back.

"Vega's my daughter?"

Tera nodded. Betty squeezed her arm. The rushing noise, the cries of the baby, drained from her ears, made the silence that followed nearly unbearable. Eve breathed in, and the truth unfurled itself in front of her in the delicate sweep of Vega's cheekbones, the shape of her eyes. Features she knew well in the mirror but hadn't recognized on a stranger.

From outside came the sound of a truck engine roaring down the drive, the swing of headlights illuminating Betty's and Tera's faces. JJ hollering for Ethan.

"No, boy," Tera said, her voice cracking.

They ran outside, Eve's heart pounding. JJ had driven over the rocks at the end of her driveway, the bumper of his truck just kissing her porch. She moved past Betty and Tera.

"Eve, no," Betty called, trying to stop her with a hand to her arm.

Eve shook her off. "No, Betty, this is my fight."

JJ hopped out of the truck, joined by his cousin, who tossed a beer can at her window. Eve felt someone touch her arm—Joshua. She pushed him behind her, broadened her shoulders. It was something she'd faced her entire life: the hatred, the rage, the intolerance for someone different. She'd face them alone, like she always had.

"You done crossed a line, Ethan." He advanced toward her. Eve's leg muscles tingled.

She felt suddenly crowded, and another hand touched her arm. She looked over—Sister Anna, who had labored and sweated alongside Eve to clear burned wood for the last three days, stood beside her. Sister Anna, who had gently corrected Eve when she'd referred to them as nuns: *Our proper title is* sisters. And Eve had tipped her head and smiled; she understood the importance of a name.

Sister Anna and her fellow sisters in their work jeans and plaid shirts stood in a semicircle around Eve. Jane joined them, standing just behind Eve. Everyone else who'd been working on the barn followed suit, surrounding her and Joshua and Antonne in a protective wall of their bodies. Some held shovels; others palmed hammers.

Eve couldn't swallow past the lump in her throat.

JJ's eyes took in the sisters and Jane, the others with their tools. He shifted his weight. "What's wrong with you? He ain't natural. He's a abomition."

Eve couldn't help herself. "I think you mean I'm an *abomination*," she said, and a few quiet laughs floated around her.

Tera's voice cut through the bodies. "You need to leave, JJ."

"Momma, what's wrong with you?" JJ looked genuinely perplexed.

"Nothin's wrong with me, son. But you ain't welcome here with a attitude like that. Go on."

"He'll turn Josh into a fa—"

"Joshua's exactly who he's supposed to be. You the one's got to change. Now, git, JJ."

JJ stared at Tera, his face a wavering mask of anger and disbelief. Eve almost felt sorry for him. Almost.

Sister Anna walked toward JJ and was joined by the other sisters. Tera moved to the front, looked up at her son. "I love you, JJ. But how you actin', I won't tolerate it no more." She reached up and touched his cheek, and only Eve probably noticed the minuscule tremble in her chin. "Now, git. I mean it."

JJ stared down at his momma. His cousin sneered at Eve, ready— she knew—for a fight. She braced herself, feeling the space tighten, the tension pulling them close, suffocating. Seconds ticked by, and then something broke in JJ and he backed away from Tera, stumbling when his thigh hit the fender of his truck. "Damn it," he mumbled, and jumped into his truck. His cousin did the same, opening another beer as soon as he slid into his seat. JJ stared at Eve, hatred twisting through the muscles in his jaw, and when he drove, his oversize tires crumpled the side of Eve's porch, splintering it.

Jane patted Eve's arm. "We can fix that."

Eve's heart fluttered with gratitude, but she couldn't speak. Betty stepped in. "Chili be ready soon. Go on and warsh up."

Everyone filed inside, chatting with each other like it was any other regular night and they hadn't just done something that had utterly shocked and touched Eve to her core. She stood in her yard, listening to the snort of the pigs, the cluck of chickens, her feet rooted to the ground.

"People can change," Betty said.

Tera took Eve by the arm. "Even the assholes."

Eve still couldn't move. She pressed a palm to her chest, her heartbeat frantic. "But something's wrong. Something bad is going to happen. I can feel it." Fear danced around her, ghosts in the night. Eve felt the weight of something coming like a wave above the town, hovering and ready to crash.

And then a knowing fluttered inside her ear, and it all came together in a moment. "Call the paramedics! Heff's been shot!"

CHAPTER THIRTY-SEVEN

August 1995

Donna lay on the mattress in the back of the bus and stared out the small rectangle of window, looking past the trees and to the inky black sky and the tiny white dots that made her feel every inch of her loneliness. She didn't think Tera would show up in the morning, not after seeing her with her father, but Donna wondered how serious the girl had been in the first place. Maybe she'd been all talk.

She rolled to her side, faced the wall, and let memories of the last few weeks swirl in the night. It had been nearly a month since she'd run away, and it had been the happiest she'd ever been. Giving up wasn't an option. She bit her lip, felt determination battle with the queasiness that still swam around her stomach. Why stay here any longer? A calmness washed over her with a decision: it was time for her to leave. Time to get Beth as far away from their father as possible. Time for Donna to live life on her own terms.

She fell asleep to the sounds of tiny claws skittering across the floor and the hoot of an owl—her protector for the night.

~

Something touched her hair, and Donna shot out of bed, hit the back of her head on the bus wall, and struggled to get to her feet with stars swimming in the shadows. She lashed out blindly, fists hitting soft tissue, heard a moan and the sound of wind knocked out of lungs. Scrambled on her hands and feet as far away as possible, her eyes slowly adjusting to the dark and to the girl who crouched doubled over, holding her stomach.

"I will fuck you up if you come any closer to me."

"I've heard that line before," the girl wheezed.

Donna shook her head, groggy from sleep, confused because she knew that voice. She lowered her fists. "Ethan?" But it wasn't Ethan; it was a girl with dark shoulder-length hair, wearing a summer dress with sunflowers sewn along the hem. A burst of anger like fireworks in her chest. "Is this a joke?" she said. "You makin' fun of me or somethin'?" She advanced, fists raised. She'd bust his pretty face, kick him in the kidneys.

But Ethan wasn't laughing. He sat down on the mattress, legs crossed, dress over his knees, and flicked on the lantern. His eyes were lined, mascara making his eyelashes longer than her own, a sweep of blush across his cheeks. Donna was confused, speechless. She sank onto the mattress opposite him.

"Is this your Halloween costume?"

Ethan shook his head.

Donna's mouth had gone dry, and she searched for words, tried to understand. "So you like to wear girl stuff and pretend you're a girl?"

Ethan's eyes dimmed. Like she'd said something wrong. "No," he said. "I *am* a girl."

"I don't understand."

"That's how I feel, how I've always felt." He pointed to his heart. "In here."

What he was telling her should have shocked her. She didn't know it was possible, was sure her mother would call it immoral, her father a sin. But when she searched her own heart, she knew it didn't matter what her parents or anyone else thought. Ethan was her friend. He'd accepted her exactly as she was. Never judged her for the foul things her father had done. His friendship had made her feel whole for the first time in her life. Her eyes stung. He'd been hiding this part of himself from her because he was scared she'd reject him. She leaned forward, elbows on her knees, and studied him. His makeup was good—much better than anything she'd tried, way classier than anything Tera wore. "So that's why your father's such an asshole, huh?"

Ethan nodded.

"They know?"

"When I was little I used to sneak into their closet and try on my mom's clothes. She found me more than once. Later, I found the bus and that helped me to hide it from them. But, yeah, they know."

Donna stared at the clothes rack, the makeup table, and it dawned on her like a sunrise on a cloudy morning. "Those are your clothes. This is your fort in the woods. Not some girl's."

Ethan nodded again.

She tried to take it all in, replaying their time together, the things they'd shared. Ethan crossed his arms, chewed on his bottom lip like he expected her to . . . what? Be angry? She thought about it. Was she? She was disappointed, she guessed, that he wasn't who she thought he was. And it was different, a little weird. She looked at him, at the delicate line of his jaw, the curve of his shoulder down to his arms, the way he held himself in the dress—elegant, relaxed, like it suited him perfectly. And Donna wondered what it would have been like to have gotten to know him as he was from the very beginning. Her throat squeezed shut. He hid from everyone. He was lonely like her.

She leaned back, lightly kicked his shin. "You look better in a dress than I do."

He gave her a small smile, shy. "I know."

They both laughed and Donna thought her heart might explode. She had her friend back. Different, but still the person who had stopped her father, still the person she loved.

Ethan clasped his hands in his lap, squeezed his fingers together. "I love you, too, Donna."

Everything fell into place then—not perfectly, not the way she'd hoped, but it made her feel better. Confused but more centered, more herself. Like Ethan had been the one thing holding her feet to the ground, and with him back, she felt the earth between her toes.

"I didn't know how to tell you," he said.

She nodded. "Yeah, I get it." Shame burned the tips of her ears. "I might have been just awful." She shifted, the truth of her words hanging in the space between them.

They sat for a minute in a silence that slowly absorbed the awkwardness. "Let's not lie to each other ever again. Okay, Ethan?"

"Deal," he said. He picked at a fingernail, seemed unsure once more, like he wanted to say something else. "My name—" He swallowed and she could hear it move around his Adam's apple. "My name is Eve."

She stared at him, and maybe it was hearing the name out loud, but it seemed to fully hit her then. Eve. Ethan was Eve. She nodded, eyes wet. It didn't change anything. Ethan was the same on the inside, and that was what mattered most to Donna anyway. She stuck out her hand. "Hi, Eve. I'm Donna. Want to leave this hellhole in the morning?"

Eve smiled, nodded, wiped a hand across her eyes. "Hell yeah."

"Then we better get some sleep." She turned off the lantern and lay down beside Eve; she smelled like vanilla. Sleep danced around them until Donna reached out and took Eve's hand.

Tomorrow, she'd start a brand-new life, and she wouldn't have to do it alone.

$\sim$

The bus tilted the way it did when someone climbed the steps inside. Donna's eyes flew open, pulse racing. Felt the heat of Eve's body beside her, breathing even, still asleep. Maybe she'd imagined it. Her ears tuned to any sound: the early-morning songs of birds, the crunch of tiny paws scurrying through the underbrush. It was quiet, still that early-morning hour before the woods woke up and the sun crept over the horizon, turning the black sky into dusty shades of purples and pinks.

The bus creaked; it often did. The thing was old, and sometimes a little breeze made the metal moan. She pushed up on one elbow. Maybe it was Tera, coming early because she still wanted to join them. The thought made her smile; it would be the three of them after all. But the noise had died away, and Donna's eyelids grew heavy. She lay back down, let them close. They were leaving in a few hours, and Donna needed her sleep because she had no idea what was ahead of them.

"What the devil?"

Donna's stomach turned violently at the voice, and her eyes flew open. Her father, hulking above them, face in shadow, his usual stink of Old Crow a cheap perfume slithering up her nose. Inside, she screamed, so loud it busted glass and woke all of Crystal. In her mind, she jumped to her feet, grabbed a rock, and finished bashing his head in. But on the outside, she didn't make a peep, couldn't move, her limbs frozen to the bus floor like grass on a first frost.

She braced herself, ready to feel his fists, his hands squeezing her arms, dragging her outside—his property, his possession, and nobody would be able to stop him. She pushed a sob down until it stuck inside the bones of her chest. He leaned closer; she could make out the hairs in his beard, but he wasn't looking at her. He stared at Eve, disgust twisting through his lips, up into the squint of his eyes, the V-shaped lines in his forehead.

Panic held her down until she finally found her voice. "Daddy, no!"

He paid her no mind and, with an angry growl, grabbed Eve by the ankles and pulled. Donna screamed. Eve started thrashing, trying to kick, using her fists to hit at anything; one caught Donna in the chest, and then Eve was gone, her body trailing down the aisle, head and shoulders hitting the steel legs of seats as she went. Donna scrambled after them on her hands and knees. Afraid if she stood, her legs would buckle. She heard the thump of Eve's body when her father dragged her down the stairs. Eve's cry of pain, her confusion.

Outside the bus, Eve lay on the ground on her side, curled into a ball, hands covering her face and head, body absorbing the blows. Her wig had fallen off; Donna grabbed it from the stairs, held it to her chest. "Stop, please, stop!"

But her father didn't even look at her, kicking Eve in the chest, back, stomach, neck. Over and over until Eve stopped fighting, stopped moving, and it happened so fast that Donna clutched at her throat, couldn't breathe, her screams a wheeze. The sky was a lighter gray. A bird sang from a branch above them. Donna reached around her, dug her fingers into the earth, searching for some kind of weapon, some way to stop her father.

Something flashed in the woods, and then a wiry figure sprang from the shadows, long blonde hair flying behind her. Tera raced through the meadow and threw herself onto the man, a wild thing that clung to her father's back, punching, kicking, biting him on the side of his face. He roared and bucked her off, chest heaving, saw who it was. "Bitch, get home 'fore I tell yer daddy who you with."

Donna crawled over to Eve, pulled her into her lap, tears falling, mixing with the blood that was everywhere. Eve's face was unrecogniz-able. She pushed her hair from her cheek, the strands stuck to the skin. "No, no, no, no, no. Please, God, no!"

Her father roared and Donna felt something crack against her skull, stars floating, and she was flung aside. Her father hovered above her, a crazed light in his eyes. Tera came up from behind him, raising a thick half log above her, and with a shriek she brought it down on his head. It stunned him and he seemed frozen in place. Before he could react,

Tera raised it again and again, bringing it down onto his head each time, and Donna knew that she was never going to stop.

Donna scrambled to her feet, hands out. "Tera!"

Tera dropped the log, fell to her knees. Tears streaked her face. She crawled over to them. "Why?" she cried, touching Eve's face, stopping short when she saw the torn sundress, yellow flowers stained red.

Donna clawed at the ground. Her father lay in a crumpled heap on the ground, staring at her with sightless eyes.

Tera wiped her face, smeared blood across her cheeks, and stood. She sniffed and something hardened in her eyes. "Run, Donna. Go get Betty!"

⁓

Donna ran through the woods, feet slipping on moss, toes smashing into exposed roots. Tripping once and falling so hard she thought she broke her elbow. But she got up and kept running until she heard the wind chimes. Saw the tiny mirrors reflecting the early-morning light.

She pounded on the door. "Betty!" Her voice was hoarse.

It opened, and Betty took one look at her and hugged her.

"It's Ethan, please, hurry, I think he's dead. My father . . ." She swallowed and everything stuck in her throat. "My father did it."

Betty's face turned white. "I'm callin' an ambulance." She hurried to the kitchen and Donna stood by the fireplace, listening to her dial the old rotary phone, give her address and the bus's location to the person on the other end.

"Please hurry," she said. "I think he's hurt real bad."

Together they ran back through the woods, Betty a few steps ahead of Donna, fast and determined. When they reached the clearing, Betty ran to Eve, took her jacket, and laid it over her. "Oh my dear, stay with me, stay with me. Help's comin'."

Donna winced at her father's still body. She met Tera's gaze and walked toward her, numb. Tera picked up her father's ankle; Donna did the same, and they started to pull. It took every bit of strength she had and then some. Sweat trickled into her eyes, glued her shirt to her skin. They moved him inches at a time, but she knew where they were going. Had watched Ethan throw his father's knife inside. Had wished she had something to throw in too. They didn't speak and Donna didn't look at her father, who never moved or made a sound. When they reached the crest of the hill, they flopped him onto his side and pushed him down the slope. Dragged him the rest of the way.

At the edge of the mine, Donna hesitated, stared down into the black hole. Thick clouds had moved in, spitting rain, the roll of thunder in the distance. She'd sat here with Ethan and wished her father dead. And now he was, and she felt nothing. Not free. Not released from his abuse. Only bound more than ever to his sickness.

"I ain't waitin' a second longer," Tera whispered, her voice cracking. She knelt down and started to push, straining, grunting. Nothing happened. Donna knelt beside her and pushed, too, crying, screaming, until his body fell into the hole with a crash, the sound of wood falling, settling, then nothing.

Donna leaped away from the hole, shaking, her hands, clothes, covered in blood, skin freezing, wet now from the rain. Tera stood, her face a mask, took Donna's hand, and walked her through the woods and back to the clearing, where she pulled up short and hid them behind a bush. Betty stood off to the side, looking small and so sad Donna wanted to run out and hug her. The paramedics hovered over Eve's body, working frantically.

Tera pulled her away. "You can't be here."

Donna let herself be led away from the scene. Tera turned and they locked eyes, neither one crying anymore. They stumbled through the woods and back to the road, where Tera's car was parked along the side. Donna slid into the passenger seat, shaking so badly her teeth chattered. Tera drove, silent, and Donna looked out the window, not understanding where they were going until Tera pulled up in front of Donna's cabin.

"Get your sister."

Donna climbed out of the car and walked to the door, opened it. Her mother and Beth sat at the kitchen table, eating oatmeal. Her mother leaped up from the table, grabbed the shotgun from where it leaned against the refrigerator, and pointed it at Donna. The tip wobbled toward the ground. Donna ignored her, smiled at Beth. "Hey, Bethy."

Beth stared at her, eyes big, scared; then she ran to the cabinet and hid behind the pots and pans, right where Donna had told her to go when she was scared. It felt like a blow. Donna was the monster now.

"What did you do?" her mother whispered, staring at Donna's blood-soaked shirt, the red stains on her skin, dirt crusting her fingertips.

Donna looked at her mom, and for the first time in her life, she felt sorry for the woman. Wondered why she'd stayed, decided it was probably because no one had ever thought to show her a way out. But it was too late, and Donna realized that Beth didn't need to go with her. Not anymore. "Beth's safe now. Keep her that way."

The tip of the rifle lowered, and her mother stood in front of the cabinet where the girl hid. Her chin trembled, face a pale white. "Go on. Get."

Donna did as she was told.

∼

Tera drove them to the hospital. Donna covered her bloodstained shirt with a jacket Tera pulled from the back seat. She ran through the sliding glass doors, stopped short when she saw Betty in the waiting area, sobbing, Carl holding her. She fell to her knees in front of them. Tera joined her. Betty pushed the wet hair from Donna's face. "He's gone. Go, girl. Before they come for you."

~

Tera stopped just outside town, close to the stairs that led up to Carl and Betty's cabin. They sat in silence, staring out the windshield. Rain poured now, pattering through the leaves, drenching the ground, puddles on the road.

"I came over this morning to tell you I ain't goin' with you no more." Tera slumped over the wheel. There were leaves tangled in her blonde strands, and the car smelled of wet clothes and body odor.

"Oh." She didn't know how to feel, what to say. She didn't think she'd ever feel anything again. But her stomach folded in on itself, her mouth watered, and she pushed open the car door, puked into the mud. Rain soaked her neck. She leaned back on the seat, holding her stomach, waiting for it to settle before it happened again.

Tera stared; her eyes were dull, empty. "You puking a lot?"

Donna wiped her mouth with the back of her hand. "Yeah."

"Mornings?"

Donna thought about it. "Yeah."

Tera's forehead touched the steering wheel. "Shit."

"What?"

"You use protection with Ethan?"

Donna wasn't thinking straight, confused by what Tera was saying. And thinking about Ethan set her shaking all over again. Trying to remember past anything that had just happened seemed impossible, especially a night weeks ago, fuzzy from alcohol. "Um, I don't think so."

"Shit," she said again.

Rain thundered on the metal roof, loud in her ears. Everything she thought she'd had in Crystal—friends, family, a place she belonged— was gone, folded like the house of cards she'd tried to build when she was little. "I have to go, Tera. I can't stay here." Her voice was a whisper. She didn't know how she'd make it, where she'd go, or if she'd survive, but she had to get out of there. Away from the pain that raked across her body every time she thought about her friend.

Tera stared out the windshield. "Yeah, I know." She leaned over and hugged Donna, wiry arms around her shoulders squeezing so hard that for a second, Donna couldn't breathe. She released her and got out of the car, standing in the rain, hair plastered to her face, blood washing away. "You take the car."

Donna wanted to be strong and say no. Wanted to figure out how to make it all on her own. But she couldn't. She had to get out of this town before she broke all the way through. She slid over into the driver's seat, the cloth seat wet beneath her thighs. "Thank you."

"Stay far away from this shithole. And if you ever meet another man like your father, run. There's just some men you run from. Got it?"

When Donna pulled onto the road, Tera stood watching her go, getting smaller and smaller in the rearview mirror until she was gone and Donna was alone.

CHAPTER THIRTY-EIGHT

VEGA

May 2021

Heff parked halfway between Vega's apartment and Jane's store.

"I saw that car a few nights ago," Vega said.

"Maybe Jane's right. The college kids do like to camp around here."

"What are you going to do?"

Heff smiled at her, and it was familiar to her now, comforting. They had become friends, and Vega looked forward to seeing his face, started to wonder what it might feel like to run her fingers through his hair. Having thoughts like that had become more frequent—surprising her, but not totally unwelcome. She wasn't a nun, after all.

"I'm going to write them a friendly note asking them to kindly not park there anymore and leave one of my business cards along with it. College kids are future home buyers, so it can't hurt."

Vega laughed. "You're such an optimist." She got out of the truck. "I'll only be a minute." She walked away, feeling his eyes on her and enjoying it.

When she slid her key into her apartment door, she frowned. She'd forgotten to lock it. That was happening more and more, a sense of safety in the small town, despite people like JJ.

She walked inside and froze.

Zach stood in front of her, grinning and pointing her mother's gun at her face. "Hi, Vega," he said.

Her heart raced, sweat beading up in her armpits, and all she could think about was Riley. Phantom pains in her stomach, around her wrist. She would never let this man around her son. A mental inventory of her apartment: Butcher knife in the kitchen drawer. Hammer and a wrench in her tool bag. Piece of shelving she'd intended to install in the kitchen. Thoughts of her mother, running all her life, and it weakened Vega. Their lives were so similar. She'd wanted something different for Riley, but it seemed she had no choice.

"How did you find me?"

His laugh was cruel. "You're such an idiot. That pic you sent of Riley. It had your location attached to it."

She stepped back, stunned. She'd been too sheltered. So naive. How could she have not known?

"You kidnapped my son," he said.

"No, you attacked me, and I refuse to let him be raised by an abuser. Get help, Zach." She wanted to keep him talking, find a way to distract him. Her leg muscles tensed. "Was your dad like this? Is that why you hate him so much?"

Zach pressed his lips together; the flesh turned white. "Shut up."

"What're you going to do, Zach? Kill me? Spend your life in prison? Let Riley be raised by your father?"

He smiled, and there was nothing of the man she'd thought she'd loved. "So many people are worried about you, Vega," he mocked her. "Worried for your mental health, worried about what you might do to Riley or yourself."

Chills ran down her spine. He was going to make it look like she'd killed herself. Panic unfurled in her stomach. She couldn't let that happen. Her body shook, but she took a step closer to Zach, ready to launch herself at him.

The door busted open, and Heff pushed into the room. Knocked her out of the way and lunged at Zach. Zach fired. Vega screamed. Heff's eyes opened wide; he clutched his chest, swayed, but he didn't fall. Instead, he heaved his body toward Zach, who was so surprised he didn't react right away. Heff fell on top of him. The gun skittered across the floor.

Heart in her throat, Vega scrambled for it, fingers brushing the cold metal, then gripping the handle and whipping it around at Zach, who stood above her, ready to attack.

She scooted away from him, keeping the gun pointed at his chest, and pushed to her feet. Heff lay facedown on the floor, blood spreading from his chest.

"Heff!" she cried. "Wake up!" He didn't move, and Vega was filled with a rage that tumbled down her arm and into her trigger finger.

Zach held up his hands, fear in his eyes. Vega liked it.

"You're not gonna shoot me, Vega," he said.

She thought of her mother, of Riley, of Heff dying at her feet, and she steadied her arm. Zach's eyes shifted to something behind her. Vega stiffened but didn't turn.

"Vega?" Eve, her voice calm, like she was trying not to spook her.

"He's killed Heff, Eve." Her voice wobbled, but she didn't take the gun off Zach. "He'll take Riley from me. I'll lose everything."

"Tera called the paramedics, Betty called the cops. Help is coming, okay? Put the gun down, Vega. Killing him won't help Riley."

"Yeah, this asshole ain't goin' nowhere but the clink." Tera's voice.

Vega felt a hand touch her shoulder. "He ain't worth it, hon," Betty said.

Vega slumped forward, letting the gun fall to her side. Zach rushed at her, eyes hot with rage. She felt herself pulled backward, surrounded by Betty, Tera, and Eve, the gun gently removed from her hand, and Eve stepped in front of her, gun raised. Vega cried, "Eve! No!"

From the dead, Heff's hand shot out, and he grabbed Zach's ankle. Yanked hard, and Zach fell face-first to the floor. Tera scurried into the room, grabbed electrical wiring Vega had coiled by her tool bag, and jumped onto Zach's prone body. In a matter of seconds, she'd tied his hands behind his back, then his ankles. She smiled, leaning against him like he was her prized steer.

Vega rushed toward Heff, and with Eve's help, she gently rolled him over. Betty studied the wound. There were droplets of blood on his chin, but his eyes were clear.

Betty patted his cheek. She took a dish towel and pressed it against the wound. "We need to keep pressure on it."

Vega took over, pushing her palm against the towel, blood soaking through. "Thank you," she whispered, her face wet.

"My pleasure," he said.

She brushed hair from his forehead, tried to smile but felt hot tears on her cheeks. "Guess you can add a *slash hero* to your business card."

He laughed, winced. "Oh, that hurt."

Betty patted his cheek. "I dreamed about a pig in my house last night. You'll be just fine."

Heff grunted when he moved. "Thanks, Betty, that's good to hear." He looked up at Eve. "Any, uh—" He paused, his breath coming in gasps. "Any helpful knowings, Eve?"

"Oh, now you want to know?"

He grimaced. "Seems I'm not ready to die after all."

Eve took over applying pressure from Vega, gave Heff a tender smile. "I'd listen to Betty."

They sat there for a few minutes in silence. Heff lay half-propped against the kitchen cabinets, face pale white. Each of them took turns applying pressure to the wound. The blood had slowed, and Vega felt a slight release in the tension running up her neck. She wanted Heff to be okay, realized how much she wanted him to be okay. She moved her fingers, placed them over his hand, and squeezed.

Tera sat beside Zach, holding on to the wire that bound him and looking bored.

"How long does it take the paramedics to get here?" Vega asked, anxious.

"We don't got 911," Betty said. "Ambulance comes from the next county over."

"And the police?" She gave Heff an apologetic look. "No offense."

"None taken."

"Well, that would be the once-a-month deputy. He should be along soon."

She felt wrung out, exhausted. The whole situation was absurd. "So we just wait?"

Heff squeezed her hand. "If you live here long enough, you get used to it."

Betty wrung out a wet cloth, placed it on Heff's forehead. "You're gonna be okay. Got that?"

Vega heard the worry in the quaver of the woman's voice. She tried to stay calm like everyone else, but her body was shaking.

Tera pulled out a pack of cigarettes. "Mind if I smoke?"

Vega thought of Riley. She wanted to hope that there'd be more nights for them here in this apartment. "Um, yes, I do," she said.

"Okay, then." She put a cigarette between her lips but didn't light it, thrummed her fingers across Zach's head. He'd been quiet; every time he moved, Tera punched him in the ribs. "Eve, you gonna tell this girl what you know about her or am I?"

Eve gave Heff some water but didn't look at Vega. She seemed uncomfortable—awkward, even—and that was not something Vega had ever seen in the woman.

Vega dragged her eyes from Heff but didn't take her hand off his. "About me? Is it about my mom?"

Eve's shoulders straightened, and she turned to face Vega. "It's about one of your moms."

Vega knitted her eyebrows together, shook her head. It didn't make sense. Her mother's words echoed in her head: *Your father was good enough.*

It dawned on her then, slowly, in little pieces that tied together and made sense. Ethan had been her mother's friend. Ethan had been good enough. She stared at Eve, saw Riley in the straight line of her nose, the dimple in her cheek. "You're my mom?"

Eve nodded, squeezed her hands together.

A flare of anger. "Why didn't you tell me?"

"She just found out," Tera said, giving Zach another jab to the ribs.

"Ow, bitch, stop that."

She gave him another jab, and he shut up. "Seems I got knowings like Eve," Tera said, unlit cigarette hanging from her lips. "Maybe we all died some that night."

"Maybe," Betty agreed, and Vega thought the two women shared a sad kind of look.

"Wow," Heff said from where he lay between them, a goofy smile on his face like he'd just finished the end of his favorite book. "I see it now. You do look a little bit like her, Vega."

Eve finally spoke and it was reserved and timid and nothing like the woman Vega had come to admire. Like she was preparing herself for Vega's rejection.

"I know I'm not what you expected or even what you want in your life. And I respect that. But, Vega—" Her voice broke. "Your mother was my best friend. I loved her. And if you, well, there's not much you can do about it, but I love you too."

Her mother's voice in her head, a wisp of her in the space beside Vega and the one thing she'd said about Vega's father. *Your father was good enough.* She thought of her mother at the bus, alone and lost, and her only friend a boy named Ethan. Vega wasn't as surprised as she should have been. Almost like a part of her had known it. She leaned over Heff, put her arms around her mother, and hugged her tight. Eve sighed.

From below them, Heff cleared his throat, his voice thick with emotion. "This is about the most beautiful reunion I've ever witnessed."

Vega leaned back on her heels. "Did my mom really kill her own father?" She'd asked the question before, but she had a nagging feeling there was more to the story.

Eve raised her eyebrows, shook her head. "I died during that part, so I don't know."

Betty shrugged. "Donna came to get me after her daddy beat the snot out of our Eve here. But he was gone when I got there. Always figured he'd known what he'd done and left town."

Tera, now lying with one elbow propped up on Zach's back, took the cold cigarette out of her mouth. "God shore do love a mystery."

From outside came the flash of lights, footsteps on the stairs. There was more—Vega was sure there was more. But discovering that Eve was her mom was enough.

CHAPTER
THIRTY-NINE

August 1995

The highway was a straight line, bordered by sunflowers taller than her, the sky a deep blue she thought only existed in paintings. The farther she'd gotten from the gray skies of Ohio, the more she could breathe. Sleep had been elusive—haunting dreams of Eve dying in her arms, her father's body in the mine. The waves of morning sickness that woke her early and had her nauseous most of the day. In the distance, hovering above the horizon, peaks of white—mountains spreading vast and high.

Tears on her cheeks, one hand on her belly. Her new reason to survive. It was a girl, she just knew it. And Donna would love her the way her own mother should have, keep her safe the way a father was supposed to. She'd teach her to be brave, like Eve. Strong, like Tera. Show her how to provide for herself, like Carl. And give her a home, like Betty. This girl would be a survivor.

On the side of the road, she saw a car pulled over, hazards on, blown tire. A woman with a baby on her hip, a toddler with his head stuck out the window, all of them staring at the tire. Donna turned on her blinker, pulled up behind the car, and got out.

"Need help?"

The woman turned, eyed Donna suspiciously. A yellow bruise spread across her jaw. She looked wrung out, exhausted, and weary. "You know how to change a tire?"

Donna stood up straight. She smiled at the toddler, who sucked his thumb, staring at her. "Yes, ma'am, I do."

CHAPTER FORTY

VEGA

It was a cool fall day, the leaves a million shades of red and gold, burnt orange and green. Vega pushed the stroller down the road until she found the trail that led back to the bus. Riley sat up in his seat, pointing at the sky, the ground, babbling nonsense words, turning around and shrieking in delight every time he spied his momma.

The thick wheels of the stroller moved smoothly over the uneven ground, easily clearing tree roots and rocks. Her breath steamed in the cold air. A glimpse of yellow through the brown trunks; then the trees opened ranks, and the bus was in front of her. Her chest tightened. Seeing it got her every time. Thoughts of her mom here, with Eve and Tera, Betty and Carl, the last family she had before Vega came along.

She pushed the brake on the stroller, pulled a blanket from the basket underneath, and spread it on the ground. Unclipped Riley, whose body spasmed with excitement at being released, and set him on the blanket. Sat beside him, and together they stared at the bus.

Vega knew most of the story now, except for the very end. Seemed nobody really knew what had happened to Donna's dad. Vega had decided she didn't need to know. That some secrets were best left in the past. But she knew what had happened to Donna. And for that, she was grateful.

There were voices from the woods, the snort of pigs. Vega smiled. Heff joined her, picked up Riley, and plopped him on his lap. Riley squealed, reached up, and jabbed the man's face. Heff laughed. Eve laid down her own blanket next to Vega's. Carl and Betty sat in lawn chairs.

Tera was the last to join them, tearing through the woods on an old minibike she'd spent the summer restoring. She rested it against a tree, plopped down on the blanket beside Eve. "What're we waitin' for?" she said.

Vega stood, pulling a thin piece of metal from her pocket. Something she'd asked Heff to make for her. Carl had helped too.

And without much fuss, she pulled a battery-powered drill from under the stroller and screwed the metal plaque into the side of the bus. Stood back, felt something move and click into place. Took a handkerchief from her back pocket and shined the metal.

RENEE'S PLACE.

Vega turned, smiled at her friends, her family, her heart fuller than she thought it had a right to be. The pigs roamed around the bus, squirrels clicked at them from the tops of the trees, and Vega returned to the blanket and gave Riley his first bite of Betty's buckeye cookie.

Acknowledgments

This is my favorite part. I love that the acknowledgments section is an expected part of any book. It's important to say thanks—and there are many to be said, especially after this past year. It wasn't just about book writing or research. For me and for my family, this year was about heartache and loss, celebration of life and learning how to keep moving forward even as we grieve. And as my fellow writers know, we don't write in isolation from our lives. Too often, what we experience off the page can affect how our characters behave on it. Sometimes it's good, and sometimes it makes for difficult and emotional days of writing.

So first, to my dad. Your voice, your questions, your enthusiasm and worry are all here. I remembered what we talked about. I thought about what concerned you, and it came along with me and got itself all tangled up in the story in the best way possible. Thank you, Dad. Words fall so miserably short, but love was always in abundance. I will miss you forever.

To my mom, for your patience, your unbridled support, and a deep and abiding strength that is the rock of our family. Thank you for teaching me how to find joy even in the sadness. To Jennifer and Scott and your beautiful families for doing whatever it took to be together, for long-distance and late-night phone calls, for being the best brother and sister a girl could ask for.

To Gwynne and Christi for shoring me up when I needed it most and giving me the space to write and to give this story the attention it deserved. I would not have finished it without you. To Allison, because, well, you're the family favorite, of course. And to my lovely parents-in-law, Becky and Ray, for your enthusiasm and loving support.

To Penny and Bonnie and everyone at the Tenacious Unicorn Ranch for meeting with me, answering my questions, and introducing me to the alpacas. Your work to create a trans haven in rural spaces and all the ways you support the community at large are inspirational and important, and Colorado is better because of you.

To Maxie Mettler and Samantha Hancox-Li for carefully reading and giving feedback that helped me to take this story to a deeper place. Some stories require an additional set of eyes meant to ensure that an author's portrayal of a marginalized character is done with compassion, sensitivity, and authenticity. I have worked with sensitivity readers, also known as cultural research readers, for my past two books, and I believe that their feedback made my stories and characters richer and stronger. Thank you, Maxie and Samantha, for working alongside writers to share your own experiences and to make sure that we depict characters with care and accuracy. Your work makes a difference.

To Maryalice and Don at the Pregin Ridge Studio and Retreat in Chauncy, Ohio, for providing the absolute perfect writing retreat for me to brainstorm and outline this book all those many, many months ago. Your stories (both worldly and other) sparked ideas for my characters and this book. There's a reason that all your reviews are five stars. I can't wait to come back.

To my former editor Chris Werner for helping to bring this book to life and for giving me the chance I needed to start this amazing writing career all those stories ago. Thank you so much, Chris. Best of luck to you, but you will be missed! And thank you to my current editor, Erin Adair-Hodges, for working out some last-minute wrinkles with me and seeing this book through to the finish line. To the always amazing Tiffany Yates Martin for yet again working with me on the rounds of developmental edits. I think this was the first book that didn't earn me a ten-page letter.

Maybe I'm finally getting the hang of this. To Jessica Faust, my agent and cheerleader, for making this writing dream a reality in the first place. To my publicist, Ann-Marie Nieves, for being there for all my small questions and organizing events from afar. I'm so grateful for our partnership. And to the incredible team at Lake Union: Jen Bentham, Rachel Norfleet, Kellie Osborne, and everyone else who worked to bring this book to readers.

To my dear friend and writer and early-stage developmental editor Sara Miller. Without your talent at asking just the right questions, I'd have written the wrong story. Thank you for checking in on me and letting me cry when the days were dark and everything felt too raw.

To Veena Mathad and Jerry Federico for your sincere kindness and support during everything. Your willingness to answer my questions and listen to my worries helped me more than you may know. And to my forever critique partners Mary Johnson and Elizabeth Richards: thank you for your critical eyes and commitment to helping us each grow as writers. To Kappy at Hearthfire Books and Treats for being the best local bookstore a writer could hope for, and for your dedicated support of local authors. To all my friends who show up in the good times and the sad, but who were there for me during very hard days when deadlines loomed but the writing wouldn't come—Kelly, Sara, Taryn, Sarah Chase, Brenda Hobgood, Sonia Stovall, Katy Downie, and everyone else who thought to call or text simply to say they were thinking of me. It meant more than you may know.

To Ella, Keira, and Sawyer: you special, lovely humans who inspire me with the beautiful people you are. Even though you clean the kitchen half as often as you should, you make family a priority and you love hard. Being your mother is my absolute favorite role. And finally, to Sean: thank you for being the roots of our family, for never weakening when things are hard, for making it possible for me to care for my dad and write a book and holding my hand through it all. I'm forever grateful you sat behind me in that college Spanish class.

Book Club Questions

1. This book deals with quite a bit of trauma, both personal and generational. How did the characters' experiences and their journeys throughout the story affect you as a reader?

2. Did you identify more with one of the characters? If so, how?

3. As a young person, Eve had a near-death experience that affected the rest of her life. Have you ever had a similar experience? Or experienced something that changed your perspective so completely? If so, explain.

4. Many assumptions about the characters—including some made by the characters themselves—led to negative stereotypes. Were those stereotypes changed by the end of the book? If so, how? If not, explain.

5. Were there any characters who surprised you? How?

6. Share a favorite quote from this book and why you connected with it.

7. The story follows two different timelines. Did those timelines intertwine for you, or was it difficult to jump back and forth?

8. What did you like most about the story? What did you like least? And why?

9. Did the ending satisfy you? If yes, why? If no, how would you have ended it?
10. If you could ask the author one question about this book, what would it be?

About the Author

Photo © 2020 Eric Weber

Melissa Payne is the bestselling and award-winning author of *The Secrets of Lost Stones*, *Memories in the Drift*, and *The Night of Many Endings*. For as long as she can remember, Melissa has been telling stories in one form or another—from high school newspaper articles to a graduate thesis to blogging about marriage and motherhood. But she first learned the real importance of storytelling when she worked for a residential and day treatment center for abused and neglected children, where she wrote speeches and letters to raise funds. The truth in those children's stories was piercing and painful, written to invoke a call to action in the reader: to give, to help, and to make a difference. Melissa's love of writing and sharing stories in all forms has endured. She lives in the foothills of the Rocky Mountains with her husband and three children, a friendly mutt, a very loud cat, and the occasional bear. For more information, visit www.melissapayneauthor.com.